Praise for the Stranje House Series

"Baldwin has a winning series here: her characters are intriguing and fully rendered." –*Booklist* on *Refuge for Masterminds*

"Sign me up for Kathleen Baldwin's School for Unusual Girls. It sucked me in from the first few pages and kept me reading until late into the night. Kathleen Baldwin has created a completely original–and totally engrossing–world, full of smart girls, handsome boys, and sinister mysteries."

–Meg Cabot, #1 NYT - USA Today bestselling author of *The Princess Diaries* on *A School for Unusual Girls*

"An outstanding alternative history series entry and a must-have for teen libraries."

–*School Library Journal* on *Refuge for Masterminds*

"enticing from the first sentence . . . Swoony moments also abound; after all, this is a romance as well. Yet gender stereotypes are turned upside down as the women, who each have an unusual talent, plan a daring spy mission."

–*New York Times Book Review* on *A School for Unusual Girls*

"Spellbinding! A School for Unusual Girls is a beautifully written tale that will appeal to every girl who has ever felt different . . . a true page-turner!"

– Lorraine Heath, NYT - USA Today bestselling author

"Refuge for Masterminds moves at a fast pace from the first page and doesn't stop. Although it is written with a young adult audience in mind, it is a fun and enjoyable novel and will also appeal to adult readers."

– Francesca Pelaccia, *Historical Novel Society*

"I enjoyed this story immensely and I closed my kindle with a satisfied sigh."
—YA Insider

"Think Gallagher Girls, but written by Georgette Heyer."
—*VOYA Magazine* on *A School for Unusual Girls*

"The richly detailed setting and intriguing alternate history are well-crafted, but the characters are what stand out. Narrator Tess is headstrong, melodramatic, and awkward, but she is also brave, bright, and completely real. Such secondary characters as Indian Maya and Chinese Madame Cho provide some diversity. Readers ... seeking period romance with a twist need look no further."
—*Kirkus* on *Exile for Dreamers*

"I am in love with the Stranje House novels. Seriously, in love."
—*Book Briefs*

"I could almost smell the tar and feel the rocking of the boat ... I felt right there with her. This series keeps getting better and better and the author continues to show a fascinating alternative history where small changes in events could lead to vastly different outcomes. I am loving this series."
— *Greg's Bookhaven Blog*

"Leave it to Kathleen Baldwin to surprise us along the way! . . . a fantastic binge-read-worthy series!"
— *Mamma Reads Blog*

"I loved this book. Within a few pages I felt the same sense of adventure I felt . . . as a pre-teen, that breathless eagerness to turn the page."
—*Fresh Fiction Reviews*

Also by Kathleen Baldwin

The Stranje House Novels

A School for Unusual Girls

Exile for Dreamers

Refuge for Masterminds

My Notorious Aunt Series

Lady Fiasco

Mistaken Kiss

Cut from the Same Cloth

The Highwayman Came Waltzing

Diary of a Teenage Fairy Godmother

HARBOR FOR THE NIGHTINGALE

KATHLEEN BALDWIN

INK LION BOOKS

HARBOR FOR THE NIGHTINGALE

Published by Ink Lion Books

5100 Eldorado Pkwy Ste 102-518

McKinney TX 75070

INK LION BOOKS

First Edition September 2019

Printed in the United States of America

0 9 8 7 6 5 4 3 2 1

To Rel for loving the women of Stranje House as much as I do. Your edits were brilliant.

To Gurdeep for inspiring me with emails and your advice on language.

And to Tracine and the Reader-Ladies of Cache Valley for encouraging me to get it done.

Thank you!
You all kept me smiling.

Harbor for the Nightingale

One

Miss Maya Barrington's Typhoon

July 1814, Mayfair, London, Haversmythe House
Miss Stranje hosts a coming-out ball for her young ladies

ALL THE WORLD IS SOUND. Even if I were blind, I would still be able to see. It is as if everything hums—the trees, air, stones, and people—especially people. They all sing songs.

Some songs are more dangerous than others.

Most of the guests have already arrived at the ball, and our receiving line is dwindling. Georgie, Lady Jane, and Tess left us to join a lively country-dance. Seraphina still stands quietly beside me. Her inner music wraps around her as delicately as does the silk of her cloud-blue ballgown. With her white-blonde hair, Sera is the closest thing to an angel I have ever seen. On my other side, stands our rock, our headmistress, Miss Stranje, a woman made of iron.

The footman at the doors announces another arrival. "Lord and Lady Barrington."

My father and his wife stand in the doorway. The instruments playing serenely within me crash to a stop and clatter to the floor of my soul.

He came.

I press my hand against my heart to keep it from flapping and shrieking like a strangled bird. Seraphina edges closer so that our shoulders touch. She is trying to lend me strength.

The ballroom overflows with people. Dozens of strangers clad in shimmering finery, surround us, laughing and talking, but my very English stepmother ignores them all and marches straight for the receiving line. She holds her nose aloft, and her mouth pinched up so tight that her porcelain white face looks almost skeletal. An out of tune clarinet, she squeaks toward us, every step making me wish I could stop up my ears.

People say she is beautiful. My father certainly must have thought so. I fail to see it, especially when her face prunes up as it is doing now. It is a familiar expression. One that causes me to quake nervously while simultaneously clenching my fists.

Stepmother. That is what I was instructed to call her. I cannot bring myself to do it. *Mother* is a title of sacred honor. This woman, whose soul honks like an out of tune oboe, hasn't the faintest motherly inclination toward me. To me, she will never be anything more than the woman who married my father. Never mind that my mother, his first wife, was a Maharajah's daughter. To the new Lady Barrington, I am merely the brown-skinned embarrassment her husband acquired in India. Her hate roars at me like high tide slamming against a rocky shore.

She halts, and her blond sausage curls quiver with distaste as she plants herself squarely in front of Miss Stranje. She does not curtsey or even nod in response to our headmistress's greeting.

Her words trickle out so sweetly that most people would not notice she is gritting her teeth as she utters them. "Miss Stranje, a word if you please."

Naturally, Seraphina notices. She notices everything—it is her gift. *And her curse.* She reaches for my hand to reassure me. Of the five of us, we who are Miss Stranje's students, Seraphina Wyndham is the only one who truly understands me, and I do not want my best friend to suffer if she is caught being supportive of me. So, I smile reassuringly and slip free of her fingers. This is my battle, and I must face it alone.

Sera tugs my arm as I step away and furtively whispers, "Do something. Calm her."

She, like everyone else at Stranje House, mistakenly thinks my voice contains some sort of magical power to soothe. It is much simpler than that. My grandmother taught me how to use certain tones and cadences to relax people and communicate tranquility. Most souls are more than receptive, they hunger for it. My father's wife is a different matter. I have tried in the past, and rather than succumb to my calming tactics, she resists. On several occasions, she even covered her ears and screeched at me. I remember well her accusations of witchcraft and demonic bedevilment. It was on those grounds she convinced my father to send me away to Stranje House.

I wish, for Miss Stranje's sake, Lady Barrington would let me quiet her rat-like tendency to snipe and bite. Although, I'm not worried. I am confident our headmistress has guessed what is coming and will manage my father's wife quite handily without my help. After all, a rat does not surprise an owl.

"This way, Lady Barrington." Miss Stranje graciously directs our bristling guest to the side of the receiving line.

Father's charming wife clasps my shoulder and propels me forward with her. I could not possibly soothe her now. I'm not nearly composed enough to do it. Indeed, I am battling an overwhelming inclination to yank her boney claw from my shoulder and twist it until she cries off.

"What have you done, Miss Stranje?" Lady Barrington releases me and waves her hand at my ensemble. She is objecting to Miss Stranje's ingenious innovation, a traditional sari draped over an English ballgown.

"Why have you dressed the child thus?" Lady Barrington's fingers close in a fist around the embroidered veil covering my hair. "I'm mortified! You've garbed her like a heathen. Surely, this is an affront to everyone here." She flicks the saffron silk away as if it has soiled her gloves. "How do you expect Lord Barrington and myself to weather this . . . this *outrage*!"

She barks so loud that some of our guests turn to stare.

"After the enormous sum we paid you, it is beyond my comprehension why you should do us such a disservice—"

"Lady Barrington!" Miss Stranje's tone chops through the woman's tirade. "Calm yourself." Our headmistress stands a good four or five inches taller than most women, and she straightens to make every inch count. "You sadly mistake the matter, my lady. The other guests are well acquainted with your husband's daughter. In fact, a few weeks ago she was invited by no less a personage than Lady Jersey to sing at Carlton House for the Prince Regent. Miss Barrington's voice impressed His Highness so greatly that he, *the highest authority in the land*, suggested your stepdaughter ought to be declared a national treasure."

"What?" Lady Barrington blinks at this news, but her astonishment is short-lived. She clears her throat and steps up emboldened. "Oh, *that*. I am well aware of Maya's ability to mesmerize others with her voice. She uses demonic trickery, and you ought not allow—"

Miss Stranje leans forward, her tone low and deadly. "Are you unaware of the fact that Lady Castlereagh issued Miss Barrington vouchers for Almack's?"

"Al-Almack's . . ." Lady Barrington sputters at the mention of high society's most exclusive social club. Her hands flutter to her mouth in disbelief. "No. That can't be. Lady Castlereagh approved of *her*?" She glances sideways at me and her upper lips curls as if she tastes something foul in the air.

"Yes. Her vouchers were signed and sealed by the great lady herself." Miss Stranje's face transforms into a mask of hardened steel under which most people tremble in fear. "Not to put too fine a point on it, my lady, but Miss Barrington has been granted entry into the highest social circles. And, more to the point, it is my understanding that the patronesses refused to grant you vouchers. You were denied, is that not so?"

Lady Barrington steps back, unwilling to answer, a hand clutching her throat.

Miss Stranje refuses to let her quarry wriggle away. "In fact, my dear lady, anyone planning a soiree or ball during the remainder of the season, *anyone who is anyone*, has invited Miss Barrington to attend. I have stacks of invitations, dozens of notes, all of them begging your husband's daughter to do them the honor of singing at their gatherings. Indeed, society has taken her under their wing so thoroughly I had rather thought you would be offering me a bonus, instead of this ill-conceived reprimand."

Miss Stranje turns and levels a shrewd gaze at my father, who until this moment stood behind us silently observing.

He places a hand on his wife's waist and moves her aside. This stranger, this formidable Englishman who I used to call Papa with such glee, steps up to my headmistress and takes her measure. After a moment that stretches long enough to hammer my stomach into mincemeat, he nods respectfully. "Very well, Miss Stranje. I shall send additional remuneration to you in the morning."

His wife gasps, and indignation squeals off her like sour yellow gas.

He turns to me and reaches for my hand. Every instinct in me shouts to pull back. *Do not let him touch you.* It has been many long years since I have seen anything resembling a fatherly mannerism from him. I am terrified of what I might feel, and yet even more terrified of what I might miss if I pull away.

A sharp intake of breath crosses my lips, but then all other sounds cease. I no longer hear laughter or talking from the guests in the ballroom. No footsteps. No shuffling or clattering. The hum of impenetrable silence muffles everything else as I watch him lift my hand.

My father bows slightly, the way all the other gentlemen did as they came through the receiving line. He holds my fingers loosely as if we are mere acquaintances. "You look lovely, Maya, very much like your mother." He straightens, and I think I hear a whiff of sound—a soft keening, low and mournful. Except it is so brief and distant, I cannot be certain.

"You have her fire in your eyes. She would be proud." He squares his shoulders. "I'm pleased to see you making your way in the world—flourishing on your own."

Flourishing?

Hardly.

Unable to summon enough breath for words, I dip in an English curtsey that has become a habit. When I am able to speak, it sounds embarrassingly weak and fluttery, like a frightened bird. "I am glad you think so, my lord."

He lets go of my gloved fingers, offers his arm to his wife, and leaves me. Without a backward glance, he walks away. His measured gait is aloof and elegant, no different from that of a hundred other strangers in this room. The hollow thump of his heels as he abandons me hurts far worse than anything the spiteful woman he married has ever said.

I wish now that I had not allowed him to touch me. I ought to have run from the house—anything would be better than this grinding loneliness that darkens my insides. I would rather rip out my heart than to fall into the chasm threatening to swallow me. I've been in that dark place before.

The way he dismisses me without a second thought sends me spiraling back to India. I'm there again, in the stifling heat of his sickroom. Worried, I sneaked in to see him and stood quietly at the foot of his bed. Fear thumped through me like an elephant march as I watched him thrash under the sheets, fevered with the same epidemic that had only days earlier taken my mother's life.

I remember his wide-eyed alarm when he noticed me standing by his bedpost. I was only six, but I can still hear his hoarse shout for the servants. "Get her out of here. Send her away!"

"No! No. I want to stay with you. Let me stay with you," I begged. Crying, I clung to his bedpost, refusing to leave.

"Go! Take the chi–" Retching cut his rebuke short. Next came a string of muffled curses. "Out!"

"Come, miss. You cannot stay. Your father is very sick." Servants dragged me, kicking and screaming from his room. Later, my *ayah* told me Papa wanted me to stay away so that I would not catch his illness. I will never know if that was true or not. My *ayah* may have been trying to spare my feelings. I do remember telling her I didn't care if I got sick and died. I would rather stay with my papa.

"No, *kanya*. No, little girl. You must not say such things." She brushed my hair until it gleamed like my papa's black boots. "You will live, child. I see this. The future blooms in you. You are *gende ka phool*." She pulled a marigold out of a small vase and placed it in my palms. "Protector. Sun lion." I touched the bright orange petals and thought to myself, what good is such a small flower. It is too fragile—too easily crushed.

I was right.

The next day, on Papa's orders, his secretary, a fusty man with little patience for children, escorted me to my grandmother's family in the north. My father sent me away from the only world I'd ever known. On that long trip, loneliness and hurt chewed me up. Why would he send me so far away? Was he too sick? Or was his grief too heavy for him to share in mine? Perhaps my black hair and olive skin reminded him too much of my dead mother. Or was it because she was gone that he no longer cared for me?

Why?

We traveled for days and days, journeying toward the great mountains, land of the five rivers, and all the way there, sadness gnawed on my soul.

Few Europeans had ever ventured to the old villages and cities along the rivers. People were wary and distrustful of my white escort. He had difficulty finding a guide, and even when he did, we made several wrong turns. I did not care. Numb with grief, certain my father would die, or that he no longer loved me. I was already a lost child. What did it matter if we wandered forever?

After several treacherous river crossings, our guide located my family's village on the Tawi River. The weary attaché deposited me and my trunks in their midst and hurriedly left. I sat in the dirt beside my baggage, completely abandoned. The last ember of hope flickered inside me and blew out.

Strangers, who I would learn later were my cousins and aunts, gathered in a circle around me, staring, their faces ripe with curiosity and suspicion. Half-English, half-Indian, I was an unwelcome oddity, who belonged nowhere. I sat in the center of their circle, feeling like an oddly painted lizard. Did they judge me poisonous? Or edible?

A woman's joyous cry startled me. Astonished, I stood up. In my exhausted state, amidst all the confusion, I briefly mistook her voice for my mother's. I stared at the old woman running toward me. The voice, although eerily similar, did not belong to my dead mother. It belonged to my grandmother.

She burst through her gathered kinsman, took one look at me, and opened her arms. Though I learned later she had only visited me once as an infant, she kissed my forehead and hugged me, rocking and murmuring in Hindi. In tears, she declared to all my cousins and aunts that I was her daughter returned home.

Grandmother, my *naanii*, did not care about my mixed blood. She had no qualms about teaching her half-caste granddaughter the ways of her people. Others in our village were not so quick to trust me. I was half-English, after all. But out of respect for my grandmother, they kept their opinions to themselves. *Naanii* taught me how to make bread, how to mix healing herbs, braid hair, sew, and a thousand other things.

More importantly, *Naanii* taught me to listen.

To hear the world around us.

Over and over, she told me, "All life sings a song if we will but stop and listen."

I remember standing on the banks of the river washing clothes. "Close your eyes, little bird," *Naanii* said. "Quiet your mind and tell me what you hear?"

I pointed to her kinswoman standing in the shallows scrubbing her laundry against the stones. "I hear Kanishka humming a contented tune."

Grandmother, ever patient, smiled and asked, "And the stones, little one, what do they sing?"

I laughed and closed my eyes tight, listening for subtler vibrations. "They are old, *Naanii*. Their voices are quiet and deep. I can hardly hear them. Kanishka sings too loudly, so does the wind in the trees and grass." I opened my eyes. "And the river is especially loud."

"Ahh." She nodded, wrung out the cloth she'd been laundering, and set it in her basket. "It is true. Water is bold and brash. Very noisy." She galloped her fingers through the air. "Always rushing to and fro. River thinks she is all-powerful. You must try harder, my child. Listen for the calm voice of the stones." She laid a smooth pebble in my palm and pointed to one of the large rocks jutting up, splitting the current of the river. "Do you feel it? The mighty waters push and shove with the strength of a hundred horses, yet that boulder is unmoved. Hear how deep it hums, how sure it is of its connection with mother earth."

Years later, I would hear the stones sing, but not that day. That day I heard my grandmother, not just her words; I heard the unfathomable vibrations of her soul. It was as if she was as ancient and knowing as the stones of which she spoke.

I wish I were still standing on the banks of the Tawi River. Instead, I am here in London with too many sounds roaring in my ears—the babble of our many guests, the rumble of the city seeping up through the bones of this house. My father has taken me half a world away from the person who loves me best in all the world. Even though she is thousands of miles away, I close my eyes, hoping to catch my grandmother's distant pulse. I try to block out all the other noises, searching for those melodic threads that run between us even at this great distance.

"Maya? Maya! Are you all right?" Lady Jane rests her hand on my shoulder and startles me out of my search. She and Sera stare at me expectantly. "The musicians are tuning up for a quadrille. We are about to return to the dancing. But you seem shaken, what's wrong?"

I look at Lady Jane, wondering how to answer. I am not *all right*, as she phrases it, but what else can I say, here in this jangling place. "Yes, I hear the music," I say, and try to smile as if it is an important observation, as if the frivolity of dancing lightens my heart.

"Hmm," she says skeptically, and takes my hand, pulling me along with her like the mighty river carrying a piece of driftwood. I feel her questions clamoring to be asked, but luckily, I also know Lady Jane will restrain herself. This is not the time or place for that sort of discussion. She glances around the room and spots Alexander Sinclair. Immediately she brightens, and I feel joy pulse through her fingertips.

"Come." She leads the way and, arm in arm, we face both the music and crowd together.

TWO

THE DISQUIETING DANGERS OF DINING

I DRIFT THROUGH THE NEXT two hours, closing my ears to everything except the music flowing from the orchestra. Everyone here thinks I am so peaceable and tame. Infinitely calm. They think this because, in the past, I have used my voice to quiet their hearts, just as my grandmother used hers to soothe mine. They have also seen me meditate, but they do not know why I do it.

No one knows the truth.

Inside me, races a wild storm. A typhoon thunders against my ribs, rattling my soul, and I fear the day I can no longer hold it back. Shortly before my father took me away to England, *Naanii* instructed me to let the storm escape a little at a time. How? If I open the door, my fury will roar like a lion and leap out to devour what is left of my tattered world.

No, I must hold the storm inside.

I manage to do so, until the supper dance with Lord Kinsworth. He will perform a duet with me later this evening, and so he thought it best if we sat together at dinner. By all outward appearances, Lord Kinsworth is a very pleasant young man. At least, that is what Lady Jersey says of him. Lady de Lieven begs to differ with her friend's assessment. "Pleasant? Are you mad? He is an absolute Adonis. There isn't a female in Britain who doesn't catch her breath at the sight of him." She made this bold claim and added, with a girlish sigh, "Too bad, he's so young."

I wish someone other than me would notice that regardless of how handsome he is, the man is dangerous. I can't remember meeting anyone so elusive. Lord Kinsworth is impossible to decipher, and I do not like that. On the other hand, I must admit he does sing quite well. Fearlessly, in fact. His throat opens with a clear rich tone, full of depth and power. He holds nothing back there. His voice is incredible—so warm it would melt the butter on our bread plates.

I also concede that I hear kindness strumming through his being. I suppose some people find kindness an even more alluring trait than his commanding shoulders or his powerful physique. Not I. And frankly, the fact that he could easily pick me up with one arm is not reassuring either. Yes, kindness can be alluring, but shouldn't that arouse suspicion? I don't trust kindness. Not at all. A lion may purr and his mane might appear soft and inviting, but only a fool dares pet that lovely beast. There are always teeth attached. I am much more comfortable with people like Miss Stranje, whose stern no-nonsense demeanor lets me know exactly where I stand.

What's more, I care nothing for Lord Kinsworth's honey brown hair or his absurdly blue eyes. He must be dangerous, else why would his inner music always be running away, staying just out of my reach, laughing at me, as if we are playing a game of hide-and-seek.

It bothers me.

Dancing with Lord Kinsworth epitomizes our questionable friendship. Dance is so much like a chase. I step forward, he steps back, he moves toward me, and I step aside. No one in this merry jig is ever truly captured.

Afterward, he leads me into the dining room for supper and sits beside me. We silently busy ourselves spooning up creamed asparagus and cheese soup. Footmen remove our bowls and ready our plates for the main course. I glance sidelong, to the far corner of the table, at my father and his wife. They are chatting amiably with their dinner partners. My father does not even glance in my direction.

"You're awfully quiet tonight." Lord Kinsworth leans into me, nudging my shoulder with his. At the same time, he is irreverently twirling his dinner fork. "Not nerves, is it?"

"Nerves?" I blink out of my trance and struggle to grasp his meaning.

"Are you apprehensive about our performance after dinner?"

"Oh, that." I smile. Our upcoming duet had not even crossed my mind. "No. That is the least of my concerns. Are *you*? Apprehensive, I mean."

"Of course. Can't you tell?" He gives me an innocent grin, a grin he probably used his entire life to charm nursemaids, his mother, and every girl within a hundred miles. "I'm quaking in my boots."

He is not telling the truth. Nor is he wearing boots. I hear laughter beneath his mockingly serious words, and now he begins spinning his fork on one finger. A very un-English thing to do. The woman across the table stares at him with a disapproving frown. He spins it faster. Before the thing should go flying across the table, I gently retrieve his fork and set it beside his plate.

Hunting for something to say, I come up with a feeble compliment. "It is very generous of you to have agreed to sing with me."

"Generous?" His brows lift as if I've surprised him. "I assure you, generosity has nothing to do with it."

"No?" *If not that, then what?* I cannot keep the edge out of my tone. "Are you doing it out of pity?"

"Pity? Hmm. Let me think." Part of my veil has drifted onto his sleeve, and he toys with the silk embroidery. "Yes. Perhaps."

How does he do that? How does he make his face a mask of seriousness, and yet I can almost hear a boy laughing in the wind? Whatever the case, he has ruffled the last of my hard-won calm. I adjust the silver knife beside my plate until it lines up squarely. "Pity?"

"Naturally. What else could it be?" His brows angle up and, despite his cheerful curls and square jaw, he pulls a long mournful face. "I felt pity for all these poor souls who would otherwise be deprived of our duet."

He is jesting. "Oh," I say, embarrassed because I can never find my footing with him. The moment I think he is about to sing one song, he strikes up a different tune. My hands drop into my lap. "I see."

"Why else do you think I would've spent all those long hours practicing with you?"

Were those hours so very torturous?

I blink at him, aware of the fact that as I struggle to respond my mouth is foolishly opening and shutting. *Difficult man.* He doesn't mean for me to answer—I'm sure of it. And yet, he waits expectantly, compelling me to speak. I turn away from him and focus on a vase of roses situated in the center of the table. "I thought you enjoyed singing?"

To this, he merely hums and lifts his shoulders in a shrug.

My gaze snaps back to him. "You perform quite well, for someone so indifferent."

"You make it easy, Miss Barrington. Singing is like dancing. With the right partner, it is almost effortless. A pleasure." He turns his attention to the footman, who offers to serve us slices of roast beef.

Roast beef. I smell rosemary and bay leaf, but also the flesh of some innocent unsuspecting cow. In my country, cattle are a symbol of prosperity and life. It is forbidden to kill them. I cannot bring myself to even look at the platter. Whereas, Lord Kinsworth indicates he would like an additional helping. Of course, he would, wouldn't he? After all, Lord Kinsworth is an Englishman. An inscrutable beef-eating Englishman.

I do not belong here with people like him. I do not belong in England. It is a cold and unfeeling place. As soon as I reach my majority, and find some means to support myself, I am going back to India. I am fully aware that as a half-caste they will not fully accept me there either, but at least the people in India are not impossible to understand.

I wave the beef-bearing footman away and cross my arms, waiting for the roasted parsnips. A few moments later parsnips arrive, bathed in butter and herbs, followed by platters of fresh green beans garnished with almonds, bowls of pickled cauliflower, plover's eggs in aspic jelly, and a dozen other offerings. Miss Stranje spared no expense. This is a feast worthy of a king, which is fortunate, given the fact that our honored guest, His Highness, Prince George, Regent of England, sits at the head of the table.

During the dessert course, Prince George rises to offer a toast. "To the brave young ladies of Stranje House. We are dazzled by your loveliness, charmed by your elegance, and eternally grateful you know when to shout."

An uncomfortable chuckle goes around the table, followed by pale-cheeked grimaces as the memory whistles through us all like a high-pitched flute. He refers, of course, to the day our shouts warned Prince George and his admirals of a bomb about to explode. The gentlemen who were on the platform that day, men who might have died, admirals and statesmen—they bolster themselves against that dreadful memory and stand to honor us.

My cheeks grow warm with shyness, and I lower my gaze. Lord Kinsworth stands, too. For once, it does not feel as if he is laughing. He raises his glass when the Prince bellows. "To the young ladies! To their health and long life!"

A cheer shakes the air, making my heart pound faster. I am uncertain where to look, but I peek sideways, down the table to where my father stands. Curiosity ripples from him. His brows pinch as if he doesn't understand what the Prince means. How could he? He wasn't there that terrible day, and yet my father joins in and raises his glass. His head tilts to the side, and our eyes meet.

Instantly, I turn away. Confusion tumbles through me, two storms colliding, one warm, one cold, forming a cyclone within me, whirling out of control. I hum quietly to calm my jumbled emotions.

Lord Kinsworth glances at me and leans down so that only I can hear. "Cheer up, Miss Barrington. You needn't wear the hero laurels long. Any minute now, and you can chuck them aside."

I do not know what to say to that odd comment. "I am not a hero."

"Quite right. Begging your pardon. What is it they call you?"

Many things, I'm sure.

I open my mouth to reprimand him for his rudeness, but he is already rattling on. "A hero-ness? No, that's not the word. Ah, I have it—a heroine. Yes, that's it."

"No. Neither one. That is to say—" I am at a complete loss, and fully aware of the fact that I am sputtering. Prince George signals for all of us to sit down. Lord Kinsworth ignores my stammering and moves to help me with my chair.

"My lady," he says, being absurdly gallant.

Finally, everyone is seated. I am still struggling to find a suitable comment to put Lord Kinsworth in his place. Except my chance vanishes when the Prince lifts his cup again. "And to peace."

"To peace!" We echo this sentiment. Millions have died in battles with Napoleon. This war has bruised us all and wounded dozens of nations. Let us be done with it.

Our cheer fades, but the Prince continues to hold his cup aloft. An ominous thrum radiates from many of the men at the table. Admirals, Captains, Lords, they all lean in, apprehensive about something, listening closely, holding their breath. I sit back, and grip the seat of my chair, joining in their dread of what he might say next.

Miss Stranje straightens. Her features harden as if she, too, is steeling herself for the worst. Lady Jane stares intently at the Prince, her tensed muscles whirring with alarm. Lord Kinsworth falls eerily silent. He slouches, pretending to be relaxed, but I feel the fighter inside him, ready to spring up and swing his fists.

"*Peace.*" The Prince Regent begins with a childish tremor, dragging out the word as if by slowly scraping his sword from its scabbard we won't notice the threat. "We have been at war with Napoleon Bonaparte for eleven long years. Eleven years our men have given their lives. The time has come to end the bloodshed." He nods sagely, staring into his wine. Then, with a resolute sniff, he lifts his gaze to ours. "To that end, we have agreed to meet with Napoleon in order to negotiate a settlement."

We?

British government?

Or does he mean *he* intends to negotiate?

I am not the only one around the table who tallies up his remarks and sucks in a wary breath. *What sort of settlement?* He wants peace, but all down the table I hear only war drums pounding in my ears.

The Prince Regent gauges their reaction and begins bleating at us like an injured goat. Surely, I cannot be the only one who hears the tantrum in his cadence. "P'rhaps you do not grasp what a remarkable turn of events this is. Yes, yes, *remarkable*. In a few weeks' time, we may finally achieve the peace England and, indeed, all of Europe has so desperately desired over the last decade." Prince George makes this claim as if he believes such a thing is possible.

He is a child wishing upon a star. There can be no peace. Negotiating with Napoleon is tantamount to surrender. Does Prince George plan to surrender England to Napoleon?

Low murmurs punctuate the beating war drums. Admiral Gambier slams down his cup and rises, striding out of the dining room. His wife hurries after him, looking fearful, as she should. In other countries, they might lop off the admiral's head for rudely walking out on the ruler.

Lord Kinsworth slants toward me. "Interesting kettle of fish His Highness dumped on the table, wouldn't you agree?"

I survey the worried faces surrounding us and whisper, "A rather *dangerous* kettle of fish, I should think." *More like a kettle of foul-smelling poisonous snakes.*

"Uh-oh!" Lord Kinsworth's sudden alarm causes me to start. He grabs his spoon and holds it as one would a weapon. "Your strawberry ice is melting, my dear." He reaches over, stabs my ice and scoops up a spoonful from my plate.

The gray-haired lady across the table huffs loudly. "Manners, young man. *Manners*."

Without a morsel of shame, Lord Kinsworth chuckles and conspiratorially whispers into my ear, "I wonder how Lady Dreyfus will react when Boney's troops march into town and snatch the food from *her* plate."

He doesn't wait for my retort, which is a good thing since I cannot think of one. Instead, he helps himself to another spoonful of my ice and holds it up in tribute to the indignant lady. Closing his eyes and humming with pleasure, he leans close to me and adds, "This is a miracle, Miss Barrington. You really ought to give it a try."

He is incorrigible. I shake my head in a scolding manner, but cannot keep the corners of my lips from quirking up. "I would, my lord, except you seem to be devouring it for me."

With an impish grin, he sets down his spoon and gestures for me to taste it for myself. It is only then, after I have scooped up a spoonful of strawberry ice and it is dancing divinely on my tongue, that I realize Lord Kinsworth has managed to distract me from both the confusion my father caused and the gravity of Prince George's dreadful announcement.

THREE

WHAT SONG OF WOE IS THIS?

A glooming peace this morning with it brings.
The sun, for sorrow, will not show his head...
For never was there a story of more woe
Than this of Juliet and her Romeo.

AFTER DINNER, despite the Prince's unsettling announcement, Miss Stranje continues with her plan for Lord Kinsworth and me to sing for our guests. "Are you certain?" I ask, fighting to moderate the slight quiver in my throat. "The ballad, after what the Prince said . . . I'm not sure it is quite—"

"We shall stay on course, Miss Barrington." Miss Stranje moves past me, graciously herding the guests to their seats. Seraphina takes her place at the piano, behind her a violinist and violoncellist warm up. The low rumbling notes of the violoncello vibrate through me, adding to the shakiness of my legs. Lord Kinsworth and I turn and face a very gloomy gathering of England's high society. The room throbs with so many heated emotions, confusion and worry, fear and anger, the force of it nearly topples me.

The ballad we practiced is a retelling of Romeo and Juliet. It will not lift our guests' spirits. In hushed tones, I confide this concern to Lord Kinsworth, "I wish we had chosen a different song. Perhaps we ought to switch it to something else."

"Difficult this late in the game." With a guiding hand on my back, he situates us closer to the piano. "I suspect this song may be the very thing they need." He winks at me as if we are sharing a secret. "It'll be cathartic. Let's give them someone else's troubles to think on."

I hope he is right. I am still staring at him, considering the idea, when Sera and the other musicians begin playing the introduction. *Very well.* If this sad story is to distract them from their turmoil, let us make it exquisitely sad.

Lord Kinsworth opens the song with a bravado I envy. His bold cheerful notes startle our listeners. They sit up in their chairs as Romeo teases Juliet upon their first meeting. We are dancing again, he and I, only this time it is with our voices. Juliet cleverly evades Romeo's advances, until he holds up his palm and sings to her of kisses. *Sings to me.* Lord Kinsworth mimes the actions of the song and holds his palm up—awaiting mine.

Impertinent. We did not practice it that way, but what can I do except lift mine to his? Impossible to miss the breathless quality in my answering refrain. I cannot stop the slight tremor in each note as he steps closer, pressing his palm to mine.

I must not let him fluster me. Singing with more force, I struggle to calm my silly heart. He is an expert charmer—so very like Romeo. And everyone knows, it did not end well for them. I do not run from the room. I can't. Twice today, I ought to have fled. Instead, I stay and harmonize with him.

I am forced to admit to myself, the way our voices intertwine, I would not run away even if I could. It is pure heaven. My traitorous vocal cords follow his as surely as if he were the Pied Piper and I, a witless child.

The ballad is another chase of sorts, a furtive dance of hidden passion. In and out of joy we run, teased with the promise of happiness and hope, until the end. When Juliet discovers Romeo is poisoned, saltwater stings my cheeks.

Save me! It means these tears leaking from my eyes are real. Lord Kinsworth has wrapped me so tight in the imagery that I cannot escape grief. It is fiction, I know this, but he has cast me under his spell so thoroughly that, like Juliet, I cannot bear thinking of life without the warming touch of his voice.

They feel it, too. Lady Jersey's cheeks are wet as I raise an imaginary dagger. Even my father's eyes are watering. I plunge the invisible blade into my heart, and sing, "Oh happy dagger, this is thy sheath. There rust and let me die."

The ballad concludes with Juliet's soaring declaration of grief, and the violoncello dragging a low mournful sob across the strings. This is how our song ends. The Prince of Verona does not ride in and scold us for our folly, nor does he summarize the tragedy. It is over.

A weighty silence nearly suffocates us all.

The audience does not leap to their feet and applaud. Instead of clapping, most of the ladies are blotting their eyes. Several gentlemen pull out handkerchiefs and dab at their own cheeks. Lady Jersey hunches forward, and her shoulders shake as she surrenders to racking sobs.

This is a disaster.

We have grieved them when they so desperately needed cheering.

I turn to Lord Kinsworth for reassurance. He seems distressed, as well. A rare thing for him. I strain to understand. It cannot have been the ballad—we practiced it at least a dozen times. Was I off-key? It felt as if every note hit its mark.

What can be vexing him? I would swear I hear trepidation whirring in his soul. *And his heart*—his heart is pattering like running feet. How can this be?

Any second, I expect Lord Kinsworth to paste on his cocksure smile or don his lopsided grin. Surely, he will turn me upside down with one of his teasing remarks. Except he doesn't. When he finally looks at me, his lips are pressed in a tight straight line, and . . .

Oh. He is unhappy. *With me.*

My stomach sinks, and I rest my hand on the edge of the piano to steady myself. I don't know what I did, but clearly, I am the cause of his consternation. He steps back, forcing his shoulders to relax, and bows. Except it is far too extravagant. Flamboyant. The sort of thing an actor might do. He means to be amusing, but I brace myself for what may come next.

"Fair Juliet . . ." He hides behind a performer's mask, pretending he is still playing the part of Romeo. "T'was an honor to have sung at your side, m'lady. Ne'er was there a voice that called more sweetly to the heart than thine." He winces as if stung by his own tomfoolery.

I incline my head, silently accepting his compliment. *If, that is what it was.*

His gaze flits off to the distance, anywhere but to me. "And now, I must be off. For lo, I hear the lark heralding the morn."

It's obvious he does not intend for me to answer, but I cannot stop myself from uttering Juliet's response. "Nay, my lord, 'tis not the lark. It is the nightingale, you hear."

He laughs, low in his neck, like a man being choked. With a curt nod, he strides away as if he has urgent business elsewhere.

Perplexing man! What are you running from?

Most of our guests drift toward the ballroom, but Lady Jersey remains in her seat, struggling to dry her eyes. Lady Castlereagh, ever stoic, takes the chair vacated beside Lady Jersey and rests a consoling hand on her friend's shoulder.

Here sit two of the most powerful women in England. Lady Jersey pretends to care about nothing except the latest fashion when all the while she has a finger in every political pie cooked up in Britain. And dear Lady Castlereagh, everyone thinks she is the most formidable of the patronesses, a stickler for the rules. In reality, she is a tenderhearted woman who quietly sacrificed all to support her husband. Lord Castlereagh holds the very thorny office of Minister of Foreign Affairs, and he would be lost without her.

These great matriarchs of society have been remarkably gracious to me, the least I can do is go to Lady Jersey and apologize for upsetting her. I approach and wait until Lady Castlereagh gives me a nod of approval to speak. "I am very sorry, my lady, for causing you such distress. In light of the evening's events, I do wish we had chosen a different song–"

Lady Jersey waves away my apology.

Lady Castlereagh speaks for her. "Nonsense, Miss Barrington. I doubt either of us has ever heard anything so moving. Isn't that right, my dear?"

"Yes. Yes." Lady Jersey crumples her handkerchief and straightens her back. Tears left wide tracks in her powder. Yet she looks even more beautiful because the tears have washed away her artifice. And now, an intensity throbs from her, so strong that it weakens my knees.

Miss Stranje, Lady Jane, and Sera come up quietly and stand behind me.

"*We* will not–" Lady Jersey takes a shuddering breath, her hands tighten into fists, and she strikes them against her lap, digging her knuckles into the red silk. "–we *must* not make their mistake." She stares up at me as if I grasp her meaning. "Romeo and Juliet."

In truth, her words baffle me, but I nod in agreement. What I do hear and understand is the river of strength and conviction flowing out from beneath each syllable. With that river, the sound of a thousand horses thunders in my ears. It is with *that*, I wholeheartedly agree.

Lady Jersey looks past us, squinting at the Prince Regent standing across the room. Her jaw flexes. "We must save Romeo from his poison."

She whips back to Lady Castlereagh and me, her tone

punctuating each word like an iron hammer. "And if that fails, we shall *not* fall upon our daggers."

"Certainly not." Miss Stranje takes a soldier-like step forward. "Not now. Not ever."

Eyes glistening fiercely, Lady Jersey lifts her chin and meets Miss Stranje's warrior gaze. "For we are made of sterner stuff than Juliet."

Lady Castlereagh claps her hand over Lady Jersey's fist in a silent pact of agreement, and the two of them turn to us expectantly.

Are we, their protégés, strong enough to face what may come?

Sera nods solemnly, and Lady Jane steps up beside me, her chin raised courageously. Across the ballroom, Tess and Georgie are lining up for a country dance, and both of them cast concerned looks in our direction. I answer for all of us, echoing our mentors' brave words, hoping that the coming storm will not prove them false.

"For we *are* made of sterner stuff."

FOUR

ODE TO A FLOWER

SILENCE FOLLOWS our solemn vow. For a moment, all we do is breathe and take solace in one another's company. Our reverie dissolves when Mr. Chadwick, son of the magistrate from our home county, intrudes on our circle and formally bows. Although he is our friend, Quinton Chadwick is not privy to what Miss Stranje is actually training us to do in her school. Sera and the others worry that he is too inquisitive. I think it shows he is a clear-headed fellow with keen powers of observation.

It is only natural that he would be suspicious. Anyone, who knows us as well as he does, has ample cause to wonder. There is something solid and refreshing about the young man. His inner music rings as true as church bells echoing across a valley.

Tonight, he hesitates politely. "Your pardon ladies, but I believe Miss Wyndham promised me this set."

Sera's cheeks turn a vibrant shade of pink.

"Haaas she now?" Lady Jersey resumes her aristocratic

drawl and lifts her quizzing glass to scrutinize young Chadwick as if she, and she alone, will decide who dances with whom. The great lady is toying with him.

"I did, my lady." Sera pipes up, not loudly, but with enough shaky determination to make her wishes evident to us. "I promised him." She rests her hand on his offered arm.

"I seeee. Very well." Lady Jersey lowers her glass. "Off with you, then."

Sera allows him to lead her away to the promenade. As they leave, Alexander Sinclair saunters up and bows to all of us as if we are queens. "Ladies. Unless I miss my guess, you are knee-deep in, er, uh, plans. I, for one, am terrified of vexing you, truly I am."

He does not look terrified at all. Nor does he sound worried in the least. Alexander Sinclair always seems as if he is about to tell everyone a walloping-good joke. He is the opposite of Lady Jane.

"However," he says, bowing again, putting on an air of seriousness. "I must insist on extracting Lady Jane from your midst. By my reckoning, a plum-awful riot is likely to break out in your ballroom if she doesn't come and fulfill her obligations on the dance floor."

"Humph. A riot started by you, no doubt." Lady Jersey tilts her head up so she can peer down her nose at him. "And see here, young man, we are not *knee-deep* in anything. If you intend to court Lady Jane, I insist you learn to mind your tongue."

He responds to her scold with a relaxed grin. "Therein lies the problem, my lady. My wretched tongue seems to have a mind of its own."

"And all the subtlety of a . . ." She sniffs derisively.

"An *American*."

He bows again. "Why thank you, my lady. High praise indeed."

Lady Castlereagh chuckles and taps Jane with her fan. "I suggest you take your cheeky young man away before Lady Jersey runs him through with the dagger she has stowed in her reticule."

The instant they leave, Lady Jersey turns to us and abandons her haughty accent once more. "Don't look now," she whispers. "But Prince George is embroiled in a rather heated argument with Admiral St. Vincent—*no*, don't all of you turn around at once. Wouldn't you just love to be a fly on the Admiral's ear."

"Goodness gracious. Oh, my dear . . ." Lady Castlereagh subtly glances over her shoulder. "Not only is Lord St. Vincent Admiral of the Channel Fleet—the fellow also has Wellington's ear, as well as most of Parliament. This does not bode well, not well at all. I shall find Lord Harston and send him over to see what's ado. Harston is a clever-boots at sidling into sticky conversations."

"Hmm, yes. A pity it will take so long to find Lord Harston in this crowd. It would be quite advantageous to know what they're saying right now." Miss Stranje says this while staring straight at me. I know what she wants—she wants me to spy on them, to eavesdrop.

With a sigh, I acquiesce. "If you wish."

"I do." Miss Stranje brightens and turns to her friends. "Miss Barrington is a *marvel* at overhearing. Observe how skillfully she blends into the scenery. She becomes nearly invisible."

"Does she now?" Lady Jersey's eyebrows lift with interest. "Go on, then. Go!" She flicks her hands at me, shooing me off to the task. "Let us see this magical feat."

Miss Stranje is exaggerating. I am not really a marvel at this, and it certainly isn't a feat of magic. It is a skill I acquired while living with my father and his new wife. *A necessary skill.* I taught myself how to become invisible, how to blend quietly into the furniture, how to move from room to room without being heard. I had superb motivation. If the new Lady Barrington didn't see me, she couldn't bark her disapproval at me.

However, the ability to slip past my stepmother hardly qualifies me to disappear in a ballroom crammed full of people. Especially dressed like this. It is a challenge, but I manage to drift across the room without drawing attention. One must breathe softly, holding one's inner music very quiet, while at the same time avoiding anyone's direct gaze. Fortunately, most everyone in the ballroom is preoccupied with watching dancers, or flirting and chatting with one another. It is so crowded that the traitorous Lady Daneska and Ghost could stroll through the room unseen. It is also to my advantage that Miss Stranje instructed the servants to set up dozens of magnificent flower arrangements, and several lush rows of potted shrubberies.

Prince George and Admiral St. Vincent stand away from the crowd, taking advantage of the breeze by a window next to a bank of greenery. They are ludicrously mismatched. The Prince is fat and bloated. I doubt the poor man has seen his toes this decade lest his feet are propped on a stool. The Admiral, on the other hand, is older but lanky and muscular, with a beaky hooked nose and birdlike quickness to match.

I move toward them with cautious flowing steps, gliding silently past potted palms and massive ferns. Like an unnoticed breeze, I weave alongside a hedge of greenery and wedge myself against the wall, tucking between a panel of velvet draperies and the bank of flowering jasmine. The cloyingly sweet fragrance tickles my nose, but I stay. Completely hidden, this is the perfect position for me to overhear their conversation.

I peek between the leaves, and see Prince George is *red-in-the-face* mad at the Admiral. So much so, he forgets to use the royal '*we*.' "Now listen here! Parliament may force me to pick the Prime Minister they prefer, and I may not have any say-so over taxes, but I still have the right to declare war, do I not?"

"Yes, Sir, you do. But—"

"No buts. I do, and you know it. And since that is the case, it stands to reason I have the power to declare peace. I will do what I jolly well think is best for England, and there's an end to the matter."

"That's the point, Your Highness. Negotiating with Napoleon Bonaparte isn't what's best for England. The man cannot be trusted."

Prince George's cheeks get even redder. "By all accounts, he is a man of his word. Face facts, the Bourbons are dead. They are no more. Napoleon Bonaparte is the Emperor of France."

"Emperor—*fah*!" Admiral St. Vincent nearly spits his opinion at Prince George. "He's a self-made *tyrant*, set on conquering the whole blasted world. A *madman!* You simply cannot do this, not without Parliament's consent."

Prince George puffs up like a vexed cobra, a fat, very dangerous cobra. His words snort out as if he's blasting a trumpet. "You forget yourself, St. Vincent. Parliament is not my nursemaid. And by–"

Lord Harston strolls between them and interrupts.

A crafty fellow, Lord Harston. Anyone might think he and Prince George had known one another since birth. He resides at Carlton House as the Prince's guest, and the two attend all the same gatherings and are often seen together gambling at Brooke's. But the truth is, unbeknownst to Prince George, Lady Castlereagh strategically positioned Lord Harston in the Prince Regent's sphere, and tasked him with protecting England's acting monarch. He serves as the Prince's bodyguard of sorts, while at the same time Lord Harston gathers information for Lord and Lady Castlereagh. Lady Jersey refers to him as our man inside the palace.

We were all shocked to learn that until recently, Lord Harston was secretly betrothed to our own Lady Jane. They are not engaged now, of course. He stepped aside so that Alexander Sinclair could court her. Lord Harston surprises me. He is a man full of contradictions, a dandy yet a devoted patriot, generous yet shrewd, and about as unlikely a parental sort as ever existed. Nevertheless, fate has cast him in that role, too. His sister was Lord Kinsworth's mother, and upon her death, Lord Harston became Lord Kinsworth's legal guardian.

"May I be of service, your Highness?" Lord Harston leans in protectively to the bristling Prince. "You seem distressed, Sir. Is anything amiss?"

Prince George sniffs and tugs on his vest. "It's nothing. A trifle." He replaces his puffy irritation with a genial mask. *Only a mask.* I still hear trumpets blasting inside Prince George, except now they blare beneath a blanket of good manners. "The Admiral here has merely forgotten himself. That's all."

"My lord." Lord Harston inclines his head in a respectful greeting to Admiral St. Vincent. "I'm sure we are all friends here, are we not?"

Admiral St. Vincent does not answer immediately. "Merely expressing my concerns, that is all."

"Of course. I know exactly what you mean. These are trying times. *Trying times*, indeed." Lord Harston nods in agreement. "And I'm sure no one is more concerned about our country than our devoted Prince Regent."

"Just so." Prince George lifts his chin. "And now *we* must be off. Must mingle. We mustn't neglect our *other* friends."

The two men bow as his Highness waddles away. Lord Harston calls after him. "Save me a chair at the card table."

"Ha-ha! Ha-ha." Prince George doesn't turn his great huge self around. Instead, he raises one plump pointer finger into the air. "You know us too well, Harston—too well."

As soon as the Prince is out of earshot, Lord Harston turns to the Admiral. "I say, St. Vincent. What was that all about? Are you trying to make an enemy of the future King of England?"

"Trying to save England, so we have a future. You know as well as I do, this is a colossal blunder—this insane idea of his to break bread with Napoleon and hammer out a settlement."

"Can't be as bad as all that, can it?" Harston's inner music is subtle most of the time, like a leopard weaving through tall grass. I know this cautious sound—he's hunting. "Surely Prince George can't agree to anything on his own? They're just going to discuss the matter, after all."

"If you believe that, I'll sell you my goose that farts golden eggs."

Lord Harston had the good grace to chuckle.

Admiral St. Vincent postures like an angry man, but he is also afraid. The slight tremor in his voice gives him away. "He has the bull-headed notion he can speak for Britain without consulting Parliament."

"Surely not. He can't, can he?"

"Theoretically, yes. He can. Things are changing, but the current laws aren't definitive. What he most certainly *will* do is plunge us deeper into this war than we already are, not to mention the fact that he'll divide Britain's loyalties." Admiral St. Vincent warms under Lord Harston's sympathetic ear. "Napoleon knows this, and he'll try to bribe Prinny, you know he will."

Our man on the inside, sips his wine and casually asks, "Did His Highness happen to mention when this meeting is supposed to take place?"

The Admiral rumbles like a storm cloud threatening to thunder. "No, he did not. But he alluded to it being as soon as three or four weeks."

"*Three weeks*? But Parliament will have adjourned the week before." Lord Harston's calm bursts apart. He tries to cover his off-key outcry by taking another sip of his wine.

"Exactly."

"Where? Do you know if they're meeting on French soil or British?"

The Admiral shakes his head and curses under his

breath. "Refused to tell me. A *secret*, says he, *between rulers of the two greatest empires in the civilized world*."

Their conversation has me peering into the shrubbery so intently I almost fail to notice Lord Kinsworth passing my bank of greenery. I spring back against the wall and hold my breath, praying he didn't catch the movement in the bushes.

He strides straight for his uncle. "There you are, Uncle. I've been looking high and low for you."

"Ah, well, you see there's your problem. You should've hunted here in the middle." Lord Harston doesn't sound as jovial as his words might lead one to believe. "Lord St. Vincent, I believe you know my nephew, Lord Kinsworth."

Lord Kinsworth bows. "At your service, my lord."

Admiral St. Vincent gives him a cursory nod. "Splendid performance tonight, lad." His mumbled compliment sounds cursory. "Now, if you'll excuse me, I must be taking my leave." He takes a step, but turns back, working his jaw hard before he speaks. "Listen here, Harston, if you've any influence with His Royal Highness, I urge you to exert it. If he goes through with this harebrained scheme you know as well as I do, Britain is done for."

Lord Harston raises his chin and draws a deep breath. "I'll do my best."

Lord Kinsworth stands next to his uncle, watching Admiral St. Vincent stalk away. "Working tonight, I see."

"Always, my boy. Always. Although, I must agree with St. Vincent–splendid performance tonight. Your rendition of the Bard's ill-fated lovers choked me up. And that spirited young filly you sang it with, she's–"

"You needn't repeat your warning." Lord Kinsworth

cut him off.

What warning? I frown at them through the jasmine hedge.

"Oh yes, I heard you quite clearly the first time you lectured me about her." Lord Kinsworth's irritation pours out. "*The Barrington chit is unsuitable. A foreigner. Not to mention she's one of Miss Stranje's students, which means she's trouble. Think of your offspring.* So on, and so forth."

Unsuitable? Everyone must feel as my stepmother does. Knives of anger zing through my stomach. I hate it here. Miss Stranje should never have brought me to London. No, it is not her fault. It is my father's. He should never have brought me to England in the first place.

Trouble–he says. Ha! I choke back a vicious half chortle. Oh, yes. I am trouble. More than any of them could ever imagine. I am a typhoon about to explode. I press back against the wall, my hands knotted into throbbing fists.

Think of your offspring.

I swallow my heaving breath and hold it tight. How dare they speak of children–*my future children.* Those words wound me worse than anything else they said. Lord Harston must think that my heritage and skin color will hinder them here in the land of pasty white English cream puffs.

My stomach churns, tumbling like mud and stones and uprooted trees in a flash flood. I feel sick. Sick enough to burst. I hate him. I do. Even if it is true, it is a heartless thing to say.

Lord Harston tries to laugh it off. "Come now, Ben. I wasn't as dictatorial as all that."

Ben?

That must be Lord Kinsworth's given name. *Ben*, I roll the sound of it over my lips even though I will never say it aloud. We are not friends, Ben and I. We will *never* be friends. Apparently, I am *unsuitable.* I am *trouble.* Trouble for him, and *a brown curse to my future children.*

"You were tyrannical!" With a loud exasperated gust of air, Ben presses his point. "In fact, I'll lay odds the Queen Mother is less dictatorial–"

"You needn't fly up in the boughs about it. What I'd intended to say, before you cut me off so rudely, was that when the young lady sings, I find myself completely transfixed. She's extraordinary. Quite remarkable."

I peek through the bushes again, not hating him quite as much as I did a few seconds ago.

Ben doesn't say anything. He frowns, glancing in my direction as if he senses my presence. I draw a sharp breath and jump back against the wall. I wish I could vanish from this wretched hiding place. I don't want to hear the next flippant remark he is sure to fling into the air. Worse yet, I do not want him to catch me here. It would be impossible to sneak away now. Not this close, not without being seen. If he discovers I've been lurking among the potted plants, eavesdropping, I will die of embarrassment.

Fortunately, his uncle reclaims his attention. "I watched the two of you sing, it looked as if you are already forming an attachme–"

"Delighted the song pleased you." Lord Kinsworth doesn't sound delighted at all. "Now what do you say, we take our leave?"

"*Now?* The night is still young." Lord Harston seems

genuinely surprised at his nephew's sudden desire to go home. He sets his wineglass on a passing footman's tray and takes another glass filled with sparkling white wine. "I've matters yet to attend to, and I promised to meet Prinny at the card tables later. Why would you want to leave so early? It's barely past one."

"Stifling in here, don't you think?" Ben tugs at his shirt collar.

"It's as pleasant as one can expect this time of year. What's wrong? It can't be the heat. Come stand nearer to the window." Lord Harston tugs Ben a few steps closer. I sink deeper into the curtains, hoping they won't notice me.

"I thought you were enjoying Miss Barrington's company?" his uncle asks. "It may please you to know I've revised my opinion on the matter entirely. Just this evening I spoke with the young lady's father and—"

"What!" Ben demands too loudly. Luckily, his outburst overshadows my own involuntary squeak. "You didn't?" he demands.

My sentiments exactly. *Why did his uncle speak to my father? What did he say?* Ben is right, it *is* stifling in here. I push my veil away from my neck, feeling as if I might melt into the floorboards. In fact, it would be better if I could. Anything would be better than the dread snaking up to swallow me.

He spoke to my father! Why? It takes every ounce of strength I have to keep from shouting my questions.

"Of course, I did!" Lord Harston matches his nephew's raised voice. "When it comes to your future, I refuse to leave anything to chance. Admittedly, the gentleman was not very forthcoming. Scrutinized me as if I was a thief come to steal his prized possession. That alone gave me cause to approve her."

Ben—er, that is I meant to say, *Lord Kinsworth*—is ordinarily as carefree as swallows whistling on a summer breeze. This minute, however, he roars like a stormy winter sea. "When it comes to *my* future—I wish everyone would leave well enough *alone*."

"Lower your voice, Ben. You're making a scene."

He doesn't. He raises it. "I don't need a guardian!"

"Until you reach your majority the law says otherwise."

Lord Kinsworth shifts to a low growl, and even from my side of the jasmine hedge, I can almost feel his jaw flexing. "You're as difficult as my mother was."

"My sister loved you dearly. It was her dying wish that I watch out for you, and I'll not go back on my promise to her."

"By all means, Uncle Gil, if you see I'm about to gallop over a cliff, grab the reins and turn me around. But that isn't the case here. And I certainly don't need your help with women!"

"Huh." Lord Harston grins like an ornery camel about to spit. "I hadn't thought so either. Not until I saw the moonstruck way you looked at Miss Barrington."

"Moonstruck? Ha! Not ruddy likely." Lord Kinsworth crosses his arms and steps back assuming a stance identical to his uncle's. "I've never been moonstruck in my life." Standing to his full height, he has several inches on his uncle. He must think that gives him an advantage as he presses forward. "Even if I did have a moment of weakness, I'm quite capable of watching out for myself in that regard."

Lord Harston steps out from under his nephew's imperious glower and lowers his guard. "Are you, Ben?"

"Yes." Lord Kinsworth relaxes, too, and his arms fall open. "For pity's sake, Uncle Gil, I'm tired of being choked to death. Give me some freedom."

"Freedom?" Lord Harston squints at his nephew studiously. "That's what you want?"

"Yes!" Ben's answer rings out like a shot.

Lord Harston doesn't flinch. He merely tilts his head inquisitively. "And India? What is it about India that interests you so much?"

I want to know the answer to that, too, so I strain to hear, pressing deeper into the hedge.

"I don't know." Lord Kinsworth shrugs. "I suppose it to be a mysterious place. Interesting. Brimming with color and life. At any rate, it's bound to be better than old dull gray England." He brightens, and the jovial boy in him returns. "India would be an adventure."

"Is that what you're after, Ben? *Adventure*." Lord Harston isn't mocking; there is *not even a hint* of amusement. It surprises me because ordinarily, I sense an undertow of humor in him. The two of them have that in common. Instead, Lord Harston seems sincerely interested in the answer. "That's what you want?"

"Yes!" Ben says in a single breath as if a thousand dreams come rushing out of his lungs. "Yes. More than anything." He braces himself against the window, staring off in the distance. "I can't stop thinking of my father, and how he died of pneumonia before he had a chance to see anything of the world except Shropshire. As far as I can tell, he never left the estate except for a few brief excursions to London when he was my age."

"Your father was a good man. Honorable. Reliable. Kinsworth treated my sister very well."

"Yes, but sheep and wheat–that was the extent of his life. My father died in the same house in which he was born. After that, you know what my mother was like. She fretted over every scraped knee I got. I need only cough once, and she would start dosing me with remedies. Wouldn't allow me to go away to school. She hired tutors instead. Every time I went out on my pony, she fussed as if I was endangering everything she held dear."

Lord Harston turned the wineglass round and round in his hands. "Well, you were, weren't you? You were everything to her."

"That's not the point. You don't know what it was like after my father died. Whenever I *was* obstinate enough to actually go riding, she'd send two grooms with me and wait in the yard, pacing, until I came back. She was terrified of losing me, and she was always so unhappy. Did my best to try to make her laugh, but the gloom always returned."

"She loved your father deeply." Lord Harston's voice drops so low I can barely hear. "Theirs was a love match, you know?"

"A *love-match.*" Lord Kinsworth rakes a hand through his hair. "Oh, yes, I know. I heard that sad refrain often enough–*how lovely they were together. A right pair of turtle doves.*"

"Well," Lord Harston set his goblet down with a click. "Truth is, they were."

"Except it wasn't lovely. It was *suffocating.*" Ben straightens and paces. "Loving him was her undoing. And his." Ben usually handles everything as if something amusing lurks beneath the surface. But now he sounds agitated, and it worries me. In India, I'd seen caged tigers pace the same way he is doing in front of the ballroom window.

"Ahh, now I see." Lord Harston opens his lips as if suddenly handed the key to a vault filled with jewels. "*That's* why you're running away from Miss Barrington."

"What are you talking about?" Ben stops abruptly. "I'm not running away."

"No? It looked like you were."

Lord Harston is right. It did look like it. I wriggle my face into the jasmine, gently moving aside some of the glossy leaves so I can see more clearly.

Ben slants a surprised expression at his uncle. "You were watching me?"

Lord Harston issues a loud exasperated sigh. "I thought by now you understood–it's my job to be observant."

"About your job–"

"Oh no, you won't get away with changing the subject." His uncle shakes a scolding finger. "Back to Miss Barrington. One minute you seem enthralled with her and the next you're sprinting in the opposite direction."

Lord Kinsworth puffs air through his lips as if his uncle has gone daft. "Don't be ridiculous. I didn't sprint." He smirks, cavalier again. "Look around you. This is a ballroom. One does not sprint from women on the chase."

"Oh, I see. She's the one chasing you, is she? If that were the case, I suppose I would run, too."

It is a barefaced lie! I am not chasing Kinsworth.

Of all the arrogant, roguish . . . I squeeze the velvet curtains in my fist, but as soon as I realize what I'm doing, I stop. The moving fabric might draw attention.

"It's more complicated than that." Lord Kinsworth rubs his chin. "I only let her *think* she is chasing me. Not that it matters. Either way, she'll never catch me."

His uncle frowns. "You're confusing me, my boy. Who is chasing whom? Miss Barrington doesn't seem the sort of young lady to run after a man, or lay a trap for him. Now that I've studied her out a bit more, I'd be willing to wager she's too reserved and gentle for that sort of thing."

"Are you blind, Uncle Gil?" Lord Kinsworth, *the scoundrel*, laughs at his uncle for defending me. My fingers itch to squeeze something until it snaps. Something like his big neck.

"Perhaps you drank too much wine at dinner." Ben resumes his pacing, this time faster than before. "Can't you see? Miss Barrington is the most dangerous kind of female. She doesn't need to lay a trap. Oh no. She's the sort who can trick a man into thinking he *wants* to give up everything. Blink twice, and she'll have you believing you actually *want* to live out the remainder of your days locked away with her, in a dull gray stone house, surrounded by nothing but bleating sheep. Worst of all, she lures you in with a song. All that gentleness—that *is* the trap."

Lord Kinsworth steps back waiting for his uncle to respond. When all he gets from his guardian is a shrewd measuring squint, he lowers his voice and calmly tries to explain further. "You understand, don't you? She's like an exotic flower. If a man gets close enough, he'll drown in those big brown eyes of hers and never wake up again."

"Ah." Lord Harston clicks his tongue sympathetically. "Hmm, yes, I see. That kind of woman *is* dangerous, indeed."

Dangerous?

Perhaps I ought to demonstrate exactly how dangerous. Just as I'm ready to rip a handful of jasmine off this blasted hedge and heave it at both of them, Lord Harston says, "But I don't understand, Ben. If all that is true, why do you keep buzzing around her?"

I freeze, crushing the jasmine blossoms in my palms. *Yes. Why?*

Lord Kinsworth presses his lips together and glances up to study the ornate ceiling. Before answering, his pursed lips relax into an innocent lopsided smile, a smile that surely won him forgiveness from every female he'd ever wronged. Completely disarming, his wretched smile softens the tension in my belly, causes me to slacken and slump against the wall. People think my voice is magical, but my skills are nothing compared to what he can do with a simple roguish grin.

Even so, it is his words that cause me to slide down the wall and hug my knees like a confused child.

"Because, Uncle, have you ever seen so bewitching a flower?"

FIVE

THE LION'S MARCH

A BEWITCHING FLOWER.

What kind of words are these, that both tease and burn my ears? Why do they confuse me? I am an expert at perceiving the truth behind what someone says. I learned years ago to listen for the tiny fractional notes that betray a person's true meaning. And yet Lord Kinsworth eludes me. I hear his words, the nuances, the clever shifts in his tone, but the truth beneath it all escapes me.

I should be pleased he likened me to a flower. Shouldn't I? The way he said it warmed my heart, softening it like sunshine on butter. Yet, a moment later and it is as if a swarm of monkeys shakes the trees of my mind, chattering and screaming. His words trouble me. No doubt, he only meant them as flummery, a joke, a feeble excuse for the attention he had so unwillingly bestowed on me.

Confusing man!

Why is it most men, indeed most people, are as easy

to read as a sheet of music, but this one is forever confusing me? But then, I suppose my father is equally inscrutable. Mayhaps it is because I have difficulty hearing either of them with full impartiality.

Impartial.

Caring—that is my mistake.

Caring is dangerous. Lord Kinsworth made his reluctance to associate with me perfectly clear. I rehearse his list of my faults, ending with his notion that I am a threat to his precious freedom.

What utter nonsense!

Not that I care. Because I don't. He cannot be trusted. Men cannot be trusted. Now that I think on it, I dislike him calling me a flower.

I dislike it intensely. Flowers are fragile things. They wilt too easily. They fall to pieces on the ground and get smashed underfoot. Other girls might be flattered to be likened to a flower—not I. My heart cries out against it.

I am not a flower.

I am a roaring lion.

I am a raging storm.

He does not know me—this is what I tell myself. I care nothing for this man's opinion. Remember who you are. Rise lion and stalk through the tall grass. Blend into the scenery. Find a way to escape this maddening clump of jasmine.

And so, I do. I slide under the curtain, and flatten myself against the wall, easing away from them behind the curtains until I reach an open door and slip unnoticed out onto a balcony where I am welcomed into the arms of darkness.

A soft breeze cools my temples. The night breeze also

carries with it the stink of London in summer, of too many people, and too little fresh air. I miss the forests of home, the wind from the rivers. I even miss the ocean air that sweeps up over the cliffs near Stranje House. But Miss Stranje brought us to London for a reason. Our enemies are here. And our friends. She needs me here in this rancid place, to prowl among traitors and fools. She needs me to listen for the murmuring lies and whispers of truth, and bring them in my sharp teeth to lay at her feet.

For now, I am her loyal lion, and she has given me a task to fulfill. I breathe in the sour air, turn away from the comforting quiet of the night, and reenter the ballroom to make my report to Miss Stranje and the others.

I whisk silently through the crowd. Avoiding anyone's gaze until I am stopped short. Without looking, I know who has stepped in my way. I would know Lord Kinsworth's music anywhere. I step aside intending to go around the obstacle. But he matches my step, blocking my way.

"And what were you doing on the balcony, young lady?" He pretends to take a fatherly tone. It is the actor in him. Unbeknownst to Lord Kinsworth, my *real* father would've sounded distant and unconcerned. "It is not safe for a young woman to be prowling around dark balconies without an escort."

"I have no need of a guardian." Those were his exact words to his uncle, and I dared to throw them back at him. *A foolish risk.* I cover my mistake with a brusque wave of my hand. "I assure you, my lord, I can take care of myself. Aside from that, it is no business of yours if I should decide to take a breath of cool air, now is it?"

He is not used to such sharpness from me. I catch the startled expression that dashes across his features, but he banishes it immediately and squints suspiciously. I can tell he is wondering if I overheard him from the balcony.

"Now if you will excuse me." I try to dodge around him, but he forestalls me.

"How much did you hear?"

"*What?*" I cannot control the heat scalding my cheeks. *He knows.* What a fool I am. And if he didn't know before that I was eavesdropping, he does now. My traitorous blush will have given me away. I lower my face, afraid to meet his scrutiny. "I have no idea what you mean, and I really must go find Lady Jersey. She is waiting."

Her venerated name ought to force him to stand down and stop questioning me.

"Oh, but I think you know exactly what I mean." He holds his position like a great hulking wall of iron.

I swallow, struggling to know how to answer. My mouth turns dry as the Thar Desert. I can only shake my head.

"I've heard rumors," he says, with a sly upturn dancing at the corner of his eyes. "Nothing more than whispers. Conjecture. A scrap of gossip here and there . . ." He waits, towering over me. "Naturally, everyone knows the story of Miss Stranje's odd brood of young ladies saving the lives of the Admiralty. But there are those of us who wonder exactly how that feat came about."

Those of us? Who wonders? Who besides him? Surely, his uncle has a notion. After all, he is in the business of spying himself. But who else has Lord Kinsworth heard speculating about our activities?

"It was a simple matter of luck—that's all." I press my shoulders back, refusing to let him intimidate me. "Good fortune."

He has the decency to laugh. It is a warming laugh, the kind of easy chuckle that sets the hearer at ease. Except I know better than to lower my guard. He is treading too close to the mark. I shrug and smile back at him as innocently as I can manage.

"Very pretty." The edge of his mouth stays in a wry upward curve. "But you cannot charm your way out of my question, Miss Barrington. What *exactly* is Miss Stranje training you to do?" He stares at me intently, studying the way my neck tightens and my lips part despite my struggle to control them.

He stands too close, so close that he will sense a lie before it leaves my mouth. I will have to tell him the truth, or at least something near the truth.

It startles me when he speaks before I can answer. "You smell like jasmine," he says, and his gaze jerks back to the bank of flowers near where he and his uncle had stood.

I must answer quickly before he figures it out. "Miss Stranje is training us to navigate the treacherous waters of your complex English society."

"Hmm." His mouth twitches to the side. "You mean how to navigate gatherings like this one? Or do you mean soirées? Musicals, perhaps? Or the theatre? Oh yes, that does sound treacherous."

"Now, you're just mocking me." I spin indignantly and skirt around him.

"Wait." He has the audacity to grab my arm. "They *can* be treacherous. Especially if you're referring to political waters."

I stare at his hand on my arm. The silk of my sari does nothing to shield me from his touch. His hold is not tight. Barely enough pressure to arrest me. He loosens but doesn't let go. Not right away. He, too, stares at where his fingers graze my skin, white on brown, rough on smooth.

I did not expect his hands to feel so . . . I shake off these wayward thoughts and focus on what I can learn. Lord Kinsworth must do more with his time than loiter in ballrooms and play cards at Brooke's. He does work of some kind. His hands are too solid and calloused.

I look up to find I am no longer the only one blushing. His lips part, his focus floats like a warm cloud enveloping us both, as his hand slides gently down my arm before he lets go.

I must strike while I have the advantage. Lowering my voice, I intone chords I should not employ, dangerous chords, but the lioness in me has returned. I want to repay him for his audacity—for his attempting to guess about Stranje House, for stopping me from walking away as if he has some right to do so, for calling me a flower. And for a hundred other unspoken offenses. So, I draw on soft enticing notes, notes that will make him hungry.

"Take a good look at me, my lord. Pray tell, do you see a young lady who knows about your complicated English politics?" The scent of jasmine fills the warm air between us, and the softness of my words flows over him like an achingly slow river. "I am only sixteen, my lord." I pause, letting the innocence of my age unsettle him.

Never mind that childhood abandoned me long ago when I was six. I blink up at him, and he is trapped. Now, I strum the last notes of this ballad, filling my voice with flower-like innocence. "What can I know of such things?"

It takes him a full half-minute before he remembers to breathe.

I quickly curtsey before he can completely recover. "And now if you will excuse me."

As I walk away, I hear him ask aloud, "What, *indeed?*"

No longer darting here and there to avoid notice, the lioness inside me smiles in triumph, and I stride boldly across the ballroom. I have performed the task Miss Stranje gave me, *and* I have bested Lord Kinsworth.

I glide through the throng toward Miss Stranje and the others. When I arrive, Sera takes my arm. "Maya?" She squints sideways at me. "You look . . . *peculiar.* What happened?"

I remembered that I am a lion, not a wilting flower.

Lady Castlereagh and the others glance up from their discussion with Lady Jersey. Miss Stranje takes one look at me, and her gaze flies beyond me, no doubt she is assessing the young man I left standing across the room. I do not need to turn around to know what she sees. I can hear his confusion tumbling through the air from here.

A gratifying breeze.

Lady Jersey follows Miss Stranje's gaze, and then they both turn to me. "What do you think of him?" Lady Jersey asks me.

"I do not *think* of him," I answer too sharply and feel my cheeks redden.

"Of course, not." She chuckles and pauses, leaving

my lie hanging between us. The others shift and shuffle, holding back half-cocked grins. "But I was asking what you thought of his character." Lady Jersey employs a more commanding tone. "His uncle has proven to be a valuable asset. And we are considering bringing his lamb, *as it were*, into the fold."

Lord Kinsworth–one of us?

"No!" I blurt out before I can stop it. "He's too . . ." I struggle to find the right word. "Too impetuous. The man does not take anything seriously. He can't be trusted."

Lady Jersey steps back assessing me, then skewers me with another question. "Can't be trusted *with what?*"

I catch the side of my lip in my teeth. How am I to answer? *Secrets?* No, that's not it. Ben would keep their secrets. *Loyalty to England?* That's not it, either. He would remain true to his country.

Lady Castlereagh leans closer to me, and a soothing lullaby hums beneath her words. "My dear, are you concerned the young man might fold under pressure?"

I shake my head. "No, he's not easily ruffled." *On the contrary, he's altogether too devil-may-care if anyone were to ask me.*

Lady Jersey collapses her fan into her palm with a sharp thwack. "For pity sake child, I'm not asking if we can trust our hearts to the lad. He's sure to be a rapscallion in that regard. Never you mind, we'll discuss that later when you are not overwrought. For now, you must tell us what *Prinny*–excuse me, I meant to say, what His Highness, Prince George, and the Admiral were arguing about."

I am not overwrought–I want to argue. Except they are

all leaning in, having steeled themselves to hear my report on the other matter. So, I stand straight-backed and report. "Admiral St. Vincent was warning the Prince not to trust Napoleon, and to forego meeting with him. Prince George did not appreciate the Admiral's advice and declared rather vehemently that he would go forward with his plan with or without Parliament's consent. *Parliament is not my nursemaid*, is how he phrased it."

"Did he now?" Lady Castlereagh harrumphs.

Miss Stranje kneads her knuckles against her chin. "Did they mention when this meeting is to take place?"

"They are not sure. It could be as soon as three or four weeks."

"Did they say where it will be held?" Lady Castlereagh no longer hums like a caring mother as she had a few minutes earlier. Lullaby gone; she charges forward with the bull-like rumble of a general preparing for battle.

"They do not know." I try to soothe them with a calming cadence, like the washing in and washing out of a gentle sea. "Lord Harston asked the same thing of the Admiral. I am certain he intends to find out."

Lady Jane appears to be deep in thought. She uncrosses her arms and draws a circle in the air between us, marking a place on an invisible map. "What if *we* set up their meeting place? We could offer them neutral ground. Someplace out of the way, safe for both leaders, but with specific controllable access points, a rendezvous location we could manage. We might suggest Ravencross Manor, or perhaps, Stranje House."

Georgie grins. "Splendid idea. Stranje House has ample spyholes. And if we should need to evacuate the Prince Regent, we could use the secret passages."

Lady Jersey flicks back the enormous ostrich feather bobbling over her brow. "Hhmm. An interesting stratagem. That would allow us to maintain some small measure of control over the situation."

"It's better than the alternative." Lady Castlereagh squares her shoulders. "But it must be handled with the utmost care." She nods. "The Prince will need to think it's his idea."

Seraphina frowns. "How can we convince him–"

I shiver. Despite all the chatter, the music, and dancing surrounding us, I hear the unmistakable sound of Tess running toward us. Dread gallops alongside her like a shrieking dark horse. She bursts into the middle of our circle, white-faced with worry, and points at the double doors on the east wall. "She's here! I saw her."

"Slow down. Take a breath." Miss Stranje grasps Tess's shoulders and calmly asks, "Who? *Who* is here?"

We all know the answer. There is only one person on this wretched island who could make Tess's heart thunder with such intense alarm.

"Daneska," Lady Jane murmurs and unconsciously lowers her hand to the wound still healing on her leg.

Tess's shoulders sag, and she nods.

"No. It can't be." Georgie stares at the double doors. "She wouldn't dare come here. Not after–"

"She would," I say softly. "Lady Daneska has many traits, timidity is not one of them."

"It is precisely what she *would* do." Sera's lips flatten into a thin line. "We should've expected it. I'm ashamed I didn't–"

"No. Even she is not that foolhardy." Georgie grabs Tess's arm and squints hard as if she can ferret out a mistake. "Was it a vision? How can you be certain it was really her? It might've been—"

"It was her! Not a vision." Tess shakes free of Georgie's hold and glares at her. "I'd know Daneska anywhere. She was in disguise, but there's no hiding those eyes."

It's true. Lady Daneska's eyes are a startling ice blue, and as empty of warmth as the hollow drums that thud in her soul. My opinion has nothing to do with the fact that there is no love lost between us. I am at peace with the fact that Lady Daneska has always hated me. It's understandable—she cannot gull me with her sugary lies.

Miss Stranje is already moving toward the doors. So are we all. "Where did you see her?"

Tess hesitates. "She's gone now. The minute I saw her, she took off running."

"But you're faster." Lady Jane limps more markedly than before hearing this news, but she hurries to catch up to Tess. "Daneska could never outrun you."

"Where was this?" Our headmistress bears down on Tess. "*Where* did you see her?"

"I. . . that is, *we*, Lord Ravencross and I, um, were—"

"Tess!" Her startling tone halts Tess's evasive dance as effectively as a hawk's screech. "Out with it."

The breath Tess has been holding rushes out in a resigned sigh. "If you must know, we were in the upstairs hallway." She looks down and fidgets. "It was dark up there, and we were having a . . . a private moment."

Miss Stranje closes her eyes and turns her face heavenward for a split second. "*Kissing*. You were kissing."

"Yes, all right. But that's all. Just kissing." She glances past Miss Stranje's shoulder to all of us. "We're engaged.

It's perfectly normal."

Lady Castlereagh waves away Tess's defense. "We shall discuss that later, young lady. Tell us what happened."

"I thought I heard footsteps and so *Gabr*—Lord Ravencross and I dashed into that little nook at the end of the hall and hid. We saw someone tiptoeing out of our library. At first, I thought it must be one of the maids, except it couldn't be because she was wearing a ballgown. I leaned out to get a better look, but Lord Ravencross pulled me back into the alcove so we wouldn't, *um*, get caught." Her cheeks reddened.

"Go on." Miss Stranje sounds both disapproving and impatient.

Tess is done feeling guilty. Her music no longer sounds wary and off-key. She meets our headmistress's glare without a flinch. "You keep that room locked, do you not?" Miss Stranje nods, and Tess continues. "Knowing that—I had to find out who had sneaked into the room where we keep our papers. I thought it might be that shifty traitor Alice coming back to steal more information to sell. So, I crept out to see. By then, she was all the way at the other end of the hall. The floorboards must've creaked under my foot because she glanced back. Light from the stairway window shone on her face. It was Daneska!"

Tess stared earnestly at Miss Stranje. "I know it was. She had on a black wig, but it was her. She whipped down the stairs, and I bolted after her. When I got to the first floor, she was nowhere in sight. I hunted everywhere—every nook and cranny, every cupboard and shadow between the third floor and the front door. She must've hidden somewhere in the house and then slipped out. Ravencross is still searching. But I know her, Daneska is gone."

"Stands to reason that plaguey girl would be here." Lady Jersey snaps open her fan and flaps it as if she is the one overheated from having done raced up and downstairs hunting Daneska. "Mark my words, our conniving little countess is behind this peace with Napoleon nonsense. She's bound to be the one carrying Bonaparte's messages to Prinny. And no doubt, pandering to our Prince's enormous vanity as well. Who else but that little trollop could convince our thimble-headed—"

"My lady!" Miss Stranje cuts off Lady Jersey's dangerously seditious tirade, and flashes a warning to her friend, reminding the lady that they are on the edge of a very crowded ballroom.

Lady Jersey smiles serenely and brushes out her skirts as if she'd only been mentioning the weather. "What I meant to say is, who else could convince oouur beloved Prince that no haaaarm would befall him if he were to ally himself with that poisonous little toad Napoleon." If it weren't for the anger jangling beneath her forced genteel accent, the lady would've succeeded in making *poisonous little toad* sound like a compliment.

"Whether it was Lady Daneska's doing or not, we must press forward. We may only have two weeks." Lady Castlereagh taps her chin. "That doesn't give us much time to convince His Highness that he ought to meet Napoleon at Stranje House rather than risk doing so on French soil."

Lady Jersey fans herself, this time it is not for effect, little beads of sweat are forming on her brow.

SIX

A FAR CRY FROM PEACE

THE MUSICIANS PLAY lively gallops and jovial country-dances. For two more hours, our guests dance and laugh. We play the part of blissful debutantes, smiling and nodding at everyone as if funeral marches aren't playing in our hearts. And all the while, we weave through the crowd silently scouring each face in the hope of finding a certain traitorous young lady. Daneska may have changed her wig, so we must look carefully at every face.

Mr. Sinclair and Lord Wyatt are assisting Lord Ravencross, searching the darker parts of our townhouse, the servants' quarters below stairs, the attic, the grounds in back, surrounding alleyways, and streets. Georgie carries messages back and forth between all of us. She hurries through the ballroom doors and shakes her head at Miss Stranje. Which can only mean Lady Daneska has vanished.

Escaped.

And yet I feel her presence tiptoeing among us, breathing dark tunes like an angel of death.

The next hour trickles by as slowly as a desert creek. The Prince Regent wobbles out of the card room, reeking of brandy, and makes his way to Miss Stranje. The music grows softer in anticipation of the Regent leaving.

"We have had a splendid evening, Miss Stranje." His Highness lifts Miss Stranje's hand elegantly, and with a soldierly click of his heels, he says, "Had a spot of luck at cards tonight." He touches the side of his nose as if sharing a secret. "Daresay, Lord Dreyfus will be slightly less plump in the pocket after our last hand of whist. What! What. Ha-ha!" He pats his gold-embroidered coat pocket and leans closer to her, slurring his words. "All in all, 'twas a jolly affair—no, wait! P'rhaps not so *jolly* come to think on it. *But splendid.* Yes, that's what we shall say. *Splendid evening.* Well done, Miss Stranje. Well done."

Our headmistress sinks in a respectful curtsy, and we do the same alongside her.

He twirls his hand high into the air in a flamboyant wave. "Farewell, ladies." Lord Harston does his best to guide the Prince toward the doors, but Prince George wheels back around, throws his arms wide and shouts, "And a fine good evening to one and all!"

Everyone in the room drops into a courtesy in response. He laughs heartily as if bidding the entire roomful of guests farewell is a hilarious joke. He and his entourage finally funnel out of our ballroom.

Lord Kinsworth trails behind Prince George and his uncle, but he turns back before leaving and casts me a soldierly salute. I have no idea what he means by it. Nor do I care. Let him think whatever he chooses. It makes no difference to me.

I only wish his mock salute hadn't looked as if he found something highly amusing. If he has truly guessed the purpose of Miss Stranje's school, it ought not to amuse him. Quite the opposite, ours is a serious business. Life and death. Oppression or freedom. The survival of his English homeland may very well depend upon us. There should not be fireflies of laughter flitting about in his eyes. If I had something to throw at him, I would be sorely tempted.

Now that the Prince Regent has departed, everyone else is free to do so, and soon after our guests trickle out.

It is nearly four o'clock in the morning before we are able to retire to our bedrooms. Lady Jane, Sera, and I share a room. Drooping with exhaustion, we help each other out of our ballgowns.

"I wonder what Lady Daneska stole from the study." Lady Jane pulls a white cotton nightrail over her head. "And how in blazes did she escape from Tess."

Sera climbs under the covers. "We'll figure it out in the morning. I'll go over the workroom. When it's daylight, we'll be able to spot what's out of place." Her voice trails off, and her breathing falls into an even and regular pattern.

Lady Jane turns out the oil lamp. In the darkness, I rest my head on the pillow, but it is useless. I'm over-tired and unable to sleep. Events of the night race back and forth in my mind—Lord Kinsworth's unsettling words, the Prince's dangerous plans with Napoleon, and my father.

Papa.

I watched him thank Miss Stranje as he and his wife were departing. I thought, for a moment, that he glanced over his shoulder in my direction. Although, it was only an instant, less than an instant, a blink, and he turned away. Perhaps, I'd imagined it. If he did look back, he did not linger in doing so. There was no wistful, "*farewell, my daughter. I am terribly sorry for abandoning you to the care of others.*"

His words from earlier skip around my head, taunting me. "I'm pleased to see you are making your way in the world—flourishing on your own."

Flourishing?

That is a bit farfetched. Yes, I am surviving. And, yes, thanks to his wife, I have developed a few skills that the English find advantageous in their political maneuvers. On occasions, I am even assigned tasks the other girls know nothing about. I suppose one might say, I am useful.

Useful.

I roll over in disgust.

Useful is a thousand miles away from *flourishing.*

As for making my way in the world—this world, my father's world—it isn't true.

I ache to go home. I don't belong here. My father should never have brought me here. I suppose one might think I am *adapting*, growing accustomed to England's unrelenting cold, learning to live with how the chill bites into me in the winter. Even in the summer, gray skies smother this bleak little island too often.

I would trade everything I have to feel India's sun warming my skin. I long to hear the women in our village singing as they bake bread together. I miss the noise of village children laughing and playing, the chortle of brown doves early in the morning, and the whoop of cranes overhead in the evenings.

Most of all, I miss my grandmother. I miss the way her wisdom hums through my soul, the calm reliable rhythm of her heart as she holds me in her arms. Oh, how I want to feel those arms around me, right now. She is a blanket of peace that quiets the echoing loneliness that has always haunted me.

Lady Jane murmurs in her sleep, reminding me I am not all by myself. Although, I doubt being physically alone has anything to do with this ache in my heart. Sera curls tighter in her kitten-like coil of sleep, snuggling deeper under the covers. How dear she is. The night feels a little less lonely. I *do* have a few friends here.

It is my great good fortune to have chanced upon the young women of Stranje House. They are treasures of light hidden here in this gray land. True friends like Sera, Georgie, Tess, and Lady Jane, are rare in this world. I smooth the coverlet up over Jane's shoulders.

Perhaps this is what it feels like to have sisters or cousins. I have no way of knowing. My grandmother and her family are thousands of miles away on the other side of the earth.

I may never see them again.

Unhappy thoughts.

I clasp the bedding and pull it up to my chin. I must not drown in these thoughts. Grandmother taught me how to manage sorrow. "Sadness is like a flash flood," she explained. "Storms come. The river flows faster and faster. Then in a mighty rush, a wall of water rolls upon you, carrying uprooted trees and all manner of debris. You must not let it drown you, child. To escape a flood of anguish, clear your mind, and focus on one sound. One sound only."

And so, I sort through all the noises of the night, searching for one lone noise worthy of my devoted attention. This is the quietest hour in London. By this time, most of the gentry have gone home. Their carriages do not clatter over the cobblestones. In another hour or two, the streets will fill with workers rolling their carts or walking to shops and places of business. I close off Lady Jane's restless tossing and turning, and Sera's muffled breathing. The house creaks, as all houses do. The windows purr as the soft breeze ruffles through. There are mice in the walls, and–

Something is out of place.

It is offbeat pulse emanating from the fourth floor above us, a rustle, a half step against a loose floorboard. *Faint.* Very faint. The housekeeper and the maids are forever whispering about ghosts on that floor. I doubt I am hearing ghosts tonight, and yet something is stirring in those unoccupied rooms, something with cat-like stealth.

Still as a corpse, I lay, and quiet my heart, slow my breathing, blotting out all other sounds. The longer I listen, the more I begin to think I am sensing a presence rather than hearing anything of substance.

There! A hollow otherworldly stirring, like death's dark robes dragging back and forth across the floor.

I close my eyes to concentrate more closely. Now I recognize that empty tune.

Lady Daneska.

"Jane. Wake up. Jane!" I jostle her shoulder and then nudge Sera. "Sera! I hear Daneska."

"Can't be," Jane grumbles in her sleep and pushes my hand away. "We searched the house. Go back to sleep."

"It's her. I know it is."

She sticks her head up from the pillow, her short hair sticking out every which way as she listens with half-shuttered eyes. "I don't hear anything."

Sera wriggles out from under her cave of pillows and sheets. "What did it sound like?"

How can I explain the way a person's soul emits sounds? I shake my head. "It is more of a feeling. I sense her."

Jane flops back down on her pillow. "It's late, you're exhausted. Your mind is playing tricks."

No longer certain, I whisper, "But couldn't she be upstairs? I feel so uneasy."

"Most likely, it's the effects of too much excitement." Sera pats my arm sympathetically and lays back down. "It was a difficult night. We're all terribly tired." The end of her sentence drifts off, but she rambles on sleepily, "I'm quite certain Lord Wyatt searched those rooms. . . yes." She struggles to keep her eyes open. "Several times."

I nod. She and Jane are probably right. It is unlikely that Lady Daneska could've hidden that effectively. Sera smiles drowsily and burrows back under the covers. Jane is already snoring softly.

It may be my imagination. Except I still hear it. And whatever it is, it is as out of place here as I am.

Perhaps the servants are right, and this house has a ghost. I've never met one before, and as I have no fear of the dead, if there is a phantom upstairs, I intend to see it.

I slip carefully out from under the covers and tiptoe into the hall. I hear it more clearly out here. The hollow echo is unsettlingly off-key, like the dull clang of the monk's gong calling mourners to prayer. Each beat seeps into one's sinew and bone, reeking of emptiness and loss. This cannot be Lady Daneska I'm hearing. She has never seemed sad to me. Never to be pitied. Malicious, yes. Full of greed and wanton ambition, most assuredly, but she has never sounded woeful.

Perhaps I am merely dreaming, but like a hapless dreamer, I am drawn forward, transfixed on that unearthly sound.

Following it, I climb the winding staircase in murky darkness, treading as lightly as possible to keep the steps from creaking. A narrow shaft of faded moonlight filters from the upper rose window, casting shadows along the walls.

Members of the household staff avoid the next floor, the fourth floor. The maid told us it is because Lady Haversmythe was thrown from this balcony three years ago. They think her ghost lingers here. The between-stairs maid always crosses herself whenever she passes this landing to go up to the attic, where a few of the braver servants reside. The more senior servants have rooms below stairs. The scullery maid is so afraid of the haunted floor that she prefers to sleep on the hearth in the kitchen.

Never mind all that, if I want to find the source of this troubling sound, I must search this floor. One lone candle in an old brass holder sits on the hallway side table. I consider using the striker and lighting it, but then I would be seen long before I see whomever or whatever is interrupting my peace. I prefer to have stealth on my side. My eyes are adapting to the dim light, and this floor looks much like our own, three bedrooms, and a sitting room at the far end. I can make my way without a candle.

The presence hums louder with every step I take.

I have heard the plaintive songs of snow and ice at night. This is a darker vibration, colder, and far more bleak. I shiver—despite the heat of summer. The haunting murmur that chills the air fans the curiosity raging within me. I should turn back, and yet I cannot. I am as driven as a bloodhound following the scent of a bear. I must hunt down this sound, even though the creature I find might tear me to bits.

My toe bumps against the corner of a chest of drawers. I wince but clamp my lips tight to keep silent. It's darker here in the first bedroom. The heavy drapery blocks out any trickle of moonlight, and for a moment, I regret not lighting that candle.

I try to calm my thundering heart and listen for the way objects bounce or absorb sound. I regain my bearings and more carefully pick my way through the room. There is a thick carpet on the floor, soft beneath my toes, and my shoulder brushes against an armoire.

I'm close now. Except there is no breathing. This near, if this creature is human, I ought to hear breath sounds. Instead, there is only that off-key thud picking up speed, thumping faster.

It's cold in here for July. I've heard ghosts can cause a chill in the air. So can fear. Deciding to go back for that candle, I turn.

She flies at me.

Silent as an owl snagging a mouse, she slams me

against the wall and whispers in my ear, "I knew it would be you."

She whisks the cover off of a dimly flickering oil lamp

Not a ghost.

"Lady Daneska," I say in casual greeting. As if I am not at all concerned about the sharp blade she holds to my throat. I'd expect nothing less from her. She presses the dagger, and I feel the cold nip of steel against my neck. Death does not frighten me. I wait. Listening.

It surprises me to hear fear pulsing through her. No. *Fear* is not the correct word. Raw anguish. I have heard something like it before. Years ago, I saw a small Muntjac deer feeding in the underbrush beside the river near our village. A leopard pounced on her, and I will never forget how that deer screamed. It was not loud. It was the strangled cry of the lost. A pitiful hopeless sound, filled with the certainty of death. How can that be? Why would such a dreadful tune be coming from Lady Daneska?

She holds the knife–not I.

Scarcely moving my mouth, I ask, "What is wrong?"

Even in the dim light, I can see how much she hates me. She practically vibrates with the desire to kill me. But I also see that she is afraid. Through clenched teeth, she says, "I need your help."

Surprise jumps out of my throat–a breathy choked laugh. "Me? My help?"

Is she delirious? Has she been poisoned? Gone mad?

This can't be real.

I blink, trying to wake up, thinking surely, I must be dreaming. Lady Daneska would never be so desperate that she would ask for my help.

She rams her forearm into my chest.

That felt real enough.

"Do you think I like this?" she hisses. "Coming to *you!*" Some of her spittle lands on my cheek.

I wipe it away. Let her cut my throat. I don't care. "What do you want?"

"What do I *want?*" She pulls back only slightly, but enough that I have room to breathe. "I *want* you dead." Her chin juts out. Her French accent has slipped, crashing hard into her native diction. "All of you at this dratted school–*dead.* Out of my way. *Yah,* that is what I want." She pulls back, composing herself. "A better question would be, *what do I need?*"

There it is. Desperation whistling through her again. This is not the same Lady Daneska I knew before. Something in her feels broken. Maybe it always was, and I failed to notice. Without thinking, I employ a soothing gentle timbre. "What is it you need?"

"None of your tricks." She presses forward with the knife, but it is as if part of her melts. "None of your tricks," she says again, this time without any heat.

"What is wrong, Daneska?" The softness in my tone is not artifice, I genuinely want to know what is disturbing her so intensely.

She takes a long breath and draws back. "Do not think I won't use this on you." She holds the knife between us. "I will. If you force my hand."

"You know me well enough to know I won't fight you." This is true, although since coming to London I have secretly been studying combat with Madame Cho. Even so, my skills are no match for Lady Daneska's. "*Force your hand?* How? You have a knife. I cannot do anything except listen."

"No? You dare not even try?" She squints suspiciously and pushes her face closer to mine. "Too bad. I had hoped to cut you here and there. Just enough to teach you that I am your master."

Her bravado annoys me. She is afraid of something. "A master does not usually plead for help."

"Fool!" Hate returns to her eyes. "I do not plead. Does this look like I am pleading?" Fast as a snake strikes, she cuts a jagged line down my arm. Stunned, I watch as a lightning strike of dark red etches through the white sleeve of my nightdress.

A second later, it burns.

Burns as if she'd seared me with a red-hot poker instead of a dagger. A scream rises up from some bottomless well. My mouth opens—but Daneska clamps her hand over my lips, turning it into a muffled whimper.

She snarls into my ear. "Hush, unless you want me to cut the other arm."

I close my eyes. Shutting her out. Shutting out the screaming pain. Quiet. I need quiet. I will sink into the peaceful dark.

Away from her.

Away from England.

Away from this wretched nightmare.

"No!" she jerks my chin, forcing me to open my eyes. "No. You cannot faint. You're no good to me asleep. Stand up. Do you hear me? And listen." She digs her fingernails into my jaw. "You will listen to me or, by all that's holy, I'll make you hurt like you never hurt before. Do you understand?"

I fight my way to the flickering light on the surface and manage to nod, *once*.

"Good." Her grip relaxes slightly. "It's true I want your help. But you will see, I do not plead, and I *never* beg. I have come to offer you a trade."

A *trade?*

She is a madwoman. I remain silent. I do not want anything Daneska has to offer.

As if she's reading my mind, she says, "I know exactly what you want. I know what you crave more than anything else in the world." She eases her hand away.

I cannot tolerate her smugness. She knows nothing about me, so I say, "You, in chains?"

The plush darkness of the bedroom with its Turkish rugs, thick bedding, and heavy draperies swallows up the sound of her tinkling laughter.

"Bird brain." She flicks my forehead. "You don't really want that. I'll wager that not once tonight did you think to yourself, '*Oh I do so wish I could see Lady Daneska bound up in chains and thrown off the nearest bridge.*' Is that not so?"

I dislike that she would win that wager. *And*, I dislike that she mimicked my voice as if I am high-pitched and squeaky. I never squeak. She stands there waiting, glancing from the bloody tip of her knife to me, as if she expects me to answer her absurd observation or she'll stick me again.

"Very well," I use an intentionally low even-keeled tone. "I admit that I did not think it, not in those exact words. Although, I do rather like your idea involving a bridge."

She wipes the blade on my cheek. "Do not jest with me, my dear silly princess—"

Princess.

My eyes flare at her mockery. Blood drips from my fingers despite the fact that I am making a fist. She smiles and pokes my earlobe with the tip of her dagger. "*Princess*. That is what a Maharajah's granddaughter should be called, is it not? *La princess*? Of course, it is. You are royalty, are you not? Oh, but no. Pardon me. I have forgotten. All of that is behind you now—your grandfather was overthrown by the English. In this country, you are *la nullité*. A little nothing. The foreigner. A mere curiosity. It must be hard to have fallen so far."

"You don't know anything about me."

"*No?*" She pulls back as if I've wounded her. "I know this, you used to cry yourself to sleep when you first came to Stranje House."

"I did no such thing." I refuse to look at her.

"No? Ah, well, perhaps not every night. But I know you used to miss your grandmother, is that not so?"

In those early days at Stranje House, I had not thought Lady Daneska noticed me at all, except when she needed someone besides Sera to torment. I stare into the shadows surrounding us, wishing ghosts would come flying out. At least then, Daneska might stop badgering me.

She exhales with considerable irritation. "I know you miss her. You played such mournful songs on that annoying lap harp I wanted to bash your head with it."

"I'm surprised you didn't. Why are you bringing this up?"

"Because my little turtle dove, I know you want to go home to India."

Breath freezes in my lungs, and I stare at her unblinking.

How can she know the thoughts that spun through my mind earlier tonight?

"Oh, don't look so surprised. Anyone could've guessed that much."

I swallow. "Is it so obvious?"

"Don't be a widgeon. It's not as if it's written across your face in ink." She thumps my forehead with the butt of her dagger. "*C'est la vie.*" Her voice raises pitch, turning back into her haughty fake-French self. "In my opinion, *anyone* from *anywhere else* would want to leave this pathetic little island and return home."

"If England is so pathetic, why does Napoleon want it? Why do *you* want it?"

She waggles her knife at me. "You know why. *Power.* Britain has too much of it. And they need to share." That edge of desperation thrums through her again. "Enough questions. Do you want to go home or not?"

"Are you offering me passage to India?" I know now Daneska won't kill me, she needs something from me. I nudge her back so that I can clasp my bleeding arm. "In exchange for what?"

"*Ahh, oui.*" She plasters on her French accent. "Now we are speaking the same language, *no*?" She laughs. Georgie once told me she thought Daneska's laughter sounded like breaking glass. It does, but it also reminds me of the cackle of the myna birds outside Calcutta, empty of any real emotion. "Passage home, yes. *Bien sûr*, but we are offering you much more than that."

"We?" I'm afraid of her answer. The blood in my hand is warm and sticky, the smell sickens me. Suddenly, I have trouble feeling the floor beneath me and start to slide down the wall.

She holds me up, forcing me in place with her body. "Emperor Napoleon and his friends."

His friends. Our enemies.

"You mean the Iron Crown," I mumble. She presses close and her breath, heavy with the scent of wine, fills my nostrils. I concentrate on that sour smell, rather than the tarnished-penny tang of my own blood. "What do they want?"

"First, let us discuss what *you* want. You want to go home, but do you want to go home to an India ruled by Britain? To your homeland held in servitude by that pompous plum pudding of a Prince? Or, would you rather return to a free India, to your own province ruled by your family as it was for centuries? As it would still be if Britain hadn't decided the land of spice belonged to them."

She waits, squinting at me in the dark. I'm terrified the truth shows on my face. I *do* want all those things. *Heaven help me*, I do.

She smiles. "That is what Napoleon does, you know. He restores local rule. All he requires is that the rightful rulers swear fealty to him. If they do, the Emperor will leave them alone to rule themselves. Do you not remember he allied with your people against the British at Mysore?"

Mysore. Now she has overstepped.

I frown. "You know perfectly well, Napoleon wanted to rule India as much as the English. And anyway, Tippu was not '*my*' people. He was a greedy warlord, no better than the French and English—always attacking the surrounding dynasties."

She shook her head. "Napoleon is not greedy. That is

not how he thinks. The Emperor wants peace and prosperity for all people. For his people. He wants freedom from tyrannical rule."

I nearly laugh aloud. The man crowned himself Emperor. In England, they call Napoleon *the little tyrant*. He is hardly the noble benefactor she's painting him to be.

"I'm telling you the truth." Lady Daneska argues against my unspoken skepticism. "I can prove it. In my country, he set up duchies and gave the dukedoms to local leaders who were faithful to the cause, men such as my father. Everything was grand and wonderful until the British came and stuck their muskets in where they didn't belong. They killed my father and took his dukedom away."

Gloom ripples across her features, quickly displaced by drumming anger. Then that underlying moan of desperation returns. I want to ask her again what she is afraid of, but I know she won't answer.

Instead, impatient and weary, I ask flatly, "What is it you want from me, Daneska?"

She looks away, at the amber darkness pooling around us. "Napoleon feels we made a . . . a *mistake* trying to bomb the shipyards."

A mistake. Ha! It was a colossal blunder. It enraged the entire Admiralty. They are more determined than ever to capture her beloved Napoleon. Not only that, but Alexander Sinclair's new warships will be finished soon and ready to speed troops across the English Channel.

"The bomb was not Napoleon's idea, was it?" If not, it does not take a mastermind to conclude the Emperor blames Daneska and Ghost for it going wrong.

She drags in a deep breath, afraid of saying too much.

I blurt out my theory. "Ghost concocted the plan, didn't he?"

Her head tilts enough that I can tell the answer is *yes.*

"And Ghost blames you for it failing?"

Her eyes flash wide, and that deathly music thrums from her so loud I nearly cringe. Daneska clenches her teeth, then spits her venom. "It was Jane's fault. If she hadn't meddled . . ."

Her words drop—a twisted lie—writhing and squealing at our feet.

Ghost might blame Lady Jane, but ultimately, he would hold Daneska responsible. If it weren't for her, Lady Jane would never have escaped from his ship. The Grand Master of the Iron Crown would not take kindly to his plans being crossed. And being the vengeful creature he is, Ghost would exact punishment.

"Did he hurt you?" I ask softly, lacing each syllable with gentle healing salve.

She quietly pleads, "No tricks, Maya. *Please.*" But she does not fight it. Or threaten me. Her shoulders droop. The wound inside her spills open, convulsing like a dying bird.

"No tricks. I promise." The thing I do with my voice is not a trick. It can be a mercy. A kindness. It is a soothing balm, not a trick. "You could run away from him."

"Run from Ghost? From the man who knows how to disappear—how to make the world think he is dead? The same man who knows every hiding place in Europe? Each and every stratagem for escape? Are you mad? He'd hunt me down and—"

"We could help you."

"*You?*" Humor flits across her face, then vanishes. "He blames all of you. You have no idea what he's like, what he might do . . ."

"I saw how badly he cut up Lady Jane."

"Yes, and he intends to kill her for her part at the naval yards. He'll do it, too, if we don't turn things around for him. He'll slaughter everyone at Stranje House—all of *you*! And your deaths won't be easy. Trust me. Lucien knows how to make a person pay for their sins against him."

She shudders, and I can tell it is not an act. Her strength melts, and she looks up at me with eyes bulging with terror. "You've no idea what he's capable of." She licks moisture onto her lips and blinks her fear away. "If Napoleon does not take England, Lucien means to burn it to the ground, the whole bloody island. But first, he plans to set a plague loose in London and—"

"*Plague?* What? No!" Memories hammer through my mind. Memories from my childhood that I'd blotted out long ago. The stench of death. Flies buzzing after the carts that clattered through the city to collect the dead.

"He can't do that." I blindly argue against the horror. "How? He wouldn't. It's unthinkable. I'm sure he was angry when he threatened those things. Ranting. People say things when they're in a rage—"

"Angry?" Daneska stares at me as if I'm the one who has run mad. "You think he swore to do all those things in the midst of a rage?" She shakes her head. "You don't know him. You don't know him at all. Lucien doesn't rant. He *plans*." She waits for me to absorb her words. "He *makes* things happen."

I gulp down the fear she is spreading to me.

She lowers her knife and leans closer. “He and his men will do it. I’ve seen his papers. He has a plan, and he *will* carry it out. Genghis Kahn catapulted diseased corpses over the walls of cities he wanted to conquer. Ghost will do no less. He will destroy England if you don’t help me.” She catches herself. “I mean, if you don’t help Napoleon.”

Her words leave me stunned. So numb, I can’t even feel the cut on my arm. “Wh-what would you have me do?”

SEVEN

A CHORUS OF INHARMONIOUS SCHEMES

"I TOLD NAPOLEON about your gift. I explained that you can use your voice to manipulate people–"

"I don't manipulate people."

"Very well. The way you are able to use it to calm people and allay their concerns. I lied to him. I told him that yours is an ancient art from India. The occult fascinates him. So naturally, he was intrigued." She stops briefly as if vexed that he should admire one of my skills. "He relies too heavily on *numerorum mysteria,* magical numbers and dream interpreters–all that nonsense." She waves her hand as if she thinks *all that nonsense* stinks like rotten fish.

I clamp my teeth together, holding back my annoyance. Never mind that using sound to influence the mind truly is an ancient art. "*And?*"

"*And* we want you to work for Prince George."

"That makes no sense."

"Oh, but it does, because you will secretly be working for us. I will go to Prince George and convince him to use your talents. It won't be difficult. He raves about your singing." Daneska purses her lips for a moment as if it annoys her that Prince George should like my voice.

"That hardly means he would—"

"Hush." She pinches up at me. "One need only look at his palace in Brighton to know he is enamored with Asia, and India, in particular. I will act as if it is an idea he has already conceived. I'll pretend to be outraged that he would use your voice to bend Napoleon's thinking to his will." Daneska pantomimes a damsel-in-distress expres-sion.

I roll my eyes up to the ceiling.

"Don't mock me." She flicks my cheek. "I shall plead with him to not allow you in the room when he negotiates with Napoleon, insisting that it would give him an unfair advantage to use you as an unofficial mediator. Naturally, that is exactly what he will want to do." She leans in, a sneering hyena barring her teeth. "But you will actually be there to persuade our Royal Duckling to comply with Napoleon's terms."

I shake my head. "Prince George will never agree to it. Never! A girl acting as a mediator? Unofficial or not, it is unheard of. The whole thing is beyond the pale."

"Is it? Who better to act as a mediator than an innocent who has ties to neither country? An innocent who helped save His Highness's enormous royal ass from being blown to pieces only a few weeks ago."

Put like that . . .

Still.

Me?

"The whole idea is mad." I stamp my foot and press against the wall, lifting my chin to avoid her scornful leer. "You'll never get him to agree."

"Oh, won't I?" She flashes me a wicked grin. "You have your methods of persuasion. I have mine."

That, I do not doubt. Lady Daneska is, by English standards, extraordinarily beautiful, and when she applies herself, she can be charming. *Fatally so.*

While contemplating her outlandish plan and trying to keep all the blood in my arm from draining onto the floor, it occurs to me that Daneska's scheme would fall in quite neatly with the Patronesses' desire to control the situation. Except for the fact that it will trap me squarely in the middle of their tug-of-war. If I bend Prince George to Napoleon's will, Miss Stranje and the others will hang me as a traitor to England. On the other hand, if I persuade Napoleon to leave England unbreached, Daneska and Ghost won't help me return to India. *No, indeed.* I'm quite certain they will murder me.

Either way, there are unavoidable complications. "What makes you think you can trust me?"

"Because, *mon chérie*, you want to go home more than anything in the world. Isn't that so?"

I bow my head, hating that she is able to hold me hostage with my own desires. My inner turmoil is chattering so loud in my head that I fail to hear Sera approaching.

"Maya? Is that you?" The fear in her voice is not lost on Daneska. Sera's candle is a hesitant yellow orb lighting the hallway outside the bedroom.

I start to call out a warning, but Daneska clamps her hand over my mouth and holds the point of her knife to my heart. As soon as Sera turns into the room, Daneska lets go of me and springs at Sera snaring her into a hold with the dagger gleaming across her throat.

Startled, Sera yelps and drops the candle onto the Turkish carpet. Daneska slaps her hand over Sera's mouth, muffling the scream.

"Fire," I shout, even though I am stamping out the small spark that had ignited. "Fire!" Surely, a cry of fire will rouse the others from their beds.

"Hush!" Daneska glares at me. "Quiet! Or I slice the mouse open!" She grips Sera so tight they are both trembling– Sera with fear and Daneska with fury. "Say you'll do it."

It's not my silence she is demanding. She wants to know if I will betray England.

"Agree!" She snarls at me and the blade in her hand quivers.

I nod, agreeing to her scheme. "You needn't hurt her. I will do as you ask."

"If you cross me, I swear I will come back and kill her first. I will, you know. I will kill you, too, but first I'll cut her open and make you watch her blood drain out. I'll start with her because you like her best. Jane will be next." She lowers the knife an inch. Enough that Sera takes a gasping breath. "You shouldn't play favorites, Maya, little *Princess*."

She calls me *Princess* to mock me, but also to remind me of who I am–who I was–who I could be again if I help Napoleon succeed.

There's a clatter on the stairs. Someone heard my cry

of fire. Daneska shoves Sera hard, toppling both of us. She rushes to the window, whips aside the curtains, and climbs out on a length of cording she must've tied in place earlier.

"You're bleeding." Sera's palms come away from the wound in my arm covered in thick red ooze.

"Go after her!" I try to shake off the queasiness overwhelming me.

Sera ignores me and reaches for the oil lamp so she can inspect my injury. "Pointless to chase her. Daneska will have planned her escape too carefully."

She's right. I sag against the wall, and Sera peels back the drenched fabric of my sleeve. "We'll need to bind this up quickly. You're losing too much blood."

The pain and turmoil from the past twelve hours pour over me like a mountain of sand. "I'm tired," I say, letting my head loll back against the carpet. "I will rest here on the floor for tonight."

"Maya!" Sera pats my cheek. "Maya."

Vaguely, through what feels like a dense fog, I glimpse Jane kneeling down beside Sera, and I think I hear Miss Stranje rushing into the room, and Tess and Georgie. Surrounded. I am surrounded. For some reason, that gives me the peace I've been hungering for all night. I surrender to a deep sleep.

I awaken the next morning in our bedroom, and there is a poultice tied around my arm. Six anxious faces are standing around my bed, and a very grumpy Doctor Meredith turns me on my side. He presses a long horn-shaped cone against my back and leans down to listen.

A moment or two later, he sets the cone aside. "Miss

Stranje, I've no idea how your young ladies incur such ghastly cuts. I might expect this sort of knife wound on a dockworker or a soldier. But I've never seen the like on a young lady before." Then he frowns deeper. "Except for the gash on your Lady Jane, over there."

The doctor narrows a stern glare at our headmistress, but she is not one to be cowed.

"I ask myself that very same question." Miss Stranje holds her head erect, and her lofty tone indicates she will not tolerate any scolding from him. "It seems high-spirited young ladies, such as the girls in my school, are always finding themselves in one scrape or another. If it weren't so, they wouldn't be in my care, now would they?"

Fortunately, this doctor doesn't know about the cut on Madame Cho's throat, and never will. Madame Cho has taken to wearing high collars on her Chinese dresses to cover the scar Daneska left on her neck. "High spirits. Yes, well, I suppose that might explain it," he says, but his brow remains fixed in a disapproving frown as if he suspects her of mistreating us. No doubt, he has heard the rumors about the harsh methods she uses to reform those of us in her *school for unusual girls*.

With a sigh, he puts away his suspicions, along with his medical implements, and closes his leather carrying case. He will probably confide his misgivings to his wife or some other confidant, thereby perpetuating the myth that surrounds Miss Stranje's school. She encourages such rumors because they provide useful camouflage for her school's real purpose.

The doctor heads for the door. "Whatever the case, you managed the wound satisfactorily. Miss Barrington will bear a scar, but her overall health appears to be sound. She'll need rest, and some milk soup with meat and greens in it, to build up her blood." He continues giving instructions as he walks out, adding that we are to send word to him if my wound should fester.

Miss Stranje shows him out, and the others close in around me. "What happened?" Tess demands. "What did she want?"

Lady Jane reaches for my hand. "I'm so sorry I didn't listen to you. I should've believed you—"

"What did she want?" Tess looks furious. Her heart is drumming wildly. She's not angry with me. It's Lady Daneska who has upset her. These encounters are particularly difficult for Tess, especially after Daneska betrayed and nearly shot her. It is even more distressing because Lady Daneska was once Tess's closest friend.

"My help." My throat is dry and scratchy. The words inch out like a hoarse whisper.

"Here. Drink this." Sera places a cup of tea in my hands.

"She came to *you* for help?" Tess crosses her arms. "That doesn't sound like Dani. What sort of help?"

Sera sits on the bed beside me. "What did you to agree to do?" She remembers everything, Sera does. She's reciting Daneska's exact words. Which means I have no choice, but to tell them the truth.

I swallow some tea, and it soothes my throat. "It was more of a trade than an agreement." I sip the tea again, uncertain how much to tell them.

EIGHT

SING ME A SONG OF DUPLICITY SING ME A SONG OF DECEIT

"TELL US EVERYTHING." Lady Jane's brow furrows as if she hears a troublesome rat skittering across our bedroom floor. "Every detail. Start to finish."

Georgie glances toward the door. "Perhaps we should wait till Miss Stranje returns. I'm sure she will want—"

"No!" Tess is still brooding. "Tell us now."

With an air of authority, Madame Cho says, "We wait." None of us dares question her. I am relieved. I dread having to explain that Daneska asked me to betray them and that, because it meant I might be able to return to India and see my grandmother again, I was tempted.

"Wait for what?" Miss Stranje strides through the doorway and her students jump aside, allowing her to approach my bedside.

Tess grumbles, "Daneska asked Maya for help."

"And they made an agreement of some sort." Georgie climbs onto the far side of the bed like a child eager to hear a bedtime story. "I can't imagine what she wanted from Maya."

"Hmm." Miss Stranje raises one eyebrow a little too high and turns to study me with too many questions written across her birdlike features.

Sera traces her forefinger over the patterns on our quilt, a distraction as she tries *not* to guess at what Daneska might have offered me. Lady Jane catches her bottom lip. I know she must be numbering the possibilities, drawing conclusions. I can no longer bear to look at any of them.

My hand shakes as I set the teacup on the nightstand rattling it against the saucer. "She asked me to sway Prince George to do what Napoleon wants."

"Oh, is that all," Tess scoffs.

"You told her no, didn't you?" Georgie leans across the bed and props herself up on her elbows.

I lower my head. "I agreed to do as she asked."

Georgie pounces up. "But you wouldn't! You can't. Well, I mean you probably could do it, but—"

Sera smacks her hand against the quilt. "She agreed to do it to save Lady Jane and me. Daneska threatened—"

Miss Stranje holds up one finger, and Sera stops short. Our headmistress asks in a too calm voice, "First, what did Lady Daneska offer you?"

Ah. There it is.

The lethal question.

And when I answer, it will taint me in all of their

minds. I would much rather everyone continued to think I only agreed with Daneska to save Lady Jane and Sera. It's partially true. Except, when they hear what Daneska offered, they will wonder if I can be trusted. Will I betray them? That question will be on all of their minds. I cannot fault them. Truth be told, *I wonder* if I can resist the temptation. As things stand, I might never see my grandmother again in this life. It will be a miracle if I even hear from her.

I rub my forehead thinking of the hundreds of letters I've posted to India.

All of them unanswered.

I doubt they ever reached her. Mail couriers seldom trek to those distant northern villages. If my *Naanii* has tried to write to me, her letters never arrived here either. We are lost to one another except for the thin ribbon of a song that still stretches between us.

What did Daneska offer me?

Hope.

And now, I must dash it away.

I pick at a nubbin of thread on the quilt. "Lady Daneska offered me passage back to India. She also promises that Napoleon will restore my family to their rightful place as rulers among my people." I take a breath, there is no need to repeat the part about me becoming a princess again. I don't care about that anyway. But now I must tell them the truly treacherous part. "In exchange, she wants me to serve as a mediator between Prince George and Napoleon."

"Mediator? How? Why would he—"

I do not wait for the rest of Georgie's question. "Lady Daneska is certain she can convince Prince George to ask for my assistance during the negotiations. She will tempt him with the idea that I can use my voice to influence Napoleon on his behalf, when in fact, she expects me to be swaying Prince George to comply with Napoleon's wishes."

There.

I said it.

Shame falls over me like a woolen blanket. Suffocating. Except, no! I throw it off—I have no reason to feel this way. I have not betrayed them. Not yet. I raise my chin and study their faces, watching, as they digest the level of enticement I am facing, as they comprehend the betrayal that could be brewing in their midst.

In a few moments, I will have no more friends in England. These few who had nearly become my sisters will never think of me the same. How can they ever again rely on someone who can so easily be tempted by their enemy?

They will always wonder.

Except Sera relaxes and smiles serenely at me, bright with trust.

How can she do that? How can she be so sure of me, when I am not?

Even though I doubt myself, the heaviness on my chest lifts knowing that at least *she* feels certain of my loyalty. I take a deep breath, and my heart thrums with unexpected joy.

Lady Jane, too, shows no alarm. Instead, her lips curve into one of her knowing grins. "Brilliant," she mutters and leans in to whisper. "You told her, yes, didn't you? Say you did. Reluctantly, of course, but you did tell her yes?"

All I can do is stare in wonder at her.

"Of course, she did." Miss Stranje contemplates me steadily. "Well done. Obviously, you realized that Lady Daneska had unwittingly provided us with the ideal means to influence His Highness's ill-conceived *tête-á-tête*. This turn of events is beyond anything the patronesses could've hoped for."

Georgie, too, chimes in. "For once, Daneska is playing into our hand."

"It took backbone for you to play along with her." Tess stands back from the others, but her praise is genuine, and in my case, a rare thing.

I am stunned that not one of them worries I will betray Britain instead of Lady Daneska. My mind falls blank, and I am at a loss for words.

Then it occurs to me they must not have fully grasped the consequences of what they expect from me. "You do realize Lady Daneska will kill me when I turn the tables on her."

"Oh, yes. I'm sure she'll try, my dear." Miss Stranje says this with headmistress-like matter-of-factness. "But we shall be fully prepared. We'll put precautions in place." She pats my hand as if the threat is a small matter. "Don't you worry."

"Humph." Tess purses her lips. "No one is ever adequately prepared for Daneska. Or Ghost."

Miss Stranje ignores Tess's gloomy comment and brushes down her black skirts. "I am sorry, Maya, that you sustained an injury at Lady Daneska's hands. But it is a scar you can wear proudly. You have brought us remarkably good news, and now I must hurry to inform the patronesses. We've much planning to do."

As soon as Miss Stranje leaves the room, Georgie scoots up and sits right beside me on the bed. "Where was Daneska hiding? How did you know where to find her? Did she say anything else? Mention the Iron Crown? It's so unlike her to ask for help, especially from you."

I never know which of Georgie's questions to answer first, and before I can sort through them, Tess pushes into the tight circle. "Daneska would never ask for help. *Never.* Not unless—"

She straightens suddenly. "Ghost!" His name shatters over us like a falling icicle. "He threatened her, didn't he?" Tess's voice trails off. The sadness in it is unmistakable. It amazes me that even though Daneska has betrayed her and shot at her, Tess still feels compassion for her former friend. "Did he . . .?"

"Hurt her?" I glance away and sigh. "Yes, I believe so. She didn't tell me *how* and I shudder to guess. I told her we would help her escape from him, but she laughed at me. She seems to think it is impossible to hide from him, that he would hunt her down and kill her."

"He would," Tess says solemnly from where she has retreated in the shadows.

"Very likely." Lady Jane stands at the foot of the bed. "How very sad for her."

"Sad, yes." I try to wet my lips, but my mouth has suddenly gone dry. Ghost will hunt me down one day, too. I hear my grandmother's voice calming my galloping heart. *Face only one problem at a time, little one.* So, I take a deep breath. "But I do not think Ghost is the only reason she won't let us help her. I don't think Lady Daneska is willing to leave him for another reason. She worships one thing above all else—"

"Power." Georgie sighs heavily.

"I believe so," I say quietly. "She is convinced Napoleon will be victorious over England and since Ghost rules the Iron Crown—"

"She'll stay with him to the end." Lady Jane flops down on the bed as if Daneska's choices are too much to bear.

"To the death," Sera adds mournfully and leans her forehead against the bedpost.

"Not necessarily," Georgie says, almost to herself.

Jane sits up and stares at her quizzically.

"We mustn't forget the possibility that Napoleon might win." Georgie looks around at our astonishment. "No, don't look at me as if I've spit out a goat. You know it's true. We may not want to think about it, but it could happen. I'm a scientist, and in science, we learn to consider all possibilities."

Tess huffs loudly. "We don't need science to figure out that if Napoleon wins, we'll all be dead."

Two hours later, following one poultice change, a bowl of milk and bone broth soup, and an interminable half-hour of Georgie and Jane fussing with my hair until I wanted to scream, they help me into a suitable day gown, and we descend the stairs to await an audience with three of the Patronesses.

They arrive not five minutes after we take our places in the drawing-room. Lady Jersey sweeps in on a cloud of perfume and swishing silks, trailing a high collared cape despite the summer heat. "We came as soon as we got your note, Emma, dear." She leans in to kiss both of Miss

Stranje's cheeks as is the European custom, unlatches the frog of her cape and lets it flutter into the arms of the footman trailing behind them.

Lady De Lieven and Lady Castlereagh glide in serenely behind her. Lady De Lieven is my favorite of the patronesses. Her inner music fascinates me—she vibrates with the closed-door hum of secrets, yet she always seems on the verge of laughter. It is as if she finds our twisted messy world rather humorous. I wish I were more like her. Georgie and Lady Jane admire the entertaining Lady Jersey with her flamboyant way of speaking. Sera and Tess prefer Lady Castlereagh's company. Although, she is stern and a stickler for the rules, they trust her direct manner and lack of artifice.

Miss Stranje greets them all with sisterly warmth, and as soon as the servants depart, she closes the parlor doors, and they all turn to me.

"She wounded you. You poor dear." Lady Castlereagh smooths her gloved hand over my bandaged arm as if her touch might heal.

"Tell us everything," Lady Jersey demands exactly as Tess had earlier, having no time for wounds or sympathy. Her country is in jeopardy, and she intends to get down to business. "How does that irritating little vixen think she can convince our dear Prince to allow you in on his peace negotiations with Napoleon?"

I repeat Lady Daneska's plot to trick the Prince.

Lady De Lieven tilts her head thoughtfully. "It might just work."

"Doubtful," Lady Jersey grumbles.

Lady De Lieven smirks at her. "Admit it. You are only nettled by the fact that her gambit might actually succeed."

Lady Jersey sniffs disdainfully. "No, I dislike that the scheming minx thinks she can twist our Prince Regent around her little finger. He's not as gullible as all that."

"Isn't he?" Lady de Lieven says wryly.

"I fail to see why he would trust a foreigner like Lady Daneska or even Miss Barrington when he won't even trust one of us to be there." Lady Jersey tilts her head apologetically in Maya's direction. "No offense intended, my dear, but despite Lady Daneska's chicanery, I doubt our prince will trust anyone, much less a young lady who he barely knows."

With a slight shake of her head, Lady De Lieven steps forward. "No, no. Lady Daneska is playing her cards quite cleverly. You know how enthralled he is with Maya's mesmerizing voice, and he fancies everything about India—"

"Ahem." Lady Castlereagh clears her throat, putting a halt to their bickering. "There is one person he *does* trust. A close personal friend."

"Ah, yes." Lady Jane glances up from her contemplation. "Lord Harston."

"Exactly." Lady Castlereagh smiles with pleasure. "Suppose we were to help Lady Daneska's stratagem along? Give it a *leg-up*, so to speak?"

"How?" Lady Jersey seats herself in the middle of the divan, like a queen preparing to hear out her subjects.

Lady Jane seems to have already leapt to some sort of disturbing conclusion because she is glancing at me with palpable concern, and inside she grows as silent and wary as an alerted doe. All, except Lady Jane, are gathering closer together, leaning in to hear Lady Castlereagh's idea.

The great lady speaks gently but with a strong air of competence. "We have already decided to bring Lord Harston's nephew, young Kinsworth, into our confidence. In fact, just this morning, our beloved Prince invited that very gentleman to come and share his uncle's rooms at Carleton House. If we were to arrange an engagement between Lord Kinsworth and Miss Barrington, she would no longer be an unattached foreigner. She would be betrothed to a peer of the realm, who happens to be the nephew of the Prince's closest friend."

"Brilliant idea." Lady De Lieven pats Lady Castlereagh's shoulder.

I had heard what Lady Castlereagh said. Every bit of it. Every heart-stopping syllable. Each stomach-punching word. And yet, when they all turn expectantly to me, I ask an inane question, and not in a low moderated tone. "*What?*" squeaks out of me like a strangled cry for help.

"An engagement, dear," Lady Castlereagh answers calmly as if it is a trifle, and I am behaving like a slightly feeble-minded child.

"No. No. No," I whisper in mouse-sized peeps and shake my head. Or, at least, I would be shaking my head if all the feeling wasn't draining from it and flooding down my neck like a river overflowing its banks, thundering toward my feet.

Not him!

I can't even speak now. So much for my persuasive abilities—I cannot even save myself. This entire plan is doomed from the start. I can't. *I can't.*

I can't marry him.

Sera is chafing my hand. "I don't think she wants to

do it."

Her touch pulls me back to earth. I draw in an enormous breath, a great ungraceful gulp. It as if I haven't breathed for days, and maybe I haven't. Whatever the case, it helps.

I close my mouth and eyes and simply breathe. Steadily. In and out. My heart finally stops banging like a madman's drum.

This time I speak with as low and as soothing a tone as I can manage. "I cannot do it."

"Can't do what, dear?" Lady Castlereagh looks at me with her sweet innocent bunny rabbit expression, even though I know she is as shrewd as a mongoose.

"I cannot marry Lord Kinsworth. Aside from my feelings on the matter, he'll refuse to do it." I know this because I heard his eloquent speech detailing his fear of losing his precious freedom on my account. I cannot tell *them* why, because it will expose the fact that I eavesdropped on far than needed after Lord Harston's conversation with Admiral St. Vincent.

Lady De Lieven chuckles as if I have told a joke. "We aren't asking you to marry the young man, Miss Barrington. Engagements can be broken. It will merely be a pretense. You needn't go through with it."

Lady Castlereagh's mouth rests in a patient motherly smile. "She's right, dear. Although, from what I have observed, the young man is not indifferent to you."

"For heaaaven's sake, we must aaaall make sacrifices for the greater gooood." Lady Jersey is affecting her drawl again, which means I have annoyed her. "Aside from that, you could do faaar worse, young lady."

"Sally!" Lady De Lieven raps her on the sleeve with

her fan. "Have a care."

"Don't ring a peal over my head. You know perfectly well, it's true. There isn't another young lady in Mayfair that wouldn't have him. You've seen the way the debs drool when he walks past them at Almack's. Not to mention the young man is plump of pocket and a peer of the realm. I simply cannot fathom why Miss Barrington should be so missish about it."

"I *could* do better," I argue under my breath. "I might marry someone who loves me. Someone who thinks of me as more than an exquisite flower to be avoided at all costs."

I glance up. Apparently, they heard my nearly silent protest. Lady Jersey and Lady Castlereagh exchange knowing looks, and Lady De Lieven presses a finger to her lips covering a smile.

This is not a laughable matter, I want to say. *This is my life. My future.* Before I am able to muster those words, Miss Stranje places her hand on my shoulder protectively. "Lady Daneska put Miss Barrington through a distressing ordeal last night. She looks rather pale at the moment, and I'm afraid it is time for her to rest. That will give her a chance to ponder our . . ." She was going to say *proposal.* I'm sure of it. "Our suggestion." She pats my shoulder. "Before we continue further with this plan, it might also be advisable to consult with Lord Kinsworth on the matter."

"No!" I glance up, pleading. I don't want them to discuss it with him. They mustn't. The idea of these women ordering him, nay commanding him, to play the part of my fiancé is humiliating. I cringe, imagining his response, and my stomach clenches into a screeching knot. "No."

My plea falls on deaf ears. Before I can argue more strenuously, Miss Stranje has me up and moving toward the door. She signals Tess and Sera to assist me upstairs to my room.

Except, they cannot dismiss me yet.

"Wait!" I wheel out of Sera's grasp. "I haven't told you the worst part."

"There's more?" Lady De Lieven sits down for the first time that morning.

"Yes. It is the very reason why we must proceed as if all our lives and our families' lives depend upon it. It is why you simply cannot leave this situation at the mercy of a preposterous engagement scheme." They all appear surprised at my outburst, but I focus on Miss Stranje.

"Go on," she says with deadly calm.

I alter my tone, hushing the panic rising like a whirlwind, but I do not quiet the force of the wind blowing through me. "Lady Daneska warned me if the parley with Napoleon does not proceed as Ghost plans, he will burn England down. But not until after he has made us suffer. He intends to release a plague on Britain."

They all draw back as if I have stung them.

Nine

Sound the Trumpets

"A Plague." Miss Stranje murmurs her dread into the deafening silence. She sits beside Lady De Lieven and stares at her hands clasped tightly in her lap. "Dear God."

"He wouldn't." Lady Castlereagh shakes her head in disbelief. "You're certain Lady Daneska was telling the truth?"

"Yes, that must be it. We all know how she loves to lie." Lady Jersey raises hopeful eyes to me.

I meet her gaze steadily. "I am not as capable as Sera is when it comes to discerning falsehoods, but I will never forget Lady Daneska's eyes as she told me these things. Her pupils widened with dread. Her voice quavered and, during that particular confession, I did not hear one false note." I lower my gaze to avoid witnessing their disappointment. "I *wish* she had been lying."

A rustle of fear blows through them, the way wind shivers through the trees to warn of a coming storm.

"I asked Lady Daneska if he had threatened such horrific acts in a fit of anger. She assured me that, no, Ghost had calmly calculated his methods of revenge. She heard him discuss it with his men, and saw his plans."

"But it's impossible." Lady Jersey bolts up from the divan and paces, her train twisting behind her. "Can't be done! No one person can accomplish such a terrible thing."

Lady De Lieven pales considerably. "He is master of the Iron Crown, Sally. He has a secret army at his beck and call."

Lady Jersey kicks her train angrily out of her way and takes another vicious turn across the carpet "Even so, to inflict a plague on an entire country—impossible!"

"Sadly, it isn't," Georgie says, matter-of-factly. "There are dozens of ways to do it. Ghost will have studied history. Ancient Scythian archers wiped out enemy camps by dipping their arrows into diseased corpses. Greeks and Romans contaminated water supplies with animals carrying the plague. Genghis Kahn catapulted diseased dead over the walls of besieged cities." Georgie's head is bowed in concentration. "Do you know which plague he intends to use?"

"I didn't ask." I shake my head, stunned at how easy spreading a plague might be.

"What does that matter?" Tess's fists knot tight. "A plague, *any* plague, will devastate our entire country."

Georgie dives in to argue the point. "Don't you see? If we know what disease is coming, we can anticipate the type of infirmaries to set up and how many. We'll know which treatments might be most useful to keep it from spreading, and—"

"What we *need* to do is find Ghost." Tess grips the top of Lady Castlereagh's chair, squeezing it until her knuckles bulge. "And kill him before any of this happens!"

"Ideally, yes." Georgie is still hunting for solutions, oblivious of Tess's agitation. "But in lieu of—"

"Stop!" Miss Stranje holds up her hand, and we all fall silent. "This news changes everything. *Everything.*" I've never seen her look so pale. "Ladies," she says, taking a deep breath and glancing pointedly at the patronesses. "I'm afraid this scenario goes beyond the scope and means of our sisterhood."

"Agreed." Lady Jersey speaks now without even a hint of a drawl.

Lady De Lieven nods solemnly.

"It most certainly does." Lady Castlereagh chews her bottom lip for a moment. "I shall apprise my husband, and he will undoubtedly bring Captain Grey and Lord Wyatt into the matter. We will need all hands on deck, and that includes all diplomatic operatives. I don't see that we have any alternative, Miss Barrington, but to go ahead with the engagement. I'm sorry, my dear, but it is more important now than ever." She raises a finger. "Moreover, you are *all* sworn to absolute secrecy regarding this wretched plague." She winces as if even speaking the word stings her tongue. She turns to Lady Jane, Tess, and Georgie. "You do understand, don't you?"

"Yes, of course," Lady Jane answers for all of us.

"We know how to keep a secret," Tess grumbles.

"No doubt." Lady Castlereagh stands, short in stature and older than the rest of the patronesses, but the fortitude that rings through her is unmistakable. "Nevertheless, you must use extra caution this time, even when discussing it amongst yourselves. Be wary of any servants who may be within earshot. We must take care no one catches wind of this terrifying threat. It would spread like wildfire. The panic would be catastrophic."

With that warning, we are all dismissed; I am sent to bed to recuperate, and the others to the ballroom for a defensive arts class with Madame Cho. I am curious as to what deadly technique she'll be sharing today behind those locked doors. Whatever it is, it will be useless against the plague.

The Patronesses stay to confer with Miss Stranje for a half-hour longer, before leaving in a loud clattering flurry. "See to it immediately," Lady Jersey orders. I had wanted, in the worst way, to eavesdrop on their conversation, but this bland London townhouse has no secret passages. If I had leaned outside the door, Miss Stranje might have suspected and caught me. More likely, since I am still weak from last night, collapsing or dripping blood on the floor would have given me away.

So, I remain in bed, laying here wondering about a great many things. None of which I can do anything about. Plagues are too ghastly to dwell on, Napoleon's negotiations with Prince George twist my stomach into a boiling lump. Hours pass, and my thoughts drift and tangle around an imaginary conversation between the Patronesses and Lord Kinsworth.

I picture him pressed into a straight-backed chair, surrounded by his uncle and the three great ladies. Miss Stranje may even be there. The minute Lord Kinsworth protests their outrageous scheme, *as I know he will do*, Lady Jersey shall puff up like a scalded cat. I can almost hear her caustic tone.

"Listen here, young man," she will say, and bustle

closer to him, leaning in until she is only inches away from his face. "I don't give two farthings about your dreams of freedom and adventure. Fah!" She will rap him on the forehead with her fan. "Your whims are nothing compared to the lives of thousands of British citizens."

"*Less* than nothing!" She'll rear back with her hands on her hips. "This is utter foolishness. Snap to it, young man. We expect you to do your duty for King and country. No matter how onerous you consider the task, you must pretend to be engaged to Miss Barrington. We need you to do it. Your Prince needs you to do it. And so, you shall!" She will fan herself as if his pigheadedness has overheated her. "And there's an end to the matter."

Lady Castlereagh will pat his hand. "Cheer up, young man. Miss Barrington is not as bad as all that."

Lord Harston will clamp his hand on his nephew's shoulder. "Chin up, lad. You said you wanted into the business. This is the price. It isn't as if you actually have to get leg-shackled to the chit. This engagement is only a pretense after all, not the end of the world. Play along for a few months or so, until this matter with the Prince is resolved. Then, as agreed upon, she'll give you the heave ho. You'll be free. Nothing to it." He'll snap his fingers. "A piece of cake."

"*Cake?*" Lord Kinsworth will respond, as droll as ever despite the sweat beading on his brow. "Wasn't it on account of *cake* . . . that they sent Marie Antoinette to the guillotine?" He'll follow that remark with a comical expression and whisk of his hand across his throat.

Lady De Lieven will laugh aloud.

Lady Jersey will tap him with her fan again, this time on his shoulder. "Don't be cheeky, boy."

"Not cheeky. Clever." Lady De Lieven will defend him, because the rogue will have charmed her with his wit.

His uncle's brow will furrow. He knows Ben hides behind humor when he is troubled. "If it's going to be that distressing, my boy, you needn't go along with it. I'll take your place. I can pretend to court the girl for a week or two, and–"

"No." Lord Kinsworth will shake his head. "No, you're right. I asked to be a part of your world. If this is the price, so be it." He'll probably stand and grasp his uncle's arm. "I'll do it! I will make this sacrifice to prove my loyalty to you, and to King and country."

"We all have to make sacrifices." Lady Jersey will sniff disdainfully, thinking she is the one who brought the misbehaving young pup to heel.

Lady Castlereagh will smile proudly at him. "Very good of you, Lord Kinsworth. Most noble."

Noble.

I grit my teeth. *Oh, yes, how very noble. Ergh!*

My stomach begins to weave and bob as if I'm aboard a ship at sea. I squeeze my eyes tight and try to imagine a less odious scenario. Except, no matter how hard I try, it always turns out with him doing his duty, sacrificing himself for the good of mankind, being so very noble, *nauseatingly noble*, as if the prospect of pretending to be in love with me is horribly revolting.

I have the most ferocious urge to rap him over the head for it. And, with something much bigger than Lady Jersey's fan.

The cad.

This whole situation is his fault. He is the one who

wanted into the diplomatic spy business. He is the one who offered to sing with me. It is he, who as if he is Romeo in the flesh, and continues to tease me mercilessly.

Scoundrel.

I will make him pay for his wretched nobility. If he thinks this is going to be some easy little farce, he is sorely mistaken.

"What are you thinking about?" Sera has slipped into the room and I didn't even notice.

"Nothing." My face reddens at being caught daydreaming about him. It *must* be red because my cheeks grow dreadfully hot. Maybe she won't notice.

"It's him, isn't it? You're thinking about your fiancé, Lord Kinsworth."

Drat. Sera notices everything.

I sigh loudly. "He isn't my fiancé."

"Not yet. But I expect he will agree to it."

"He is such a scoundrel."

"Really? I wouldn't have thought it. He seems a perfect gentleman. He impressed me as such when he came to your rescue that first time you sang at Carleton House. What has he done? Did he try to—"

"No. No. Nothing like that." I smooth the bedding out from where I have twisted it into knots. "He flusters me. That's all."

"Oh." She lowers her head and her beautiful white hair falls forward like a silk curtain. "I know *that* feeling."

She must be thinking of Mr. Chadwick. It's not the same. She can't possibly understand the humiliation I will face. "It's mortifying."

She jerks her head up. "Mortifying?"

"Yes! I wish the patronesses weren't trying to force me into this pretend engagement." *Forcing him.*

"I see." She looks genuinely sorry for me, and I do not mind because she is my closest friend. "Do you dislike him that much?"

"Yes!" I say a little too forcefully. "He . . . he is most annoying."

She slants her eyes at me, studying my face. She knows I'm not telling her the whole truth. Sera always knows things like that. She watches my face for telltale twitches and out of place grimaces.

"Hmm. Then I expect the next few weeks are going to be exceedingly uncomfortable for you. Here." She hands me a folded note. "Miss Stranje asked me to bring you this. It's from him. It would seem the patronesses have succeeded in convincing Lord Kinsworth to go along with their plan. The note asks if he might call on you this evening after dinner."

Tonight?

"No." I shake my head. "I cannot. I am unwell."

She checks the bandage. "There's no more bleeding. You are well enough. Read the note."

"I would rather not." I reluctantly unfold it.

"Miss Stranje already wrote back and told him yes. It's all very formal. He and his uncle will meet with Miss Stranje beforehand. I believe that is how this sort of thing is done. Our parents granted her legal authority to act in their behalf in matters such as these."

Marriage contracts.

"Tonight." I swallow—try to swallow—but my throat has gone completely dry.

She seats herself on the edge of the bed beside me.

The blue walls with their ivory latticework wallpaper seem to close in around us. I slump forward and lean my head in my hands, humming to myself, trying to calm the typhoon winding up inside.

"You are worried. That is only natural." Sera rests her hand on my shoulder, the healing warmth of her palm seems to help still the torrent inside me. "They are asking a great deal of you."

It is as if she hears my thoughts. I know she cannot, but it seems that way. I look up and forget to control my tongue, forget to hide my fear. It is all I can do to hold back the storm. "I don't think I can go through with this. The whole thing is impossible. How can I convince Napoleon of anything? Why do they expect this of me? I'm just a girl from a mountain village."

She does not push away from my qualms. She holds steady, and so my storm quiets somewhat. I try to explain with more tranquility. "It is a small thing to ease someone's discomfort, to help them to relax, or convince them to change their mind about an inconsequential matter. My skills of persuasion will be of little use with a man as headstrong as Emperor Napoleon. Think of it, Sera. He has risen to become the most powerful man in Europe. He swayed countless people to follow him, to the *death*, if need be. How am I to sway him?"

She does not answer, she waits as if she knows that is not the end of my tempest.

"And then there is Lord Kinsworth . . ." I sink into my hands again. "He does not want to align himself with me. He wants the exact opposite—freedom. He's going to be insufferable about this, I just know it. And, I . . ."

I fear his foot-dragging will strike too near the still-bleeding wounds of my father's indifference. "I don't know if I can bear it."

"You can." Sera tugs one of my hands into hers and holds it in her palm. "In many ways, Maya, you're the bravest of us all. Think of it, in France, you disguised yourself and pretended to be a lowly serving girl. *You* infiltrated our enemy's forces. And you did it so well that even Lady Daneska didn't discover you. You lived and worked inside the Iron Crown stronghold—around Ghost himself." She squeezes my hand tighter. "*You* did that to save Sebastian."

My throat tightens as I remember how afraid I was. But it had to be done. The alternative was unthinkable. The other girls were brave, too. "All of us played a part," I rasp, my throat tightening as I remember that ghastly time and how close to death we all came.

She takes a deep breath that matches my own. "Yes, but you—*you* marched into the lion's den, and didn't look back."

The lioness.

She nods as if she has overheard my thought. "If you can do that terrifying thing, you can do this. It will be easy to pretend to be engaged to Lord Kinsworth after that."

She is right.

"Even if he flusters you."

I look up and smile at her. Sera is wonderful. Sometimes she seems almost angelic—it makes one wonder. This much I know for certain, she is a true friend. A true friend, in this world where very few souls actually sing with love.

"Thank you," I say quietly, wishing I had better English words to express the gratitude and kinship I feel. In my country, we rarely say *thank you.* We bring food if one of us is sick. If a wagon wheel is broken, we gather around to help fix it. There is no need to say *thank you.* We strengthen one another, we help one another because that is how a village stays strong. That is what people who care for one another do.

Today, Sera has become a sister to me.

Instinctively, we bow until our foreheads touch. This reverence lasts for only a moment, but it is enough. I know she senses my gratitude.

I will do this thing my sisters need me to do.

And if Lord Kinsworth annoys me, or flusters me, or humiliates me in any way, he shall feel the sharp sting of the lion's claws.

TEN

THE GROOM'S TUNE

I DID NOT EXPECT to see the Patronesses, nor Captain Grey or Lord Wyatt along with Mr. Sinclair and Lord Ravencross standing in the drawing-room this evening. The way they have gathered in their finery one would think this sham engagement, this farce for political purposes, was genuine. I dressed like an Englishwoman for the occasion, in a pale gold silk gown. If I am to pretend to be engaged to an English lord, I suppose I ought to dress the part.

Apparently not.

The minute the ladies catch sight of me, they rush me back upstairs, ordering me to don my sari and veil. Lady Jersey scolds me in hushed tones all the way to the foot of the staircase. "You must remind the world of your exotic heritage at all times. Aaat aaahll times!" she drawls. "It sets you apart. It will remind Prince George of why you will be an asset when he meets with Napoleon."

"But he is not here."

"Ah, but child, he will hear. By tomorrow afternoon,

all of London will have heard about this evening." Lady Castlereagh pats my hand and shoos me onto the stairs.

"London loves her gossip." Lady De Lieven suppresses a smirk.

"Yes." Lady Jersey acts as if this is a compliment rather than a slur on her beloved London. "Precisely the reason why you must conduct yourself as if you are a mysterious foreign dignitary—an Indian princess if you will."

I cringe at the word.

Lady De Lieven must have noticed. She places an arresting hand on Lady Jersey's forearm. "My dear, that is exactly what the young lady is, a Maharajah's granddaughter. Remember?"

"Ah, yes. Well, then, do try and remember who you are."

I scurry up the stairs and return some minutes later, properly wrapped and draped in a veil trimmed with elaborate gold embroidery. If they want a princess, they shall have one. I enter the drawing-room, and the gentlemen stare for a moment before remembering to bow. I curtsey in return, and Lady Jersey gives me an approving nod.

I have not yet taken a seat when Miss Stranje hurries through the doorway, her black bombazine skirts rustling. She must've completed the necessary contracts and arrangements with Lord Kinsworth and his uncle. She wears a pleasant smile as if their meeting proceeded satisfactorily. I turn toward the entrance, expecting Lord Kinsworth to walk in, dragging behind his uncle, sulking like a beaten dog, whipped into grudgingly doing his duty.

Instead, Lord Harston fills the doorway. "Ah, my dear Miss Barrington. How lovely you look this evening. Allow me to be the first to wish you felicitations and welcome you to the family." He bows effusively.

I curtsey, confused. Lord Harston is doing it up a bit brown. Everyone here knows, don't they, that this is all an act? I glance around the room. Perhaps they don't. Lord Ravencross is frowning as if he doesn't approve, but then he is not prone to joyful expressions except when he looks at Tess. Mr. Sinclair glances from Lord Harston and back to me, looking confused. Perhaps it is because Lord Harston was once engaged to his beloved Lady Jane. Mr. Sinclair turns to her, his face ringing with questions. She acts as if nothing is amiss. Lord Wyatt seems genuinely pleased, and I wonder if perhaps the situation has not yet been explained to him or Captain Grey.

Mr. Peterson, the butler here at Haversmythe house, carries in three bottles of champagne. A footman follows, laden with a large tray of more than a dozen crystal flutes. The delicate glasses clink softly as he sets down the tray. I glance at the doorway, and there stands my *would-be* fiancé.

Not beaten.

Not whipped.

Beaming!

Lord Kinsworth is grinning like the rascal just gobbled down the last ginger cookie in all of England. He strides confidently across the floor and bows to me as if I am the only woman in the room.

I squint, studying him, as I perform my curtsey. For once, his inner music is not elusive. I do not have to strain to find it. It is so loud and clear that I daresay everyone in the house can hear it, even mice in the attic rafters must be startled by the sound. Where I expected to hear dark brooding thuds, exuberant horns are trumpeting with excitement.

My ears must be deceiving me.

This is all wrong.

I draw back expecting some sort of trick. He cannot possibly be pleased about this engagement the Patronesses are foisting on us. What is he playing at? What game is this?

He turns to the butler, who is quietly displaying one of the bottles of champagne to Miss Stranje for her approval. "A moment, my good man." Lord Kinsworth indicates the bottle. "I'm afraid this is a bit premature."

Everyone's attention snaps his way, but he smiles sideways at me as if we share some sort of private joke. "You see, the young lady has not yet given me her consent. Miss Stranje, I believe on occasions such as this, a young lady and gentleman might be granted a few moments alone. Is that not the custom?"

Miss Stranje inhales deeply and steps forward, donning her most formidable headmistress expression, not that it dampens Lord Kinsworth's buoyant spirits in the least. "Yes, I understand that is sometimes allowed," Miss Stranje says as if she has no intention of granting his request. "However—"

"Excellent!" He ignores her hesitancy and smiles broadly at all fourteen faces staring expectantly at him. "Rather than displacing all of you, I think it might be more convenient if Miss Barrington and I take a stroll around your garden?"

"The garden. Hmm." Our headmistress squints hard

at him. "Yes, well, I suppose *that* might be acceptable." She consults her timepiece. "You may have fifteen minutes, and not one minute more. We have Miss Barrington's reputation to consider."

"Of course." He bows and offers me his arm.

As we walk out of the drawing-room, Tess warns him, "Mind the wolves."

"Wolves?" His shoe catches briefly on the Turkish carpet.

Tess answers with a wry smirk.

"Our dogs," Georgie explains.

"Oh, a jest. I see." He grins amicably.

Several quiet chuckles follow us out of the room. On our way through the foyer, the back hall, and out to the garden, I decide not to tell him that our 'dogs' actually are half wolf. He will find out soon enough, and when he does, I shall relish his alarm.

He opens the garden door, and we step down into the yard.

The sun sits low on the horizon, draping the sky with streaks of burnt orange and magenta. In the evenings, the haze of smoke and ash that hangs over London during the day drifts lower to earth. Tonight, at least, there is a breeze to alleviate the heaviness in the air. In this dusky light, our lawn turns a deeper green and shadows appear almost as dark as the wolves' black fur. Hollyhocks, their tall stalks laden with white blooms, stand like cheerful sentinels along the path.

As we walk deeper into the garden, Lord Kinsworth pats my hand on his arm. He doesn't know, but the wolves are watching from the shadows. They dart silently from hedge to hedge, stalking us to see if we are friend, foe, or prey. Suddenly Phobos springs out from the bushes and blocks our path, his teeth bared. Tromos leaps out, too, and stands guardedly behind her mate.

"Don't move," I caution. Phobos and Tromos know me, but I fully expect they will growl and snap at Lord Kinsworth.

"Oh!" he says excitedly, not heeding my warning. "They really are wolves. And black wolves, at that!"

Phobos studies his quarry, looking from me to Ben, sniffing the air warily and then he takes a menacing step toward us. I worry he might attack Ben. Lord Kinsworth is a stranger, after all, and the wolves have puppies to protect. Instead, Phobos's back relaxes, and trots up to the intruder and sniffs his hand as if they are old friends. A moment later, Phobos yips to his mate, and she yips in answer. Immediately, two black pups tumble out from where they were hiding in the hedge.

"Good gracious. You have an entire wolf pack." Ben stoops down to greet the newcomers. Moonlight, a silver cub, scoots out behind her brothers, her makeshift wheel and harness snag briefly on the bushes, but she yanks it free. "What in the world is that–? Oh! I see. The little one is lame, and this contraption allows her to walk."

"Miss Fitzwilliam designed it. Mr. Sinclair made a few improvements and helped her build this latest version." I explain all this, still astonished, and a little aggravated, to see the wolves accepting him so quickly. Charm, as effective as his, is dangerous. The puppies, even Moonlight, are enthusiastically sniffing him, barraging him with licks and whimpers for attention.

"What an ingenious device." He stands and brushes off his hands. Phobos and Tromos circle our legs, trying to nudge their exuberant offspring back into the hedges where they are training the young ones to hunt mice and voles. Moonlight knocks against me while trying to evade her mother, and Lord Kinsworth clasps my arm to steady me. "I envy the lot of you," he says, running his hand up and down my arm. His heart hums dangerously close to mine. "You and the other young ladies at Miss Stranje's school, you're almost like a family, aren't you?"

"Yes." Although, it was only this very afternoon that I realized how close a family we are.

I look up and see he is grinning broadly at me. Too broadly. He whispers, "Miss Stranje told me everything."

Everything?

I click my tongue. "I sincerely doubt that."

"She told me enough." Louder, he says, "How lucky you are. What adventures you all must have had. Why didn't you tell me you were . . ." He lowers his voice again and leans close. "Spies?"

I step back, aghast. Miss Stranje could not have told him that. She wouldn't have. *Never.* My mouth opens, but I cannot find the right words. Finally, I fling out an inane retort. "If I had, I would be doing a very bad job of it, now wouldn't I?"

He smirks. "I suppose."

"Aside from that, we are not *spies.*" I try to unclench my teeth and sound less snappish. "Miss Stranje would never have said such a thing. I know her. She wouldn't have said it. The very notion is absurd. We are no such thing. Not really. We are . . . we are diplomatic . . ."

I suddenly realize that I do not have a word for what we are. Lord Wyatt and Captain Grey officially work for the government as diplomatic attachés. But Miss Stranje and the Patronesses, what are they? As their understudies, what are we? "We are, um, we are students . . . and she is teaching us how to, um, how to help out. Here and there. Behind the scenes, so to speak. Diplomatically."

He shrugs. "Yes, she tried to tell me something along those same lines. But isn't that exactly what a spy does?"

"No! Not exactly." I cross my arms, and *not* because I'm cold. "A spy tries to procure information from the enemy. They sneak behind the lines into enemy camps and infiltrate—"

"You and the others, you've never done that?"

I look away, hoping that in the dim orange of the setting sun, he can't see my cheeks heating up. "No."

He takes my shoulders in his palms and turns me toward him. "You're a terrible liar."

"Lying is not my specialty."

"No. And yet, for this assignment we must lie. We must pretend to be in love."

"Engaged," I protest. "Not necessarily in love."

One side of his mouth curves up, and I know he is up to something. "Perhaps not, but it will be a great deal easier to convince everyone our engagement is real if we pretend to be smitten with one another."

"*Smitten?*"

"Ah, you don't know this word." Mischief sneaks into his eyes. "It means passionately in love."

"I know the word." I squint at him, doing my best to look severe.

He tugs me closer. "And do you also know it is customary for couples to kiss when they get engaged?"

Kiss? He cannot mean it. I swallow air a little too loudly. "I may have heard such a thing. But we cannot. In my culture such a thing is forbidden. Besides, it is completely unnecessary. We are merely pretending to be engaged."

"But we are in England. Your father is English. And our customs allow for such small discretions."

"Indiscretions, you mean." I cross my arms.

"Come, Maya. You said yourself you are not a good liar. To that end, the more authentic we make this engagement of ours, the easier it will be for you."

"I see. Easier *for me*. And *you*—are you so very accomplished at the art of deception?"

"No. As a matter of fact, I am not. All the more reason if we are to convince the world we are truly engaged, I will need a great deal of help from you."

"Oh, yes, it will be hard to convince them because everyone knows you are terrified of losing your freedom?"

His hands, which have been roaming far too intimately up and down my arms, still. His head tilts and his jubilant music stutters. "How did you—?" Then it dawns on him at what time and place he exposed his feelings on the matter. "You overheard me at the ball, didn't you?"

I say nothing.

"Of course, you did. Very good." He chuckles and regains his absurd confidence. There is singing in his soul again. "Yes, but don't you see—that's the beauty of this arrangement. Because of your . . . *your work* at Stranje House you have countless adventures ahead of you, and now, so do I. This is temporary. Neither of us will be permanently entangled. It's the perfect arrangement."

Perfect?

I press down the rumble rising in my throat. Now, it all becomes clear. I want to roar at him. The scoundrel thinks he is free to dally with me and then walk away without looking back.

I will not allow it.

He leans down to kiss me. When I draw back, he uses a deeper, more seductive tone. "Come, Miss Barrington, you know I am right. We ought to kiss. We must fall as close to the truth as possible if we are to persuade Prince George that we are in love."

It's the possibility of actually *falling* for him that frightens me. I endured enough pain when my father walked away without a backward glance. I will not suffer it from Lord Kinsworth.

I swallow, hunting for my lion claws, and something to say that will foil his little scheme. Except his words are eerily similar to advice Miss Stranje often gives us regarding prevarication; *always stay as close to the truth as possible.*

Very well. Here's the truth.

"No. I don't want to kiss you." I try to edge away from him, but his hand holds me in place with barely a touch. "It simply is not done. In my country, such behavior is a crime. We would both be thrown in prison or whipped." I tilt my head, glancing sideways at him to see if he is sufficiently terrorized.

"Prison, huh?" He thinks on it a moment, but then stuns me with that irrepressible grin of his. "Lucky thing we live here."

His music is playing cat and mouse games, I know if I look up, he will wear me down with that impish grin of his.

"And anyway, I have never kissed anyone before." I stare down at the toes of my shoes, afraid to meet his gaze. "I don't know how."

"It is a small matter. One puckers one's lips and–" A chuckle bursts apart his demonstration. "Surely, you've kissed your mother and father? Or they kissed you?"

"No. My mother died before I can remember, and my father . . . he doesn't . . . didn't . . . he isn't one for displays of affection either." I frown at Lord Kinsworth, schooling my features to appear frank and aloof, just as if this conversation isn't wounding me to the core. I cannot even remember my grandmother kissing me.

Scorching shame brands my cheeks, and a hollow ache drums in my soul. I shake my head, unable to speak.

"I see." He squints at me as if such a thing is incomprehensible. His music changes timbre to a low mournful bansuri flute. "I'm sorry," he says sadly and means it. "That's not right, Maya. Not right at all. You should have been cossetted and hugged and . . ." He stares at me as if truly seeing me for the very first time. "Kissed."

What would that have been like?

"Do you mean that?" I look up, unable to keep hope out of my voice.

"Yes. Are you blind to your qualities? Can't you see?"

I should've been hugged and loved and–

Suddenly, I want to know what it is to be held, to be kissed, truly kissed. I want to know with all my heart.

He caresses my cheek with his palm. "If you will allow me . . ." His voice is as smooth as hot chocolate on a cold morning, warm and pleasing to my ears, flowing with deliciously earnest notes. "I shall be honored to teach you."

Honored.

He tilts his head toward mine, waiting patiently until I raise my chin, and when I do, trembling, he lightly presses his mouth against mine. Our lips touch for one breathless lingering moment.

"You see?" He smiles drowsily and leans closer. He means to kiss me again, and I am glad. Now I know why they put people in prison for this—it is addicting. This time he covers my mouth with his, and somehow it feels as if my lips are melting into his.

The world around us begins to soften. The amber sky, the rooftops, the rocks, all the hard edges are disappearing. Strange music murmurs in my ears, a faint blissful chorus, and it seems to lift me, as if we are afloat in a swirling mist of sunset and bliss. He is still kissing me, and I am holding onto him to keep my balance.

I like kissing.

I like it very much.

He stops, and I tip up on my toes for more.

"Maya," he whispers. Gathering me tight in his arms, he falls to kissing me some more.

ELEVEN

A ROARING RIVER

"A-HEM."

That voice, that icy tone, it arrests us mid-kiss.

Kinsworth winces and turns slowly to look down the garden path. As for myself, I hide my face in the folds of his cravat and peek out.

Miss Stranje stands a few yards away, frowning, and tapping the watch that hangs around her neck. "Young man, your time was up four minutes ago."

"Is it?" He has the good grace to blush. Even in this light, I can see the red blotches climbing up his neck. "My apologies. We shall return to the drawing-room immediately."

"I should say so." She waits for us, drumming the toe of her shoe against the stone path. I hasten to repair his smashed cravat and fluff up the wrappings of my sari from where he crushed me to his chest. Miss Stranje waves us forward, impatiently. "Come along!" she snaps.

As we walk back to the house, Tromos trots up beside her. She ruffles the big wolf behind the ears but keeps walking. "You great wooly soft-heart," she scolds. "I see I shouldn't have counted on you to keep them at arm's length."

"You mustn't be too severe on them. Your wolves very nearly attacked me." Lord Kinsworth pats my hand resting on his arm and winks at me.

She sniffs. "If they had, it would've been no more than you deserve."

He laughs at that. "I suppose you're right."

"I shall be more watchful in the future, my lord. You may count on it."

That means *no more kissing.* My heart sinks at the thought. "But you allow Lord Ravencross and Tess—"

"I do nothing of the kind." She bristles, and her posture grows even more rigid. "Aside from that, I have known young Ravencross since he was in leading strings. And he has proven himself trustworthy on several occasions." She squints at Lord Kinsworth, shrewd-eyed as a hawk surveying her prey. "I shall be watching you, my lord."

"So, you said. And I believe you." He ought to be uneasy under her scrutiny, but he isn't. His smile is slow and easy, that same roguish *I-will-win-you-over* grin he always employs when he's in a pinch.

Our stalwart headmistress does not melt and smile in return like all the other women in his life. No, she frowns more severely and marches us at an even faster pace toward the drawing-room. Which dampens the euphoric chorus humming so contentedly inside me. Dampens, but does not extinguish it.

"What happened to your arm?" Ben glances down at my shoulder next to his. "Earlier, I noticed you're wearing a bandage."

"Oh, *that.*" I'd hoped my sleeves had hidden the wound well enough that it would not draw anyone's notice. "It's nothing. A small accident."

"That's a rather large bandage, for a *small* accident."

I am spared having to answer because we have reached the doorway and Miss Stranje prods us forward. We trudge sheepishly into the crowded drawing-room.

Mr. Sinclair chuckles. "If red faces are anything to go by, it would appear congratulations are in order."

Lord Kinsworth rubs the back of his neck in answer, and the red bloom on his cheeks deepens.

Lady Jersey lifts her glass of champagne. "To the happy couple!"

Cheers surround us. Clapping and huzzahs fill our ears. Ben edges closer to me, pressing even tighter on my hand that rests on his arm. Lord Wyatt slaps his back and calls him a "Lucky fellow."

It occurs to me that Lord Kinsworth has not yet actually asked me to marry him, but why would he? This is all a pretense. I glance sideways, up into his face, hoping to catch a glimmer of the warmth he'd shown me earlier. I don't expect it. I expect him to be devising witty quips and putting on a jovial show for our guests. Instead, I find him staring at me. Staring intently, as if suddenly something, *most likely our engagement,* troubles him.

"*Yes. Lucky,*" Kinsworth murmurs, blinking, struggling to shutter his uneasiness away. He tries to laugh in the face of such feelings, laugh and run away, just as he always has before. Except, this time, no laughter comes. No jest springs to his lips. Fear is scraping and sawing away his confidence. Some minutes back, he smothered the trumpets, and now he is breaking the flutes. He is desperate to run. I hear panic thrumming inside him.

His distress over our engagement stings my pride, but I know what I must do for him. "My lord, this is only temporary. A few short weeks." I use a cadence so gentle it is almost a lullaby. "Soon you will be free again, very soon."

"Will I?" He swallows and drags in a breath as if I have pulled him to safety from a roaring river. "Will I ever be free?"

"Yes." Reassurance glides over my tongue like warm milk. "Yes, you will."

The roaring river, the thundering noise in his soul, quiets. He leans nearer and breathes in deeply as if the scent of pomegranate oil in my hair is healing. "I'm not so sure," he whispers.

What?

Startled and confused, I watch as his uncle clasps Ben's shoulder and pulls us apart. We are dragged into the arms of our friends, who enthusiastically offer us their well-wishes. I try to concentrate on their conversation but cannot stop pondering what he meant.

Does he worry he'll never be free of me?

Across the room, he repeatedly glances in my direction. It is as if our kissing has thrown him off-balance somehow.

How can that be true?

I thought *he* was the experienced one.

After all, *he* was the one *teaching me* the magic of kissing. And he did a wondrous fine job of it, too. *Superb.* I cannot stop smiling stupidly as I remember how lovely it felt to have his arms around me.

Is it possible he underestimated the power of an embrace of that sort? I certainly did. It is a mystery, this kissing business. Somehow our lips seem to be connected to our hearts. Right now, even though he is clear across the room, I can feel how disconcerted he is. I see, now, that kissing entwines two souls. It weaves our inner beings together on some unseen eternal loom.

If that is true, Lord Kinsworth may be right. I nervously twist the fabric of my veil around one finger. There may be no escape from our entanglement—not without paying a price, not without ripping apart that newly woven bond, not without the pain of loss.

Loss.

I am all too familiar with that particular malady. *Achingly familiar.* But familiarity has gifted me with an advantage. Here is what I have learned about loss—I will survive it.

Judging by the look on his face, Lord Kinsworth is not as certain.

We are toasted and patted on the shoulders, teased and jostled good-naturedly until Lord Harston raises his glass high and calls for our attention. Chatter lessens, and we glance in his direction. He stands before the fireplace and pastes on a broad smile. "This is as good a time as any to make another announcement."

A hush falls over the room, and we all turn to listen. Lord Ravencross mutters, "What *announcement*?"

I wonder the same thing. Despite Lord Harston's jovial demeanor, his inner music carries an ominous undertone. "My friends, just this afternoon our beloved Prince told me he intends to leave the heat of London and remove to his palace on the Brighton shore." He lowers his glasses and swirls the remaining champagne. "And since Parliament adjourns next week, he plans to make the journey a day or two afterward." He looks up and pretends to smile. "It seems he is in something of a hurry to meet with, uh, other dignitaries, and . . . friends there."

Brighton Palace. England's southern coast. The perfect place to hold a clandestine meeting with Napoleon.

More than one among us draws in a wary breath.

Lord Harston taps the rim of his crystal, regaining our attention. "Not only that, but His Highness has invited myself, as well as Lord Kinsworth and his betrothed, Miss Barrington. We are to join him at the palace, for the . . . uh, the pleasures of the sea, and to participate in the festivities with his *other* guests." He lifts his champagne as if this is marvelous news, and we all ought to raise our glasses to it.

"To Brighton." Lady Jersey stoically joins in the salute.

"Oh dear," Lady Castlereagh murmurs. "It's so much sooner than we expected."

"It could be worse, my dear." Lady De Lieven pats the shorter patroness's arm. "At least, we know where, and, we'll have people in attendance." The side of her mouth quirks up, and she lifts her glass to me. "To Brighton."

Less than a fortnight.

I'm not ready.

Not ready at all. I glance around, hunting for Lord Kinsworth, wondering if he feels as uneasy as I do. Except he has moved from where he last stood. He is pushing through the other guests. He bumps Mr. Sinclair's shoulder and skirts around Lady Jane in a great hurry to corner his uncle. "A word, my lord, if I may? *In private.*"

Lord Harston looks surprised. "Well, certainly my boy, but can't it wait?"

"No. It can't." Lord Kinsworth is taller and broader than most men. That gives him the means to efficiently guide his uncle forward, but he stops beside Miss Stranje and issues a similar request.

Miss Stranje does not look happy. "If you insist." She bristles and suggests they might return to her study.

What is he doing?

He is agitated. Even from this distance and surrounded by so many people, I hear that much quite clearly. If Ben is having second thoughts about our engagement, I have to find out and put his mind at ease again. I excuse myself from Lady De Lieven and hurry across the room toward them.

"Oh, good," He says, and snares my hand, clasping it firmly on his arm. "This concerns you as well."

His strides are so lengthy he practically drags me along beside him. As soon as we are out of the foyer and two or three yards down the hall, well out of earshot of the drawing-room, I ask him, "Are you regretting the engagement, because if so–"

"No," he answers sharply and glances down at me. Lord Kinsworth rarely frowns, but right now, his face is pinched tighter than I have ever seen it. "Of course, not."

"Then what–"

He hurriedly tugs me into the study, and Miss Stranje snaps the door shut.

"Yes, my lord, what is it?" Her dress rustles as she spins to confront him. "What is so urgent that you obliged me to abandon our guests?"

He stands to his full height, unintimidated by her stern expression. "It's this assignment. It's too dangerous."

She steps back as if he has surprised her. "You're afraid? I wouldn't have thought—"

"No! Not me. Of course not. It's too dangerous for *her*." He glances down at me.

My jaw nearly comes unhinged. I want to laugh. Except I'm still gaping in disbelief.

"I see," Miss Stranje says. "You are concerned for her safety. Commendable, but you needn't be. Miss Barrington is well trained in the art of self-defense, and she possesses several other skills that protect her quite admirably."

He steps forward as if *he* is the headmaster calling *her* to task. "I know about the wound on her arm."

Miss Stranje spins to me. "You told him?"

I shake my head. "Never. I wouldn't."

He clicks his tongue. "No, in fact, Miss Barrington lied. I had to waggle the truth out of someone else. And before you ask, I will not betray who. To be fair, I tricked it out of him, by pretending I knew more than I did. The point is, I found out she was wounded by Lady Daneska. Isn't she one of the people responsible for exploding a bomb meant to kill half of the Admiralty?"

Miss Stranje rears up like a raven ruffing out her feathers. "*Who* shared these speculations with you?"

"Me." His uncle winces. "When I explained his assignment, it seemed a pertinent detail. Kinsworth will be at Carleton House, and as Lady Daneska is known to visit there on occasion."

This uproar has gone on long enough.

I yank my hand off of Lord Kinsworth's sleeve. "I am perfectly capable of taking care of myself."

"Oh, yes? Then how is it you were stabbed while taking such *perfect* care of yourself?"

"Cut. Not stabbed. And you don't understand. It was a calculated ploy." I press my lips together, remembering that I should breathe evenly and moderate my voice. "Fortunately for us, the ploy worked. I won her confidence. And because of it, we obtained important new information."

His posture softens, but his words do not. "So, you're saying, you won this traitor's confidence by nearly bleeding to death?"

"Nothing as dire as that." I try to smile as if he has comically exaggerated the matter. "It was a minor cut. You can see for yourself I am perfectly healthy."

"So, you say." He looks askance at me for an overlong moment, as if he knows I am lying. "I have every intention of keeping you that way. Alive and unharmed."

Some young ladies might find his words endearing. *Sweet.* He wants to protect me. Part of me flutters and blushes at his concern. But another part, the part I depend upon for survival, rears up in alarm. His *sweet* words slam down around me like a wall of iron bars.

The lioness inside me roars in rebellion.

I have endured many things, but a cage is not one of them. *Naanii* treasured her own freedom too much to have ever hampered mine. And my father, he may not love me but, beyond bringing me to England, he never sought to control me. His wife tried, and when she failed, sent me away to Stranje House. Miss Stranje is a stern headmistress, exacting, but she prides herself on teaching us how to *escape* cages, not endure them, whether they be restrictions imposed by society or actual dungeons.

More importantly, if Lord Kinsworth continues trying to protect me, this mission to save England from Napoleon is doomed.

I begin my rebellion by using a deadly resonance that vibrates deep inside the hearer. "You have no say over me, Lord Kinsworth. None whatsoever. I think you must have forgotten I am not *actually* your fiancée. This is only an act. A part we must play to save our country—no matter the danger." Hard words, delivered with a tongue of iron, a hammer meant to split stone. I move closer, bearing down on him. "My lord, listen to me carefully. I will go where I am needed, and I will do as I please."

"But . . ." I see how stricken he is. It claws at my heart to hear his soul deflate like collapsing bagpipes.

I do not want to hurt him. Wounding him, I bleed, too.

If only there were another way, except there isn't. I must put a stop to him thinking this way. Our mission will fail if he continues trying to protect me. So, I steel myself to deliver the final blow. "What did you think you would do? Confine me—as your mother did you?"

He flinches as if I have kicked him in the stomach.

"It will not work with me, my lord. A caged nightingale cannot live." *It may sing for a time, but in the end, the wild bird will bash itself against the bars until it dies.*

He holds out his hand to me. "I don't want to cage you. Only protect you."

"There is no difference. You of all people should understand that." I hear too many winds of hope still blowing within him. It grieves me, but I must push him further. "Did you think my kissing you meant more than it did?"

His eyes widen, and he steps back.

I clench my fists, forcing myself to finish this, to cure his romantic notions once and for all. "I only kissed you to aid in our deception. Those were your own words, were they not?"

Ben's shoulders sag, beaten.

I want to rush to him, to wrap my arms around him, and tell him it isn't true. I ache to tell him our kisses sang songs in my heart that will remain forever. But I cannot. Instead of comfort, my tone must harden to steel. "And now, my lord, we shall proceed with the plan and do what must be done in Brighton. If we are to succeed, you must never again question my safety. If I must die in the service of my friends, I am content to do so."

All three of them stare at me. I am fully aware I employed the sword tongue, but I did not expect *all* of them to look slain. Only Kinsworth.

How long will they stand there in a stricken stupor? I am exhausted inside. I feel like crumpling up in the corner and crying, but I must speak again. This time, to warm them to action, I must sing them up some fortifying honey and tea. "There now. All that is settled, shall we return to the drawing-room?"

Miss Stranje blinks. "Yes," she breathes out softly. "Yes. I suppose we ought to, yes." She brushes past me, still a little shaken, and opens the door.

I follow her out, not waiting for Lord Kinsworth, who appears to be still recovering. His uncle leans close to Ben's ear, but I catch his muffled words. "You warned me she was dangerous. You were right."

"You're too late." Lord Kinsworth's music awakens and begins to play again. I catch the breathy strains of a bansuri, low, hushed, solemn eve, and yet faintly playful. Which alarms me. At least now, there are no trumpets. But he says, "Perhaps, uncle, you should've tried harder to keep me from galloping over that cliff."

TWELVE

INVASION OF THE CHOIRBOY

THE FOLLOWING AFTERNOON Miss Stranje summons all of us, Georgie, Tess, Lady Jane, Sera and me, upstairs to the study, the room Lady Daneska was seen exiting last night. She puts us to work trying to find what might be missing, or what documents Daneska might have seen.

An hour later, after finding nothing amiss thus far, Lady Jane plants her hands on her hips. "She was probably hoping to find the formula." She is referring to the undetectable invisible ink formula Georgie perfected.

Georgie glances up from checking through her equipment case, a large black satchel crammed full of devices she insisted on bringing to London: calipers, compasses, scales, beakers, and whatnots. "Good thing I keep the ink and the formula hidden in a lockbox in the back of my wardrobe."

Tess scoffs. "That's the first place I'd look if I were

her."

"Well, she didn't. I checked." Georgie latches her tool case. "And there's nothing missing here, either."

Sera brushes off her hands. "Our maps and papers appear undisturbed, too. That doesn't mean Lady Daneska didn't read them and carefully replace them."

We have all been taught how to do precisely that, and since Daneska was once a student at Stranje House, she is certainly capable of doing so.

"Right. I haven't found any evidence of what she was after either." Miss Stranje turns the key and locks the study door. "We had best move on to the problem at hand." She unrolls, onto our worktable, two large detailed drawings of Prince George's Brighton Palace. "These plans may have been the objective of her search. Regardless of whether she found them or not, you must all memorize these floor plans."

Prince George's Brighton Pavilion, with its onion-domed roof and minarets, looks more like a Hindu temple than a palace. Except, according to these drawings, the inside is decorated from top to bottom in the fantastical style of a Chinese pagoda, with enormous vases, Chinese statues, brightly painted wallpapers, and turned up cornices everywhere.

"Obviously, there are no spyholes or priest holes in a palace this newly constructed." Miss Stranje uses the plume tip of her quill, a long quail feather, to indicate three narrow passages. "However, there are a series of private hallways running down the center of the building. Here. Here. And here. They can be accessed from outside through the servants' entrance, here, near the kitchens."

Lady Jane pulls out a chair and sits down. "That

means Lady Daneska and Ghost can enter as they please." The rest of us join her at the table.

Our headmistress squares her shoulders. "It is entirely possible Lady Daneska may be invited in the front door. But yes, we must assume the Iron Crown will know about the passages. We must also presume their spies will have infiltrated the palace staff." She directs our attention back to the drawing, tipping her feather to a large room marked music chamber. "The Chinese wallpapers cleverly conceal the entrances, but you should find a door hidden along this wall. And in the Grand Salon, there is one located near this corner."

She sets the quill down and stands back surveying all of us. "If you find it necessary to enter one of these passages, use extreme caution. You must not get caught in them—especially unaccompanied. The architect, Mr. Nash, installed these passages primarily for the servants' convenience. They do use them, and you may be sure they will report it to their masters if they see you."

She pauses, making sure each of us grasps the seriousness of her warning. "That is not my only concern. In a palace of this sort, especially considering the company Prince George keeps, guests sometimes use backstairs and private passages to sneak into other peoples' rooms for trysts. Should anyone catch you in those secluded corridors, it could ruin your reputation. Even more problematic, if Ghost and Lady Daneska are in the vicinity, you may be certain they and their cohorts will use the passages for *other* purposes. If a member of the Iron Crown discovers you in those dimly lit hallways, it may very well cost you your life."

At our resounding silence, she clasps her hands together. "Excellent. Now, let's move on to the difficult part."

Difficult? Was memorizing the layout of an immense palace and discussing the risks involved not difficult enough?

She continues with her customary determination. "You all heard Lord Harston's announcement. His Highness only invited Maya and one companion to reside inside the palace. Stranje House is a full day's ride from Brighton. The rest of us will follow along and take lodgings as near to the palace as possible so we may be of assistance. Miss Barrington, I cannot act as your chaperone. My duty lies outside the palace walls. I must be free to move about unchecked, that will allow me to orchestrate the external situation more efficiently. You may count on all of us to be present at the Prince's gatherings, but between times, you will be somewhat cut off. Bearing that in mind, I leave it to you to choose who you would like to accompany you. Madame Cho has offered, and she would be an excellent advisor and companion. However, you may think it more prudent to bring someone who can mingle easily with the other guests and help you gather information."

I would prefer to have all of you there with me.

"Learning to make a difficult decision, such as this, is an integral part of your training." Miss Stranje leans forward and taps the oak table with her fingertip. "You must ask yourself this question, *what assistance will I need?* Once you determine your needs, you will know what choice to make. For example, if you think you may require strategizing or lock-picking, you would be wise to bring along Lady Jane. On the other hand, if you foresee you may need help climbing out of a third story window, it's rather obvious Tess would be your logical choice."

Sera sits beside me and suddenly her inner music jumbles. Her normally quiet, albeit highly-structured melodies gallop wildly and collide. She hangs her head and hides behind the white curtain of hair that always refuses to stay tucked back in a knot.

Miss Stranje continues advising me. "Consider carefully, and choose the person most able to assist you in this critical assignment."

I don't need time to consider. I already know who I ought to bring, and I know she would like to help me, but I also feel her reluctance.

I look around the table at them—my sisters. My mentors. My friends. "I wish I could bring all of you with me."

Georgie nods and stares at the map. "Yes, we are stronger together. But since we can't all come, I'll pack a supply of ink and developer for you. You can send us messages every day."

Her invisible ink will be very helpful. I smile with gratitude and, remembering her English ways, I remember to say, "Thank you."

"You'll need time to consider." Miss Stranje starts to turn away. "I will return—"

"Wait. I already know," I say.

She whirls back, her brow pinched in surprise. "You do?"

"Yes. I need someone with me who is far more observant than I am."

Everyone turns to Sera. She shrinks down in her chair.

She is afraid. I apply a bolstering cadence to my request. "It would be a great help to have someone beside me who notices crucial details, someone who catches the subtle nuances in people's expressions."

And someone who knows how to calm the raging storm inside me.

I lean close and quietly offer her an escape. "But if the risks overset you too much, if you are not comfortable, I shall not require it of you."

I hear the shadow of a laugh from behind the curtain of her hair. She raises up with a twist to her lips and looks pointedly at me. "You know perfectly well I am *never* comfortable. Ergo, I may as well come with you."

Tess and Lady Jane laugh aloud.

"Well done." Miss Stranje hums with approval, looking from me to Sera. "Excellent choice. Now, let us turn our attention back to these drawings of the palace. We must all learn this layout by heart."

We lean over the sketches, and not two minutes pass before there is a scratch on the study door. She hurriedly rolls up the papers, and we scramble to take out our textbooks and pretend to be studying.

Miss Stranje cracks open the door to our butler, Mr. Peterson, who strains to peek into the room. At being given only a narrow slit with which to peer into our inner sanctum, he sniffs. "Begging your pardon, miss, but there is a young man calling. He insists he must speak with you on a matter of grave importance. If it were anyone else, I would've sent him on his way. However, as he claims to be a magistrate's son, I thought it circumspect to allow him to wait in the front parlor."

"Pray, does this magistrate's son have a name?" she

asks, even though Sera is already cringing, and it isn't hard to guess who our caller is.

"Yes. Mr. Chadwick, miss. Seems a quality young gentleman, good manners, well-groomed, but if you prefer not to meet with him, I shall turn him away."

"No, I'll see him." Miss Stranje studies the card the butler handed her. "Thank you, Mr. Peterson. Please, tell him I'll be down in a few minutes."

She closes the door and wheels on us.

Sera snaps her history book shut and grips it tightly. She stands without shoving back her chair, and I catch it to prevent it from toppling.

"What can Mr. Chadwick want?" Sera turns and paces toward the wall as if she intends to disappear into it. "I've given him no cause to think—"

"Calm yourself, Miss Wyndham." Miss Stranje guides her back to the table. "It may not have anything to do with you. His note specifically asks if he might speak with me." She flips his calling card over so Sera can read the message scrawled on the back. "In all likelihood, he has more questions about the two deaths that occurred at Stranje House last month. He never did fully accept the coroner's conclusions. Even so, I would like you to come down to the drawing-room with me. You are the perfect distraction for him. We must keep him from becoming any more inquisitive about our school than he already is."

Sera gnaws at the corner of her lip for a moment. "Yes, all right, but we should all go. More of us to divert him."

"Very well." Miss Stranje retrieves the card and pats Sera's hand. "Do try to cheer up, Miss Wyndham. I assure you Mr. Chadwick does not bite."

Sera heaves in a much-needed breath. "I'm not so sure."

Miss Stranje gives Sera's shoulders a quick squeeze. "As men go, my dear, he's fairly harmless. Nothing like that rascal, Lord Kinsworth." She squints, sending a hawk's shrill scree of disapproval in my direction, before turning back to Sera. "You'll see. Mr. Chadwick is an amiable young pup. Distract him with your smile, and we shall sail through his visit undetected."

Undetected.

I am not so certain, and I can tell Sera is not convinced either. As female *political intriguers*, we rely upon passing ourselves off as innocent debutantes who have nothing but frivolity on our minds. Trouble is, Mr. Chadwick has a sharp intellect and is nearly as observant as Sera. His inner music plays with all the complexity and mathematical genius of Mozart. It seems odd to me that Miss Stranje thinks Mr. Chadwick will be easily distracted from the truth.

As we leave the room, I caution her quietly, "I would not underestimate him."

Miss Stranje stops, purses her lips and arches one eyebrow rather high, before responding. "Very well, Miss Barrington. I shall try not to be blinded by the fact that I've known him since he was in the cradle and his parents are bulwarks of the community."

I understand why she is inclined to trust him. He is that kind of person. One need only listen for a few minutes to the crisp bright symphonies resounding from him to recognize the trueness of his heart. Never mind his tousled curls, which would rival those of an archangel, the threat lies in his extraordinary cleverness.

Sera and I lag behind the others as we descend the stairs. "I heard what you said," she whispers. "You're right. He already suspects far too much. Miss Stranje is cloaked in mystery and riddles, and his insatiable curiosity is bound to keep him hunting for answers."

THE MOMENT SERA steps foot in the parlor, I hear a shift in Mr. Chadwick's music. Mozart stutters to a stop, and suddenly a serenade intrudes, yet there remains a steady and logical rhythm. He bows. "Miss Stranje. Miss Wyndham. Ladies."

"Mr. Chadwick." Our headmistress gives him a genteel curtsey, and we all follow suit. "Lovely to see you this fine afternoon. What brings you to our door?"

He bows again as if that might help answer. "Forgive the precipitousness of my visit. I should've sent a note around first. Your butler took some convincing. Quite the watchdog you have there, Miss Stranje. His protectiveness makes me worry less for your safety."

"How very kind of you to concern yourself with our welfare, but I assure you we are perfectly safe here in Mayfair." She takes a seat in the largest armchair, and we arrange ourselves on the sofa.

"Are you?" His question rings with genuine concern.

"Yes, of course. Quite safe. I shall speak to Mr. Peterson about being more hospitable to our callers." She smooths out her black skirts. "That is why you're here, is it not? To call on Miss Wyndham?"

"No," he blurts. "Er, I meant to say, I had hoped for a private interview with *you*, Miss Stranje."

"Me? Whatever for?" Her lips press together briefly

before she forces a smile. "I see the footman has provided us with a tray. Would you care for some refreshment? Some tea, perhaps? A biscuit?" She holds out a plate to him, but glances sidelong at me with a slight flare to her nostrils, meaning she is reconsidering my warning.

"Thank you, no." He sits in the chair closest to her and leans forward earnestly. "I was hoping you might spare me a few moments in private? I've a few things to, *er*, discuss."

Sera clutches my hand and shoots me a look that fairly screams, *oh no, this is trouble*. Is she afraid he'll propose? Before our coming-out ball, I questioned her about him. "Why do you always run away from Mr. Chadwick? Anyone might think you dislike him."

She turned to me, her eyes wide, and her inner song skittering like swallows caught in a whirlwind. "No, I don't dislike him at all. How could I? He's . . . he's . . . it's just that when I'm around him, I feel excessively—oh, what is the right word? *Uncomfortable*? Yes. No, that's not right. *Rattled*? No, that's not it either. I can't describe it. I only know that around him, I find it difficult to . . ."

"Breathe?"

She gulped for air in response to my question. "Sometimes. Except it's more than that, I can't seem to . . ."

"Hide?" I ask, because that is what she does. Sera is forever hiding. Hiding her brilliant mind. Hiding what she knows. What she feels. There is an entirely different world tucked away inside her. An *extraordinary* world. I know, because every now and then, I catch glimpses of its divine melody.

"Yes!" She brightened. "Exactly. When I'm in his

company, I'm likely to say whatever springs into my mind. It's most disconcerting. I'm not myself at all around him."

I wonder if she is mistaken. Perhaps the only time Sera is truly herself is when he is around. Mayhaps something about him frees her to be forthright, to stop hiding.

As we sit crammed together on the damask sofa, I am eager to see what might spring forth from her today.

Mr. Chadwick looks at Sera as if she is an angel seated among ordinary humans. "Naturally, I would very much like to call on you, Miss Wyndham. Would tomorrow afternoon suit you?"

"Perhaps," she answers, in a breathy whisper.

His customarily buoyant demeanor shifts to a more somber requiem as he turns back to Miss Stranje and awaits the answer to his request for a private audience.

Miss Stranje tries to lighten the conversation. "You're wearing such a serious expression I find myself growing concerned. You obviously have something on your mind. Is something amiss, Mr. Chadwick? I trust your mother and father are well?"

He shakes her inquiry off. "My parents are fine. I wish to speak to you about another matter—one of grave importance."

"Oh, my. How very mysterious you are today." She smiles. "Don't tell me, you've received bad news from Fairstone Meade. Have you come to inform me Stranje House has burned to the ground?"

"No." He flicks her question aside. "Nothing of the sort."

"Well then speak up, young man. What is it? Anything you have to say to me you can say to all of us. We have no secrets here."

No secrets. I nearly laugh.

Whenever our headmistress lies, the music of her soul turns chilly, as if it must blow through a frozen horn, hard, icy, and brittle.

"No secrets?" He shakes his head and appears saddened. "Begging your pardon, Miss Stranje, but I rather doubt that." His skepticism does him credit.

She looks down, smoothing out her black skirts, a pensive expression on her face, as if he has wounded her by calling out her lie. Except, Miss Stranje is not wounded. Not in the least. Her true music is playing a rather threatening march.

"Very well. Have it your way." He rises abruptly and begins to pace. "I'd hoped for a private word, but they may as well hear this, too." He glances sideways at us, and a quick frown of regret passes before he continues. "I have given considerable thought to recent events. In particular, the two deaths surrounding the attempted abduction of Miss Aubreyson, followed by the inexplicable disappearance of Mr. Sinclair's steamship—"

"My dear boy, it didn't disappear. Ships simply do not simply up and vanish." Miss Stranje chortles as if he has made a joke, although it blows rather icily over us. "I explained all that."

"Yes, I remember your account. Pray, be at ease. I mean you no harm. I assure you this visit has no bearing on the coroner's inquest. The matter is closed. Since then, however, I have given the, *uh*, the circumstances more thought. My father is completely unaware of the direction my thinking has taken. However, the facts of your case, when coupled with the unfortunate explosion that occurred recently at the navel yards, aroused certain suspicions. As a result, I took the liberty of investigating in more depth."

"I see." Miss Stranje pours herself a glass of lemon water, as calmly as if he is merely commenting on the excessively warm weather instead of alluding to our covert activities.

He stops and faces her, his arms at his side, very stiff, very formal. He certainly doesn't look much like the *amiable young pup* she described earlier. Rather more like an earnest young soldier about to raise his weapon and take aim. "It is my understanding, Miss Stranje, that your father served in the foreign office, did he not?"

The foreign office.

His implication is obvious. *He knows*. I swallow hard.

"*Uh oh*," Georgie says under her breath and presses back against the sofa. Tess edges forward, her fists clenched, and I worry she might attack him at any moment. Sera sits still as a marble statue, but Lady Jane perks up and leans over the arm of the sofa as if she is intrigued.

Miss Stranje does not smile. Her hawk's beak sharpens to a crisp point. "Yes, as a matter of fact, my father served in the foreign office at the request of William Pitt. How did you find out?"

"It's a matter of public record." He waves away her question as if it's a gnat. "Almost anything can be found in the Records Office, if one knows where to look."

"What a clever lad, you are." She bites into a dry shortbread.

"Captain Grey also serves in the foreign office, does

he not?"

She no longer pretends to be amused by his cleverness. "I couldn't say. Perhaps you ought to ask *him* next time you see him." A talon is poised in her voice. I hear it threatening him to tread carefully.

Mr. Chadwick pushes on bravely. Or ignorantly. I'm not sure which. "And Lord Wyatt is a diplomatic attaché, which means he serves directly under Lord Castlereagh."

Miss Stranje drops the shortbread onto a plate with a decided plunk. "My goodness, but you certainly seem to have spent a great deal of time in the Records Office."

"Not only there, but also at our parish offices." He sighs and taps his hand nervously against his thigh. "The truth is Miss Stranje, I also discovered Mr. Sinclair is not your cousin, as you claimed. You have no cousins in America. Your family is landed aristocracy, and as such, your genealogy is detailed in parish records. The inventor is not related to you. I checked before coming to London."

"I see." She sits back, assessing the young man, her lips pressing and un-pressing. A blaze of anger melts Miss Stranje's cold tone. "What is it you want from us, Mr. Chadwick?"

Sera draws a quick breath and grips my hand even tighter. Madame Cho stands and abruptly closes the parlor doors. She crosses her arms and blocks his exit. I recognize the stance. She is ready to break this *amiable young pup's* neck if Miss Stranje gives the signal.

Mr. Chadwick stands his ground unflinching. "I want in."

The clock on the mantel ticks like a sledgehammer.

"In?" Our headmistress says, in a low steely tenor. "In

what?"

He leans forward. "Please, Miss Stranje, do not mistake me for a country bumpkin with no education. I am a man with enough sense to know I can do something more with my life than rusticate on my father's estate."

Miss Stranje only relaxes enough to sit back against her chair. Her spine remains ramrod straight and her tone could split apart brick. "There is a great deal to be said for rusticating, Mr. Chadwick. Your father is an excellent gentleman, a credit to our county, and, indeed, the entire country. His service as a magistrate is noble and invaluable to all of us. Your mother is one of the finest women of my acquaintance. I am pleased to call her a friend. Furthermore, Mr. Chadwick, I still haven't the faintest idea of what you are requesting of me."

"I think you do." Instead of cowering, he stands squarely before her. "You know exactly what I'm asking."

She says nothing.

The symphony within him plays as clear and strong and pure as any I've ever heard. "I love my parents," he says calmly. "I admire them prodigiously. My father would like me to follow his footsteps and become magistrate one day. To that end, I considered studying law, but—may I speak plainly?"

Miss Stranje drum her fingers on the armrest. "Apparently, no one can stop you."

I glance sideways at Sera's face and am surprised to see, not admiration, but anguish. Her eyes are watering with pain. "How can this be?" she demands, her composure shredded. "How? Your parents have given you everything, blessed you with a superior education—yet you are unhappy?"

"No, Miss Wyndham, I'm not unhappy. I simply crave something greater. I was certain you would understand. Can't you see? I want what *you* have."

"*What I have?* Are you mad? You want to be an outcast, despised by your parents, sent away from your home? I would've given anything to have parents as understanding and kind as yours. *Anything.*"

He rakes back his hair and shakes his head. "I'm deeply sorry, that isn't what I meant. Not the outcast part. No. I was referring to *this.*" He gestures at Miss Stranje, at the five of us on the sofa, and even at Madame Cho. "I know what you are doing, Miss Stranje. I've done the math. This is no ordinary girl's school."

She waits, letting silence force him to speak.

He takes a deep breath and recites his tally sheet. "First, you are an exceptionally good shot, Miss Stranje. You felled one of the marauders at a distance that would challenge a seasoned hunter. In and of itself, that might not have aroused my suspicions. As you mentioned, my mother is also an excellent marksman. But when I accidentally startled Miss Aubreyson, she tossed me over her shoulder without a moment's hesitation. She also threw a knife and dropped her attacker at twenty paces. A French-born sailor, I might add. A man who surely possessed the requisite fighting skills. According to my hypothesis, those assailants were thugs sent after something Miss Fitzwilliam possessed or knew, something of value to the French. Next, much to my delight, I discovered Miss Wyndham, here, has perfect recall. Not only that, she seems to notice the finest of details, crucial details. And from those scant details, she draws impressively logical conclusions."

He stares at us as if we are a row of awe-inspiring Roman goddesses rather than five outcast girls who had nowhere else to go except for Miss Stranje's reform school.

He turns back to our headmistress. "Next, I took into consideration your American guest, Mr. Sinclair, who built that marvel of a steamship. You must've forgotten I saw it the night you were shooting down Chinese lanterns."

She straightens the cuff of her sleeve. "I did not forget. I remember quite distinctly the night you intruded upon our birthday celebration."

The night Lady Daneska captured Tess, cut Madame Cho's throat and left her for dead. The night Lord Ravencross nearly drowned trying to save Tess. Oh yes, all of us remember that night.

He clears his throat. "A most peculiar birthday celebration. Then you hid the steamship in your cove until it's equally peculiar disappearance."

"You are grasping at straws, young man," Miss Stranje snaps, but most of her vehemence seems to have drained away.

"Not straws. Facts. I was present at the Naval yards. I heard Lady Jane cry out to warn His Highness and the Admirals of the bomb. Did no one else find it noteworthy that a young lady was the first to sound the alarm?"

The five of us, wedged together on the sofa, exchange veiled looks.

"No one ever suspects a young lady of such complexities, do they?" He paces toward us, radiant with admiration. "The five of you possess extraordinary skills, and unless I miss my guess you are all being trained to do more with your lives than sit and darn socks and paint watercolors." He swings wide his arms. "You are doing something worthwhile. You're fighting Napoleon. You're using your mental acuity. You ask, what do I want. The answer is simple. I want to help you."

"Impossible." Miss Stranje shakes her head. "You are a young man with a gentleman's responsibilities."

"Phfft! A *gentleman's responsibilities*." He throws up one hand and begins to wear a path in the Turkish carpet again. "No, no, you must allow me to work with you. I'll go mad doing nothing. I'm not like the other gentlemen here in town. They seem oblivious to the fact that a tyrant is rampaging across Europe, and that any day he'll mount an attack on us. They go to their clubs, drink their port, and gamble as if tomorrow may not bring an end to England as we know it." His hands tighten into fists. "What I *want to do*—what I *must do*, Miss Stranje, is serve my country."

She stirs in her chair. No longer queen. Her soul echoes with the heavy song of a teacher, a friend. The hawk disappears and she growls, as wary as Tromos for one of her cubs.

He opens his palms to her. "I have a decent mind. I beg you, put me to work."

More than decent, although, I dare not say so amidst this skirmish.

Miss Stranje glances at Madame Cho. They have known each other for so many years they often speak as sisters do, in wordless expressions. Madame walks away from the door and sits in a straight-back chair, folding her hands in her lap.

Miss Stranje rubs her temple for a moment. "I run a

school for young ladies. I'm in no position to take on a male student."

"I thought of that." He perches on the edge of the chair beside her. "But your Captain Grey, he might be able to put me to work, to train me. I'm a quick study, you'll see."

"I've no doubt of that." She sighs. "No doubt at all. The problem is, there is so much to learn, and usually . . ." She brushes away the idea with her hand. "This is highly irregular. Ordinarily, we start training our protégés when they are in their early teens. There are languages to master, combat skills, and–"

"But I'm not yet twenty-one. I'm already fluent in three other languages, French, Prussian, and . . . Latin." He shrugs. "I don't suppose Latin is of much use, but I'll learn more if needed." He leans forward, almost in a manner of prayer. "Ask Captain Grey for me. *Please.*"

She pushes back from his entreaty, stands, and now she is the one pacing. "Ours is not an easy life, Mr. Chadwick." She looks past him to Sera. Her face draws down into a profound sadness. "I had hoped for better things for you. Then, there are your parents to consider."

He nods. "I understand. But the truth is, if they had their way, they'd keep me closeted at home for the rest of my life. I can't do that. God help me, I love them, but I can't sit at home with them and do nothing."

"But they love you!" Sera squeezes her crossed arms tight against her middle and looks stricken.

"I know," he turns to her. "Too much. There is such a thing you know."

"No," she shakes her head. "No, I don't." I stare at the two of them. As alike as they are in intelligence, in some respects, no two people on earth could be more different.

"Try to understand—I feel trapped." He claps his hands together as if he has caught a fly. "Wrapped in a cocoon so tight, it's suffocating me."

I have heard Lord Kinsworth sing this same tune. I wonder, do all Englishmen feel trapped?

Sera is nearly in tears. She looks from me to Miss Stranje and back to him. She doesn't understand. How can she? Mr. Chadwick has the nurturing family she has always dreamed of having, and yet, he is willing to leave them behind for our life as exiled children.

He stands and reaches out to her, but she refuses to look at him. Saddened, he steps back to the fireplace and leans against the mantel. "England's fight with the colonies soured my father on all war. He insists Parliament ought to have settled the colonists' grievances peaceably. Which is a good point, but this battle with Napoleon is different. If Britain doesn't do something soon, we will be under attack on British soil. We stand to lose everything."

Miss Stranje braces herself behind her chair, poised behind it like a captain steering a ship. "If it is a battle you're seeking—"

"No. If I've guessed correctly, the work you do is on a more . . ." He hunts for the right word, drawing with his finger on the mantle. "Your fight is on a more subtle level, is it not? That is where I believe I can be of the most service."

Miss Stranje stares at him for a long uncomfortable minute. The inner music in the room is so discordant it gives me a headache. When she still does not answer, his hands fall to his sides. "I ask only that you consider my petition. Whatever your answer, you may rely upon my discretion. I would die rather than tell anyone your secret."

"That, Mr. Chadwick, is not an oath to be taken lightly. Given what we do, it may very well come down to it."

The next morning, another visitor surprises us, arriving at an hour when visitors are rarely expected. Miss Stranje sits at the head of the table, briefing us on the day's schedule while we finish our breakfast. Mr. Peterson glides in and interrupts, wearing his out-of-joint butler nose high in the air. He leans down and murmurs next to her ear. She immediately glances at me. A fleeting arrow of worry whistles my way, but she turns quickly, and without explanation, excuses herself to go meet our unexpected guest.

Lady Jane casts a sideways glance at Georgie, who has the best view of the doorway. She strains to peek out, but when that fails, she sags back against her chair. "Couldn't see. Can't be one of the patronesses, not at this hour of the morning."

Jane sips the last of her tea. "Of course not, if it had been one of them Mr. Peterson wouldn't have been so secretive."

"She looked at Maya before leaving." Sera toys with her empty juice glass, and tilts her worried gaze toward me. "It has something to do with you."

Jane studies me shrewdly, mimicking our headmistress more and more every day. "Lord Kinsworth, perhaps?"

I shake my head. "Doubtful. As Georgie said, not this

early."

Madame Cho sets her fork down with a decided plunk. "Enough chatter. We will find out soon enough."

We find out almost immediately—or at least I do.

Miss Stranje met our guest in the parlor and, although she shut the doors, his loud accusation carries rather clearly. "I should've been consulted."

Papa!

My spoon drops with an embarrassing clatter, and I sink lower in my chair.

"What about the marriage settlements?" he demands.

"Your father?" Georgie mouths.

I cannot even bring myself to nod in agreement.

Miss Stranje's reply is too calm and melodic to hear through the doors. My father's retort is not calm, not calm at all. "I'm well aware of the fact that I signed your ruddy contract. Contract or no, I'm her father!" Every word seems to blast through the house and shake me to the bone. "Lord Kinsworth ought to have applied to *me*! Not to you. You're nothing but her headmistress."

Nothing but my headmistress?

How can he say such a hurtful thing? The woman has been my salvation in this country. She welcomed me. Gave me hope, where I had none.

I feel my cheeks flame red, and I want to crawl under the table and hide. Sera reaches for my shoulder, but my shame makes even her gentle touch scorch. I pull away covering my mouth as if that might somehow shield me from his embarrassing words.

"No dowry?" My father is practically roaring. "Why would you tell him such a thing? I will provide a dowry for my daughter. To suggest otherwise is an insult."

Miss Stranje says something I cannot hear.

"Of course, I remember your terms." He is still loud but at least speaking in a more civil tone. "Yes. Yes! All right. No, I don't wish to drag the matter into court."

Their voices lower. I cannot help myself, I stand, and like a sleepwalker, I stagger from the dining table, toward the agitated hum of voices. Except my feet refuse to move any closer than the hallway.

Lord Barrington flings open the parlor door and stalks across the foyer, shoes clicking, crisp and slick with the shiny polish of an English gentleman. He brusquely demands, "My hat."

Mr. Peterson scurries to obey.

"Papa?" My voice humiliates me with its limp weakness.

He whips around, takes two forceful strides in my direction, and stops, irritation ricocheting off him in peppery gunshots. "And you, Maya, this engagement is acceptable to you?"

Is he asking me if I want to marry Lord Kinsworth?

Or is he wondering if I find the financial terms suitable?

How do I answer? The truth is a hundred miles from either question.

He grows impatient with my hesitation. "Does it please you? Yes, or no."

I blink, wanting to say a thousand things. I want to pour out the truth. But he has no time for the truth. Or me. I stare at the cold veined marble floor, listening, seeking steady songs of stone and earth to bring me peace, to give me comfort. But the marble is as foreign and lost here in this place as I am.

"Maya?" His voice is softer now, and it seems to echo

with the same vibrations as does the marble, and my own lost heart. I look up. *Are you lost, too, Papa?*

I must be brave.

For both of our sakes, I must be the lion.

I find my tongue again, searching his face and soul for the papa I used to know. The man who used to laugh and throw me high into the air. "Yes," I say with the gentleness of a marigold, the little sun lion. Still, I listen, ever hoping to hear an inkling of the father I used to know. "Yes, it pleases me."

Now, it is he who blinks. His shoulders bow slightly. He takes a deep breath and presses his lips together. Once again, I hear that strange woeful music, the same plaintive tune I heard at the ball. "Very well. This has all happened rather suddenly. I hadn't expected it. . . not so soon."

He accepts his hat from Mr. Peterson and smooths his fingers around the brim before slapping it on his head. "My felicitations."

Felicitations?

He wishes me happiness—the man who has withheld it for ten aching years. I choke back a lump of disappointment. "Thank you, Papa." I say very properly, as if he is a stranger, an English stranger. And the words nearly strangle me.

He swallows hard and rushes away, dragging a mournful cry in his wake. A cry that only I can hear.

THIRTEEN

PICK A PATCH OF PRETTY POISON

SEVEN DAYS LATER, Sera and I are bouncing along in a coach bound for Brighton. We are in a caravan of sorts, the Prince's entourage, three carriages, and a dray filled with His Highness's necessities.

Lord Kinsworth and Lord Harston accompany us, but they ride alongside the coach for the time being. Our bandboxes and luggage sit on the seat and floor beside us. The top of the coach is stacked high with luggage belonging to several other guests. The road is long, bumpy, and with every passing mile my confidence in this inane plan shrinks.

"I don't see how this can work. How can I possibly influence either of these men?" The windows are open, so I speak softly, only loud enough for Sera to hear.

She is struggling with traveling sickness and stares steadily out the window to steady herself. "It is a great deal to ask of you."

At that, I almost laugh. "A *great deal?* It is an impossibility. I have no idea why Lady Daneska thinks I can influence the Prince. Nor why the rest of you think I can sway Napoleon, which is even more outlandish."

"Not really. We've seen your powers of persuasion at work." She looks positively green but straightens and fans dust away from her mouth.

I hand her a corked bottle of ginger and lemon water. "Here, drink some of this." "You've seen me use my voice to persuade guards, maids, cooks—people of far less intellect than the Emperor of France, or the Prince of England."

"Not so." Sera starts to shake her head but stops and squeezes her eyes shut for a moment. "We've seen you influence entire audiences, and Prince George was among them, along with several admirals, dukes, and key members of Parliament."

"That was different. Singing provides me with certain advantages."

She swallows a swig of lemon water, and her normally solemn lips spread in what almost appears to be a smile. "If that is so, perhaps you should *sing* for Napoleon."

I wave her jest away.

She leans forward, somber and earnest again. "Maya, there have been times when you've used your gift on those of us at Stranje House." She grasps the seat as we bounce over a rut in the road. "Are you saying we're of low intellect?"

"No! I never used it on any of you unless you were agreeable—willing to cooperate."

"You used it on Lady Daneska, and she is never cooperative."

I sigh. "Perhaps."

"And Lady Daneska has an exceptionally sharp intellect."

"Yes, and a sharp knife as well." I rub my arm where the cut Daneska gave me is beginning to heal. "I have not always succeeded with her."

Sera sits back, nervously drumming her fingers on her knee. "If you have doubts, perhaps we ought to consider an alternative solution."

"An alternative?" I squint at her. "What do you mean?"

"I don't have Lady Jane's gift for strategizing, but it seems to me if our objective is to keep Prince George from conceding to Napoleon, there might be other ways to achieve that end."

She has a point. I've been pinning myself to the situation instead of taking the broader view and looking for another way around the problem. "Why didn't you say something when we were planning all this with Miss Stranje?"

She glances at the floorboards for a moment. "I thought you were amenable to the task at hand."

"Amenable?" I gape at her. "How can you say so? I was forced into it."

"Were you?" She refuses to look at me and returns to gazing out the window. "Even the engagement?"

"Yes!" I cross my arms, irritated that she should suggest I *wanted* to go along with this outrageous scheme. "Most assuredly."

"I saw signs indicating you felt otherwise." She peeks sideways at me. "For instance, your obvious attraction to Lord Kinsworth."

"Obvious. How?"

She hesitates, hiding for a moment, but then she takes a breath and surprises me with her directness. "Very well, since it is just you and me, I will tell you. There are other symptoms, things I find it difficult to explain. Suffice it to say, the colors that normally surround you change when he approaches. But I have more solid evidence. In his presence your pupils widen, your cheeks flush, your voice changes tenor, and the fingers of your left-hand flutter ever so slightly, almost as if you are playing a harp or counting the time musically-speaking."

"My fingers?" I clutch the offending appendages. "They do not."

She shrugs.

I sit back and glance out the window at him, worried he might have overheard her. Except Sera's voice is feather-soft. It could not possibly have carried over the clatter of our coach.

Lord Kinsworth does sit very fine atop his horse.

Oh, dog's breath!

She is right. My fingers twitched.

This farcical engagement has muddled my thinking. Tantalized me. Lured me into this dangerous and insanely impossible situation. All in the vain hope of finding out what it might feel like if such a relationship were possible.

I open my mouth to deny her allegation, except I haven't the heart to try to deceive her. It would be useless anyway. Sera always knows when I am lying.

She watches me, tapping her pointer finger atop one of the bandboxes stacked beside her.

"All right," I say, admitting defeat. "I see your point."

"That wasn't the only reason." She sits a little taller,

her inward music playing a little more bravely. "I considered Lady Daneska's offer to be a powerful incentive. Even if you fail to persuade Napoleon on our behalf, she might assume you did as she bade. In that event, it is possible she might actually provide you with passage home to India. Should Napoleon win, I daresay she won't want you remaining in England or France and becoming one of his favorites."

"Phfft." I spurt indignantly. "I would never become one of his favorites. He's a horrible tyrant. Not to mention, if Lady Daneska thought I threatened her position, she would be far more inclined to cut my throat rather than pay for my very expensive six-month voyage back to India."

"True enough." Sera stares thoughtfully out the window. "It seems your life is at risk no matter the outcome of Prince George's meeting with Napoleon. And if Napoleon doesn't get what he wants I daresay Ghost will see to it all of us suffer."

The plague.

"Exactly." I try to swallow, but dust and the thought of plague clog my throat. We travel on in an unspoken cacophony, wheels thumping and kicking up gravel, the jangle of horse harnesses, and the coach creaking and swaying to the rhythm of my future demise.

A half-hour passes, and I can take this dreariness no longer. "You mentioned an alternative solution?"

She nods and chews the corner of her lip before answering. "Except there was another reason I didn't say anything sooner."

"And that is?"

"I cannot see another way around the problem."

"Neither can I." Still bound on a journey to my grave, I prop my elbow on the window and watch Lord Kinsworth ride his horse. He does not look as if my set down the other day quelled his spirit one wit. In point of fact, he seems positively jubilant. I can almost hear his music prancing as boldly as his horse. He glances in my direction and with a cheeky wink, tips his hat to me. *The rogue.*

Sera sighs. "You're lucky. He's a fine-looking gentleman. I see why so many debutantes preen and giggle when he enters the ballroom. He's strong, broad-shouldered, has a sturdy jaw—"

"A *sturdy* jaw?" I glare out the window at Lord Kinsworth. "A stubborn willful jaw, you mean."

"If you say so. Is he willful? He seems to have a rather pleasant countenance. Playful, I would say, always on the verge of a smile."

"Or a smirk." I frown at her. "You seem to have studied him quite carefully."

She shrugs. "I study everyone carefully. That *is* why you brought me along, remember?"

"Yes." An exasperated puff of air passes through my lips. "But I'm not *lucky*. You know as well as I do, my relationship with Lord Kinsworth is all an act."

"Is it?" And now she smirks—Miss Seraphina Wyndham, a young lady who does not have a smirky bone in her body. She twists her lips as if she is holding back a private joke.

"Yes! It is an act—all of it. A complete farce." I breathe out my irritation and turn away, watching Lord Kinsworth rein in his horse, a large spirited blood-red mare fond of rearing or kicking up her heels when her rider tries to hold her to a pace she does not like. The ornery horse bucks, but Kinsworth maintains his seat and pats the animal's sleek red neck, using soothing tones to coax her into cooperating. Soon he has sweet-talked the bay into a pleasant canter, and they disappear from view. *Typical.* He charms even his horse.

If only my problems could be so easily resolved. I turn back to the black interior of our coach, considering Sera's suggestion that there might be another way around our problem. "What if Prince George were unable to attend the meeting?"

"Unable?" She perks up. "Why? How?"

"I don't know—suppose he could not travel to the meeting place. What if all of his horses were to go lame?"

"*All* of his horses?" Sera's eyes widen as if I've lost my mind. "That could be dozens, or more. What are the chances that all of his horses would go lame? Even if they did, to bring England into his clutches, Napoleon would be willing to come to him."

"*Drat*. Bonaparte would, wouldn't he." I trace my finger over the black leather of our seat, thinking, stewing, and lacking even a morsel of an idea. Out of pure frustration, I blurt, "What if the Prince were kidnapped?"

"Maya!" Her eyes widen, and she leans close to whisper, "You mustn't even suggest such a thing. Kidnapping a ruler of England is a hanging offense." She shakes her head. "No, no, I take it back. It would be *a drawn-and-quartered, head-on-a-spike* sort of offense. Far too risky. Out of the question."

"Nonsense. Everything *we* do is a risk." I wave away her objection, but offer a new proposition. "Perhaps our dear Prince could merely be waylaid somehow."

"Waylaid?" She sniffs skeptically and retreats, sinking

back into the bandboxes and luggage surrounding us as if she is afraid talking to me is too dangerous. "How?"

It is difficult to suppress the desperation I feel, but I fight to keep my voice calm and soothing. "There must be a hundred ways."

"A hundred," she mutters.

"Well, at least, *dozens*." I smile with a confidence I don't feel. "All we need is one. Only one. Surely, we can think of one useful stratagem."

Two hours later, when the Prince and his entourage stop at a coaching inn, neither of us have thought of one single solitary satisfactory plan.

We follow the others into the inn for tea and a bit of refreshment. The moment I step into the inn, I am overwhelmed. The building is packed with so many strangers, too many sounds and smells. We make our way through the crowded public rooms, to the back of the building. The Prince rented two private parlors, one for himself and his attendants, and the other for the rest of us. Our private parlor is not much better than the common rooms. We are a large company of travelers, and the room is hot and stuffy despite the luxury of having a window.

I sit at the long trestle table, but the noise is too much, and my head throbs. I rise abruptly and explain to Sera, "I should like to take a walk."

Both she and Lord Kinsworth spring up, ready to accompany me. "No, no," I wave them away. "I shall be quite all right on my own. Stay. Enjoy the bread and stew. I need to walk in the fresh air to clear my head."

Neither of them looks convinced.

"Please, I need a moment or two of quiet." I point out the window at the roses and hollyhocks blooming outside. "I shall take a turn around the garden and come back in short order. You will be able to see me quite clearly from your table."

"As you wish." Sera reluctantly sits back down and sends me a suspicious frown, as if she thinks I might try running away.

Even though the idea of escaping has a strong appeal, I do my best to reassure her. "I promise to return in a few minutes." Sera nods, and reluctantly resumes her place on the bench, staring down at her bowl of mutton stew.

Lord Kinsworth accompanies me to the door. "I shall join you shortly."

I hurry to dismiss his offer. "No need."

He leans close and tickles my ear with a whisper. "Must keep up appearances." He straightens and bestows a conspiratorial grin upon me. "Besides, I need to walk off my sore muscles. Rosy has been giving me a beating."

"Rosy?"

"My horse." He pats his thighs to indicate the pain.

"Oh." I should not have looked at his legs. It is a most unladylike thing to gawp at a man's leg muscles, even if a gentleman is rude enough to discuss them and point them out. It happens before I catch my error. Instantly, my cheeks heat up with embarrassment. I quickly turn away and inspect the door frame. Well, that is a silly thing to do. So, I gaze across the room, to where his uncle is flirting with Lady Devonshire. Then I peer at a platter of cheese and nuts on the side table. I look at anything except him and his knowing grin. Even in this noisy room I can hear his inner music rippling with laughter.

I turn to flee, but he reaches for my hand. “Here, take this. You’ll be hungry otherwise.” He presses a warm scone into my palm. I accept it and hurry from the room, rush into the hallway, and leave through a side door, scurrying down the steps until my feet finally touch the earth. The air is warm but not nearly as stifling as London this time of year.

I breathe in deep, and a gentle wind blesses my face with cooling flute-like fingers. The trees call to me with their creaky ancient songs. And so, I walk in that direction, listening to the flowers and rows of cabbages, corn, and potatoes, all murmuring blissfully in the garden. Bugs and bees and butterflies twirl by me singing busy little tunes.

This is freedom—if only for a moment.

Freedom from the dark failure looming ahead of me. I glance over my shoulder at the inn. Lord Kinsworth is watching me from the window. I suppose I felt him watching me long before I turned and saw him standing there, following me with his gaze. I nibble at the buttery scone he gave me, breaking off a morsel and savoring it until the sweetness melts away in my mouth.

Jackdaws, with their raucous squawks, frighten a flock of sparrows. The smaller birds swirl up in a whirlwind of chirps.

If only I could hold onto this moment forever. Before long, I find myself in a stand of trees, wending through the underbrush on a narrow sheep path, listening to the voices of grasses, and...

“What is this?” I stoop down. “Can it be?” Kneeling, I remove one glove so I can examine a broad-leafed plant growing among the weeds at the side of the path. Mindful of the prickles along the stalk, I bruise one of the leaves and sniff my fingers. "Ah-ha! It is you." I know this plant. At the top of the stem sits a clutch of tiny white berries, but it is the leaves that interest me.

This little plant might save my life. It offers a possibility, an *alternative solution*, as Sera calls it. I pull out a handkerchief and pluck several sprigs, carefully laying them in the open cloth.

"What are you doing?"

Startled, I answer hastily, "Nothing." Except it sounds guilty. I swallow my chagrin at having been caught unaware. Why didn't I hear Lord Kinsworth coming?

I should have.

The lioness in me growls inwardly. I have failed my training. I ought to have noticed his approach. In my excitement at having found a possible solution, I must have stopped listening to the world around me. Or perhaps he'd been exceptionally quiet. I'm not sure which.

Sometimes I wonder if Lord Kinsworth understands more about inner music than he lets on. I am almost certain he knows how to hide his life sounds. Admirable, since even I have trouble quieting my inner music. It took years of practice to learn to be truly silent.

He leans over me, trying to peek at my deadly collection. "Well, obviously, you are doing *something*."

"Nothing of importance." I quickly wrap the leaves into a tidy cloth bundle, stand, and point at the plant near our feet. "I noticed this rare herb and thought it might be useful, so I collected a few of the leaves." I force a cheery tone, and don an aloof cadence. "And what, may I ask, are you doing out here in the woods?"

"Hunting for you," he says, with a cocky grin. "Medicinal herbs? You have knowledge of such things?" He watches me a bit too closely as I tuck the packet of leaves into my pocket.

"Of course." I slip the glove back on my naked fingers and brush out my skirts, pleased that I do not have to lie to him. "In my country, depending upon where one lives, it can sometimes be several days' journey to the nearest doctor. Even as children, those of us in small villages learned about herbal remedies."

I do not tell him I also have an extensive knowledge of poisons, having made a careful study of it under Madame Cho's tutelage. Nor do I mention that this particular plant is never used for a cure. Although, it may prove an extremely helpful curative for my problem with Napoleon and Prince George.

I take his arm, and we stroll back out of the woods.

FOURTEEN

LYRICS FOR A LIE

LORD KINSWORTH COVERS my hand as it rests on his arm and toys with my fingers. "What sort of ailments does that particular plant cure?"

Fiddlesticks!

I thought I'd neatly escaped any problematic questions. *Why is he looking at me like he knows I'm up to something?*

I stammer in an attempt to avoid a lie. "Oh, um, it is a cure for any number of problems." *Such as the problem of how to stall our beloved monarch from meeting with the tyrant who wants to take over the world.*

"I see." He rubs his chin. "Does it help with fever and ague?"

"Doubtful."

"Is it for stomach complaints, then?"

I press my lips tight, knowing a tea made of these

leaves might cause a myriad of gastric disturbances, and shake my head. "No."

"What then?" He lowers his voice as if the flowers and trees might be embarrassed should his next question be overheard. "Female problems?"

I almost laugh. "Hardly."

"Gout, perhaps?" He stops walking and studies me with such obvious suspicion that he leaves me no choice. Either I must tell him the truth, in which case I might hang for treason, or I must lie. I choose the latter.

"Well," I pause for a moment, thinking. "It does tend to purge the blood. So, I suppose it *might* help with gout." *Purge* is an overly gentle way of stating the effect of this herb, a pale word in comparison to how the veins will burn and pump blood with such force into the extremities it will feel as if one's hands and feet are going to burst.

"Does it, now?" He leans in, overly interested. "You're quite sure?"

"As certain as one can be with herbs." I kick a small stone in the path.

His face brightens suddenly, and he swoops me up, swinging me in a wild circle. "My dear Miss Barrington, you are a wonder. An absolute wonder!"

"What are you doing?" I shout at him and thump his shoulder. "Put me down this instant!"

He laughs, completely unchastised, and allows my feet to touch the ground in front of him. He still has hold of my arms as he grins broadly. "You truly are a marvel. I mean it. You are probably not aware of this, but our Prince suffers terribly from painful attacks of gout. I shall tell him of your remedy."

Frog's teeth.

It had only been a thought, a wild possibility to debate with Sera. And now he was turning the idea into reality.

"Oh, no! No, you mustn't." I try to pull out of his grasp. "My poor skills are not worthy of a member of the royal family, much less the Prince Regent himself. The very idea is ludicrous."

He shakes his head. "Maya, Maya, you are too modest. His Highness will be thrilled to hear of it." He tugs me closer. "We must go and tell him straightway."

"No. Wait. Stop." I wrench out of his arms. "You mustn't—I beg of you."

He tilts his head, watching me intently. "You're afraid, aren't you?"

Afraid of being executed for accidently poisoning the Prince? Yes!

I nod and hang my head.

"All right, then." He lets go of me. "I won't mention it to him, not just yet. But next time Prince George is groaning in agony I must. I must! To withhold a possible cure would be cruel. Some mornings the poor man cannot even bear to get out of bed. His whole foot swells and his big toe turns red as a plum. I've seen it! His physicians set leeches on him, bleed him, and pack his feet in compresses of every sort. You've no idea how he suffers. He hides it admirably." He takes off his hat and stares at the interior before slapping it back over his honey-kissed curls.

Genuine concern rings through his words and guilt crashes over my head. In a dozen or so days, Lord Kinsworth seems to have developed a deep empathy for our eccentric Prince George, a man who many people consider a blight on Britain.

I plunge my hand into my pocket clutching the bundle of leaves, wishing I'd never run across them. These wretched herbs will only make the poor Prince's pain worse. I cannot go through with this. But if we don't stop him from meeting with Napoleon, Britain will be crushed under the Emperor's boot. Not just Britain, her people, my father, Miss Stranje, Captain Grey, Lord Wyatt, Sera, Georgie—all of my friends. And even though he does not yet realize it, the Prince himself. I want to roar with frustration.

Except I cannot.

I clamp my lips tight to keep silent, pressing my heels into the dirt to keep from running away. I am bound by duty to my father's country. Bound by loyalty to Miss Stranje and the faith she has placed in me. Bound by love for my friends.

No longer the lioness, I am the caged nightingale.

And if I must sing myself to death, so be it.

I weigh the costs, Britain's future against the Prince's pain. Grinding my guilty conscience between my teeth, I tell myself, if I am very *very* careful, it will only mean two or three days of discomfort for him. And Lord Kinsworth's compassion may prove to be the perfect means of delivering Britain's salvation, but I need to make sure he stands clear of any repercussions.

I wet my dry lips and choose my next words with caution. "My Lord, the Royal Physicians are far more knowledgeable than I, and even *they* have not found a cure." I shake my head. "I'm not an apothecary or a physician. I simply cannot offer a treatment to His

Highness—especially not one of my homemade tisanes—it's unthinkable. It would be the height of presumptuousness. And what's worse, suppose something were to go wrong?"

I clutch Ben's forearm, allowing fear to chase panic over my tongue. "What if he has a dreadful reaction of some kind? It could happen! One must always be prepared for such things when dealing with herbal cures."

"True." Ben's normally jovial eyes darken as he perceives the risk and adds up the ramifications. "That could be troubling." Not a minute passes before he brightens again. "I know how to handle this. We must tell him the truth. I shall convey your concerns and reservations. If Prince George is willing to take the risk, I will call upon you to prepare the remedy."

I lower my head and draw a ragged breath. "Very well. If you think that is the best way to proceed." I close the gap between us. "But you must promise me you will convey my concerns to him in a serious manner."

"I promise." He moves even closer, leaving only a few inches between us. In hushed tones he says, "You are a great favorite of his, you know. He told me so in confidence, when he hears you sing it is a balm to his soul."

The nightingale's song.

I shudder, contemplating the effect the brittle leaves in my pocket will have upon Prince George, and how very un-balm-like this remedy will be.

Ben leans down and cups my chin. "Come, come, you mustn't fret. I have every confidence in you. The Prince will adore you for trying. Think on it, Maya. Offering him a cure can only continue to improve your standing in his eyes."

I look up at him, knowing fear wails from deep in my soul. Fear of what will happen when the Prince gets so sick he feels like ripping his stomach out.

Lord Kinsworth's smile is gentle and soft and caring, there is no teasing boy ready to laugh and dash away as he studies me. His manner turns languid and warm. His heart music enfolds me as if he is softly strumming a guitar. He leans closer, and I can tell he wants to comfort me with kisses.

I dampen my bottom lip in anticipation. I have not forgotten our first kiss. Cannot forget it. The memory teases me. Taunts me. And despite my dreadful lies and our false engagement, I want him to kiss me again. It is a mistake, I know. I remind myself he does not love me. He will break my heart someday. Yet, my lips seem to thicken and warm just thinking about touching his. But we cannot kiss.

Not here. Not now. Not ever.

We shouldn't.

We mustn't.

We have strayed into the garden. The inn is only a stone's throw away. I inch back and glance furtively at the inn's window overlooking the flowers. We are clearly visible to anyone in the parlor who might be standing near it.

Lord Kinsworth does not seem to care that we might be observed. "It's all right. We *are* engaged," he whispers huskily and smooths a lock of hair behind my ear.

His breath lightly caresses my cheek, and I can't help but lean toward him. "Yes, but–."

"Kinsworth!" A shout comes from that ill-placed window. It is Ben's uncle. Lord Harston leans out and motions for us to come back. "Look lively, lad. The Prince wishes to leave in ten minutes. We must see to our mounts."

Lord Kinsworth grabs my hand and tugs me along the path. "I meant to tell you, His Highness seems to be in a great hurry to reach Brighton. It may mean his parley with Napoleon is set to happen sooner than we anticipated."

How soon, I wondered. *How long before that dreaded day? Three weeks? Two? I'd hoped for four.* We race back to the inn, my heart thundering like a frightened herd of chital antelope.

Too soon. this is all happening too soon.

By the time we reach the front of the inn, Sera is already climbing into the coach. "There you are!" she scolds. "We're leaving, and you've not had anything to eat or drink."

I climb in, and the footman closes the coach door. "Lord Kinsworth gave me a scone." I seat myself and try to catch my breath. "There is still some lemon water in our provisions. I shall make do."

As soon as we are settled in place and I can manage to steady myself I confide, "Lord Kinsworth says the Prince's parley may be happening sooner than we expected."

She groans. "How soon?"

"He does not know. But I may have come upon a solution."

She tilts her head quizzically. "Did you?" It isn't really a question. It is a prompt. Sera sits quietly, waiting for me to explain.

"I believe so." The gravity of the whole idea pulls my words into airy wisps. I bolster my shoulders and correct my posture. "I'll explain as soon as we are out of earshot."

The driver whistles to the team and snaps the traces. Our coach wheels crunch over gravel as the Prince's caravan rolls out of the inn yard. Sera switches to the seat directly across from me and leans forward. "You found something in the woods."

I press back against the leather seats. "How did you know?"

Sera leans away, retreating behind wayward strands of hair, and sniffs defensively. She thinks it vexes me when she figures something out before I reveal it to her. Except I am not vexed, not at all. I'm curious.

"How?" I ask again.

She points to my knees. "There are two spots of moisture and dirt on your skirts where you must've knelt briefly on the ground."

"Ah. So, there is." I hasten to brush the evidence off my carriage gown. "Yes, well you are right, I found something quite unexpected."

Our coach jerks as it circles out of the drive and lurches onto the main road. We are underway, and the clatter of the hooves and wheels cloaks our conversation.

"A plant of some sort?" she asks.

I don't inquire how she deduced the nature of my discovery. I merely raise my eyebrow in question.

She shrugs. "The glove on your right hand is not soiled, indicating you removed it to pluck something. Whereas the fingertips of your left glove have a slightly green tinge. I can only conclude that you handled a plant briefly with your left for some reason."

I pull out the handkerchief and unwrap it to show her the leaves hidden inside.

"What is it?"

I study the prickled sprigs. "I don't know the English name for this plant, but in my part of the world it can be used as a . . ." I stop and frown, not wanting to say the word.

"A poison?" she supplies.

I nod.

Sera draws back, sucking in her breath. "You don't mean to kill him, do you? I know the Prince is a stumbling block for England, but you can't. It's too—"

"No, no!" I sit to attention and quickly fold up the packet of leaves. "I wouldn't. It's all a matter of cautiously applying the proper dosage—a little, and he will merely get sick. Too sick to travel to his meeting with Napoleon."

Sera shrinks back against the seat. "Too much, and what happens?"

I chew my lip for a moment and stow the leaves back in my pocket. "Too much, and you may visit me at London Tower. You will find my head there, *on a pike*."

She curls into herself, chin on her fist, lips pressed into a taut line.

"It makes my stomach knot up, too. But it is the only solution we have at the moment." The words sound more brusque and confident than I feel.

She winces, and rightly so. I know I'm clutching at straws. No, not straws. Only one straw. One very flimsy lethal straw, but it is all we have.

"We have to do *something*, Sera. Britain hangs in the

balance. If Napoleon doesn't destroy it, Ghost will. We have to stop this meeting or at least delay it. It is not just Britain we have to consider. Captain Grey, Lord Wyatt, now Mr. Chadwick, and even Miss Stranje, their lives are all forfeit if Napoleon succeeds. If Prince George goes through with the parley, it does not matter whether he concedes to Napoleon, or not—I am dead. I will be considered a traitor to Britain, or to Lady Daneska. *Done for* either way."

My heart slows to a dull funereal beat, as if it is already thudding out its last farewell. I remind myself *I am not dead yet* and take a breath. "If this solution works, I may stand a chance of surviving, and England might remain under British rule."

She shakes her head and shoves away the silky white strands that have fallen across her eyes. "But you can't. What if he dies?"

"He won't, if I am careful."

Extremely careful.

I do not add that caution aloud, nor do I mention that I wish Georgie or Madame Cho were here to help me calculate the proper amounts. Even if they were, I wouldn't allow it. By helping me, if it goes awry, they would be complicit. It is best if I take the risk alone.

Sera folds her arms tight, brooding, thinking so hard the silence in the coach feels crowded and noisy. At long last, her attention whips back to me. "How do you intend to administer it?"

"Originally, I'd thought to use my poison ring and sprinkle it in his wine or food, but Lord Kinsworth has supplied me with a safer option." I explain my fiancé's eagerness to bring my 'cure' for gout to the Prince, and that I warned him about the risks of a detrimental reaction. "So, you see, when the Prince falls ill after having been properly warned, perhaps he will merely be angry with me. There's a chance I won't stand trial for treason."

"A small chance." She leans forward her hands clasped as if in prayer. "You do realize, even if you succeed in not killing him, this tea of yours will only postpone this wretched meeting for a few days."

I sag against the seat. My head back in the noose.

Sera falls silent, too, weighing our predicament, sinking deeper into the recesses of her mind, her inner singing is a far-away echo. So distant and drowned in a misty fog that I can scarcely hear the dismal notes.

She is hiding again, and we are both surrendering too much to the gloom. I scramble to provide a distraction. "Sera, you have not yet told me how you feel about Captain Grey taking Mr. Chadwick on as one of his protégés. Did it surprise you?"

She does not answer right away. She takes a deep breath and squares her shoulders as if arriving at some sort of momentous decision. "Quinton is brilliant. I'm certain he will be of great use to Captain Grey and the diplomatic corp."

"Undoubtedly." I smile at the praise she bestows on him. "Although, I do wonder how he will manage to hide the truth. The life of a spy requires deception and, like you, there is no guile in him."

"Like me?" Sera raises her eyebrows, and her mouth opens as if I have inadvertently made some sort of outrageous statement. She pulls back and shakes her head. "You don't know, do you? Of everyone at Stranje

House, I thought *you* would have known, or at least guessed."

"*Guessed* what?"

She frowns at me. "I keep secrets all the time. And apparently, *no one* realizes it. Not even you." She crosses her arms defensively, and adds, "Don't look so surprised. It's not as if I use trickery. One needn't be deceptive if one simply remains silent."

Her words ring true, and for the second time today, I have been caught completely off guard. I stare at her, my closest friend. The friend who knows me best. And yet, she has secrets, secrets I know nothing about.

How had I missed this?

I close my eyes and listen more closely to the wispy tendrils of sound that emanate from her, the tiptoeing children, the muffled wind-like chant of her soul. "Oh!" I finally understand and raise my eyes to hers. "You hide your secrets behind those shadowy curtains in your heart. But Mr. Chadwick, he–"

"Has no such shadows." Sera smiles with more than a hint of sadness and nods. "Not yet. Several months ago, Tess had a dream, and it's possible that one day he will. For now, though, you are right. He is all innocence and uncloaked light. He has not yet learned how to bury his secrets. To be fair, I think he was under the impression we are privy to everything Captain Grey does."

"He has told you something?"

She nods. "I've been keeping mum for his sake. But I believe our present situation warrants me telling you." She stops for a moment, and I can hardly breathe in anticipation. '*What secret*' I want to shout. Except I dare not speak a word for fear it will turn her skittish and she will not tell me.

She wets her lips and quietly begins. "It is this—if your plan works, if this potion of yours can hold the Prince off from meeting with Napoleon for three or four weeks as we'd originally been told—there may be a more permanent solution on the horizon. A solution Captain Grey and his men have devised."

My mouth falls open. "You mean something other than my being drawn and quartered? And you didn't think to share this with me until now?"

She catches her lip for a moment. "It was a secret Mr. Chadwick should've kept. I remained quiet for his sake. He only told me because he thought I already knew."

"Knew *what*—exactly?"

"The Navy has nearly finished building Mr. Sinclair's new warship. He, Captain Grey, Admiral St. Vincent, and Lord Wyatt convinced the Admiralty to allow them to take a small crew and do a test run once it is completed. She'll be out of drydock in a week or two. As soon as we send them word of when the meeting with Napoleon is to take place, they intend to sail the warship out of the Thames at night. They'll head south, down through the Channel, taking the steamship toward Brighton. Their plan is to intercept and sink, or capture, the vessel Emperor Napoleon is sailing to the parley."

It is a far more reliable solution. A much sturdier straw.

Hope.

For the first time in days, I have hope.

FIFTEEN

THE NIGHTINGALE'S NEW CAGE

THE PRINCE IS, indeed, in a great hurry. We stop briefly at one more inn for a light supper and to change the horses, and then travel on until late that night. The sound of gulls screeching in the night air awakens me. Fog swirls in gusty ribbons around our coach as we finally slow on the cobbled streets of Brighton and arrive at the palace. Our horses snort and paw while they are made to wait until His Highness disembarks, followed by the occupants of two other coaches, until our vehicle can reach the porte-cochere.

I watch from the window as Prince George makes his way into the palace. He is limping and leans heavily on Lord Harston's arm. Lord Kinsworth follows and casts a worried look in my direction, but it is the dead of night, and while the portico is well lit, we remain shrouded in darkness. I doubt he can actually see me as he hurries through the massive doors behind his uncle and the Prince.

It seems hours until our coach rolls forward, and at last, the footman opens our door. The night air is heavy with gnats, and a fine salty mist floats eerily around the lanterns. A servant guides us inside the grand palace.

Despite the many candles lighting our way, it feels as if we are sleepwalking through some sort of fantastic Chinese dream world, flickering with deep pinks, stunning reds, and gold filigree glimmering everywhere. Gigantic carved lotus blossoms, the size of barrels, grace every column.

Miss Stranje's drawings did not do this palace justice.

We wind through a maze of rooms and halls, and I struggle to recall the map we memorized. Sera probably remembers, but I am overwhelmed by dimly lit glimpses of this wildly imaginative palace. It is unlike anything I have ever seen.

I stop—startled by the face of a dragon coiled around a pillar.

It stares back at me, and a full tick of the clock passes before I comprehend the creature is not real. Granted, I am exhausted from traveling, but my grandmother used to tell stories of dragons, terrifying creatures, who long ago, roamed the countryside and flew across our skies. Only I never expected to come face to face with one.

I stumble forward and find his leering grin is mirrored across the hall on yet another dragon embellishing a column. We are surrounded by carved palm fronds, giant lotuses, coiling snakes, and a host of other mythical creatures.

At last, we are shown into a small guest bedroom in

one of the wings of the palace. Sera and I are to share this room. A maid helps us unpack, and we hurriedly prepare for bed. Just as we are about to turn out our oil lamp, a soft rap sounds at our door.

A droopy-eyed servant stands on the threshold with a note bearing Lord Kinsworth's seal. I open it and hold it over the lamp, inspecting the missive for hidden messages. Finding none, I read:

> *The Prince is in the throes of a severe gout attack. I explained the dangers of your herbal remedy, but His Highness says, he doesn't care if your potion kills him. He insists you make it for him a soon as possible.*

My throat instantly goes dry, and I hand the edict to Sera. She reads it and frowns. "But it is too soon."

I remember to breathe. "Yes, but what else can we do?"

I turn back to Lord Kinsworth's servant. "Tell my lord that the herbs need to cure before a draught can be made. I will set them to drying immediately, but I cannot possibly prepare the tisane until tomorrow morning. This is very important. You must convey those exact words to Lord Kinsworth."

"Yes, miss." He bobs his head and hurries off down the hall.

"Morning." I groan and shut the door. "I must make the potion in the morning."

Sera shakes her head. "I will help you."

"No." I lay out the leaves, pressing them between the pages of a book to help them dry more quickly. "You should stay as far away from this scheme as possible. If something should go wrong—"

"Make certain it doesn't." She crawls into bed.

The next morning, I ask our maid if the palace has a still room where I might prepare a special tea for His Highness. The girl stares at me as if I am an ostrich poking my head up in a nest of doves. I have never understood why it is hardest for the servants to accept me as a member of the peerage. One would assume they would be less snobbish about such things, but such is not the case. "Well?" I snap. "Do you have such a place? I will also require a mortar and pestle."

She stops blinking and stammers, "N-no stillroom, as such. B-but we've a mortar and pestle certainly, miss, in the kitchen. An' I expect chef might allow you to use one 'o the tables seeing as yer preparing something for *Hisself*. Shall I ask, miss?"

"Yes. Please do, and be quick about it. Prince George is demanding this potion, and I daresay he does not care to be left waiting."

"No, miss." She hurries out of the room, having only tied back one side of the curtains.

Sera sets down her hair brush and goes to finish the task. "I'll wager she's never heard that request before. They don't know you here, Maya. I really think I ought to go with you."

"No. You mustn't be seen anywhere near this potion." I place the now brittle leaves in a small muslin bag. "I can manage perfectly well on my own."

A lie.

Twenty minutes later, I stand, with shaking hands, at one of the long wooden tables in the palace kitchen, trying to crumble the *not-quite-dry-enough* leaves into a large mortar. Dozens of servants scurry about this enormous kitchen, and every single one of them gapes at me as if I am a cobra in their cornfield. And maybe I am. After all, this is poison I am mixing.

I do my best to ignore them and go about my work. I take up the pestle and begin crushing the leaves. I refuse to pay any attention to their gawking until a hush falls over the kitchen.

A pastry chef drops a pan, and the clatter echoes throughout the room.

"What is this?" utters a footman. "M'lady, are you lost?" I finally look up, but he strides past me.

Lady Jersey swishes into the kitchen. Her silk skirts rustle as she wends her way between the tables toward me. "Nooo, young man. Certaaainly not. I am never lost." She dismisses him with a wave of her hand.

"Theere you are, my deeaar giurl. I've been looking all over for you." She smiles briefly at me and glances up at the towering palm trees which disguise the enormous columns stretching up to the high ceiling and an expansive skylight. "Eexxtraooordinary. So, this I what a kitchen looks like? I confess I have never been in one before. How delightfully bright and airy they are. I daresay, one could hold a musical evening in a room of this size."

I laugh aloud. "Sadly, most English kitchens are far from being this grand, my lady. They are generally below ground, have low ceilings, soot on the walls, and very little light. This one is exceptional."

"Humph." She seems disappointed to hear it. "You've set down a challenge, young lady. I shall have to visit mine to see how they compare."

I suppress a smile and return to grinding.

"I heard what you are doooing." Her lips pinch up.

The pestle stills in my hand. "Sera told you?"

"Phfft. Of course, not. That young lady is as close-lipped as a fox at a hound picnic."

I do not understand this expression, fox at a hound picnic, but many English expressions elude me. I shrug. "Then who told you?"

"That fine-looking young buck who is in love with you, that's who." Her accent has vanished.

"If you mean Lord Kinsworth, he is not in love with me." I grip the pestle tighter.

"Don't be daft. Of course, he is. Any fool can see that." She flicks my shoulder by way of a scold. When I say nothing in return, she bristles. "I did not come all the way here and invade Chef Carême's kitchens to discuss your rickety love life."

She awaits my response, like a cat watching to see which way the mouse will dart. When I say nothing, and continue mashing the leaves into an oily clump, she leans in. "I could tell by how carefully Miss Wyndham side-stepped my questions that this remedy of yours is not as simple as your beloved Lord Kinsworth thinks it is."

"He isn't my beloved." I grind the pestle harder.

"Piffle. He most certainly is." She sniffs the concoction in my mortar and wrinkles her nose. "Smells ghastly."

I say nothing.

"Smells *dangerousss*," she hisses. She has guessed the truth. If it were anyone else, I might be afraid. Lady Jersey likes to intimidate people, or at the very least make them underestimate her. She wants them to assume anything other than the truth. Hence, the flamboyant diva she pretends to be. But beneath her ostentatious trappings, stands a brilliant, caring woman whose integrity chimes as solidly as a church bell. She will understand my reasoning.

I carefully set down the pestle, and watch as oil oozes from the concoction. "It has been known to purge the blood."

"Purge it? Judging by the smell, I say it would curdle it."

My voice lowers to a gentle register, not a whisper, which might arouse suspicion, yet soft enough not to be overheard. "It might make him a trifle sick." I look at her pointedly. "For a day or two."

"Ohhh," she mouths and nods almost imperceptibly. "I seeeee. How very inconvenient for him. And are you quite certain it will only discomfit him for a few days?"

Am I certain?

I frown at the slimy green pulp and take a deep breath. "As certain as one can be. It is a wild herb. Soil may change its properties. And these leaves were picked only yesterday. They have not dried properly. It is impossible to predict their potency."

She exhales sharply, and mutters, "You'd jolly well better make a good guess then, my girl." Lady Jersey never mutters, which only serves to make me more nervous. I bite my bottom lip and pulverize the leaves even more vigorously. When they are finally mashed beyond recognition, I set down the pestle.

"How can I help?" Lady Jersey acts as if she is about to roll up her silk sleeves and knead dough.

I peruse the nearby shelves, hunting for items I need

to prepare the mixture. Reaching for a small pitcher, I answer, "We also need a straining cloth, a kettle of boiling water, and a cup of cherry brandy."

"More than a cup, I should think. I could use a glass myself." Instead of helping me locate the items, she puffs up and snaps her fingers at a passing footman. "You there! This young lady requires a clean straining cloth, a kettle of boiling water, and a bottle of the Prince's favorite cherry brandy."

Before she has finished issuing these orders, two kitchen maids gather at the young fellow's side. Any moment I expect a mutiny at two strangers ordering them about their kitchen. But Lady Jersey claps her hands, "Step lively, lad. His Highness is waiting."

The footman dispatches the maids in various directions and then dashes off to procure the liqueur. Meanwhile, I lean over the mortar sniffing the ground leaves in an attempt to determine the strength of the herb. It is pungent, to be sure. I dip the tip of my finger in and taste it. My tongue curls at the bitter oil.

Lady Jersey watches my face. "Good heavens. That bad, is it?"

"The brandy will help," I assure her, hoping it is true. If only Madam Cho were here to advise me.

The maids return, and set a steaming kettle on a trivet with the cheesecloth beside it. The footman presents the wine to us.

"That will be all." Lady Jersey sends them away, and I stare at the deadly mush pooling in the white marble mortar and realize I have begun to sweat. Was it that lone drop of poison on my tongue? Or nerves?

I swallow hard. "God save us all," I say under my

breath.

"Amen." Lady Jersey uncorks the brandy and pours herself a glass. She hands me the bottle and with a trembling hand I pour a small amount over the mixture. The green sludge bubbles for a moment, but soon settles. The alcohol has emulsified the oiliness. I scoop the paste into the cloth, knot the top, place it in the pitcher, and pour hot water over the herbs to let it steep. A nose-stinging wreath of steam rises from the mixture.

When the hot water turns green, I remove the cloth bag. "It's ready."

"Not quite." She pours a generous splash of brandy into it. "He'll like it better with a little more of this." Lady Jersey signals a footman to prepare a small tea tray and turns to me. "You, my dear Miss Barrington, will deliver it to him."

I gulp down my misgivings at watching him drink the stuff, but these are girlish fears, and I know what Lady Jersey would say in answer.

There is no room for fear in our business.

A plausible excuse comes to mind. I wet my dry lips and argue, "I cannot possibly deliver it. According to Lord Kinsworth's note, Prince George is laid up in bed." When Lady Jersey doesn't even blink, I add. "In his *bedchamber.*"

"Nonsense. Don't be missish, child. There've been troops of people in and out of that room already this morning. Advisors, maids, lords, and ladies galore. I, myself, stopped in to wish him well." She leans closer and pinches my arm, talking through her teeth in a low but somehow pleasant voice. "You will do as I say. Paste a smile on that pretty face of yours, and personally deliver this *excessively helpful* tea to Prinny."

Her meaning is clear. This is what I must do to avoid suspicion of wrongdoing. I curtsey obediently. "Yes, my lady."

She straightens, sniffs, and flicks her hand for me to be on my way. "And take that annoyingly observant Miss Wyndham with you."

Not fifteen minutes later, Sera and I trail behind a fast-walking footman as he guides us to the opposite end of the Pavilion where the Prince Regent's apartments are located. Every hallway spews a new style of chinoiserie. The patterns are as confusing and volcanic as my nerves. Here, bamboo latticework is plastered atop a startlingly blue background. Turn a corner, and one is plunged into a ruby-red gilt-work jungle.

Walls do not usually make much noise, but these are an exception. They vibrate with the screams of imaginary parrots and shrieks from wild creatures peeking out of lavish bamboo forests. My steps slow as I try to make sense of it, and I nearly fall behind.

"There you are!" Lord Kinsworth rushes out from an open doorway at the far end of the hall. "I thought you would never get here." He waves the footman inside, and motions to Sera and me. "Come quickly. He's in a bad way. Traveling worsened his swelling."

The Prince's outer apartments are papered in a muted green, the color of dry summer leaves. The green is painted with silver line-drawings of winged dragons. The dragons rise skyward out of a cacophony of impossibly ornate flowers, all hand-painted in silver.

The faint odor of putrefying flesh wafts into the sitting room. Sera sniffs. Rightly so. My nose wrinkles, too.

Combine that stench with the chaotic visual noise from the décor, and it is enough to make anyone feel ill.

"This way." Lord Kinsworth ushers us into the Prince's bedchamber and the smell of sickly flesh increases. "His Highness is most anxious to try your remedy."

"Indeed, we are." The Prince's voice booms through the smaller chamber. He lounges on a massive bed with pillows propping one foot higher than the other.

This is more than a simple case of gout. His elevated foot is red and swollen to twice normal proportions. It resembles a misshapen persimmon, bulging to the point of bursting. Three leeches are attached to his swollen ankle.

Inwardly, I groan as Sera and I drop into a low curtsey. The poor man must be in agony.

His bed is surrounded by attendants. Lord Harston is here, and nods to us in greeting. "Rise." Prince George waves his hand. "Let us dispense with the formalities. Up. Up. Both of you, up."

As we straighten, Sera leans close and says under her breath, "Dropsy." Judging by the amount of swelling, she is right. If I could discern a cause, beyond his excessive drinking, I might be able to help with an actual cure. That is, after this misguided treaty business is over.

Sera nudges me to say something to our host in greeting. I swallow a dry wad of guilt. The bitter taste of that lone drop of tisane is still weighs heavily on my tongue. To speak without sounding overly nervous, I summon thoughts of my grandmother's kind face, and conjure memories of the fresh wind that blows up from the river near our village.

I draw in a calming breath. "I have brought the tea,

Sir, as you requested. I hope it serves you well. Lord Kinsworth has assured me that he rightly cautioned you that it is a blood-purgative. As such, the effects are unpredictable."

The Prince's physician, who until now stood stoically off to the side, struts forward. He looks me up and down, and with a disdain for my foreignness with which I am all too familiar, he asks, "What herb did you use to brew this, this . . ." He turns up his nose in the direction of the teapot on the footman's tray. "Tea."

I incline my head, not bowing, but acknowledging his right to question me. "I am not familiar with your English name for this particular herb."

"Surely you must have some of the leaves left. You must bring them to me at once so that I may determine their origin and nature."

"I cannot, sir. I used all of the leaves in my possession to make this tisane."

"It won't do." He bristles and shakes his head. "I am loathe to administer anything with which I am unfamiliar. Unless I know exactly what science is at work, I must forbid–"

"Nonsense!" shouts the Prince, his face reddening. "You cannot forbid me. I've had enough of your confounded science. Leave us. Out! Out with you!"

"But, your Highness–"

"Go! We are sick to death of your useless leeches and bloodletting. Be gone!" Prince George flops back against the silk pillows, and his physician scowls, casting vicious frowns upon my head as he leaves the room.

Prince George lifts one weary finger and crooks it. "Bring your concoction, Miss Barrington. Whatever floats in that pot of yours, cannot be one wit worse than these demon-toothed leeches."

I cringe inwardly but manage to smile and summon the most soothing voice I can muster at the moment. "I pray for your comfort, Your Highness."

At that, he chuckles. "M'dear innocent Miss Barrington, thank you. But as m'sainted lady mother will tell you, given m' reluctance to forego fleshly vices, one cannot expect assistance from heavenly quarters."

Not knowing how to answer. I look to Sera, but she is staring intently at the Prince's swollen foot and ankle.

It is Lord Kinsworth who comes to my rescue. "Surely, a merciful God will hear the plea of an innocent like our Miss Barrington."

"Merciful, *is He?* Let us hope you are right. Confound this foot! We've half a mind to cut the ruddy thing off. Trouble is, in two days' time, we need to be shipshape and ready to travel if we are to negotiate peace with Bonaparte."

Two days!

Too soon.

Napoleon is coming too soon. I turn to Sera, and she squeezes my hand. "Let us hope the tea provides relief."

"I'm sure it will be just the thing." Lord Kinsworth signals for the footman to set the tray down.

The prince props himself up again and flicks two fingers at the tea service. "Do us the honors, Miss Barrington. How much of this stuff must I pour down m' gullet?"

"For the sake of caution, let us start with one cup and see how Your Highness fares." With shaky hands, I fill his teacup. And I pray. Nay, it is more than praying, I am begging earnestly, that this greenish-brown poison will not kill the monarch of England.

Full to the brim, walking with the solemnity of a nun bearing a cask of saintly bones, I carry the dangerous teacup forward, and with a steadiness I do not feel, present it to him.

He whisks it out of my hands and takes a fearless sip. With hardly a grimace, he looks up at me as if he is surprised it didn't taste worse. He smacks his lips. "Cherry brandy. M' favorite. Well done, Miss Barrington. Well done."

I stare at him attentively, and so does Sera. I think we are both fearing a sudden constriction of his throat. When all seems well, I step back.

He then tosses down the rest of the tisane as if it is nothing more than a swig of brandy. "There. That's done." He plunks the teacup on his side table and collapses on the pile of pillows, closing his eyes. "Now, t'would seem a bit of rest is in order. We would like a bit of privacy. Wake us at two, gentlemen. And, Kinsworth, if you would be so good as to escort these young ladies to—" He walks his fingers through the air. "To wherever it is they wish to go. Take them away."

Thus, we are dismissed.

Sera holds my hand, and we walk quickly toward the door. It is all I can do to keep from running out of his apartments and tearing down the hall. I think we both worry there could be screams of agony erupting at any moment.

"Wait!" It is the Prince.

His command arrests us, and neither of us turns.

"A song," he says in a drowsy voice. "Stay. Sing for

me, little nightingale. One song. Something restful."

Nightingale.

Panic rises in my throat. I feel the cage doors slamming shut, trapping me.

SIXTEEN

GRANDMOTHER'S LULLABY

Sing, little nightingale.
Sing.

WITH A SIGH, I accept my fate and turn back. I will sing for him. The Prince commands it. What else can a caged bird do?

He, who holds my fate in his hands, utters a single word that melts my heart. "*Please.*" Prince George says it with a groan, as pain stomps heavy boots across his chest. And I ache for him.

In that moment, I see the truth. I am not the only one trapped. Whether it is of his own making or a consequence of his position in the world, Prince George is imprisoned in a cage, too. A gilded cage, but he suffers nonetheless.

And so, I search my memory for a tune to ease his pain.

There is a ballad my grandmother used to sing when I felt sad or unable to sleep, a song about a lonely river winding gently through the mountains at night. I find English words to interpret this ballad about Mother Moon leaning down to listen to the sad melody Daughter River sings; tumbling over rocks, whistling over fallen trees.

Deeply moved, mother moon pours out a bright stream of white flowing milk for daughter river to drink. Silver-skinned fish hum happily in river's now rich waters. Brother wind dips close to wash his cheek in the river's sweetness. Night birds swoop playfully in river's lapping waters.

No longer lonely, daughter river rushes on her way, singing with joy . . .

Prince George's fists uncurl, and he sinks deeper into the pillows. The song is not yet over when he begins to snore. Lord Kinsworth signals for us to tiptoe out of the bedchamber. I back out, still singing but allowing my voice to drift softer and softer until his snoring completely overpowers it.

Lord Harston follows us into the outer room, and bows slightly to me. "Bravo, Miss Barrington. Even though I was standing on my feet, you nearly had me falling asleep. Those notes, that voice of yours, so entrancing. How do you do it?"

I cannot tell him the truth, that it is an art one must study from childhood. Instead, I lower my eyes and blush. "I merely sing from the heart, my lord."

He rubs his neck. "Be that as it may, with a voice like that, you could ask for the moon you sang about, and a fellow would be inclined to start building a frightfully tall ladder." He chuckles at his own jest.

Lord Kinsworth laughs, too, but also noisily gulps a knot of fear.

I do not know whether to join in their awkward laughter, whether to feel complimented or insulted. Choosing neither, I smile serenely at Lord Kinsworth. "You need not fear, my lord, I would never ask for the moon."

"Ha-ha. Just so." His humor is forced. "Now, where may I escort you, ladies? Would you like to visit Parade Street or walk along the Steyne?"

"Not I. Perhaps another time. Having arisen early this morning to prepare the herbs, I should prefer a short nap." I turn to Sera. "But if you–?"

"No, no." Sera chirps with uncustomary sureness. "I am tired as well."

Lord Kinsworth looks crestfallen, when I should've thought him relieved. "Very well, perhaps another time. I shall escort you to your rooms."

Sera scoops her arm through mine. "You needn't trouble yourself, my lord. I'm certain we can find our way. Thank you, gentlemen." She dips in a quick curtsey and tugs me backward toward the open double doors.

"As you wish," Ben says, a pinch to his brow. *Confusing man.* One minute he is all attention, and the next he behaves like a man caught in a noose.

It is not until we are in the hall and well away from him, that Sera offers an explanation for her hurry. "I need to keep you away from him. He is falling too much in love with you. It is unacceptable. Given our vocation in life–"

"Our vocation!? What about Georgie and Sebastian? Or Tess and Ravencross?"

She shrugs. "Georgie is a scientist, not a spy. I doubt she'll spend her life in the diplomatic world, unless, of course, Lord Wyatt survives all this and they marry. Then who knows. As for Tess, I believe she will be the one who follows in Miss Stranje's stead and trains the next generation of young ladies to do what we do. If so, it would be fairly convenient married to Lord Ravencross, living directly across from Stranje House."

"But I thought Miss Stranje was grooming Lady Jane to take her place."

"I think she was. Then along came Alexander Sinclair. He will need to be in London, amidst engineers and inventors of his caliber. Like Lady Jersey, Lady Jane may provide a London connection for future students of the diplomatic arts. But you and I, we are destined to a different life. For us, falling in love is a detriment. Too great a risk. And your Lord Kinsworth has a gentle heart despite his claim that he hungers for adventure. You mustn't let him fall too deeply in love with you. Think of the bruise—"

"Don't be silly. He is not in love."

"You know perfectly well I am *never ever* silly." She purses her lips before exploding into one of the sternest speeches she has ever delivered to me. "You were too busy singing to observe the way he looked at you. I did." She tightens her hold on my arm. "Not that every other man in the room wasn't prepared to, as Lord Harston put it, build a ladder to the moon for you, but Lord Kinsworth's expression was different. He watched you as if he expected you to sprout wings at any moment and flutter off to heaven. The man is smitten, Maya. And it won't do. It won't do at all." She stops for a breath.

"Aside from the hurt you will cause him, he is a distraction. We need to—"

"Yes, yes, I know. We need to get word to Miss Stranje. We thought we had a week or more before the parley. But now, only two days. If the herbs do not slow him down, we are done for. England is done for. And I . . . *I am dead.*"

"Precisely."

We quicken our pace, and I whisper in her ear, "Not to mention, I was terrified Prince George would awaken at any moment, convulsing with pain from the tea."

"Right," she says, and we walk as fast as humanly possible without kicking into an outright run. "Your singing seemed to relax him greatly. But his circulation is dreadful. Did you notice how bad his dropsy is?"

"His foot was so terribly swollen—I was afraid it might burst. He cannot possibly walk on it. And the tea may complicate his symptoms." I shake my head, picturing his stomach convulsing and the poor man trying to hobble over a chamber pot. "Tea or no tea, I don't see how he can attend the meeting with Napoleon. Not in two days."

"It seems unlikely. But I can tell by the scars on his foot, leeches have been used successfully in the past. He very well may recover in time. We have to get word to Miss Stranje."

"Agreed. I shall slip out this afternoon and—"

"No, we should go together. You will be safer if I am with you, and together we will draw less suspicion." She stops at our door, her hand on the knob, and even though she is smaller than I am, she takes on the air of an older sister. "Shopping, we will say—or walking down to the Marine Parade to take in the sea air."

"I am the oldest of the two of us," I remind her. "You needn't feel as if you must take care of me."

Her shoulders relax. "Oh, good. Because I am dreadful at it. Although, you may have forgotten, but . . ." She opens the door, and we step into the room. "I have been Miss Stranje's student two years longer than you."

I do not answer. Someone else speaks for me. "*Ma oui.* Two years is practically a lifetime. *Bonjour,* my darlings."

"Daneska!" I blurt.

Sera retreats a step.

Lady Daneska lounges in a chair, as if it is perfectly normal for her to intrude upon our privacy. She flicks her finger at Sera, giving her an order, "Do shut the door, *ma petite souris.* We wouldn't want everyone in the world to overhear us, now would we?"

Sera complies, grumbling, "I am not a little mouse."

"No? A white mouse, then. *Souris blanche.* But I did not come here to discuss your character failing, *mon chéries.*"

"Why did you come?" I snap and step between her and Sera. One never knows if Lady Daneska already has her dagger drawn.

"Why do you think? To see how fares our arrangement."

I catch my lip before responding and decide the truth is our best defense. "Prince George is very sick."

"So, I heard. And you took your portly Prince a tea to help him recover. How very gracious of you."

I look away, biting my lip, and shake my head. "His swelling is quite severe. We believe he has a serious case of—"

"Yes. Yes. Dreadful dropsy. All this, I know." She waves away my concern and stands, turning her back to us, gazing out the window. "It is nothing new. Prinny will recover. He always does."

I think to myself how easy it might be to grab her from behind, tie her up, and . . . *and what?*

What would we do with her?

Hide her under our bed? Throw her off a pier?

Sera glances at me, and I know she is thinking the same thing. We both step forward, but Daneska whirls around. "Prinny will recover. He must. And you will see to it."

"My lady, I am not God. I cannot work miracles." I test to see what she knows. "Two days is a very short time—"

Anger distorts her perfect features. "Then make more tea for him. Sing to him. Do whatever you must, *Princess*."

She calls me Princess, not to honor, but to antagonize me, and remind me of our arrangement.

Her frown narrows, her voice, too, focuses, like a tiger growling before she pounces. "Mark my words, Georgie-Porgy will be well in two days, or you will not rise to see the sun on the third." She opens her hand, and from a slit in her glove, a dagger springs into her palm. "And neither will your precious little white mouse."

She twirls around us as if doing a country dance and nicks Sera's arm. A small prick, but enough to distract us, and enough to remind us of how lethal her blade is. In a trice, she opens the door. "I am watching you, my darlings." She blows us a kiss before disappearing into the hall.

"She is aware the parley is only two days away." I stare at the closed door, knowing there is no point in chasing after her.

Sera blots away the dribble of blood on her arm. "I suspect she and Ghost are the ones coordinating this misbegotten meeting of the monarchs."

"She is," I mumble, hunting for a bandage to tie around Sera's arm. "But I'm not certain Ghost has much to do with it. The night she asked me to help her, I got the impression Daneska views this as our last chance to save England from Ghost's fury. Not that she cares. It is simply that she would prefer Napoleon takes captive a habitable Britain, rather than one burned to the ground and seething with disease. I think she envisions herself sitting on the English throne one day."

"You believe her then?" Sera's voice lowers to a nearly a whisper. "About the fires and plague?"

"I do. More importantly–she believes it."

"It's monstrous." She sucks in air as if smoke and pestilence have already made it difficult to breathe. "Why would Ghost do such awful things? This is his homeland. How can he hate England so much? Why?"

"Why, indeed." Sinking onto the nearest upholstered chair, I shake my head. "Tess told me once that Lord Ravencross's father was brutal to both of his sons, beating them mercilessly whenever they failed to live up to his expectations of an English lord. Beyond that, I have no idea. Some people, like some animals, are born vicious. Others are molded into hatefulness. I only know that Daneska fears Ghost. And it is unlike her to be afraid of anything."

Sera wordlessly sinks onto the chair beside me and

leans her head on my shoulder. We both fit comfortably on the one seat. She is so small. So fragile. It feels as if we are both helpless children. Then, I remember Sera is brilliant. Her gifts far surpass any of the rest of our talents. She may be small, but the force of her acumen makes up for it.

And I may be the nightingale, armed with only a song, but at heart, I am also a lioness. God willing, we shall prevail. Straightening from my fearful slump, I pat her knee and say, "Come, we must take word to Miss Stranje and the others."

She looks up at me, as a little sister would. I do not deserve such admiration. I stand and brush out my skirts, precisely the way Miss Stranje does. "It will do us good to see our friends."

She brightens, and we quickly don our pelisses. Cloaked, armed, and ready for the out of doors, we slip quietly out of the palace, carefully avoiding notice. Miss Stranje had given us the address of her lodgings. We take the long way down North Street to Black Lion Street, purposely avoiding Parade or Marlboro Street where members of society might be walking. The day is cloudy but fine, the air crisp, and I find the cry of seabirds oddly comforting.

Until then, Sera and I had walked in silence, but she startles me by saying wistfully, "I miss Stranje House, too."

How did she know?

At my missed step, she glances at me with some annoyance. "Honestly, Maya, must you always look so surprised? I saw you watching the gulls circling above us, the same way you do at Stranje House." She loops her arm through mine. "You do realize, don't you, your face is an open book? Anyone would've noticed your nostalgia."

"I was not being nostalgic. Nothing so maudlin." I bristle a bit, knowing she can so easily guess my mood. But I let her keep tugging me along because Sera is the most good-natured person I know. "I simply find their cries reassuring. That's all."

"Oh, I see." She smiles. "Is that because you had seagulls in your homeland?"

River birds, yes, but not many seagulls that far inland. "Oh, very well. I *do* miss Stranje House," I admit with a sigh. "The seagulls would fish early in the morning, while I meditated, and I suppose I grew accustomed to the sound."

"Ah. There, you see? Perfectly logical."

"I suppose."

We come to a standstill in front of the New Ship Inn, both of us staring at the imposing white façade. "This must be the place."

A footman opens the door for us, and we enter through the columns into what resembles a very elegant, but spacious captain's compartment of a ship. The walls are oak-paneled and set off with gleaming brass sconces. The long-nosed innkeeper directs us to Miss Stranje's apartments. He informs us that they are residing on the third floor, in one of the eight exclusive apartments overlooking the sea. As soon as we are out of public view, we scurry up the staircase like excited children eager to see our friends.

The door to their suite opens, and we are met with exclamations of joy and a flurry of hugs. It is as if we have been parted for weeks rather than days. Georgie and Lady Jane ply us with a thousand questions.

Before we can answer, Miss Stranje raises her hand. "Ladies! We would've seen Miss Barrington and Miss Wyndham later tonight at the Prince's festivities. It should be obvious to you they would not be here at this hour of the day if they had not come bearing urgent news."

"True!" Sera blurts. "Lady Daneska paid us a visit. This very morning, after we returned from attending the Prince, she was waiting inside our bedchamber."

"Did she hurt you?" Tess pushes forward, looking at us closely for telltale marks or cuts.

"No," Sera assures her, not mentioning the small nick she had sustained. "She threatened us, but no."

I wave away the rest of their questions. "We've come with more serious news. We learned from the Prince himself, the meeting with Napoleon is to take place, not in two or three weeks as we'd thought, but in *two* days."

Two days.

They fall back, stricken.

Lady Jane huffs out her frustration. "Two days. That's not enough time." She turns to Miss Stranje, and I surmise from her singular consternation that Lady Jane is also aware of Alexander and Captain Grey's plan to intercept Napoleon with the new steam-powered warship.

Miss Stranje's brow remains furrowed. She reveals nothing, but asks me, "You said you attended Prince George, for what reason?"

I back away, not wishing to tell her about my treachery. Sera speaks up for us both. "He is suffering from a severe case of dropsy. Maya made a tea for him from an herb she found in the woods near one of the coaching inns. It . . ." She looks to me, not wishing to divulge the fact that I concocted a somewhat poison tea.

I cannot look directly at our headmistress. I tip up on my toes, straining to see Madame Cho's face. She stands quietly behind everyone else, watching me as if she already suspects the truth. "This tea," Madame Cho says. "It may not relieve his discomfort?"

I look down and nod.

"I see." Miss Stranje stiffens. "Is there a chance it might make him worse?"

"Possibly." I glance up, hoping for absolution, but she does not give it.

Our headmistress frowns. Gargoyles are friendlier looking than she is when she glowers. She exhales loudly and studies an oil painting on the far wall. Anyone might think those two ships engaged in some unknown battle are of more importance. "Tell me it is not . . ." She turns her sharp-eyed stare on me, the one that makes me feel like a mouse kneeling before an owl. "Tell me the concoction you gave him will not make him *permanently* ill."

Did I give him a lethal dose of poison?

"It won't. It shouldn't. I was careful." I look to Madame Cho. "But the herbs I used were from an unproven source. I measured twice and tried to evaluate the potency as well as I could."

Madame Cho purses her lips and grants me an almost imperceptible nod of understanding. Understanding—*not approval.* If I have killed the monarch of England, the blame will land squarely on my neck. Along with the executioner's axe.

Miss Stranje says nothing for a few seconds, massaging her brow as if I have given her a severe headache. "Of course, you were cautious. I would expect nothing less of you." It does not sound as condemning as I had expected. Even so, a bell of worry clangs behind her shrewd eyes, ringing unmistakably beneath that rigidly restrained tone. "While this was not a decision I would've made, it may serve the purpose." Instead of chastising me for taking such a dangerous risk, she turns to the others. "It may buy us a few extra days." She holds up her hands, suppressing the other girls' sudden brightening. "We need to plan for all contingencies. First, however, word must be sent to Captain Grey."

She shakes out her skirts and clasps her palms together. It is what she always does before donning her schoolteacher persona. "Georgiana, would you be so good as to compose a love note to Lord Wyatt?"

Georgie's eyes widen. "What? But isn't that scandalous? How many times have you told us, only a young lady of low—"

"Yes. I'm aware of what I have told you. This is an exception. Today, we must breach societal standards because it is exactly what the situation requires." Miss Stranje holds up one finger. "Write something sentimental and scandalous. Something no young lady should write to anyone except her properly betrothed fiancé. Then, if you would be so good as to prepare your special ink so that I might write our actual message between the lines."

"Oh." Georgie grasps our teacher's strategy. "And afterward, shall I post it?"

"No, the post would be delayed too long." Miss Stranje reaches for her purse. "There are any number of runners for hire at the Old Ship Tavern next door. Give the missive to a capable runner specifying Lord Wyatt's direction along with these coins. Be sure to hire a man with a horse." She drops two shillings into Georgie's palm. "We don't want any delays."

Tess frowns. "Two shillings? That's too much."

"The point is to overpay. Tess, you will go with Miss Fitzwilliam to make sure she does not get into any difficulties. Do try and pretend to be girlish—giggle and titter as if you are up to no good."

"Giggle?" Tess grimaces as if she's just been asked to muck out the stables.

Miss Stranje rolls her eyes heavenward. "Yes. It shan't kill you."

"Might," Tess mutters.

I remind Miss Stranje, "Lady Daneska's men will be watching, I'm sure of it. She was very well-informed as to our movements."

"No doubt. She will have had you followed." Miss Stranje focuses in on me like a swooping bird of prey. "Precisely why it must appear as if Miss Fitzwilliam is foolishly sneaking out to send a note to her lover." Our teacher surveys all of us. "Much better, don't you think, than having Lady Daneska's spies believe I am sending a warning to Captain Grey. Which she will expect me to do, of course."

Lady Jane steps forward excitedly. "And you will, won't you?"

"Naturally. Except, I shall hire a more experienced runner, a runner suspected of being a spy, one of our men posted at Castle Tavern."

"Ah! Now I understand. Castle Tavern lies in the other direction from The Old Ship Tavern." Lady Jane grins broadly. "Perfect."

"Why? *Why* is that perfect?" Tess demands. "Their spies are going to follow you both."

"Yes! That's the beauty of it." Lady Jane trumpets with delight. "This way, she splits up their pursuit."

Sera, her inner melodies much more sedate, turns her head sideways contemplating the scheme. "You expect both notes to be intercepted, do you not?"

"I do." Miss Stranje smiles approvingly at Sera. "Although, in my missive, I will use an invisible ink that is much easier to discover—lemon juice or something rudimentary. One pass over a candle, and they should be able to see the hidden text. Text that will lead them to believe we know far less than we do."

"Games. I hate games," Tess mutters. "Give me a dagger and someone to fight. Anything is better than these blasted charades."

"These *charades* are intended to save lives, my dear." Miss Stranje clasps Tess's shoulder. "You and Georgiana should be seen sneaking out of our hotel shortly after I depart for Castle Tavern. Mind you, I want the two of you to make a hash of it. Do not be too clever. Be clumsily sneaky, but neither should you be too obvious."

She whirls to Sera and me. "You two will leave the hotel at the same time I do, but take a roundabout route back to the palace, choose a few back streets. Lead them on a merry chase."

"Brilliant." Lady Jane rocks up on her toes. "Daneska's spies will be forced to divide their efforts even further."

"Yes." Miss Stranje does not share Jane's enthusiasm. She sighs wearily. "Hopefully, after our misleading missive has fallen into enemy hands, this ruse will have thinned them out enough to give my runner a chance to escape after he is captured. I should not like to see a life taken unnecessarily."

"No." Lady Jane's exuberance crashes to a halt. Deflated, she drops into a nearby chair. "Nor should I. Daneska's men can be so very brutal."

Her music darkens, and I know she must be remembering the night the Iron Crown captured her, that terrible night when Ghost and Daneska tied her to a chair and tortured her. I rest my hand on her shoulder in a feeble attempt to offer comfort. She smooths the sprigged muslin of her skirt, slowing her hand as she passes it over the scar on her thigh, a reminder she will always carry from that dreadful night.

Georgie, deep in thought, raises a finger. "One point perplexes me. If both runners are captured, how will the real letter reach Lord Wyatt and Captain Grey?"

"Ahh." Rather than being annoyed, Miss Stranje seems pleased Georgie asked. This is one of the things I love about our headmistress—she encourages our questions. "If you and Tess play your part well, it is possible your runner may not even get waylaid. But should he be stopped and questioned, as soon as your letter is inspected, his assailants will most likely conclude the lad is innocent of any subterfuge. And in actuality, your man will be. In all likelihood, they will give him back your foolish sounding letter and allow him to go on his way. Don't forget, whoever is following him will have witnessed you and Tess sneaking about like silly schoolgirls, tittering about your beaus. With any luck, your runner may avoid suspicion altogether."

"Quite possible." Sera takes a deep breath. "Lady Daneska's shrewdest men will already be trailing after Maya and me, or Miss Stranje."

True enough. The three of us will be the ones in danger. Miss Stranje glances at Sera and me, her lips press tight with worry. She says nothing, but her uneasiness hums as loud as a hive of wasps, and that says more than enough.

SEVENTEEN

REQUIEM FOR SPIES

IT IS LATE AFTERNOON, everything is in place, and we are ready to execute Miss Stranje's plan. Now, it is up to Sera and me to exit the inn and lead away at least one of Daneska's spies. We follow Miss Stranje out and make a great show of bidding her farewell in front of The Ship. A breeze catches the wind and blasts over the cliffs. As I press my cheek against Miss Stranje's, we are hit with a delicate mist of sea spray. "Be careful," she whispers in my ear. "And watch over Sera."

Her words land on me like warming praise, but also a weighty burden. "I will," I say, wishing she wouldn't trust me so much. I do not deserve it, not when half of me feels like running away. If I had the wherewithal to buy passage back to India, I am afraid I might do it.

But for now, I remain steadfast. No, not steadfast—I cannot claim such a virtue. But for now, at least my feet continue moving in the right direction. I have obligations here, obligations to my friends, and to my father's country. Never mind if those obligations are perilous, one does not desert one's friends.

Rather than returning to the palace by way of Black Lion Street, Sera and I turn to the west and walk briskly toward Middle Street. Without a doubt, we are being followed. This is easily ascertained when we take a sudden turn, and the footsteps break from their quiet rhythm, hesitate, and then weave into step behind us. We test our theory two more times, and our follower maintains his pace.

In keeping with our training, we must enter a building and try to identify our pursuer. The first establishment we find with the necessary features for the task is a narrow shop on North Street containing only one window—a window the spy trailing behind us will most certainly attempt to peek through. A placard on the door reads, J. Marchant, Private Writing Master. The interior is too small for our spy to risk following us inside.

It is ideal for our purpose, maps and framed documents hang on the walls, counters are stacked with papers, handwriting samples, and booklets. The proprietor, a fusty old gentleman with an old-fashioned powdered wig, peers at us over his spectacles. Our presence is obviously an annoyance. I set my reticule on the counter. "We should like to purchase a map of Brighton."

He perks up. "You mean Brighthelmstone," he corrects. "T'was the name of the original settlement."

"Yes, but I should prefer a modern rendering."

He smirks and hands me an exquisite etching of Brighton's new streets and surrounds.

"Oh, I see." I bend over the map. Everything is labeled, even the New Ship Inn from which we have just come. "This is quite good."

"Yes," he smiles fondly at the parchment, but then his nose lifts as if the etching is too fine for the likes of me. "And the cost is two shillings, miss."

"Two shillings? That is quite dear." Having noted a shadow crossing his window, I cease dickering, purchase the map, and furtively slide the coins across the counter. With any luck, our spy will suspect we are exchanging a secret communication with the writing master.

As we leave, I lean close to Sera and ask, "Did you get a look at the man following us?"

She lengthens her stride. "No. His broad-brimmed hat shaded his face, but there was something familiar about his stride."

"I thought so, too. He will likely check inside the shop before resuming his chase. Perhaps if we double back—"

"My thoughts exactly." She tugs me into the narrow gap between buildings, and we peer out from around the corner, watching the writing master's shop. Waiting.

A few moments later, a man emerges with his hat tugged low and his high collar coat obscuring his face. He hurries down the street in the same direction we had taken. We bide our time before slipping out to follow him, allowing him enough distance that he won't notice us.

At this juncture, I wish at least one of us had brought one of the clever parasols Miss Stranje provided for us. Lacey little sun-shades, each armed with a retractable blade in the tip. Before setting out on this venture, we decided against it, thinking the frilly concoction might be too easily spotted in the event we should need to evade someone. A decision I regret.

But we are not wholly unarmed. Naturally, we always have our wits. And, of course, we each carry a pair of daggers strapped to our legs, hidden beneath our skirts.

"Now." Sera pulls me onto the street, and we follow our spy. He rushes ahead in a vain attempt to catch up with us. When he gets to the end of the cobbled road, he looks both ways, and doesn't see us. His fists double in frustration. A moment passes before he turns right, which must mean he assumes we took North Street back to the palace. We follow at a distance. But when he rushes down North and doesn't see us, he stops and stands for a moment rubbing his chin.

We press into a doorway, watching. He reverses his direction, coming straight toward us. We are sunk—about to be discovered. Sera grips my hand as if it is a lifeline.

His footsteps thud distinctively on the cobblestones. Any minute, he will pass by and we will be caught. Both of us hold our breath. I silently try to open the door latch behind us, but it is locked. I vow to pay attention next time Jane tries to teach me how to pick locks.

Except then, the sound of our pursuer's boots changes tenor. The familiar thump-thump on the walkway diminishes. Sera and I blink at each other in surprise. His footfalls are headed away from us. I dare to peek out. "He's gone."

Sera edges out behind me. "Must've turned the corner."

We stay close to the smooth stone wall as we approach the gap between buildings. I bob out to check and instantly pull back. My breath trips down my throat in an awkward gulp. "He's in the alley."

Glancing up and down the walkway, she takes stock of our surroundings. "It leads to Church Street."

"Maybe he's given up." I paste on an air of composure, brush out my skirts, and step away from the wall, so we don't look suspicious to passersby.

She taps the toe of her boot nervously against the walkway. "If so, he might be heading back to report to Lady Daneska."

"Quite likely." I check to make sure my knife is still in place before suggesting, "If we follow him, maybe we will discover where members of the Iron Crown are hiding."

She agrees, and we cautiously peer down the alley. Our spy is almost to the end of it. Surely, he will look over his shoulder before turning. Except he doesn't. Instead, he waits for a carriage to pass and darts across Church Street, entering an even narrower passage between buildings.

We steal farther down the alley and find a shadowy niche from which we can observe our quarry. He stops and pushes back his hat, revealing a familiar profile. Sera and I both stifle exclamations.

"The footman!" Sera says under her breath as if it's a curse.

"No wonder we recognized that stride." It is the same servant we had followed that very morning into the Prince's bedchamber. The same fellow who had assisted me in the kitchen.

"Traitor." Sera's voice trembles, not with fear, but outrage. It catches me off guard because she is so rarely stirred to anger. "How could he do this . . . why?"

"Money," I suggest, even though it could be a dozen other reasons. I watch, noting the fellow cannot be very well-trained because he fails to doublecheck over his shoulder before rapping on a door. Instead of being invited in, a tall broad gentleman steps out to meet him.

"Can't be!" Sera lurches back into the deep shadows and reaches for my hand.

She is right to be frightened. The man has the same fearsome height and coloring as Lord Ravencross, but even from this distance, the vibrations pulsing from him cause my stomach to tighten in a way Lord Ravencross's never could. It is as if a sudden storm gathers around us, rumbling with anger.

The sky does not darken, but my soul does.

"Ghost!" I gasp the name of our enemy, transfixed by the force of his hatred. Sera and I stand, stock still, staring in disbelief.

In that moment of shock, a hand grasps my shoulder. Startled, I spring into action. In less than a breath, Sera and I have both drawn our knives. We wheel on the perpetrator and pin him to the wall.

"Whoa!" His hands lift in surrender to the twin blades aimed at his throat.

"Kinsworth? What–?" I blink, unable to comprehend his presence. "What are you doing here? How?"

"I saw you on North Street–"

There's no time for him to finish answering. Our scuffle has aroused notice. Sera and I immediately stand down, turning our attention back to the passage across Church Street.

The footman and Ghost have spotted us.

Ghost jerks the footman up by his collar, growling curses at the man, pointing at us, showing his inept spy that we have turned the tables on him—the hunted became the hunters. The hapless servant dangles in Ghost's grasp, gesturing wildly, shaking his head.

Ghost has no interest in the man's excuses. His black glare remains on us.

The heat of his anger crackles over the cobblestones. A burning wheel, it rolls straight for us, scorching everything in its path.

I cannot look away.

Amidst his thunderous fire, I hear the telltale ping of cold steel. Ghost draws his knife. The blade flashes. And even though it should be impossible from this distance, I hear it slice through the footman's neck. Cutting gristle. Ripping through muscle. Bursting airways. Still, Ghost stares, not at his handiwork. *At us.*

At me.

"No, no, no," Sera whimpers beside me.

"God in heaven," Kinsworth mouths in a hushed tremor.

Ghost lets go of his victim. The footman's body drops to the ground. A spray of red arcs through the air, spouting like a demented fountain, making it rain blood, turning cobblestones to wine.

Ghost steps over the carcass, heading toward us, as if the footman's body is nothing more than a crumpled rug in his path.

"Run!" Sera tries to shake me loose from the hold Ghost has over me. But all I can see is death. All I can hear are silent screams of terror.

Run. Her plea brushes past my ears, moth wings fluttering by in the dark tunnel of my stupor.

"Maya!" Kinsworth commands sternly. The sound of my name on his lips stirs me from this nightmare.

He doesn't have to say it.

I run.

The three of us tear down the streets of Brighton—dusk and death chasing our souls. There is no thinking. There is simply the drawing in and out of breath, and the drumbeat of evil pounding in our wake.

We do not look back.

No casting anxious glances over our shoulders. We run. Only that. It does not matter if Ghost is chasing us. We must also outrun the horror of what we saw. We scramble over the paving stones, trampling beneath each footfall the hideousness of the slaughter we witnessed.

Sera stumbles. Kinsworth scoops her up, setting her back on her feet. Still, we run, except now I hold her hand, and guilt stings my eyes. There is a shaking in my chest. A fist-like thumping. A terrible knowing.

"It's our fault." Sera puts tear-speckled words on my wild thoughts.

"No, it's not!" Kinsworth pulls us to a stop as soon as we are inside of the palace gates. He checks behind us to make sure *he* is not following us, and then he steers us through the doors. "Come, we must get you inside."

"If only . . ." My eyes water and I cannot catch my breath. "If only we had been more careful—"

"No! Listen to me." Ben grasps my shoulders, keeping his voice low enough that only the three of us can hear. "His doing. Not yours. That footman chose to associate with a monster."

"Ghost." Sera quietly supplies the name of our monster.

"Ghost?" Lord Kinsworth lets go of me and rubs the back of his neck. "I've heard stories, but . . . he's real? Napoleon's henchman?"

She nods.

"Leader of the Iron Crown." I cannot keep the tremor out of my voice.

"If he's here in Brighton, your lives are in danger." Lord Kinsworth shepherds us up the stairs. "And from the look on his face, he intends to kill you."

"Not yet." Sera shakes her head as he guides us down the hallway. "I don't think he will yet. He needs Maya at the meeting with Napoleon. I think he . . . he meant it as a"—she shudders—"a warning to us. To Maya. A threat of things to come if she doesn't do his bidding."

Lord Kinsworth grumbles with frustration. "But if you are right, at best it is only a temporary reprieve. I will contact Miss Stranje immediately, so she can take you home. The situation here in Brighton has grown too dangerous."

We are alone in the long hall leading to our room. At Ben's high-handed edict, I stop and plant my foot firmly. "You will do nothing of the kind, Lord Kinsworth. We discussed this before. I will complete the task set before me. Miss Stranje expects nothing less, no matter the danger."

Sera crosses her arms, siding with me. "Aside from that, my lord, what makes you think we would be any safer at Stranje House? It is not an impenetrable fortress. Ghost has broken into the school in the past. He snuck into the manor, captured Tess, and carried her out to sea."

I lift my chin defiantly. "Safety is an illusion, my lord."

Lord Kinsworth's jaw clenches as he considers our argument. He stares at the painted vines crawling up the pink wallpaper. "Very well. You have a point." He admits this with an irritated huff. "But no more excursions without me. At least, you will be safe here inside the palace."

Sera and I both stifle the urge to laugh in disbelief. "*Here?*" I try not to gape as if he has suddenly lost his mind. I point at our door. "You mean, in our rooms. Where, when we unlocked our door after visiting Prince George this morning, we found Lady Daneska sitting inside? This is where you believe we will be safe?"

"Maya is right. Nowhere is safe from Ghost." Sera lowers her head as if it grieves her to admit this.

Ben rubs his neck again. Apparently, this whole discussion has given him a roaring headache.

I am finally breathing calmly. "Don't worry, my lord. We have been trained for this sort of thing. We will be prepared. Preparation is our safest course."

"Yes. Yes. *Preparation.*" He studies the carpet for a moment before brightening. I recognize that look. He has a plan. "I have it! This evening, after everyone has retired, I will come and sit guard in your room."

At our aghast expressions, he adds, "Nothing untoward, I assure you. I shall sit vigil in a chair."

I press my hand to my throat. "You most certainly will not. Oh, I know your intentions are noble, but my reputation would be in tatters, should anyone find out."

"They won't." He waves away my concerns as if I am being overly missish. "Besides, Sera will be there. You'll be properly chaperoned."

Sera gawps at him. "In our sleeping quarters? Have you run mad? As it is, I'm scarcely old enough to be considered a proper chaperone. But for two unwed young ladies to allow a gentleman into our sleeping quarters is . . . is . . ."

"Beyond the pale." I pat her arm reassuringly. "Lord Kinsworth doesn't understand." I square my shoulders and face Ben, who must be either surprisingly innocent or alarmingly naïve. "My lord, I'm afraid you sorely overestimate the benevolence of English society. If we were to allow you to stay in our rooms, tongues would wag viciously. Not only would my reputation be destroyed, but Sera's as well. We cannot possibly permit you into our bedchamber at night, no matter the circumstances." I curtsey. "Thank you, though, for your kind offer."

A puff of irritation passes over his lips. "Well, if that is the case . . ." He marches toward our room and leans against the wall, folding his arms stubbornly across his chest. "I shall be obliged to set up camp outside your door. It will not be as comfortable, nor as safe, but one cry from you inside, and I will kick the ruddy thing in and charge forth."

"To his death," Sera mumbles.

His chin juts forward. "That may be, but I'll run my sword through his gizzard first."

I cannot bear the thought of Ghost cutting Ben's throat as he did the footman's. Not that it would be as easily done. Kinsworth is nearly as tall and strong as Ghost, but he is an inexperienced fighter.

He pulses with unspent fury. The need to protect

marches through him like a troop of war horses.

I rest my fingers lightly on his clenched arms, testing a tone I hope will relax him, a soft low strum meant to lure him into a confidence I wish I felt. "There will be no need for swords through gizzards." I smile as if the two of us are standing on a peaceful shore, watching a gentle tide wash in and out. "We will be safe for now. Sera is right, Lady Daneska and Ghost need my help convincing the Prince to concede to Napoleon. We must consider our dear Prince George. He is feeling so poorly–he needs your protection and care more than ever." I infuse my words with gentleness and affection, and I hear his marching horses slow and fall asleep.

Warmth flows over him, like the sun breaking forth over a meadow after a thunderstorm. In its wake, I hear a gentle humming, as if blossoms are opening and raising their heads. Then, a deep violoncello begins to play, slowly at first, then with a melody so deep and full, it makes me want to melt into his arms.

He clasps my fingers in his, and another kind of warmth fills his eyes.

Want.

I swallow. Painfully aware of the notes I hear winding, swirling, dancing up from my own soul, singing in harmony with his. Our duet fills my mind so completely, it holds captive all other thought. Leaving me breathless. Words fail on my lips. And all I can see, are his. All I can hear is the symphony playing between us.

When I falter, unable to speak, he smiles.

That knowing smile of his is my undoing. He speaks and each word matches, with stirring precision, the beguiling notes of his violoncello. "They are going to play a waltz tonight. You must promise it to me." His voice resonates deep and smooth, a sweet wine that curls alluringly inside me. He might ask anything, and I would agree.

"Yes," I say, scarcely able to whisper, wishing he might kiss me.

The hall is empty except for Sera. Perhaps—

She unlocks our door. The click of the latch reminds me, we are not alone. Nor are we safe. This is a dangerous time to fall in love. I let go of his arm, but he keeps hold of my gloved fingers and brings them to his lips. Through the lace of my glove, I feel the press of his kiss on my fingers. "Until then," he says, and glances in our room to make sure we are not afflicted with unwanted visitors.

Until then.

As he walks away, Sera asks me, "Do you suppose he still intends to stand guard outside the door?"

I turn to her, blinking, realizing I failed to secure his promise not to do so. "I have no idea."

"I rather think he might."

"Good heavens! He manipulated me with his voice, didn't he? It should be him in the parley with Napoleon, not I."

"Was it his voice?" she asks, skepticism wrinkling each word. "Or something else?"

EIGHTEEN

SERENADING A SERPENT

"I PLACED A NOTE for Miss Stranje in our prearranged hiding spot. I sent details as to where the Iron Crown is hiding. But . . ." Sera hesitates, her hand trembles as she tries to pin my hair into place. "I didn't mention, uh, the *footman.* Miss Stranje and the others will be among the after-dinner guests tonight. We can tell her in person about, um, about *what we saw* on our return to the palace." Sera cannot bring herself to say the word for what we witnessed.

Murder.

Except, no, it was worse than that. It was cold-hearted butchery.

She carefully smooths my hair and weaves flowers into the thick coil. I watch her in the looking glass. Our eyes do not meet. She avoids my gaze because she does not want me to say anything about the gruesome death we witnessed. Judging by the unsteadiness of her hands, it still haunts her.

It certainly haunts me.

I sigh, wishing I could make it right for her somehow. If only things were different. "Just for one night," I say aloud. "Don't you wish we could be like other girls?"

"Other girls?" Her hand stills. "In what way?"

"You know, behave as other girls might do on a night such as this. Be frivolous. Carefree. Happy. Think on it, Sera. Here we are in this glorious palace. We've been invited to dine with the Prince of England. Other young ladies would be giddy with excitement, wouldn't they?"

She finishes with my hair, and I turn to grasp her hands. "And you . . . look at you! In that pale green silk, you look like a fairytale princess come to life. Shouldn't we be prattling on about our beaus? Speaking of this gentleman, or that? Speculating as to who might ask us to dance? Our greatest worry might be over a bead missing from our slippers."

She lowers her gaze to our hands. "You mean, act as if we are ordinary girls?"

"Yes. Exactly. *Ordinary* girls."

"Even though we're not?" It is a hard truth she speaks. I let go of her hands.

"I wish we could be," I mumble. "If only for just one night."

She looks up, her face alight. "We could pretend." With an impish gleam, she surprises me, and dives into the game, chattering as if she hadn't a care in the world. "Your gown is ever so pretty. Wouldn't it be lovely if Mr. Chadwick were among the guests?"

We both know he is still in London, training with Captain Grey, but I eagerly play my part.

"Yes. That would be quite diverting. Perhaps, he will

join us later this summer." I lean closer, as I imagine other girls do when sharing a secret, even though I'm quite certain she already overheard this tidbit. "Lord Kinsworth made me promise to save the waltz for him."

She laughs—a gentle, sweet, fairy-princess laugh. "He will be speechless when he sees you. Your hair shines like polished ebony, and the white flowers are like tiny stars dotting the night sky. You look magnificent, Maya. Truly."

"*Magnificent?*" I shake my head at that. "Regal, I might have believed." I glance down at my pomegranate red sari trimmed with gold embroidery, and the shimmering gold underdress, the colors of royalty in my homeland. "I am merely obeying Lady Jersey's and Lady Castlereagh's command to maintain my Indian mystique while including a nod to English fashion."

"Which is, in actuality, French fashion. But never you mind. La!" She raps me on the shoulder, reminding me that we are playing at being ordinary girls, not girls who take their marching orders from two of the most powerful women in England. "What other gentlemen do you suppose will grace His Highness's table tonight?"

"Dozens, I should think, and all of them plump in the pocket." I meant it to be a jest, to parrot what other girls must remark on. Except it slipped out before I thought the comment through. True enough, money is the thing most debutantes take into account when they encounter a potential suitor. But Sera would never be the sort of girl to consider a man's income over his character. Even when pretending.

"Oh." Her enthusiasm for the game wanes. "Perhaps I wouldn't enjoy being ordinary, after all."

"Forget their pockets," I say, trying to draw her back in, hoping to elicit that rare smile from her again. "I daresay, there will be many handsome young men. Younger sons, charming gentlemen, strong, brave, true-hearted men. Perhaps even some in their uniforms. Young men do look so dashing in their uniforms, don't you think?"

But my words trail off. Her countenance has fallen serious again.

I know my mistake. How stupid I am. Now she is thinking of the many soldiers facing the threat of Napoleon. And countless others, who have already fallen on the battlefields of Europe. Brave young men, like Georgiana's brother.

"Forgive me." I rise and hug her. "I am not very good at pretending, am I? But might we not still hope that your charming Mr. Chadwick will be there? And as for me, I intend to enjoy every single minute while waltzing with Lord Kinsworth. It is something to be happy about, and heaven knows, we have enough troubling matters. Can we not spare one evening for our happiness?"

"Yes." She straightens her shoulders. "For this one night, we shall be blissfully happy—like ordinary young ladies." She glances at the clock on the mantel. "And now we had best slip on our gloves and hurry, or they will close the dining room doors, and we shall not be allowed in at all."

We hurry down the hall, walking briskly down the stairs, and glide into the banqueting room gallery. Lord Kinsworth is there to greet us. "There you are. I was getting worried."

I smile, still pretending I am any other girl in England and he is my dashing suitor. I say nothing to relieve his anxiety. After all, ordinary young ladies are seldom concerned about members of the Iron Crown murdering them in their bedrooms. When he whispers that I look ravishing, my heart flutters joyously, and I almost believe, *for a few blessed seconds*, that I am an ordinary young lady.

Lord Kinsworth leans in and confides, "The Prince was still in bed when last I checked. I was told Lady Jersey and her husband will be acting as hosts for the night's festivities."

"The Prince must be very ill to miss a gathering such as this?" I pose the question, even though I am afraid of the answer.

Deathly ill.

I wait for him to deny my allegation, but he merely nods as if he shares my opinion. A bad-omened wind snuffs out the candle inside me. I am no longer an ordinary girl; I am a poisoner of Princes.

I wince and turn away from this disconcerting news. Across the room, Lady Jersey catches my eye. She stands at the head of the room, greeting guests. Beside her is her husband, the 5th Earl of Jersey, a tall long-nosed man, who serves as one of the Prince's chief courtiers. His eyes are as shrewd and penetrating as his wife's.

No sooner do I glance away from them, but I am met with a most unsettling sight. It feels as if a cold glove slaps my face. Lady Daneska is here! Tittering like a cheap harpsichord with the other guests. Gowned in a stunning ice-blue silk, she strolls, innocent as a lamb, on the arm of a middle-aged duke.

A serpent in sheep's clothing.

Two young pages blow trumpets to announce dinner and open the doors. Guests line up according to peerage rank and prepare to follow our hosts into the dining room. Lord Kinsworth is only a viscount, and so, with the large number of higher-ranking nobility present, we fall into the last half of the guests. Ben's uncle, Lord Harston, only a baron, stands behind us in line with Sera.

Lord Kinsworth places my limp hand on his arm and guides us into the dazzling banquet hall. "Incredible, isn't it?"

My feet falter, and I am too astonished to answer. The dining room is massive. It looks as if it was specially created to match my dress. Everything is gilded in shimmering gold, vibrant red draperies, exquisite turquoise walls, and huge tapestries of Chinese royalty. *And the table!* I have never seen such a spacious table. Above it hangs an enormous lotus blossom chandelier, held in place by a life-sized gold and silver gilt dragon coiled on the ceiling.

"Dragons, everywhere." Sera follows along beside me.

"What perversity is this?" Lord Kinsworth is staring at the table. "I am not seated beside you."

"No?" I squint at the place cards. One look at the names on the placards and I can venture a guess at who dabbled with the seating chart. I am to be pinned between an earl I do not know and Lady Daneska. It was either Lady Daneska's doing, wishing to keep me under her thumb, or Lady Jersey expecting me to maintain a close watch on Daneska.

Lord Kinsworth frowns at the arrangement. But then, his customary good humor returns. He bows over my hand before taking his leave. "Be very careful, my dear. Make certain your dinner companion doesn't slip poison into your food."

Is he being ironic?

Does he think Lady Daneska would employ trickery similar to mine? I listen for any sour notes in his voice, but cannot detect even a hint of sarcasm. No, he is innocent of such thoughts. His kindheartedness is one of the traits I admire about him. Despite the Prince's absence, Ben must still believe the herb tea I brought was intended to heal. Does that mean he is genuinely worried Lady Daneska might poison me? Or is he merely jesting? Unlike his kindheartedness, I find his incessant teasing less endearing. Too often, it leaves me confused.

I dismiss his gibe and give voice to my own dark thoughts. "You need not concern yourself, my lord. Lady Daneska would never choose so easy a death for me."

"So easy as what, *mon chérie*?" Lady Daneska whirls up beside us and loops her arm through mine, the sore arm, the one she cut open not so very long ago. "Ah! *Thiz* must be your handsome *fiancé*, about which I have heard *zo* much." She is affecting a heavy French accent even though Lady Daneska is Prussian, from the Dukedom of Pomerania.

I smile as if we are old friends. "Yes, and he was just suggesting I be on guard lest you try to poison me. I assured him you would never choose so gentle a demise for me."

"Ho-ho, my dear, Miss Barrington, how very amusing you are." Her laugh is so brittle, it sounds as if the wine glasses are shattering. She raps me on my arm. "Ah, but where are your manners. You must introduce me to your charming fiancé?"

Why is it we must helplessly bow to English customs?

Here stands my mortal enemy, an enemy to England. A woman, who in all likelihood, will someday run that infernal dagger of hers, which she has cleverly concealed in her elbow-length glove, into my heart.

And twist it.

Yet, I must yield to social conventions and introduce this beguiling traitor to a man loyal to his country, true of heart—a man I quite like. *And if I survive this confounded dinner*, a man I hope to waltz with. A man whose kisses I crave, whose inward songs are pure ambrosia to my soul.

Lord Kinsworth bows elegantly to the wicked little serpent, oblivious to the dangerous hiss of her forked tongue.

She curtseys in return, fanning her long luxurious eyelashes at him and smiling her pert little minx smile. My fists clench into two throbbing maces. I have an overpowering urge to wallop her in the neck.

I could easily do it.

She is exposing more than enough of her lily-white throat as she slowly rises. One quick thrust to her windpipe and she would fall gasping to her death. Except, then there would be no waltzing with Lord Kinsworth later, and God only knows what scaffold they would hang me from for killing one of Prince George's guests.

Sera rests a hand on my shoulder as if to remind me there are places for thrusts to the throat, and the Prince's royal dining room is not one of them. Lord Kinsworth stares speculatively at me as if he, too, knows what I am thinking.

I flush with hot shame. My character is slipping deeper into hell every day. Now, not only am I a poisoner of Princes, I now find myself contemplating murder.

There is an odd quirk to Ben's mouth, and he breaks into a grin. One of his dangerous grins, the same roguish smile bound to win him *a sigh and a swoon* from any female within a six-yard radius, including any young ladies, their mothers, their grandmothers, their great aunts, and, *apparently*, me.

He bends close to my ear before dashing away. "Remember to save the waltz for me."

As if I had forgotten.

Our hosts take their places, and we are obliged to take ours. Ben is seated four seats down and across the table from me, near enough to see, but too far away to overhear or even guess what he might be saying to Miss Applewhite, the stunning English beauty seated next to him.

"This is your doing," I say to Daneska, feeling even more murderous than I had two minutes earlier.

She leans close to my ear. "Lord Kinsworth is right. It *would* be rather easy to sprinkle a little arsenic in your food." She titters, as if she has just shared a scandalous morsel of gossip, and indicates a large topaz ring on her pointer finger. "See, I need only flip it open over your crab soup."

"I, too, have a ring." I show her the far more subtle ruby studded poison ring encircling my middle finger.

Her eyebrow lifts only a fraction of an inch. "Ah, I see. So, you do. Shall we call a truce, *mon chérie*, and eat in peace?"

I sniff. But when Lady Daneska alters her voice to a mellow contralto, as she is doing now, I find it difficult to

contemplate using my poison ring. Even thoug
only armed with a sleeping potion. "Very well. Tr

Except, I am no fool. She cannot be trusted.

"And in the spirit of our truce, I will admit to you I had nothing to do with these abominable seating arrangements. Were it my choice, there are any number of guests I would rather be seated next to—your handsome *fiancé*, for example." She sets her lips in a flirtatious smirk and peers down the table at Lord Kinsworth. "He is a rather delectable crumpet, isn't he?"

With a huff of irritation, I snap back at her. "I thought you had your own crumpet to worry about."

She clamps her teeth together in a bitter attempt to smile. "My darling naïve girl, no one would ever describe my beloved lord as a *crumpet*."

Beloved? I shudder, remembering Ghost's latest cruel act. "No, I suppose not." I do my best to sip a spoonful of crab bisque, but it tastes oddly of blood.

I pour it back in the bowl, having lost my appetite for soup. "But I must warn you, no one who knows Lord Kinsworth would ever call him by that term either."

"No?" Her brow arches suggestively.

"No," I say flatly, refusing to let her lure me into one of her verbal gambits.

Lady Daneska is not easily quelled. She ignores my cold retort and tilts her head, studying my fiancé with even sharper interest, holding her now empty spoon to her lips as if toying with the idea of what it would be like to kiss him.

I squint at her, seriously reconsidering the merits of applying a sleeping potion to her bisque. Instead, I bait her. "I noticed today that your *beloved* is here in Brighton."

Her spoon lowers with a gratifying suddenness. Her inner music collides with a screech into the next note, and her smug falsetto ends in a discordant heap. "What?" she squeaks.

What, indeed.

I cannot keep my lips from spreading in triumph. "Oh?" I say, feigning surprise. "Did you not know he was in town?"

"Of course, I did!" Glowering at me, she mutters a string of Slavic curse words and plunks her spoon down without any grace at all. "More to the point, how did *you* find out?"

I shrug. "Sera and I were strolling along Church Street, and . . ." I did not need to say more.

"*Mon Dieu.*" She winces. She now realizes what Ghost already knows; the Iron Crown will need to move their quarters. Except, we are one step ahead of her. Miss Stranje will have already posted someone to watch and see what hole they crawl into next.

"He won't be happy." Lady Daneska slumps and stares at her half-eaten soup as if the chunks of crab meat are to blame for her problems.

She simmers with such clanging annoyance I refrain from mentioning the fate of her footman spy. A moment or two later she turns to me and in a rare hum of sincerity, asks, "Why, Maya? Why is it you cannot behave like a good little girl and do as you are told?"

A hundred answers thunder through my mind.

Hypocrite! Pot calling the kettle black. Why can YOU not do as you are told? And it depends on <u>who</u> is telling me to do <u>what</u>. Not to mention, your notion of good and mine are *drastically different. Besides, I am not a little girl.*

In the end, I give up and shrug. "Is it not obvious? My father sent me away to a reform school. What did you expect?"

One corner of her mouth curves upward as if she finds my answer mildly amusing. "I keep forgetting you are all trouble makers."

"And you are not?"

She laughs. For once, it does not sound like breaking glass. It is round and full. Genuine. Something I had never heard her do before. "Oh, my dear," she says. "You have no idea."

In that moment, I almost like her. *Almost.* But then, she turns away dismissively and spends the next two courses chattering flirtatiously with the elderly earl seated on her left. We are halfway through our roast pheasant when a hush falls over the room. Spoons and forks are set aside. Here, at the far end of the table, I cannot tell what is happening. People toward the front push back their chairs and begin to rise.

The head footman announces him, and Prince George strides into the room. There is vigor in his step and a broad smile on his noble face. He is flushed, to be sure, but other than that he looks remarkably robust and healthy.

All of us stand to bow or curtsey.

"Sit! Sit." He spreads his arms wide as if embracing us all. "My friends! Please, sit and eat! Enjoy your meal." Servants quickly move aside dishes and clear a space for him at the head of the table. "*We* are feeling quite splendid! Better than splendid. *Marvelous.* In point of fact, we have not felt this well for some years."

He strains up on his toes, stretching, searching for someone until his gaze lands upon me. "Ah, yes! There she is." He points at me. "The young lady responsible for our recovery." He reaches for a glass of wine and raises it aloft. "A toast to Miss Barrington, whose brilliant tea has done miracles for my constitution. Miracles!" Prince George's hearty laughter booms across the massive banqueting hall.

Miracles? A miracle he is well, yes.

But for England—

Disaster!

The meeting with Napoleon will take place too soon for Captain Grey and the others to intervene.

"Huzzah! To His Highness's good health." Lord Jersey is the first to join in. His wife seconds his sentiment and glances furtively in my direction. In a chorus of cheers, we all raise our glasses. Lord Kinsworth wears a proud smile and nods in my direction. I have pleased him—not my objective.

How could this have gone so terribly wrong?

That blood cleanser was so stringent it ought to have made him sick for days.

Days!

Unless . . . *unless it was precisely what he needed.* My hand shakes so violently, it is difficult to keep my wine from spilling.

Lady Daneska turns to me as we take our seats. "Well done, Miss Barrington. Perhaps you are not so naughty, after all."

No. Not nearly naughty enough.

A complete failure.

I school my thoughts. At least the Prince is not dead

or dying. That is no small consolation. Still, my heart sinks, humming the dour notes of a mournful oboe. I pick up my fork but lower it back to the plate. My appetite has turned to dust.

How many days do I have left to live?

Two?

Three?

Perhaps, as many as four?

NINETEEN

ONE WALTZ BEFORE DYING

I EAT WITHOUT tasting. My eyes stare at the glittering surroundings without seeing. People chatter, clink their silver and tap their glasses, but all the sounds blur into one sad low hum. Dinner ends, and we are ushered into the ballroom. Music is playing. Something lively. A young Austrian duke that I'd met previously in London, approaches, bows, and asks me to partner with him on the dance floor.

I want to say, no. Can you not see, I am in mourning? I have failed England. My friends are in deadly peril.

Instead, I nod and allow him to guide me out onto the floor. I have no idea how my feet remember the steps. My mind feels like a gnat buzzing a thousand miles above my body. Even the music seems far away as if it is being played in another valley. Luckily, we are too busy skipping and clapping for my partner to notice that I have no conversation. I smile politely when I see his lips moving, but I do not hear the words.

Lord Kinsworth dances past us, and leans close to my ear, "Remember the waltz belongs to me."

His words rouse me somewhat and draw my mind closer to the dance floor. I watch his broad shoulders as he moves down the line. Sometime tonight, those arms will hold me. I will be able to waltz with him before I die. *There.* That is something to hold on to. My heart remembers how to beat properly, and the music seems to play a little louder, a little brighter.

I grow steadily more aware of my surroundings. I notice Sera standing off to the side of the other guests, in deep conversation with Lady Jersey and Miss Stranje. Miss Stranje's expression shifts abruptly. Instead of a wily hawk, she swells and darkens, looking more like the terrifying Steppe eagle from my country, feathers ruffled, beak poised, and on the hunt.

My dance partner loops his arm through mine and skips with me in a circle. When our headmistress comes back into view. She is searching the guests with vengeance in her eyes. I can guess who she hunts.

Lady Daneska.

What can Miss Stranje do if she finds her? She can't very well drag the lady out of the room by the hair. She might deliver a stern lecture, but ringing a peal over Lady Daneska's head will do no good. She has chosen her path. As I have mine. Our dim futures aside, Miss Stranje's former student seems to have vanished from the ballroom.

Lord Kinsworth and his partner sashay past us, drawing my attention back to this frivolous country reel. I find myself taking an inexplicable dislike to Miss Applewhite. She, with her cherry blossom cheeks and bouncing yellow ringlets—he ought to have asked someone else to dance. She is so patently helpless, so absurdly English. Must she titter and blush at every comment he makes?

I turn to my partner and smile broadly. He is handsome, and his inner tune is a steady predictable rat-a-tat-tat snare beat. I suppose I ought to be dazzled by his elegant manners, his dark hair, his regal superfine coat, and smart-ish eyes. *I ought to be.* Trouble is, I keep glancing down the line of dancers, hoping to see unruly honey brown curls, to catch a glimpse of a certain someone's impish smirk, his eyes glinting with mischief, and the music of his elusive soul teasing and running away.

The set ends, and I have no time to escape before Lady Jersey's nephew requests my hand for the next set. I manage to smile politely, but all the time I am wondering, *how long?*

How long until they play the waltz?

The answer to that question is one hour and thirteen minutes. I know because I counted each slow-ticking second. Also, there is a massive gold-gilded clock on the fireplace mantel which I checked before, after, and during each turn in the dance set.

At last, the musicians tune their instruments for a promenade. I stand on the sidelines and rock up onto my toes, peering out across the crowd, searching for the one face I want to see more than any other, listening for the melting notes of his inner music, wondering if he, too, hears the promenade beginning.

He taps my shoulder. I know it is him before I even turn around, I recognize the way his touch ripples through me and strikes my soul, making it ring with delight. I whirl around, unable to keep from beaming at him.

Without a word, he bows and holds out his arm.

Finally.

I'm not sure why dancers must promenade before a waltz, except it is the custom, and who am I to argue with English customs? The waltz is considered scandalous by the more prudish matrons in the *beau monde*, but not so here, not in the Prince's domain. Here, it is *de rigueur*—all the rage. Prince George adores anything teetering on the edge of scandal. And so, we brazen couples march around the ballroom floor as near to the walls as possible, marking out our territory. Mayhaps it is a polite way of saying to the other guests, *step back, please, this is where we intend to perform this outrageous dance.*

Here is the delicious part, his arm is around my waist the whole time. Lord Kinsworth leans down and whispers, "I am delighted to see Lady Daneska did not poison you, after all."

I pretend to be astonished at the news. "Apparently not. Although . . ." I squint as if suddenly finding it difficult to see. "Now that you mention it, the candlelight does seem to be dimming unexplainably, and I profess to a certain amount of dizziness. Any moment, I may collapse."

He tightens his hold around my waist. "You needn't fear. I will catch you if you faint. Although, I suspect it isn't poison making you swoon. I've been told I have that effect on ladies."

I try not to smile.

Truly.

But that confounded grin of his does me in. Besides, it feels good to laugh. And why should I not? If these are to be my last days, I ought to soak up every minute of joy left to me.

The waltz begins in full, and Lord Kinsworth swoops me up in his arms. We fly around the room, soaring to the accompaniment of the music. Every measure lifts our hearts higher. We leave speech adrift on the wind. No need for words. Our souls are singing in perfect harmony, beating as if we are one person instead of two. Whirling so fast, everything else is forgotten.

There is only music.

Our music.

And this divine lightness of our souls.

I savor the feel of his strong arms guiding me, holding me as if I am a rare and delicate treasure. We glide into another turn, and he murmurs against my cheek, "My beautiful nightingale."

Once again, I wonder, if he can read my mind? What is it about him, this *rahasy*, this puzzling man who has captured my soul? His words skate through me, etching a tune of joy on my entire being, warming me, even though I shiver. And with that shiver, a new thought races into my mind, overpowering all else—a crashing cymbal, a gong of awakening.

I do not want to die!

Not now.

Never in my life have I felt this incredible sense of being wanted. How can I give up this euphoria, this happiness?

I cannot.

Losing all of this is unthinkable.

He whisks me into a close turn, and I cannot stop myself from asking him, "What if we were to run away?"

"Run—?" Kinsworth misses a step. He stops to correct it and stares down at me. "But what of Miss Stranje and your assignment? The Prince and—"

"Why are you saying this now?" I shake my head. "Earlier today you wanted to send me away to Stranje House. What if we ran away instead? Right now. Tonight."

He tries to catch up to the music, but his timing is off, he misses another step. "Maya?" He stares at me as if he cannot believe I am saying such things. "Do you know what you are suggesting?"

Yes! I am suggesting I stay alive for more than three days. I am suggesting we choose happiness over our duty. Over England. Over . . .

The foolishness of this thought crashes over my head—a cold soaking wave of reason. If England falls to Napoleon, what joy would either of us have? What future?

I am a fool.

There is only one hope. If I love Kinsworth, I must go to this meeting with Napoleon, and I must persuade the Prince to hold on to his people's future, to Kinsworth's future, to Miss Stranje's and my father's future.

No matter the cost.

I am a bird in a cage. I must sing to save my friends.

A lump swells in my throat, threatening to strangle me. The music no longer warms me. It burns. Every note, a scorching reminder of lost joy. I turn away from Ben's imploring eyes and focus on the walls as they blur past.

Deafened by grief rising from my soul, blinded by a

keening hopelessness, I fail to notice the odd stillness invading the ballroom. A few seconds pass before I realize our waltz has slowed. Two couples near us have stopped dancing altogether. I snap to attention in time to see the Prince wending his way across the dance floor. He taps Lord Kinsworth on the shoulder. Ben seems as startled as I.

"A word, Lord Kinsworth, if you please." Prince George inclines his head to me. "Apologies, Miss Barrington, for the intrusion. Your fiancé is needed on an urgent matter."

Kinsworth seems flustered. "Certainly, Sir."

"Good man." Prince George claps Ben on the shoulder but continues to address me in a cryptic hushed tone. "Bye the bye, Miss Barrington, if you would be so good as to stand ready near first light, your assistance may be needed as well." He taps the side of his nose as if we are playing a game of charades. "Mind, we are not yet certain, but it may be."

I can guess what game is actually at play. I curtsey to indicate my obedience. "I am yours to command, Sir."

Lord Kinsworth offers me his arm and guides me off the ballroom floor. "We will discuss that other, er, *matter* later."

Too late.

There is only one path now.

And because I love you, only one choice.

I lift my hand in a silent farewell as he follows the Prince through a side door.

First light will be upon us in only a handful of hours. I've preparations to make. Where is Sera? And Miss Stranje? She must be advised immediately. I hurry off to find my companions, my fellow soldiers, in this bloodless battle we are waging.

Bloodless for now.

Unless we do something, it won't stay that way for long.

I push blindly through the peacock-y guests, hunting for my friends. Listening for their voices above all the other pointless clucking. Where are they? I stop and lean up, sorting through all the noise until I hear Miss Stranje's comforting cadence, and follow the sound as a deer runs towards the stream.

The three of them are cloistered in a quiet corner of the room. As soon as I approach, Miss Stranje looks up, and concern furrows her brow. "What is it? What's wrong?"

I cannot help myself; I clutch her arm. Except I am not a child, I must be braver than that, a warrior. A lioness. I let go and marshal my emotions. "Prince George intends to meet Napoleon in the early hours of this very morning."

"*This* morning?" Lady Jersey narrows her goldfish eyes at me and blinks rapidly as if, *surely*, I must be mistaken. "You're certain?"

"Yes." I lift my chin. "He instructed me to be prepared to leave at first light."

"Oh, of all the pigs' bottoms in all the world! Why must that addle-pated twit be at the helm of . . ." She clamps her lips tight for a moment, and her neck flushes a fiery shade of red. "This won't do. It won't do at all."

She flips open her fan and waves it so fast it creates a breeze. "I lay this at your door, Miss Barrington. Good heavens, child, you practically healed the man entirely.

We were better off before your attempt to poison him. Perhaps you should concoct more tea and this time make it a bit more deadly–"

"She'll do nothing of the kind." Miss Stranje glares at Lady Jersey.

Our grand patroness purses her lips, her tinny war drums patter with irritation. But to her credit, rather than attacking, she backs off, fanning herself.

Miss Stranje pats my arm protectively as if bracing me for a fistfight, but she addresses the others. "At this point, we must rely on Miss Barrington's persuasive skills. She is our best and only weapon."

One of Lady Jersey's brows arches skeptically.

Miss Stranje ignores her. "Tonight, just before we left the inn to come to the palace, our runner returned with an answer from Captain Grey. Given the change in the situation, he and his men plan to sail the new steamship and intercept Napoleon as soon as possible. Unfortunately, it will be two more days before the ship is seaworthy. It seems unlikely they will get here in time."

"Highly unlikely." Sera rubs her chin while calculating the possibilities. "Even with steam powering the warship, they'll be sailing against the tide once they pass Margot. Unless they leave port immediately, it would be impossible for them to arrive in our waters in time to stop Napoleon."

"There you have it." Miss Stranje turns back to me. "We are relying upon you, my dear Maya." She places her hand on my shoulder, warm and reassuring, it hums through me, infusing me with some of her strength. "Do not forget how skillfully you infiltrated the Iron Crown Stronghold in France."

"Oh yes," Lady Jersey mutters. "I'd nearly forgotten the stronghold incident. Hmm," She collapses her fan and surveys me with more respect.

"Yes. And it was no small feat. Miss Barrington lived and worked right under their noses for several days." Miss Stranje consults her small pocket watch. "And now it is almost two. Which means, we only have three hours till sunrise." She snaps it shut. "I suggest you retire straightway, Maya. You must prepare for the most important battle of your life. Lady Jersey, Sera, and I will remain here to discuss options. If we devise a new strategy, we'll send word to you immediately."

Before I turn to go, Sera snags me in a brief but fierce hug. She whispers something, but I cannot quite hear her words. Fear is hissing too loud in my ears.

I slip out of the ballroom and make my way down the dimly lit corridors to our rooms. Unlocking the door, I half expect Lady Daneska to be waiting inside. Perhaps I am hoping she will be there and put an end to my turmoil. But the room is profoundly empty. I am alone. All alone, except for the distant sound of music echoing through the palace, and the muted song of darkness outside my window.

I ought to change into traveling garments, but what does one wear for a clandestine meeting with the Emperor of France and the Prince of England?

Dressing can wait.

I must calm my mind. As Miss Stranje said, I must prepare. *Meditate.* I move closer to the window. The night is a deep black and full of the thick stillness of the hour. I do not light the lamps because the moon and stars are more soothing candles. The moon perches low on the horizon, a lovely crescent with sharp points on both ends, just like my choices. There is no easy way for this mission to end.

My reverie is cut short by a tapping at the window—a tapping that cannot, should not, be possible. We are two tall stories up, and yet the tapping persists. A bird, perhaps? But no, I sense a much larger being. And the songs emanating from beyond the glass, though dark and unsettling, are surprisingly familiar.

I open the sash and look down into the face of my friend. "Tess! What—?"

"Don't just stand there," she growls. "Lend me a hand."

I clasp her wrist, and with one quick movement, she lunges over the mantel and leaps onto the floor beside me.

"How did you—?" I poke my head out of the window and stare down at the terrifying distance to the ground, and not a rope in sight. Turning, I gawk at Tess. Clothed in a midnight blue running dress and with her dark wavy hair, she looks like Mother Night herself. I give up on the question of *how*. It is, after all, Tess.

I lean out of the window again, to see if anyone is following her. "Is Lord Ravencross with you?" I heard he took rooms here in Brighton.

"No." She frowns at me as if I've gone daft. "Why would he be?"

I don't know. I am still surprised to see her climbing by herself in the dark. I wonder if her fiancé has any idea she goes out in the middle of the night and does things, like climbing the palace walls. If he knows, does it worry him? I accidentally blurt the last. "Doesn't he worry about you?"

"Phfft." She scowls at me as if I am being foolish. "He says it's everyone else who is in danger when I'm around."

And he is right. Which brings me to a more pressing question. "What are you doing here?"

She turns away and brushes the dust off of her black leggings. When she finally straightens, I see by her expression and hear in the low woeful notes plunking from her soul, that whatever news brought her here, it will be bad tidings.

"I woke from a dream," she begins.

This cannot be good.

"Tell me," I say, busying myself with lighting a lamp on a nearby table; not at all certain I truly wish to hear about a dream that made her climb a two-story palace wall in the middle of the night.

Tess fiddles with the dagger strapped to her thigh, before facing me squarely. "It's a trap," she blurts.

I drop onto the end of the bed and sit, hands folded in my lap, preparing for the worst, and calmly ask, "What do you mean *a trap*? Explain."

"I don't know. You know how my wretched dreams are." Tess shoves back a lock of her dark hair. "Nothing is ever perfectly clear. It's always as if I'm in a fog." She steps back into the shadows, drawing a deep breath as if it might banish whatever vision haunts her. "Then, suddenly, I see things. And . . ."

And she feels things.

Awful things. People dying. Tess often wakes screaming. She told me once that it is as if she is the person being killed. I can't imagine living through such horrors.

"What did you see?"

"You. You're going out in a rowboat tonight, aren't you?" She says this in an accusatory tone as if I am doing something shameful. "With the Prince."

"Yes, Prince George has summoned me." I stare up at her. "We are to meet Napoleon. I suppose the meeting could be at sea. I do not know. Although, we won't be leaving for the parley until early morning."

"You can't go. It's a trap. You have to stop them. If you don't, Ghost will capture the Prince. At least, *I think* that's what will happen. I saw Ghost there. And Daneska." She thumps her fist against her thigh counting off the participants in her nightmare. "You're there, Lord Kinsworth, Prince George, and there's a gun." She frowns and looks away.

"A gun? Who has the gun? Ghost?"

She nods, staring blindly into the shadows. Tess's inner music is often more than I can bear. Tonight, the turmoil inside her erupts like waves smashing against rocks, cymbals crashing, violins scraping wildly. "He shoots. Everything was so dark, but I saw a flash of fire from the barrel, smoke, choking smoke, and . . ." She covers her eyes with her hands. "There's blood, Maya, so much blood."

"Wait. *It's dark?*" I rap my fingers soundlessly against the bed covers. "You say it is dark in this dream. These things occur at night?"

"Yes. What of it?"

Hope sings through me. I sit forward. "Then it cannot be today's meeting. We do not leave the palace until first light. *Dawn.* You see? It will no longer be dark."

She slants her head, listening intently. I hear a little

of my hope spilling into her.

I press forward. "Most likely, your dream warns of a future event. Another night. I'm certain it must be foretelling what occurs a few days *after* the meeting with Napoleon."

"No!" She whirls in close and glares at me. "No. It felt immediate. Urgent. It has to be tonight—I'm sure of it."

"But that is impossible." I point at the window she just came through. "*This* night is nearly gone. It will be light in three or four hours."

"I don't understand." She shakes her head. "The sense of it all going horribly wrong felt so strong. I didn't even wait to tell Miss Stranje. She hadn't yet returned to the inn. I ran straight here."

Her words confirm what I have already guessed. Tess knew nothing about the sudden change in the Prince's parley with Napoleon. "What of Napoleon? Did you see him in the dream?"

Tess shakes her head. I stand and moderate my voice, using soothing notes to calm her agitation. "Miss Stranje is still in the ballroom with Sera and Lady Jersey. Would you like me to go and get them?"

"No." She slumps into a chair. "I must be mistaken. Except it seemed so real, so immediate."

I scoot a dressing chair close and sit next to her. "Tell me what you saw exactly."

"I told you. You were in a small boat with Lord Kinsworth, the Prince, and someone else, maybe more than one—I don't know. Then, suddenly, you are standing on the deck of a tall ship. A sloop of war, I think. And Ghost is there." She rakes her fingers through her hair. "Were you expecting him to be present at the negotiations?"

"It has always been a possibility. He is, after all, leader of Napoleon's Iron Crown. Although, I rather thought he'd be lurking behind the scene, hidden in some secret lair, keeping his presence inconspicuous."

One brow arches, and she looks askance at me. "Oh, he is there, all right. Very much so."

"It was always a concern. But what else did you see?"

"That's the trouble with dreams. They're so maddening!" She paces in a tight circle, the same way Miss Stranje's wolf-dogs do when they are agitated. "If only they were clear—laid out logically. Instead, all I see are flickers, bursts of things happening." She explodes her fists to illustrate the suddenness of her apparitions. "Smells. Noise. Then, there's always the blood. And . . . and . . . pain." Her face twists with unseen agony and the vibrations from her soul tear at my heart.

I bow my head, afraid to ask my next question, but knowing the only thing that would send her into a panic this intense would be death. "Who died in your dream?" My words come out as a hoarse whisper. I look up and ask more boldly, "Who died?"

Tess looks away and doesn't answer. There's no need.

It is me.

She has seen my death.

Worse, she lived through my death. And then, in cymbal crash of fear, it strikes me matters might be even worse. "Aside from me, did anyone else—?"

She still cannot meet my gaze.

"Tess," I demand, in a stern voice. "Did you see anyone else get killed?"

She shakes her head. "No, but I woke up right after you . . ."

Died.

I breathe out with relief. "It is all right, Tess." I reach for her hand. "Your vision must have been pointing to what happens after the parley. Ghost will be angry when I do not convince Prince George to submit to Napoleon's terms." Bowing my head for a moment to bridle in my own sadness, I add, "I have expected this. It is the path I must walk. The path I have chosen to walk." I hush the mourning song rising from the deep in my soul.

In its place, I force hymns of peace and acceptance into my next words. "Tess, listen to me. I am not afraid to die. I leave no regrets behind. None. Except for this one thing; I am sorry you had to experience it."

"But that's why I'm here." She yanks her hand out of mine, her jaw clenching and unclenching. "Don't you see? We can stop him—stop Ghost from killing you. We can make something different happen. We've done it before. We can change things."

Can we?

You have such an English way of thinking, I say to myself and sadly tuck a few wayward strands of her brown hair behind her ear. I remember *Naanii* bidding me farewell as we stood on the banks of the Tawi. "*Be strong, my child. The river of life takes us where it will, and we must be at peace wherever the current carries us.*"

The river has carried me here.

"I am not so sure." I shake my head. "I have witnessed the force of Ghost's anger. Ghost will take his revenge, sooner or later. It is inevitable. I have accepted my fate. At least, we know it does not happen tonight."

Her eyes widen as if stunned at my words. "No!" She surges toward me. "You're wrong. It *isn't* after the parley." She stares at my gown. "In the dream, you're wearing this!" She grabs a handful of the scarlet cloth. "This! And your hair looked exactly as it does now. It's tonight! Don't you see? Napoleon is not on that ship. It *is* a trap!"

Before I can answer, a soft knock sounds at my door.

"Quick. Hide," I whisper, and dim the oil lamp.

Silent as a breeze, Tess dashes across the room and presses against the wall behind the door. I turn the knob and crack it open.

"Lord Kinsworth." Frightened though I am by Tess's foreboding, my soul surges with joy at the mere sight of him. A wild wishful hope whistles through my mind. *Has he come to discuss my offer to run away?*

He presses gently on the door, attempting to widen the gap, but I only allow it to open an inch or two more. He leans closer. "The Prince sent me for you. We have to leave sooner than expected. You must come with me. They're waiting for us on the shore."

"Now?" My mouth falls open, and I battle for words. "But. . . it is still dark." *Just as was in Tess's dream. It is happening now.*

Death comes tonight.

My legs weaken, and I clutch the handle. Glancing sideways, I see Tess's face contorted in remembered pain.

"Maya? What is it?" Ben presses against the door again. "Is someone there?"

"No!" I lie. "No. It is only that this seems so peculiar. Do you not find it odd that we must sneak out in the middle of the night? Why the sudden change?" I wedge out of the opening and pull the door behind me, leaving it only slightly ajar. Standing this close, looking up into his eyes, I smell the fading starch of his cravat, the spicy scent of his skin, and I hear the excited thrumming of his heart. Kinsworth is eager. He has finally found the adventure he craves.

He speaks in such a rush I can barely follow. "We received another note from Napoleon. Written in his own hand and sealed with the Emperor's stamp. I saw it myself before Prince George broke the seal. *Napoleon Emperor Des Français Roi d'Italie Protecteur de la Confederation du Rhine.*" Kinsworth is proud of himself for having memorized Napoleon's crest.

"And this note, what did it say?" I cannot keep the skepticism and dread out of my voice. All too well, I remember Lady Daneska is a talented forger and that in the past she had accessed Napoleon's stationery.

Kinsworth smooths his hands up and down my arms as if I am the one shivering with excitement rather than him. "Napoleon says he has grown weary of battle. He's convinced that he and Prince George, alone, as the two heads of Europe, will be able to negotiate an amicable end to this war." He leans down next to my ear, his voice a breathless whisper. "At this very moment, Bonaparte is anchored off our coast, waiting to meet with Prince George. Think of it, Maya. It's finally going to happen. After all these years of fighting, the Prince is going to broker a peace treaty. And you and I will be a part of it. This will be something to tell our children and our children's children."

Yours, perhaps. I will not survive this night.

There will be no children for me.

He kisses me. It catches me by surprise. How did he

find my mouth so suddenly?

The kiss is urgent, his mouth warm, pulsing with exuberance, and I taste the brandy he must have recently drunk with the Prince. Sinking into his arms, his lips make me forget for a moment that I am about to face death. The longer we kiss, the more I wish this moment did not have to end.

I lied to Tess. I *do* have regrets.

I regret there will be no more of these kisses. No more time with Ben. Or with Sera, or Tess, or Georgie and Jane—my sisters. No chance to win back my father's affection. I am leaving them all behind, everyone I love. *I must.* There is no future for any of them if we do not deal with the threat to England.

But Tess's warning rings again in my ears. *Napoleon is not there.* If she is right, if this is a ruse, a trap, our going accomplishes nothing. Worse, it will seal all of our fates. We will have played straight into the Iron Crown's hand. I pull away from his kiss.

Before I can speak, he grasps my arm. "Come. We must hurry. I'm to row all of us out to the Emperor's sloop. The Prince has entrusted me to do this for him. Can you believe it, Maya? *Me.*"

"Of course, he trusts you. As do I." I touch his cheek, smoothing my fingers over his stubbled jaw, memorizing every line. "But how can you be certain Prince George will be safe? What if this is a ploy to capture him?"

Kinsworth shakes his head. "No, you don't understand how these things work. Napoleon gave his word. He may be many things, but he is a man of his word. It is the promise of an Emperor to a Prince. Such pledges must be honored. Respected." He pauses, waiting for me to relent. I cannot hide my doubt, and Ben frowns sternly at me. "I have to do this, Maya. I must—"

"But—"

"Stop. I understand you are frightened." His jaw flexes, and his head tilts in warning. "His Highness knows the risks. My uncle and I warned him of the potential dangers. But Prince George believes this is the only way to spare England. He intends to go with or without our assistance. He is our Regent, ruler of Britain, and he has asked for my help and yours. You knew this day would come, Maya. It is the reason he invited you here. A royal request. Whether you choose to do your duty or not, I am his trusted servant, and I *will* do as our sovereign wishes."

The door opens, and Tess steps out. "I am coming with you."

TWENTY

DEATH'S DARK DRUMS

FOOTSTEPS BRUSH against the carpet at the entrance to the hallway, I turn to see Sera hurrying toward us. She takes in our odd congregation, and though still several strides away, she begins questioning. "Tess? What's wrong? Why are you here?"

Tess, her mouth fixed in a grim expression, says nothing, which leaves me to explain. "The parley with Napoleon is taking place sooner than we had expected."

Sera closes in on our circle and quietly asks, "How much sooner?"

This time, Tess deigns to answer, her words rumble out as a growl. "*He* says we have to leave *now*."

"*We?* I think not." Lord Kinsworth is still frowning at Tess and her strange garb. "Does everyone know what we're doing?" He gestures at Sera. "Perhaps we should call a page and have him announce His Highness's secret meeting to everyone in the ballroom."

Tess scoffs. "Daresay, he'd be safer if we did."

Sera turns to Lord Kinsworth. "Why must you leave so soon? And that still doesn't explain why you're here." She frowns at Tess. Sera's inner cadence plinks rapidly, weaving through a complex tune, fitting all the pieces into place until she concludes it must have been a dream that brought Tess to us, a dream with a dire warning. "Oh." Her face draws up in alarm.

"Tess is concerned we might be heading into a trap." I keep my voice low and just cryptic enough to confirm Sera's suspicions without offending Lord Kinsworth any more than he already is. "She insists on coming with me to the rendezvous."

"Good." Sera takes a deep breath and straightens. "And as I told you earlier, I will accompany you, as well. I will not allow you to do this alone."

So that was what she said to me as I was leaving the ballroom.

"*Alone?* Miss Barrington is hardly alone. I'm here. And at this rate, I'll need to hire a barge to transport all of you." Lord Kinsworth turns his gaze up to the ceiling as if asking heaven to grant him patience. "Be reasonable, ladies. We can't all go traipsing down to the beach in the middle of the night."

"We *are* being reasonable, Lord Kinsworth." Sera's calm manner astonishes me. "A young lady venturing out of the palace at this hour without being properly chaperoned would be most unseemly. I assure you, Prince George will expect a young lady, such as Miss Barrington, to be accompanied by no less than her maid and a suitable companion."

Lord Kinsworth opens his mouth to argue, but Sera continues in a most officious tone. "It will only take a moment for me to collect my wrap. The air in the early morn can be quite brisk even this time of year." She has taken charge exactly as Miss Stranje would have done. "Maya, wouldn't you prefer to wear something additional, something warmer, perhaps?"

Sera pushes open the door to our bedroom, and I edge away from Lord Kinsworth. "Wait for us. We will only be a minute or two." The three of us hurry into the bedroom and open the wardrobe. I am quite certain Sera's real concern has nothing to do with warmth. It was nearly impossible to hide much in the way of weaponry beneath this ballgown. I do not mean to cast dispersion upon the many alternative uses for a lady's shawl in prickly situations, but we need to arm ourselves with something slightly more lethal than a silk wrap.

In the dim light, I glimpse the flash of metal. It is not an additional dagger Sera is holstering under her skirt—it is a small single-shot pistol primed with ball and wad. She glances up at me. "Miss Stranje has been teaching me. It isn't much. Only one shot, but it may come in handy."

Less than three minutes pass before we emerge from the room. Time enough to conceal a small pistol and strap on several extra daggers. "We are ready." I force a smile as if we are heading out for a merry picnic with friends.

Lord Kinsworth draws in an exasperated breath. I can tell he is reconsidering the swarm of females he's bringing to Prince George's secret rendezvous.

"Mustn't keep His Highness waiting," I say, much cheerier than I feel, and loop my arm through Ben's, hurrying him down the hall. Sera and Tess fall into step behind us.

"This is highly irregular," he grumbles.

My mouth twists in a wry smile. "By now, I thought you would have realized *everything* we do is highly irregular. You'll grow accustomed to it."

His inner music, usually so playful and elusive, jangles with an erratic mixture of uncertainty and excitement. I listen without comment until we step out of the palace into the thick darkness. There, in a sudden clatter of doubt, he catches his breath.

But there can be no going back now. *It is too late.*

Whether we attend to Prince George or not, he is out there in the chill of night awaiting his fate. And ours, as well. For England's fate is now inextricably tied to his.

"You wanted adventure," I softly remind Ben.

"Yes," he mutters. "So, I did." Silencing any misgivings he may have had, Ben guides us onward. Fifes and drums march resolutely through his veins, as we exit the palace gardens and enter into the shadows between buildings.

Soon, we leave the cobblestone streets and descend to the sandy beach. Sand soon gives way to a vast field of smooth egg-sized stones and pebbles lining the shore, which makes for very unsteady walking. Even the sea birds seem to be asleep at this hour. But the ocean-polished rocks teeter, clunk, and scrape with our every step, ruining the intense quiet of that hour. The only thing louder than these wobbly boulders knocking against one another beneath our feet is the washing back and forth of the sea. My foot twists and skates into seawater pooling between stones, soaking my silk slippers.

I dearly regret not switching them out for a more practical pair of half-boots. Stumbling along, I cling to Lord Kinsworth's arm for balance.

"Over there." He points to a lantern swinging rhythmically beside what looks to be a small fishing pier. We navigate across the remaining pebbles, and there in the shadows beneath the pier, standing beside a large rowboat, are Lord Harston and our Prince Regent. A wide grin spreads on Prince George's face, and his arms sweep open. "Welcome!"

Sera, Tess, and I curtsey in greeting. Lord Kinsworth bows. "My apologies for keeping you waiting, Sir. The young ladies—"

"No need to say another word, my lad. Ladies will be ladies."

Tess snorts at that remark, subtly, but still, she *snorted* at the ruler of the British Empire.

Prince George pays her no heed. Instead, he honors me with a slight tilt of his head. "Our little miracle worker. We are forever in your debt, Miss Barrington. And I see you've brought along a pair of friends. Splendid." He claps his palms together and rubs them briskly. "Let us be off then, shall we? Mustn't keep Bonaparte waiting."

Lord Harston steps over the side and helps Prince George into the large rowboat, then takes up his position on the tiller.

As soon as the Prince is seated, Lord Kinsworth lifts me into the boat. He turns back to assist Sera, and to his obvious exasperation, Tess sloshes out and climbs in on her own. "You could've waited," Ben mutters, shoving the craft out into the water. When the boat floats free of the beach, he deftly swings up over the side, seats himself and takes up the oars.

A second set of paddles rests on the thwart beside us, and when neither of the other two men takes them up, Tess leans toward him and whispers, "Would you like me to help you row?"

Lord Kinsworth answers with a stern glare and a distinct grumble. Sera nudges Tess with her elbow. "Behave."

"Very well." Tess sits back, lounging against the gunwale, and flicks her fingers at him as a leisurely princess might do. "Onward. And be quick about it."

Even over the waves of high tide crashing and our oars sloshing, I can hear Kinsworth's inner music scraping with annoyance. I chuckle. Something about Tess's predictable orneriness and Lord Kinsworth's boyish fuming floods me with a sense of happiness again. But chasing right on its heels comes regret. Regret that we are paddling toward death.

If only I could live a few more days, long enough to see Tess tease my big strong Kinsworth again. Long enough to treasure up a few more memories to take with me to the afterlife.

I turn to Sera and reach for her hand. I cannot bear the thought of her seeing me die. Or worse, if she should get hurt herself. Her white hair is blowing like silver gossamer in the wind. I whisper into her ear. "You should not have come. It is far too dangerous."

"How could I not?" Sera, who in this dim moonlight looks as fragile as a small child, tilts her head at me in wonder. "You would not leave me to face death alone, would you?"

Never.

In that moment, my heart breaks altogether.

I cannot stop the tears that leak out. Bravery escapes me. Am I the lioness? I do not feel her courage. Am I the nightingale? Trapped and dying. I do not know. Perhaps I am only a small insignificant marigold, a clawless lion flower, about to be plucked and thrown into the fire.

Panic rises in my chest—a wild fitful drumming.

Every thought turns toward leaping out of this wretched boat and trying to swim through the thrashing waves to freedom. I start to rise. I learned to swim at Stranje House, but I am not skilled at it. And given our distance from shore, the certainty of drowning causes me to hesitate. Either way, my fate is death. I sink back onto the thwart.

Tess wraps her arm around my shoulder, quieting the wild drumming. "We can change things," she whispers in my ear.

Can we? Or will the river carry us where it chooses? I do not know.

I only know we are sailing deeper into the darkness.

With the help of the ebbing tide and an easterly current, we row out to sea headed along the coast. Half an hour later, Lord Harston spots the dark silhouette of a sloop of war anchored out in deep water. "There! Up ahead. See it? Two lanterns."

Two tiny spots of light sway, one from the bow and one from the stern of a dark tall ship, and at the top of the mizzen mast a flag snaps in the breeze and catches the scant moonlight.

"Napoleon's standard!" Prince George points. "That's

the sign. The Emperor's ship." He stands at his place in the boat and shouts. "Ahoy!" Prince George claps a fist to his chest. "At last, we shall meet. The two greatest enemies of our time."

"Yes, Your Highness. Just so. A momentous occasion." Lord Harston helps the Prince regain his seat as the rowboat lurches forward.

As if the night isn't dark enough, the side of the tall ship obliterates what little moonlight we had. We are left with only the faint pinpricks of a few stars not blocked by clouds. Our gig thuds against the starboard side of the ship. Loops are smaller and more agile than galleons, but nevertheless, still impressive. *And threatening.* Leaning back, straining to see, I spot the dark shape of six canons protruding above our heads. A mooring line drops, we tie off, and a ladder unrolls down the side.

"Well, ladies, they don't seem to be lowering a chair." Lord Harston scratches at his side-whiskers. "Looks as if you will have to endure a steep climb if you wish to board."

Lord Kinsworth answers for us. "I suspect they're up to the task." He smirks at Tess and winks at me. "It will be my pleasure to assist."

"No doubt, it will." Prince George starts to laugh, but his humor is cut short as he peers up through the darkness at the long ladder dangling over the side of the ship. He takes a deep breath and grabs hold of the conveyance. "Jolly good thing you gave us that tea, Miss Barrington. Jolly good."

With a groan, he heaves himself onto the ladder. Lord Harston follows right beneath the Prince, making sure our Regent's buckle shoes land squarely on each of the narrow oak slats. After much heaving and grunting the Prince disappears onto the deck. Next, Sera takes to the ladder and begins scaling it with ease. Tess nudges me from where she stands in the darkest shadows and places a finger to her lips. Silently, she makes her way to the stern of our rowboat and stretching up, she grabs hold of the mooring line. A second later, she is climbing up the thick rope with the skill of a seasoned sailor sneaking aboard ship.

"What in heaven's name is she doing?" Kinsworth hisses in my ear.

"Shhh," I warn, with a finger to my lips. "She is doing what Tess does best. And it would be better if she were not seen."

"But–"

"Trust me." I place my hand on his cheek. "And now, if you would be so kind as to help me up this dreadful ladder. It swings so violently, and I confess, I am not as brave as Sera and Tess." I say this to distract him, although it is not a complete lie. I will never be as fearless as Tess, but this is a well-strung ladder, and surely any child can climb a ladder.

The words have the desired effect. Lord Kinsworth's chest puffs out, and as I reach for the first rung, he places his arms around me. "You needn't worry. I will be right here."

And he is.

He shields me on the ladder, grasping the rope right beside my hands, and with every step I take, he steps up on the rung directly beneath mine. His warmth wraps around me so that even the ocean breeze does not touch me. Rowing is hard work, and his fragrance teases the salt air, masculine and spicy, reminding me of wild oranges. I like his scent. I love his breath on my neck. I climb slowly, so I can savor him being this close.

His mouth is beside my ear. It tickles when he speaks. "You're doing very well, Maya." I can tell by the languorous way he says this that he is not trying to hurry me. Not in the least. He presses closer. "*Very* well."

We take the next two rungs in waltz-like tandem and, as I rise to the next slat, his lips brush against my neck. His feather-light touch hums through me, pirating away my strength.

My only desire is to turn around and kiss him, right here, right now. Never mind that we are dangling from a ladder in the middle of the English Channel on a ship that is quite probably going to be the place where I die.

Nearing my last moments on earth, it strikes as if by lightning, the realization that my life is not the sum of who loved me—but rather the sum of who I have loved.

My arms and legs will not move. I cannot take another step, not until I tell Ben the truth. I refuse to die without confessing what is in my heart.

"No matter what happens tonight . . ." I pause, waiting until I feel his cheek near mine. "I want you to know I love you, Ben. I know you think we are just pretending, but heaven help me, I love you."

"I know, Maya. *I know.*" His music bursts out from where he has been hiding it, deep violoncellos and playful oboes, vibrant, and full-ranged. Sounds I have grown to cherish, *his sounds.* They fill the air around us, so rich and full that the song swells and echoes even into the sea. He leans in and kisses the top of my shoulder. "I have always known."

Waves of love flow through me. My soul awakens more than it has ever done before. It is as if I hear whales singing in the ocean beneath us, though they might be hundreds of miles away, and thousands of schools of fishes humming—countless creatures. Life, so much life surrounding us, filling the air and the water and the land. And all of their voices seem to harmonize with his, with Ben, with us.

All I can do is nod.

It is enough.

I climb to my fate.

TWENTY-ONE

DUET WITH FATE

"ONLY A LITTLE farther," Sera calls down to us as we climb, but the wind carries away her words and makes it sound as if she is on a distant hill.

The ladder swings out every time a wave rocks the ship, and it feels as if we are suspended midair until the sea tips us back and we bang into the side. It is equally unsettling to climb past the cannons which reek of gunpowder and gun oil. A few rungs more and, even though we cannot see much in this darkness, the musty smell of oakum mixed with pitch tells me we are nearing the deck. I reach the last slat and see Sera's silhouette above us. Clambering up to the small opening in the gunwale, I grope for a handhold. Fortunately, salt and wind have etched the oak planks, and the hard-grained ridges make it easy to grip. I pull myself up, and Sera reaches out to steady me.

With my feet firmly planted on the deck, and Kinsworth right behind me, I strain to identify the others congregating near the forecastle. In this dim light, it is impossible to distinguish who might be standing in the group. All one can readily see are a few lanterns. Their orange glow outlines the silhouettes of those gathered and sends inky shadows flickering eerily across the deck. As we stride toward them, an unnerving snippet of laughter drifts on the breeze.

Merriment of any sort seems out of place on this ship shrouded in secrets. The sound bounces awkwardly through the murky dark and the mainmast creaks in answer. I glance up. Naked of its sails, with its rigging tossing in the wind, the masts span upward like a boney spiders' web stretching to capture the stars.

"Ah, here they are!" Prince George's bulky figure is unmistakable as he opens their shadowed circle to greet us. "Your Imperial Majesty, may I present to you Lord Kinsworth, the Viscount of Langlie, and on his left is . . ." Prince George goes on to introduce Sera and me, but my ears are buzzing, and his syllables blur into an incomprehensible jumble. I cannot believe my eyes.

Emperor Napoleon stands before us.

Here.

The world suddenly feels as if it has flipped upside down. I did not expect Napoleon to be here. Not really. Upon first hearing, I worried this trip might be a ruse. Tess's dream confirmed my suspicions. I *did* expect several other people; Lady Daneska, certainly. I even expected I might come face to face with the hooded specter of death. But not Napoleon. Not the Emperor of France and most of Europe. Not the general who outwitted the armies of the civilized world and now sits on thrones in Paris, Vienna, and Prague.

Sera and I immediately drop into formal curtsies. Deep curtsies and, I am so overcome with disbelief, I can scarcely rise when the Emperor signals.

"*Enchanté, mesdemoiselles.*" His accent is not purely French and bears a hoarse quality, as though he has nursed a cough for too long or shouted too many orders. Despite this inadequacy, I can tell immediately Napoleon Bonaparte knows how to tailor his voice to influence others. His tone, although direct and precise and not particularly pleasing or remarkable, carries an earnest quality that draws in the listener.

He knows I know.

And I find that even more disquieting.

Intelligence radiates from this man. Physically, he is only of average height, stocky but solidly built, and yet the gigantic force of his thoughts spin around us in a low threatening whirr. It is the sound a longsword makes when cutting through the air.

His chin lifts, and he addresses me with curiosity. "We have been told you possess a most pleasing voice, Miss Barrington. *Le rossignol.* The nightingale, yes?"

He reminds me of my cage.

His trapped songbird.

I nod.

He smiles at me. And though the gesture appears gracious, it is without humor. "A pity we do not have the time, nor the acoustics aboard this vessel to hear you sing." His eyes, though gray and deep-set, are keen and penetrating. He fixes them on me with a sense of knowing, as if he thinks we share a secret. And, I suppose, in a way, we do.

Perhaps several secrets.

After all, Lady Daneska stands on the other side of him, wearing a smug expression. She minces nearer to the Emperor as if he is a close personal friend. Gray shadows play ghoulishly across her features, and with her dark velvet cape and hood, she might serve quite admirably as a surrogate for the angel of death.

Prince George claps his palms together. "Yes, yes, Miss Barrington's singing is an incomparable delight. Perhaps, after our discussions, we might have time for one of her songs."

Napoleon glances toward the eastern horizon. "Sadly, I must forego that pleasure. I do not think it wise for my ship to be found in English waters once the sun comes up."

Prince George emits a half chuckle. "No. Daresay, that might create a bit of a sticky situation."

"Shall we?" Napoleon gestures toward the forecastle. "The captain has provided a small table for our convenience."

Prince George waddles toward an oil lamp flickering atop a small mahogany table, leading all of us deeper into the shadows of the upper deck. "Don't see what more can be said that hasn't already been settled in our letters."

"*C'est exactement.*" Emperor Napoleon slows his bold stride to walk beside the Prince. "To that end, I took the liberty of drawing up an accord—a treaty, no? Between us—leaders of the two greatest empires in the world." He indicates a small stack of parchment sitting beside an oil lantern on the table. "I'm sure Lord Harston, Lord Kinsworth, and Lady Daneska are willing to serve as our witnesses."

"Witnesses?" I hear a swarm of panic buzz through Prince George. He balks beside the table and does not even reach out to pick up the sheaf of papers. "What? You expect me to read all that? Here? In this light?"

Daneska frowns at me and bobs her chin in their direction as if she expects me to do something to calm Prince George and make him sign a binding accord, one he has not even read.

He is mumbling something, but I can barely hear him above his crashing uncertainty. "We will have Lord Harston gather the papers and take them back to the palace. We can read them in the morning under better light."

"*Non.*" Napoleon sniffs, trumpeting his displeasure. "That would necessitate my sailing into British waters once again. An unnecessary risk. We have come this far, why do you hesitate?"

"*Excusez-moi, s'il vous plaît, Votre Majesté Impériale.*" Lady Daneska chooses a sugary-sweet tone to address Napoleon first and then Prince George. "Your Highness, if I may be so bold as to offer a possible solution?"

They turn to her, annoyance thrumming loudly in both men.

"Why not have the lovely Miss Barrington read it aloud for you? This will accomplish your objectives, yes? And you will also have the pleasure of hearing her lovely voice at the same time."

Prince George runs his finger around his cravat to loosen it. "Aye. That might do. What say you, Miss Barrington, will you do us the honor? Your eyes are young and t'would be a great deal more pleasant to hear you read than old Harston here. Ha-ha," he laughs nervously.

One cannot refuse a royal request. "Certainly, Sire. It would be my pleasure."

Napoleon and Prince George seat themselves in two wooden chairs across from the table. I turn up the oil lamp to full capacity and lift the parchment. The handwriting is beautifully scribed and the capitals ornately decorated, bearing all the earmarks of an official international accord.

Taking a breath, I begin reading. As soon as I get past the named entities and the description of the articles therein, every sentence tightens the sour knot my stomach.

I cannot keep the mounting distress out of my voice. This contract will make Britain part of a Grand European Empire. Napoleon, of course, reigns supreme, as Emperor over this Grand Empire. Prince George, as King of England, must agree to be the Emperor's loyal representative. As such, his first act will be to dissolve Parliament in favor of a duchy system, similar to the ones Napoleon set up in Germany and Austria. English lords who agree to this organization will be rewarded with duchies commiserate with their current holdings, and all of these dukedoms will answer to Prince George. But ultimately both the lords of Britain and her King must serve as obedient subjects to His Imperial Majesty, Napoleon Bonaparte, Emperor of the Le Grand Empire.

His servants.

Puppets.

I look up from reading, fearing that even in this poor light they might notice my brown skin draining to white.

This agreement has gone too far. Prince George is

frowning, and rightly so. At least he is wavering. I must push him into resistance. I close off all sound for a moment, searching for the right voice that will sway him.

Ah! There it is. I allow fear to quiver across my tongue. Fear is a palpable force, even a slight tremor of it makes the stomach wobble and curl into itself. May the sound nip his childish soul and awaken him to his foolishness.

Barely above a whisper, each syllable quaking in breathless trepidation, I warn, "You will be returning England to a feudal system. Britain will be subjugated to France."

Prince George, like a frightened child, sinks in his chair.

Napoleon, a guard dog alert to sudden danger, straightens in his. "*Non!* Not so," he barks. "Have you not heard of the Napoleonic Code? *La Code civil des François.* It is lauded everywhere in the world."

Prince George mumbles a reply, "Of course."

"*Oui!* Then you know." Napoleon bolts up from his chair, vibrating with indignation. Incensed that any of us should question his equanimity. "*Le Code* is the fairest set of laws in the known world!" He takes a general's stance, bearing down on Prince George who still cowers in his chair. Napoleon does not shout. Instead, he uses a low threatening tone that compels all of us to lean in and listen closely. "This code is welcomed all across Europe. It demands only these two things: justice and peace. Is this not exactly what you wish for your country? Ask your cousins in Hapsburg how they fare under its tenets."

Napoleon claps his hand on Prince George's shoulder. "Consider what we can accomplish together, my friend. Eventually, we shall even bring those rebellious colonists of yours in North America to see the light." The Emperor lets go and paces in a tight path in front of the table. "This code will bring peace to the world—an end of war. Do you not understand? By uniting with me, we will be free to move into the modern age, develop industry, science. Increase wealth. These are the benefits of peace. And you, Prince George, soon to be King George, you and I, we will stand at the helm—premier leaders of the world."

He believes what he is saying. Idealistically, it is a pretty dream. Except it is a dream laced with veiled threats. The reality of his ideals will rot into tyranny. It will strangle England, and ultimately the world.

I must speak.

This time, I reach out with a rousing voice, lifting him up, inciting him to strength. "Your Royal Highness, if you sign this, England will no longer be free." Prince George looks up at me, and I detect an inkling of strength stirring within him. "Under these dictums, *you* will not be free either. Your Highness will go from being sovereign of the greatest nation in the world, to merely being Emperor Napoleon's royal subject." I pause briefly, waiting for the reality to fully awaken in him. "His servant."

"His *puppet*," Lord Kinsworth says, and steps forward, respect for me, glistening in his eyes. He knows our bold speaking will probably cost us our lives, yet he strides forward to stand loyally beside Prince George. "It is beneath you, Sir."

Lord Harston, too, comes forward to guard Prince George on the other side. "We are *your* loyal subjects. Yours alone."

In the ensuing silence, Napoleon whirs with rage, a longsword preparing to strike, and I hear others moving in the darkness of the ship. Rustling like rats, men skittering in the shadows of the deck.

But there is another who crawls through the darkness, and his pulse makes my blood quiver with dread. I feel his malignant power filling the air, drawing nearer and nearer, a silent poisonous fog.

Napoleon wheels on me, anger blasting away all other sounds. "Miss Barrington, do you dare set yourself against me? I thought you understood the price."

Price.

How crafty his words are—tricky. A sly two-edged sword. Consider the price of defying him, *death.* But the Emperor also reminds me of the promised reward—the price he would pay me for betraying my friends and my father's country—a chance to return as a ruler in my own land.

As much as I miss my grandmother, she would not have me return to her as a traitor.

But before I can answer, Lady Daneska interrupts, and I cannot help but notice she stands far too close to Sera. "Yes! How dare you speak against—"

"Silence!" Napoleon swings out his arm, cutting her off, yet his gaze never leaves me. His other hand rests atop his sword. "Do you not comprehend the generosity of our offer?" Again, his words are duplicitous.

A second chance for me to repent.

Someone else might assume he refers only to his offer to Prince George, but he also alludes to his offer Lady Daneska brought to me. I clutch my arm where she sliced it open that night.

That twinge of pain reminds I was once a Maharajah's granddaughter. More importantly, I am my grandmother's child. I may sing like a nightingale, but she taught me to put a voice to the storm, to speak with the force of the mighty Tawi river.

I no longer fear this man.

Sound rises from deep within me, flowing with the strength of rushing waters, yet as steady and immoveable as the boulders that stand amidst the river. When I speak, the power does not come from me alone. The storm carries a force far beyond my own strength.

"If only," I say to him. "If only it were truly peace you desired. Search your heart, Your Imperial Majesty. You have bravely challenged the greatest armies of our time. Again, and again, without flinching, you have ridden your warhorse straight into battle. But I ask you, do you have the courage to look inside yourself? Do you dare?"

His hand slides from his sword. His mouth opens in a drawn breath, and his constant whirring stills for a moment. His eyes seem to lose focus as he glimpses what lies within.

His uneasiness is faint at first, but rises steadily, reminding me of the enormous dessert horns in India, whose low guttural warnings echo across the dunes.

He pauses too long. I must put a voice to the truth he is afraid to acknowledge. Words flow from my mouth like a mournful wind that bends trees. "What stares back at you is a burning desire for power."

"No!" Napoleon shakes his head slightly as if trying to clear it of my thrall. "Power, yes. But the power to do good. The power to save the world."

"The power to control the world is not the same as

saving it," I say this with a gentleness meant to soothe. "Only God can save the world."

Running footfalls hammer the silence between us. Ghost swings over the forecastle railing, a growling seething presence. He lands on the main deck beside Napoleon. "Don't listen to this pointless drivel. If there's a God, he abandoned mankind long ago." He aims his pistol straight at my heart. "And *you* were warned."

Lord Kinsworth's sword glints in the lamplight as he quietly draws it and edges toward our attacker.

Other men, Ghost's rats, emerge from the shadows. Sailors clad in black surround us with their knives drawn. Lord Harston immediately raises his sword to protect the Prince Regent. Even Prince George pulls his weapon from its sheath.

Kinsworth lunges to strike at Ghost's gun arm. Ghost is too quick. He steps aside, pummeling Ben with a powerful backhand to the jaw that sends him staggering to the deck.

"Ben!" I surge forward, but Ghost blocks the path between Kinsworth and me.

Lady Daneska shrieks, "Shoot her!" Her knife glints in the lamplight as she reaches out to grab Sera by the hair—attempting to make good her threat to kill my friend because I disobeyed. Thank heaven, Sera dodges.

"Wait!" Napoleon signals Ghost with a raised hand and squints at me speculatively. My hold on him has vanished. Already, his mind is spinning, assessing the situation, swinging into battle. "She might yet prove useful."

But Ghost ignores his Emperor and cocks the hammer back. "No. She defied me."

Napoleon turns a stern glare on Ghost. "*Non!* I said to wait. That is an order."

Order or not, Ghost stretches out his arm and raises the barrel to my face. I feel inexplicably calm, until—

"Maya!" Lord Kinsworth clambers up from where he fell. Blood oozes from his gashed lip as he charges at Ghost. He is so intent on me he doesn't notice the sailor sneaking up behind him with a raised cutlass.

"Behind you!" I yell.

Ben wheels around, dodging the slashing blade by mere inches.

That same instant, Tess leaps over the forecastle and crashes into me. The two of us skid across the planking away from the gun's muzzle.

Any second, I expect to hear a gunshot. Instead, Ghost snarls at Tess, "You!" Towering over us, heaving with unspent anger, he brandishes his yet unfired pistol. "I should've killed *you* long ago."

From this angle, amber lamplight catches on the scars twisting up his neck, distorting this side of his cheek—scars from the burns we caused him at Calais. He aims the flintlock at Tess, who is scrambling up from having saved me.

"No! Not her! Stop!" Lady Daneska leaves off struggling with Sera and dashes toward us. "Not Tess!"

The gun goes off—an earsplitting blast. A burst of scorching light. I still lie sprawled across the deck. A gray cloud of smoke fills the air above me, but not before I see both Lady Daneska and Tess crumple to the ground.

No, no, no! It was supposed to be me.

Kinsworth yells my name. Except I can't see him. There's too much smoke. He must think I'm the one who got shot. "I'm not hurt," I call out.

His answer is a bark of pain, followed by the horror of steel clanging against steel. It has to be Ghost attacking him. *Ghost*—his vicious blade swinging at Kinsworth. My innocent Kinsworth, who is accustomed to charming trouble away, not battling it to the death.

The scuffling and thumps of their sword fight, the unbearable yelps, and curses, tear at my heart. I grope for a weapon, a rope, a stick of wood, anything I might use to help him. Every blow means slashed flesh. Ben's flesh. Bone nicked. Blood spilt.

Please, God, not his bone. Nor his blood.

Let him be fast. Let his sword strike true. And may his eyes see better in this gloom than mine. It feels as if I am blind and trapped in hell. Then, a familiar sound reaches my ears.

Kinsworth!

It is him. Still fighting. I would know that sound anywhere, his rumbly bear-like violoncello, except the bow is racing across the strings with such rapid intensity no one could jig that fast.

Warrior fast.

Ben.

I breathe in his name and hang onto his wild racing thread of sound.

He is battling to save us, and I must do the same. "Tess? Tess, where are you?" I whisper and scramble over the decking toward where I thought they fell.

Someone moans a few feet away from me.

"Tess!" I scramble to her. There's a red smear covering her arm, as she wriggles out from underneath Daneska. "Are you—" I start to ask if she is hurt, but stop.

Even in this dismal light, I can see the blood pouring from a wound in Lady Daneska's side, a dark stain spreading on her pale silk gown.

At the sound of my gasp, Tess turns and sees the awful truth. "What? Dani? No, it can't be."

Tess lifts Lady Daneska's shoulders and cradles her, hastily bunching Daneska's skirt and pressing the silk wad against the wound. Despite her efforts to staunch the bleeding, Tess's fingers quickly turn crimson. In the darkness of this night, blood turns the color of death.

Holding our dying enemy as if she were a long-lost friend, Tess utters a low moan. But it is her inner cry of anguish, the one rising from her heart rather than her lips, that tears at my soul. Keening low and soft, Tess begins rocking Daneska.

Lady Daneska groans. Her eyelids flutter for a moment, then open wide as if we have startled her from some night terror. "Am I dead?"

"Wounded," I answer as calmly as possible. "But alive."

For the moment.

As if hearing my unspoken words, she closes her eyes tight. When she opens them again, all the fight in her flies away like a bird on the wing. She knows she is dying.

Tess grips Lady Daneska tighter as if by sheer will she can make her once dear friend remain in this mortal realm. "What were you thinking?" Tess scolds, biting her bottom lip before spitting out her frustration. "Why, Dani? Why?"

"Hmm . . ." Daneska says drowsily and almost seems to laugh. "Funny, isn't it?" Except her mirth is cut short by a wince of pain. "I warned you not to care for anyone.

You see?" She tries to smile except she can't, it hurts too much. Her back arches and her lips twist in a deathly grimace. Her normally silky voice grinds into gravel. "Love costs too much."

"Do something." Tess glances over her shoulder at me, her soul screaming with grief, her eyes swimming in tears she would never let fall. *Not Tess.* "She's suffering. Can't you see? Make it stop. Make it so she can't feel the pain."

I am not magic.

Pain has its own song. I know this now. I hear it. One might think pain is a scream or a moan, but no. Those are merely our responses to the monster. Here on this ship, surrounded by a thousand noises, waves battering the hull, the clatter of swords hammering against one another, Ben fighting, other men scuffling and shouting, I hear the unmistakable crackle of pain, unseen flames licking at Daneska's side. Pain is an insatiable beast, smacking its hungry lips, hissing with heat, an ever-burning fire ready to devour.

How can I quiet so ravenous a creature?

I kneel closer to her.

And listen.

How is it, that despite the gnashing of pain's teeth, Daneska's soul hums more tranquilly than it ever has? She weakly raises her hand toward Tess's cheek but lets it drop as if the effort is beyond her. "Do not fret me dying," she says, trying to smile, her eyes fixed on Tess. "This is nothing you haven't felt a hundred times, eh, Tessika?"

Tess leans over Daneska, their foreheads touching as if in silent communion. A second later, she pulls back and turns to me. "Maya! Do something. *Please*"

Her plea reaches into my heart and awakens an idea, a possibility. What if I sing to quiet the vulturous thing that seeks to devour Daneska?

A lullaby for pain beasts.

And so, I begin to hum. Then I find words.

"Come out from the shadows." The melody is calibrated to soothe and calm, each note is intended to entice pain to rest. "Come out and walk with me awhile. The grass is soft and deep. Come out and walk with me awhile. The water is clear and sweet. Come out and walk with me awhile."

Tess seems to understand. She has always had a gift for calming wild animals. Valiantly choking back tears, she harmonizes her voice with mine. Our song embraces Daneska, and her shoulders unstiffen. She no longer gasps for breath as desperately.

But as we sing, a faint noise in the distance prickles my senses. It is a steady rhythmic beat, completely out-of-place amid the horrific chaos aboard our ship. I know this sound—a paddlewheel churning across the waves like a buttermilk press. Alarm buckles my throat and chokes off my song.

That sound is Alexander Sinclair's steam-powered boat, not the new warship the Navy is building. It can only be the smaller prototype we helped him construct, the *Mary Isabella*, a small craft equipped with a powerful ballista. A weapon I helped them devise, a huge spring-loaded bow like the ones I'd seen in India mounted on war elephants. Except this ballista is armed with spears bearing Greek firebombs.

Deadly firebombs.

What's more, Captain Grey cannot possibly know we are aboard this ship. The moment he or his crew sees Napoleon's flag, his coat of arms, they will fire on us. We will be bombarded with an explosive blaze of oil and pitch—nearly impossible to extinguish.

"Daneska! Answer me." Ghost cuts through our song, shouting for her. "Where the hell are you?" He splits the smoky air and stands before us, a pillar of blackness, with blood smeared across his hands and arms.

Kinsworth's?

Who else's could it be? My stomach drops away as if I am falling from a dizzying height. Time seems to slow, and all I can hear is an unearthly wail ripping silently through me. "Not Kinsworth's. Not his. *Please*," I murmur, and suddenly I feel as if I might lose the contents of my stomach.

Naanii's words call to me. *Focus* on one sound. And so, I press a hand against my roiling belly and quiet my mind. There he is, my beautiful violoncello, distant but still there. Still moving strong.

That's when I realize Ghost is reloading his gun and yelling at us, "Get away from her! What have you done? You pack of miserable—" An eerie whistling sound interrupts him.

The first spear from Mr. Sinclair's ballista strikes the deck with an ominous *thwunk*. A blaze explodes midship, casting its terrifying light across all of us. Cries of "*Fire!*" ricochet across the ship—stern to bow. Every shout quivering with a sailor's worst fear. The ringing of steel fades as Ghost's men run to save themselves from drowning at sea or burning to death.

Not Ghost.

"She's dead, isn't she?" His face contorts into an eerie semblance of grief, but an instant later becomes a hideous mask of anger. He grabs Tess by the hair. "Isn't she?"

Tess snaps at him, using the same tone she would with one of her wolf dogs if they were misbehaving. "She will die if you don't let go."

He releases her with a jerk and steps back, waving his gun at me. "This is your fault."

"No." Sera stands behind us, her small pistol drawn. I hadn't realized she was there, watching over us. "You shot her. Daneska is wounded because of your recklessness. No one else is to blame."

"And yet . . ." He shifts his aim to her. "All of you will pay."

"Not them." I rise to my knees. To someone else, I might look like the penitent saint kneeling before him, begging for forgiveness. But it is the lioness in me rising to protect those she loves. "I ruined your plans. I'm the one you're angry at. It's me, you hate."

I say this, but I know better. Ghost is consumed by anger. It has rotted his soul until all that howls from inside him is a chomping unquenchable darkness.

He almost smiles. Hollow drums thudding and off-key horns—it makes him happy that by killing Sera, he will hurt me.

No, you will not.

The resolve hardens inside me, a huge immovable stone. Solid. Ancient. A rock from which the lioness pounces.

"Lucien!" His given name burst out of my lungs in a mighty roar. *Naanii* taught me that to command a thing, you must call it by its true name. And so, I did. "Lucien!"

It claws through the air, leaping, like a giant panther, tearing him apart with its teeth.

Ghost staggers backward, his eyes wide with terror as I rise and stride toward him.

I do not know what demon haunts him, but it knows this man's name. Arm upraised, warding me off, Ghost snarls like a whipped cur.

I blink, seeing the truth, listening to the whimpering inside him—*not the yelping of dog.* A whipped boy, a small child beaten. *Lucien.* "Lucien, put down the gun," I warn more gently.

He cowers, filling with hate again. A shield for the wounded boy. He holds onto the pistol, his hand shaking as if he still sees a specter.

His gun goes off. Flames burst from the muzzle. The bullet whizzes past me. The blast is a thunderclap that shakes the deck enveloping us in more suffocating smoke.

Sera's pistol fires with a sharp bang.

Ghost grunts. Growls Then curses. Her bullet must have hit him.

His shot must've hit Sera, causing her to pull the trigger. "Sera! Sera!" I frantically search for her, choking, fanning away smoke.

"I'm here," she whispers, crouching on the deck near me. "Are you all right?"

"Me?" I grab her, feverishly searching for blood. "It's *you* he shot—"

She shakes her head. "No, I thought he killed you."

We turn back in time to see Ghost bolt up and stomp toward us. Through the haze, I spot Lord Kinsworth headed in our direction—*still alive!*

"*Imbécile!*" Napoleon bellows at Ghost. He stands a few feet beyond our left flank, clutching his arm, blood spreading over his shirt sleeve like spilt wine. "What have you done?"

All of us turn in the Emperor's direction.

Ghost swats away a cloud of smoke and blinks in confusion at his Emperor. Ghost seems to be favoring one side. Sera's bullet must've struck him, but to a man of his size, that small slug would be but a scratch.

He stares. A stunned half-second passes before comprehension blares across his features, and he realizes it had to have been his bullet that wounded the Emperor of Le Grand Empire.

Ghost bellows, not in an apology, but in a growl of fury at having blundered.

Another spear whizzes past us and bursts into flame near the quarter deck.

"*Arrêtez ces feux!* Get those fires under control!" Napoleon shouts in French. He does not let a little thing like Ghost putting a bullet in his arm unnerve him. His chest juts out commandingly. "*Allez! Allez!* Do it now! Or I swear by all that is holy I will kill you myself! I refuse to die at sea."

The furious battle pace of Ghost's war drum falters. Frustration rumbles through him, and his fingers twitch as if they are already tightening around my neck. Grinding his teeth, his eyes narrow at me until they become thin hateful slits bearing the unmistakable promise of revenge. And yet, the whipped boy in him yields and turns to do his master's bidding.

Napoleon peers eastward through a spyglass, where dawn is bleeding, too, a scarlet ribbon along the horizon.

He must have spotted Alexander's steamship heading for us. Alarm whistles briefly across his features, but just as quickly his inner blades recommence their whirring. "Weigh anchors. Ready the cannons." His voice becomes a bugle, calling his men to action. Any pretense of meekness has disappeared. "Bosun—cut and run! Full sails. Captain, take us into the wind. Now!"

His orders rebound across the ship. Sailors race to fulfill his commands, their feet thudding so hard the whole ship thunders. His men scurry up into the shrouds like a pack of spiders racing up their web. In a blink, the first sail is cut loose, unrolling with a snap and flapping in the wind.

Sera sneaks over to the table, gathers the sheaf of papers, and hands the stack to Tess. "Hide these. Protect them with your life."

"Yes, all right." Tess stuffs them down the front of her shirt and staggers to her feet, trying to lift Lady Daneska in her arms. "But we have to get off this ship. Now!" She stumbles, and I rush to help her.

Sera grabs the lantern from the table and backs away from us, making for the starboard gunwale. "One of Captain Grey's men is bound to have a spyglass trained on our ship. I'll signal them before they kill us all—the Prince included."

There is a farewell in her expression, a sad note I cannot bear. "No, come with us. We can signal them from the ladder."

"Too low." She shakes her head. "They'll see me better from the bow." She slants a fierce look at Tess. "Go! Get them off this ship. Hurry!"

I reach out. "Wait! Sera—" But she dashes off into the

darkness.

"Maya!" Lord Kinsworth runs across the deck and grasps my arm. "Are you all right? I was afraid he'd shot you."

"Ben!" Relief rings through me. I let him pull me into an embrace. He's breathing hard, his coat is missing, and his shirt is slashed in too many places. There's a gaping cut on his arm, another on his chest, and so much blood on him I can't help but wince. "You're hurt."

"I'm all right." He shakes off my concern. "But Prince George is wounded. We need to get him to safety."

"Right." Tess staggers to her feet, trying to lift Lady Daneska in her arms. She stumbles, and I rush to help her.

Kinsworth frowns. "Why're you bringing her? Leave the traitor here."

"She saved my life," Tess says through gritted teeth, trying to carry Daneska to the starboard rail. "I'm not leaving her here with that monster."

Prince George hobbles up behind Lord Kinsworth, bleeding from a gash on his shoulder and another on his leg, leaning heavily on Lord Harston. Ben is right, our duty is to the Prince Regent. "But. . ." I plead with Ben. "Lady Daneska used to be one of us. We can't leave her."

"The ladies are right, Kinsworth," Prince George mutters. "Can't abandon Lady Daneska. Harston can help me down."

Lord Harston rubs his chin. "One of us needs to guard from the deck. If anyone were to attack while you were on the ladder, Sir . . ." He shakes his head

"I would be honored to assist Your Highness on the climb down." I let a little of the lioness stalk across my tongue, just enough to assure them of my confidence. "I can place your feet just as Lord Harston did on your ascent."

Ben frowns at me.

"Ah, splendid. That's settled." Prince George nods at him. "Off you go, lad."

Kinsworth exhales loudly. "Very well. But I will climb back up as soon as I get Lady Daneska down." He sweeps our wounded traitor out of Tess's arms and strides to the side of the ship.

Tess hurries in front of him. "I'll help you get her settled in the boat and tend to her bleeding." She scrambles down the steep ladder as swiftly as one would a staircase.

Kinsworth swings over the railing onto the wobbly rungs cradling Daneska in one arm as if she weighs next to nothing. But I notice he holds on by curling his forearm under each slat as he descends. The cut on his arm must be severe enough that he doesn't trust his grip. And his right leg appears to be injured, too, because it trembles precariously each time he steps on it.

Tess steadies the ladder from the boat below.

Glancing toward the bow, I see Sera's lantern waving back and forth, a pinprick of courage piercing the black night.

Our turn. Prince George stares over the precipice as if the great height makes him nervous. I ease past him onto the ladder, darting down the top four rungs. "Your Highness, we must hurry. If you will but step down, I will place your feet on the slats just as Lord Harston did." I reach up to help guide him onto the ladder, but stop when the barrel of flintlock points at the Prince.

"He stays here." Ghost thrusts his gun at Prince George's head. "Dead or alive, he's coming with us to France."

"I think not!" Lord Harston whips out his sword and wedges himself between Ghost and the Prince Regent. "Go, Your Highness. Climb!"

"Fool!" Ghost lunges at Harston, so swift and so close there is neither time nor space for Harston to maneuver his saber. It clatters to the deck when Ghost grabs the Prince's would-be-protector by the throat. With one hand, he lifts the hapless lord and flings him over the gunwale.

"Harston—" Prince George mutters, frozen in place.

Lord Harston claws wildly at the air as he tumbles like a broken carriage wheel into the sea. With an enormous splash, he crashes into the waves, narrowly missing the prow of the rowboat.

Ghost picks up the sword Lord Harston dropped, shifts the pistol to his left and nudges Prince George with the muzzle. "Back away from the ladder. And mind your toes, unless you'd rather lose them." He raises the sword like an executioner about to chop off the head of my rope ladder.

Below me, Lord Harston is thrashing in the water. Kinsworth lays Daneska across one of the thwarts and rushes to the bow, extending a paddle to save his uncle. He shouts for Tess to untie the mooring line. With only a few seconds to act, instead of stepping carefully down each rung, I grasp the ropes on either side of the ladder and let go with my feet. I slide seaward so fast the twine cording burns through my gloves and bites into the flesh of my palms.

Even so, it is not fast enough.

Ghost chops the rope nearest him. In one mighty swoop, he slices straight through it. The entire apparatus swings away from the ship. I clutch the single twine cord still holding me.

I must've yelped. I'm not sure. Lord Kinsworth glances up at me and fear screeches across his face.

"Hang on!" He tugs the paddle into the hull, grasps his uncle's hand and yanks him over the prow. "Hold on!" he shouts again, and charges toward my swinging ladder, bounding across the boat, making it rock wildly.

Tess was untying the mooring lines, but now she, too, scrambles to the stern, straining to catch the dangling rope. Except, my lifeline veers out over the water in a sweeping arc.

"Maya!" Sera calls from up on the ship where she is perched on the railing. "Jump!" she shouts and puts words into action. There is no frenzied flapping as when Lord Harston plummeted into the ocean. Sera leaps, arms wide as if relishing the pleasure of being airborne. At the last moment, she straightens, her skirts billow gracefully, and like a sleek seabird diving for a fish, she splashes into the water below.

My tether has reached the height of its outward swing. Any second, momentum will carry me back over our rowboat. Ghost's sword is raised to slash the remaining rope. Sera is right. If I do not jump now, I will fall, smashing into Kinsworth or Tess, breaking or overturning the boat—killing all of us.

That will not do.

I let go.

TWENTY-TWO

UPON THESE WAVES, I CAST MY HEART

Falling.

THE LAST THING I see is Kinsworth's face. His normally relaxed features widen in alarm. The boat tips precariously as he dashes across it, and he bellows—a thunderclap of panic that distorts sound and bends the air around us. If it were any more forceful, it might have bent matter itself.

It is the last sound I hear before plunging into the waves.

The ocean swallows me up.

Quiet.

Dark.

Cold.

Saltwater stings my skinned palms, but they quickly cool. The water here is much colder than it is in the cove at home where Tess taught us to swim.

Home.

How surprising that I should think of Stranje House as my home. And yet, it feels right. Home is a place of belonging. And I belonged there. Miss Stranje and the others accepted me and cared for me despite my peculiar gifts. I did not have to be invisible there.

It is quiet underwater. Eerily still.

Wait! That is not true.

How foolish I am. It is not quiet here. Nor is it still. The sea is so full of vibrations I simply cannot sort them all. And the ocean itself has a voice, a voice so vast and deep and overwhelmingly ancient it nearly stops my heart. Air—I need air. Bubbles cascade from my mouth and nose, floating up to the surface. I push off my slippers and follow them.

Remove your shoes—that is what Tess taught us to do if we should ever find ourselves in deep water. She learned the importance of doing so from firsthand experience. She's right. It is much easier to kick without them. I also unwrap my sari, letting it float to the bottom of the sea, leaving me in the lightweight gold silk underdress. Reaching as high as I can, I cup my hands and climb up mother ocean's watery breast, swimming to the surface.

Crimson fingers of light filter through the briny darkness—hints of dawn. I kick and crawl harder and harder until, at last, I surge up through the waves and shake salt and seaweed from my eyes and ears.

A swell lifts me high enough to see Sera in the distance, battling the current, stroking with fierce determination as she nears the rowboat. The gig appears to be about fifty yards away from me. A distance, with any luck, I should be able to manage. Before the roller drops me in a trough, it carries me even higher, high enough to see Lord Kinsworth, bloodied and limping, step up onto the stern transom, tipping their boat dangerously. "Maya!" he cups his hands and calls for me as if I am lost. I wave and shout back. He sees me and points, gesturing wildly at the ship. "Look out!"

I turn and see the sloop's sails are unfurled and flapping in the wind. The ship is moving away. Too late, I spot one of the cannons turning its gaping black mouth hungrily in our direction.

An earsplitting crack explodes the sky.

My thoughts shatter.

God save us!

The blast punches through the air, sending tremors heaving through the water. Orange smoke flares overhead, spewing sparks across the surface. The cannonball plunges into the water a few yards to my right, striking with such force it rocks the ocean. Waves spray high into the air, tossing me up, flinging me into the convulsing sea as if I am weightless flotsam. A moment later, the ocean fluxes, sucking me back, yanking me into an undertow.

Tumbling into the dark depths, I have no idea which way is up. Once again, I must chase my own escaping bubbles to find the surface. Erupting from the waves, I inhale precious air, except it is tainted with the burnt sulphur taste of black powder.

Why would they waste munitions firing at us? Has Napoleon guessed we stole the accord? That may be why they want to drown us. But would Ghost command his men to sink a boat carrying Lady Daneska? Is he that callous? Surely not. Whatever the case, if one of those cannons hits our rowboat, we are all done for.

Save yourselves! Row! I want to shout at them, but I think better of it. It is doubtful they could hear me above the roar of sea and cannons. Even if they did, they might think I am calling for help. They are in trouble enough. Sera is barely hanging onto the stern. A drenched bedraggled Lord Harston seems to be trying to pull her aboard. Tess is manning the oars, hopefully maneuvering out from the line of fire. All is lost unless they get to safety.

And Ben is perched precariously on the stern, almost as if he plans to . . .

Oh, no! He can't mean to—

But he does.

"Don't!" I yell—too late. He springs forward, diving in my direction. His splash is but a droplet in this massive sea. It scarcely makes a ripple across the surface, and yet those small pulses fill me with worry. Something is wrong. His inner music wobbles, the off-key slur of surprise, a bow sliding sideways across cello strings.

The cannon blast tossed me farther from the boat, and this wretched current is carrying me away from them. I strain to raise my head above the waves, gulping nauseating mouthfuls of brine in the process, but there is no sign of him.

Where are you?

He breaks through the surface, gasping and pummeling the water like a windmill in a valiant effort to paddle toward me. An instant later, a wave topples over him. He reaches skyward as if clamoring for help. His mouth opens and closes, gagging.

He cannot swim!

I race in his direction. *Why did he dive in? Would he drown himself trying to save me?* Silently I repeat Tess's scold to Daneska. *What were you thinking?* Except I know the answer. Lady Daneska named it.

Love.

With a groan, I spit out saltwater, grit my teeth and battle the current. Ignoring the pain in my palms, the numbness in my legs, and forgetting that I need air, I swim harder and faster than I have ever done.

With a terrifying whoosh, an arrow from the *Mary Isabella* flies overhead. It misses Napoleon's sloop and lands in the water a few feet past the stern. The sloop's sails are trimmed and billowing out. The ship tacks southeast, cutting through the waves. Napoleon and Ghost are escaping.

And Britain's Prince Regent is their captive.

Two more explosions rip through the early morning air, firing in rapid succession. Cannonballs soar in an arc high above us, whistling in the direction of Alexander's steamship. There is so much noise I can scarcely hear Kinsworth.

He bolts up from the waves, sputtering and choking, floundering in his attempt to reach me. Sera stands up as if she plans to dive back in and help him, but Lord Harston restrains her. He directs her to look out in the distance and points at me. As if I am the answer. *Me*. The worst swimmer at Stranje House.

Lord Harston hollers to gain Kinsworth's notice and casts a length of rope out toward his nephew. But Ben ignores it. He bobs and splashes, doggedly intent on drowning in my direction.

I race toward him, kicking my feet and extending my arms, exactly as Tess taught us. Even so, my dress drags like a sodden anchor and the current is so strong I feel as if I am a tiny ant trying to scale the Himalayas.

I am coming.

Keep fighting, my love.

If only I were stronger. A dozen or more strokes and I might be able to reach him. Just a few more yards. Almost there.

Almost.

The next roller tumbles over him. His hand shoots up through the surface but then drifts under as if in final surrender.

"Ben!" I scream his name. "Ben!" I cry even louder this time.

So close.

Kinsworth was right there—not more than a few yards in front of me. But now he's gone.

Vanished.

Tell me where you've hidden him, I beg mother ocean. But she does not answer. Instead, I hear my grandmother's voice. *Panic will not serve you, child. In times of trouble, quiet your mind and listen.*

Impossible in this churning ocean.

No, my little lion. Hush. And listen.

So, I close my eyes for a moment, steadying my heartbeat, and breathing as slowly and regularly as possible, stroking evenly and peacefully through the tumbling toiling sea. I dive under, listening for him.

In this early light, the sea has turned a dark poisonous green, as murky and unfathomable as death itself.

And yet, I hear him.

I can scarcely believe the sound. It is Kinsworth calling to me. Not with his voice, it is the boy inside him, the one who runs away, only now he is shouting for me. His cello playing my name over and over.

I follow the sound.

I am coming.

The rising sun burnishes the waves with a coppery glint, and in the water ahead, it silhouettes the shape of a man.

Ben!

He is floating as if he has given up. But as I approach, he looks up, and his music practically sparks a fire in the water. I swim under him and try to push him up, but he is too heavy. He reaches out for me, but I must dodge him. If he should seize hold of me too tight, he'll drown us both. Circling behind him, I grab his shirt with both hands and tug him with all my might toward the surface. Finally, his head juts up above the waves, and he lunges upward, starving for air.

I try to help him stay afloat, but he is too big, his muscles too heavy, and his clothes and shoes are dragging him under. I dive down and pry off one of his half-boots.

After removing only one of his boots, both of us are desperate to breathe. Kinsworth grabs at the water, trying to climb to the surface. I help pull him up, and when we near the surface boost him as high as I can. As soon as I feel his lungs swell with air, I poke my chin up, too. Coughing and gasping, I take in one much-needed breath before we are dragged under again. It feels as if I am nothing more than a tiny nightingale trying to tow a fully-grown man. Both of us are fading in the cold and weakening for want of air.

We cannot keep this up.

Except we have no choice. Even our enemy cannot help us now. Napoleon's ship is already a furlong away. The steamship is almost the same distance in the other direction. And I'm not sure Tess and Sera can even see where we are.

Lady Jane would say the odds are against us. Georgie would make some sort of calculation, and nod sadly. "It does not look good."

Not good at all.

They are right. We are drowning in this freezing cold ocean. I don't see how we can go on. Despite the stinging saltwater, I open my eyes to look on Kinsworth one last time, to say farewell and memorize his features to take with me to the next life. We are close, face to face in this dark grave, and his lips curve in the bravest smile I have ever seen.

His cello slows to a melody that squeezes my heart with sadness. A song of regret. A descant of farewell. He, too, knows we are going to die. His fingers float up to stroke my cheek. *Cold*, his fingers are so cold. Even so, his love for me vibrates with a warmth that ignites my soul and ripples through this wicked wondrous sea.

The storm inside me is gone, no longer fueled by anger or grief. In its place, a powerful calm arises from something stronger than grief, more potent than anger. *Love.* The lioness roars inside me. She leaps up to protect. I cannot let him die.

I will not.

I smile back at him—not in farewell. My lips are

promising him we will live. My soul sings to his. *I will teach you to swim.* I show him my hands, forming the smooth long cup shape Tess taught to me.

Diving down, I remove his other boot.

Calling upon every ounce of ferocity within me, I clasp his arm and pull him toward the surface, showing him how to stroke smoothly and pull through the water. Fighting tide and fear and weakness, we surge upward. Despite his wounds, Kinsworth cups his hands and paddles with me.

There is a rhythm to swimming. A beat with which to match our hearts. I show him the whip-like kick that cuts through currents. It is no different than a jig. Kinsworth is a quick study. The fact that he looks at my legs appreciatively gives me hope.

Together we swim, and his music picks up speed joining mine in a strange symphony that only we can hear. The slosh, slosh, slap of the oars coming toward us, joins in, promising we will live.

Ben's glad music rings across the waves, and I wish he could hear how beautifully it mingles with all the songs of the sea.

Perhaps he knows.

Kinsworth is always full of surprises.

"Here!" I shout to our friends. "We are here!"

Alive.

TWENTY-THREE

THE NIGHTINGALE SINGS

TESS LEANS OVER the side of the rowboat and reaches down to pull me up from the water. It looks as if there might be a slight smile on her lips. Surely, I am mistaken. "Well done," she says.

"What?" I heard her, but Tess rarely grants approval, and I would dearly love to hear her say it again.

Her scant smile vanishes. She has guessed my perfidy and yanks me onto the gunwale. "I didn't think you could swim that well."

Seaweed is stuck in my hair. I am dripping like a watering pot, hanging halfway in the boat, my feet still dangling in the sea, but I look up at her and grin. "I couldn't. Not until today."

Lord Harston shakes his head. "Extraordinary," he mutters as he helps Kinsworth into the boat.

Despite my sloshing into the hull with all the grace of a giant soaking-wet mackerel, Sera grabs me up and grips me in a fierce hug. "I was afraid you'd drowned." She pulls back, her eyes watering, still clutching my shoulders as if she might never let go. "How did you do it? How did you find him, and get him to us? It looked as if he couldn't swim at all."

"Couldn't." Kinsworth coughs up saltwater. "She taught me." He blurts before heaving even more intensely.

The rest of them gape at me as if I suddenly turned into a mythical mermaid.

"Don't look at me like that." *I'm not magic.* "He must've had some knowledge, or he never would have dived in."

"No, Miss Barring–" Ben shakes his head and lunges to wretch over the side of the boat.

"You're delirious." I turn to Tess and Sera and smile as if they, too, realize such a thing is impossible. But they are still squinting at me, so I busy myself with wringing out sections of my sodden ballgown. "He is imagining things."

"No." Kinsworth wipes his mouth and leans wearily on the gunwale. "Never been in water deeper than my bath."

Lord Harston shakes his head. "You're pale as Caesar's ghost and bleeding quite badly, my boy." He bends solicitously over his nephew, patting Kinsworth's back as Ben coughs up more water. "Judging by the sound of your lungs, you nearly drowned." Harston thumps Ben's back with a tinge of irritation. "If you couldn't swim, I'd jolly well like to know what were you thinking, jumping overboard like that?"

Even though I had wondered the same thing earlier,

it now seems such a needless question. Wishing I could spare Ben from having to respond, I smooth my hand over his arm, humming softly, letting him know I treasure the answer.

Lord Harston glances at me, and comprehension quiets his irritation. "Never mind," he grouses good-naturedly and hands his nephew a rather wet handkerchief with which to wipe his mouth.

Kinsworth's hair hangs over his face, dripping, and I cannot see his expression until he looks up at his uncle and grins roguishly. "I thought—" He pauses to sputter out more water. "I thought, how hard could it be? *Swimming.*"

Harston laughs and shakes his head. "Guess you know the answer now."

"At least, he's alive." Tess has seated herself on one of the rowing thwarts. "Lady Daneska is barely breathing. We need to get both of them to a doctor. Lord Harston, if you help me row, we'll get to shore faster. But first, we have to get close enough to the *Mary Isabella* to advise Captain Grey to chase Napoleon and retrieve Prince George."

"Right!" Harston leaves Kinsworth's care to me and puts in the second set of oars. He and Tess speed us toward Alexander's warship.

As soon as we are within shouting distance, Sera leaves off attending to Lady Daneska, stands, and waves both arms. "Captain!" she yells and points at Napoleon's ship in the distance. But instead of giving chase, the *Mary Isabella* chug-chugs straight toward us and pulls alongside.

It surprises me to see Mr. Chadwick aboard. A quick glance at Sera's reddening cheeks and I know she is equally taken aback. He casts out mooring line, which Lord Harston catches and quickly draws in until the two crafts knock against each other.

Lord Wyatt sets his foot on our gunwale to steady the rocking and appraises our drenched attire. "Looks like you had a close call." He leans forward and frowns at the slash marks on Lord Kinsworth and the wash of new blood spreading rapidly across Ben's wet shirt. "What in blazes happened to you?"

"He fought off Ghost and several of Ghost's men," I answer while trying to stop the blood using his soaked shirt. "That's what happened."

"They outnumbered us, I'm afraid." Lord Harston's shirt is torn, and he, too, bears at least a dozen cuts and bruises. "Upshot is—they've abducted Prince George."

"Abducted by Ghost?" Captain Grey turns the ship's wheel over to Alexander. "What happened?"

"Napoleon and the Prince were aboard that ship." Sera points. "That's why I signaled for you to stop firing."

"Yes, we saw you and averted our aim. Well done." The Captain grants Sera a quick nod of approval. "But how did they get Prince George aboard a French warship in the first place?" Captain Grey is one of my favorite people. Even upon hearing this dire news, news that will shake England to its very foundation, he remains as steady and reliable as clockwork.

Lord Harston stares at the rope in his hand, toying with it nervously. "You knew Prince George was arranging a secret meeting with Napoleon. This was that meeting."

Lord Wyatt winces. "Never say he agreed to a meeting with Bonaparte at sea? On the enemy's ship? Has he run mad?"

"We tried to prevent him." Lord Harston bristles. "He would not hear it."

Captain Grey remains silent and rubs his chin. Mr. Chadwick inhales deeply and turns his gaze up to the last few stars still twinkling in the dawn sky.

Mr. Sinclair leans on the wheel and scratches at his forehead. "Whose brilliant idea was it?"

"They cooked it up between themselves." Lord Harston takes a deep breath and faces them squarely. "As I said, Prince George could not be persuaded to do otherwise. Believe me, we tried."

"Confound it!" Lord Wyatt jangles with frustration. "Not even you, Maya? You couldn't make him change his mind?"

"I was not given the opportunity. Even had I been, Napoleon promised your Regent a great many enticements. I doubt I could've succeeded against such irresistible temptations."

"Except she did succeed!" Sera rushes to my defense. "In part. Maya kept our Regent from signing the Emperor's accord–an accord that would've put Britain under Napoleon's thumb. She stopped him. That's when Ghost came out of nowhere and attacked us."

"There was an accord?" Captain Grey keys in on the salient point.

"Yes," she says. "And we stole it."

"You did?" Lord Harston looks at her, a flute of hope whistling through him, and he doesn't take a breath until she nods. "Thank God! That's proof." He sags with relief and then straightens with worry again. "Except the papers got wet when you jumped, didn't they? The ink will run, but maybe some of it will still be legible."

"I have them—dry and safe." Tess pats her midsection, where she hid the papers inside her blouse.

"Brilliant." Lord Wyatt salutes her.

"I'll take them to Miss Stranje." Tess sits on the thwart, the oars poised in her hands. "But for now, Napoleon has Prince George, and you need to go after him."

"There'll be a fight." Lord Kinsworth pushes up and stumbles wearily toward the steamboat. "You'll need me with you."

"Hold up, Kinsworth." Lord Wyatt holds up his hand. "You don't look well."

"Fit as a fiddle. Prince George was my—" Ben labors to draw in enough breath to speak. "My responsibility. I will see this through."

Captain Grey eyes him skeptically. "Admirable notion, lad, but given your present state—"

"Ben!" I lurch to my feet as Lord Kinsworth knees buckle, and he collapses beside the gunwale.

Lord Harston catches his nephew mid-fall. "Not so. Prince George was—*is* my responsibility." He strains under Ben's weight, holding him until I settle in the hull and he eases Kinsworth into my waiting arms. "Take care of him, lass."

"With my life," I murmur.

Lord Harston nods and rises. "Captain Grey, I would very much like to come with you. If one of your men would be so good as to make certain these young ladies make it to safety?"

"Go!" Tess blows an irritated trumpet of air through her lips. "We can see to ourselves."

"Chadwick!" Captain Grey ignores her and gestures to his newest recruit. "If you would assist with their rowing."

Sera is leaning over checking Daneska's pulse, but when Captain Grey calls Mr. Chadwick's name, she straightens as if someone fired a rifle.

"Certainly, sir." Mr. Chadwick climbs into our wobbly rowboat, and Lord Harston steps out, taking the mooring line with him.

"Godspeed, ladies." Captain Grey pulls out his spyglass and sights it on Napoleon's sloop. "Wyatt, throw an extra log on the fire. Sinclair set our course south by southeast. We have an Emperor to catch."

With that, the *Mary Isabella* churns past us. Spray from the paddlewheel flings a fine mist of seawater over us. Mr. Chadwick whips off his coat and wraps it carefully over Sera's shoulders, and I shield Kinsworth. His breathing is regular but shallow. I hum, hiding my worries from the tune.

Sera stares after Mr. Chadwick, red-faced, fidgeting nervously with his coat sleeve, ringing with confusion, and yet, she also chimes with a few delicate bells of excitement.

He takes his place on the bench in front of Tess. "Heave ho, Miss Aubreyson. Heave ho!"

Tess smiles. A rare occurrence for her. "Finally," she mutters. "A man who doesn't treat me like I'm some sort of wilting lily." Her oars splash into the water. "Heave ho, *yourself*, Mr. Chadwick. And do try to put some back into it."

He does.

He puts a surprising amount of muscle into it, especially for someone whom I had considered to be primarily a scholar. Soon, we are crashing through the waves, fairly flying toward Brighton.

I apply pressure to slow the bleeding on one of the largest of the gashes across Kinsworth's chest, but all I have is this miserable wet cloth. It is a losing battle. Suddenly, he groans, and he starts to shake.

"Wake-up." I pat his cheek. "Wake-up, Ben." But he doesn't wake up. He is far too pale, and the quaking is too violent. "Oh-no, this is not good. No good at all."

Sera turns from attending Daneska, takes one look at Kinsworth and worry tramples through her like the clatter of too many running feet. "He must've lost a great deal of blood."

I cannot listen to the sound of worry-feet right now. *Calm*, I must stay calm. "Yes, I'm trying to staunch it, but it is nearly impossible without a proper bandage. And now I'm worried he might be developing wound shock."

"This might help." Sera tears a long strip of muslin from Daneska's underskirt. "At least it's moderately dry. How is his breathing?"

"Steady enough. It is his shivering that worries me." I fold the cloth into a thick pad and wrap the rest of it across his wound to hold it in place. Brushing wet hair away from his forehead I gauge the temperature of his skin. "Cold. Clammy. But at least, there's no fever."

Not yet.

"Here." She hands me Mr. Chadwick's coat. "Take it."

"But you—"

"He needs it more."

I cover him with the coat and inch him higher, moving him farther from the dampness in the bottom of the boat. "Live," I whisper in his ear. "Live and be well." Folding my arms around him, I hold Ben close, hoping to lend him whatever warmth I have left. I don't know what else I can do for him, except sing.

So, I do.

The song is nothing—certainly not magic. I am, after all, only a nightingale. This is a soft simple tune, a gently murmured lullaby, that speaks of peaceful breezes and soothing sands. If there is love laced through the melody, he deserves every note. If there is hope hidden in the harmony, well, that is a gift from far beyond my lips—a gift for both of us.

A half-hour passes, and when the rising sun turns the sea to molten gold, it is not Kinsworth, but Lady Daneska, who stirs. Sera strokes our enemy's hand reassuringly. "You are safe, Daneska. Among friends. *Rest.* When we get ashore, we'll fetch a doctor for you."

"Friends?" Daneska mutters a string of what sounds like acerbic oaths in her native language. Clearly, she believes she is neither safe nor among friends.

Kinsworth's shaking lessens. He shifts restlessly, uttering incoherent murmurs of pain. I resume singing, and he rouses a bit more. His groans cease, and he turns his head, adjusting his position so that his ear rests against my chest. "Maya?" he says drowsily.

"I am here."

"Mmm," He breathes. "I hear your heart."

He will live.

"Of course, you do." I smile with relief.

"No," His eyes flutter open, and he blinks at me as if I have completely misunderstood his meaning. "I've *always* heard it." He closes his eyes again with a satisfied half-smile playing on his mouth. "Your music."

Are these delirium ravings? Or—

Suddenly it all makes sense. How his inner music was able to allude me. The way he could walk up behind me, and I wouldn't hear. Why he always seems to know what I am feeling.

I knew it!

He can hear.

"You scoundrel," I say without proper force. "All this time, and you never told me." I ought to be angry. Instead, I hold him closer and press my lips against the wet cherubic curls on his head. "We are almost to shore. As soon as we find a doctor for you, and the minute you are well enough, I am going to deliver a resounding peal over your annoyingly beautiful head—the sternest reprimand ever given. A scold, you shall never forget. Ever."

He smirks as if he is looking forward to it.

TWENTY-FOUR

THE HORNS OF SAFE HARBOR

UPON OUR RETURN, Miss Stranje turns into a veritable field marshal. She employs multiple surgeons, the best in the region. At her behest, Dr. Meredith even travels all the way from London, but our headmistress supervises Lady Daneska and Lord Kinsworth's care as if she is the queen of all medical knowledge and these men of science are merely her minions.

And anyone would think Sera and I had just returned from the dead. She will not let either of us leave her sight. Straightway, she sends for our things and moves us out of the palace into her suite of rooms at the Ship Inn. I promise, if she thanks Tess one more time for saving our lives, I might explode.

Truly, I might.

Afterall, Sera and I did have a little something to do with our escape, and Tess was merely doing what a sister does–risking her life to rescue us. The same thing Miss

Stranje would do without a second thought. That same thing any of us at Stranje House would do for one another.

A DAY AND A HALF LATER, Captain Grey tramps into our suite. I hear him greeting Miss Stranje and hurry out of the bedroom after changing the dressing on Lady Daneska's wound. "Did you catch them?" I rush to ask.

The Captain stands tall and straight, his inner clockwork as steady as always, except today his beat is somber, a little slower and sadder. "They caught the wind," he shakes his head and scuffs the toe of his boot at the carpet slightly. "Disappeared in a fog along the coast. We weren't sure if they turned north or south. Logically they would sail south toward Le Havre to take the Seine to Paris. We took that chance. It could be they dodged us somehow, or went north."

"Either way, we lost them." He takes a deep breath, and Miss Stranje closes the distance between them.

He takes her elbows in his hands and leans his forehead against hers. "We lost them, Emma. Gone. Searched up and down the French coast. Steamed as near as we dared to the Seine. By now, Boney will have Prince George locked away in Paris, holding him hostage."

"You know what this means . . ." He straightens, backs away from her, and I have never seen him look so much like a lost young man—not our Captain. Not the man upon whom we all rely. "This blasted war is going to get worse. Much worse."

Much bloodier.

At least, I think, having captured the Prince Regent, Ghost will be appeased for the moment, and he won't be catapulting plague into Britain.

"We don't know that it will get worse." Miss Stranje squares her shoulders and reaches up to cup his cheek in her hand. "You'll send out men to rescue him. That's how you found Alexander. And Lord Wyatt. We thought we'd never get Sebastian back, remember. And yet, *you did.*"

Captain Grey doesn't look convinced, so she presses the point. "You will find Prince George. You'll stop Napoleon. Surely, you will. And we can help. There is still the possibility Lady Daneska will recover. . ." She glances in my direction, the question ringing in every syllable.

"Yes." I nod. "She has a strong constitution. Her fever broke early this morning, and that was the doctor's primary concern."

"There. You see?" Miss Stranje exudes confidence. She is the anchor for all of us—our safe harbor. She primly folds her hands in front of her. "When she recovers—"

"If," he reminds her.

"*When.*" She dismisses his nay-saying and presses on. "She may be of considerable help. Most likely she will have some idea where the Iron Crown would dare imprison Britain's Prince Regent."

"Aye. She might." He steps back, rubbing his neck. As Lady Jane would say, Captain Grey is not a man to bet on uncertainties. Whether or not Lady Daneska will live, and if she does, whether she will disclose any useful information about the Iron Crown, are two enormous uncertainties.

"Keep me informed." The Captain straightens, all

soldier again. "But for now, I have come to you on an errand of sorts. Lord Harston rides to London tonight. He is charged with presenting a full account to Lord Castlereagh and the Cabinet by morning light. He will require that accord your young ladies procured."

"You mean the one they stole," she says proudly, and glides to her desk to retrieve the sheaf of papers now neatly tucked in a leather satchel. "I trust you'll send riders with him? These are the only proof we have as to what he and Napoleon conspired to do."

"Yes! Upon my life, yes. There will be riders, our best, and I will be accompanying him as well." He says this with a wistful glance in her direction. "How is Lord Kinsworth faring?"

"Oohhh," she huffs, and numbers his sins on her fingers. "That young man will not follow the doctor's orders and stay in bed. He has already torn out two stitches. Refuses leeches. Won't eat his broth unless we provide him with bread and cheese to go with it. He is an absolutely dreadful patient. *Dreadful!* The young scoundrel harasses Miss Barrington to the point of distraction. I've half a mind to tie him down or run him through him myself. I daresay, by tomorrow he shall be nigh unto impossible."

"Ah, that is good news. Good news, indeed." He winks at me and turns to go, but wheels back around. "I meant to tell you—young Chadwick handled himself commendably. I'm pleased you spoke to me on his behalf. He's a clever lad, and will make an excellent addition to the foreign office."

"*Too* clever, at times." She smiles wistfully. "I trust Lord Wyatt is well—you know, Miss Fitzwilliam will ask me."

"Aye." He chuckles. "As much of a rascal as ever. He and Sinclair are returning the ship to London." He checks his pocket watch. "They should be rounding the straits about now."

"Ah, I see. Generous of the Navy to permit you to take the prototype, considering the sum they paid for it."

"Hmm." He scuffs at the carpet. "I wouldn't exactly say they granted permission."

"Ethan!" Her tone holds a scold, but a wry smile twists her lips.

"Pax." He holds up both hands, warding her off. "I've no doubt they would have granted it if we'd had time to make the request. As soon as I got your message, we had to set out."

"Yes, well . . . and thank goodness, you did." Miss Stranje lowers her head, shaking it slightly. "Your fires disrupted Ghost's crew. I dare not think what might have happened to my girls if you had not arrived when you did."

Except she does think of it.

A cacophony of crashing notes emanates from Miss Stranje. She casts a grief-stricken look in my direction, and in that brief moment, I learn what it must feel like to have a mother who would lay down her life to save her daughter.

Captain Grey clasps her shoulder, and her music immediately resumes its harmony. "I will always heed your call, Emma. You know that, don't you?" He lets go. "And now, may I ask how long you plan to remain in Brighton?"

"A day or two, I should think. We will return to

Stranje House as soon as Lady Daneska is able to travel."

"Very good." He watches her face closely. *How very peculiar.* Captain Grey's methodical clockwork skips a beat, stumbles, and transforms into a surprisingly musical jumble. He reaches for her hand. "It is difficult to know where Castlereagh will send us next."

"I assumed as much." Her voice catches.

He does not tell her he will miss her. Instead, he holds her fingers loosely, carefully, the way one would hold the most precious jewels in the kingdom, and takes a long last regretful look at her, mourning all the lost moments of their past and future. "Until we meet again."

Our brave stalwart headmistress does not answer. She tamps down a flood of wildly wishful flutes, and hides a thousand violins of would-be kisses behind a towering wall of dammed-up love for this man. All she can do is nod stiffly and try to smile.

Does he know? I wonder. Can he hear her heart?

Their parting hurts too much.

I cannot bear it.

I rush back into Daneska's bedroom and close the door. "Life is too complicated," I whisper. "How are we to love in such a confusing world?" I sit down beside my unconscious enemy, wishing she could hear. Wishing *anyone* could hear and teach me how to swim in these waters.

THE NEXT DAY, news of Prince George's abduction spreads all over England. Runners descend on our little seaside town. Messengers ride like a horde of wasps into Brighton, knocking on doors, rousing citizens, carrying orders for admirals, lieutenants, and their underlings to report immediately to London.

As if summer has abruptly come to an early close, Brighton's streets fill with loaded drays and coaches piled high with luggage. Guests are fleeing the coast. Wives and daughters are being sent home to their country estates to hunker down in case of war and a possible invasion.

We are not packing. Not yet. Lady Daneska is too ill to travel.

Miss Stranje's prediction that we would not be able to confine Lord Kinsworth to his bed proves accurate. He is up and restless today. She invites him to join us for a light repast at one o'clock in Ship's dining room. Tess is off riding with Lord Ravencross and will not be joining us. Georgie and Lady Jane are here, but they have both been moping about because Lord Wyatt and Mr. Sinclair followed their orders, and sailed the steamship back to London.

Lady Jane drearily drags a lone strawberry through the cream on her plate. "One would think they might've taken at least one day here in Brighton."

"Nonsense!" Miss Stranje scolds while slicing rye bread. "What's more, I grow weary of these long faces." She slows the knife and stares pointedly at Jane and Georgie. "We have enough weighty matters pressing upon us without you two mooning about like lovesick puppies. I won't have it." She plops the bread down on her plate and leans forward. "Bear in mind, ladies, it is easy to be pleasant when life is handing you sunshine and roses. How one conducts oneself amid conflict is the truest watermark of one's character."

Lady Jane looks away sheepishly, but Georgie raises one finger. "But what if the war worsens—"

"Tch!" Miss Stranje glares at her, holding the knife upright as if she might use it for more than cutting bread if Georgie persists. When her most quizzical student realizes her error and presses her lips tight, Miss Stranje continues sawing the rye. "To that end, I suggest the two of you join me this afternoon for a shopping spree."

"Shopping?" Georgie turns to Jane in amazement.

"Ah, I see. So, this the sort of punishment you're so famous for?" Lord Kinsworth dares to tease her.

"Phfft." She waves him away, slaps a piece of ham on her bread, and frowns at Jane and Georgie. "Oh, don't look so surprised. It's not a punishment. Given the turn of events, shops will be nearly empty. The merchants shall be at our mercy." One eyebrow lifts diabolically. "It will be a fine test of your negotiating skills."

Given the somber chants arising from her own inner chorus lately, I suspect the shopping spree is as much for Miss Stranje's benefit as it is theirs.

"Miss Wyndham, I realize you do not care much for shopping, but if you would care to join us, you are welcome. Madame Cho will be sitting with Lady Daneska this afternoon, so you needn't feel you must stay indoors." She looks up from cutting several slices of cheese. "Unless you had other plans?"

"I, uh, that is to say . . ." Sera turns bright red. Sly as a fox our headmistress, she must know what Sera has already confided to me. "Mr. Chadwick asked if I might accompany him to the Marine Library. I meant to ask your permission, but Madame Cho said—"

"Yes, yes. I know all about it. Of course, you may go." She turns to me. "Miss Barrington, I am entrusting this young rascal into your care." She points the knife at Lord

Kinsworth. "He may take a light walk. Nothing strenuous. See that he does not overdo and tear out more of his stitches, if you please."

A gentleman strides into the dining room. One of our waiters tries to stop him, "But sir, if you will allow me to assist you—"

"My lord," the gentleman corrects the servant with an irritated tone. "Furthermore, I am quite capable of speaking to the lady without any assistance from you."

Spoon upraised, I freeze in place. I know that voice—the unmistakably familiar marching cadence.

My father.

"Papa." I plunk down my spoon and stand.

"Maya!" He whips off his hat and strides straight for me. "Thank heavens." For one unbelievable moment, it seems as if he might wrap me up in a hug. Except he stops short, standing a foot and a half in front of me, staring. His eyes glisten with mist, the way things do after the morning fog lifts.

I hear it then, a song I have not heard since I was a small child. In my country, there is a long neck lute, and its strings vibrate with joy, but there is a softly dissonant melancholy that reverberates in it, too. The song washes over me, his hidden melody, breaking my heart with its tenderness, and then Papa snaps shut the door to his soul.

He turns on his heel and marches around the table to my headmistress. "Miss Stranje, I will be collecting my daughter. I have lost confidence in your ability to keep her from scandal and mayhem."

She sets down her meal of meat and cheese, and wearing a pleasant smile, glances up at him. "Scandal and mayhem—those are indeed serious accusations."

The words slid insincerely over my father's tongue as if they were sent directly from his wife to me. I am surprised she is not trailing in behind him. One can only hope he left her at home or in the carriage.

Miss Stranje dusts off her hands on the tablecloth, as is the custom, and stands. "I assure you, my lord, there has been no scandal and only a modicum of mayhem."

"A modicum?" He pulls a copy of the Times out from his coat pocket and slaps it on the table. "We have heard *stories*."

We? Is my father using the royal 'we,' or is he referring to himself and Lady Barrington, and perhaps the maid and butler at his estate?

"Stories?" Miss Stranje doesn't appear the least bit worried. She picks up the Times and opens it out. "Ah, yes. I read this one." She hands the paper to me.

The front page is covered with the story of Napoleon abducting the Prince Regent.

"Is it true, my daughter was present when our Prince was kidnapped? That she barely escaped with her life?"

I hand the paper to Sera. "As you can see Papa, I am perfectly well."

He bristles for a moment, "Well, that is more than I can say for your fiancé." He points at Kinsworth. "*He* does not look perfectly well."

Lord Kinsworth rises. "I assure you, my lord, I am quite well. In a few days, I will be shed of this bandage and right as rain."

My father only gives him the slightest glance. "I have never understood why anyone thinks rain is *right*. Or wrong. It is wet. That's all."

"Precisely," I say under my breath. At least, we agree on that much.

Miss Stranje decides this is the ideal moment to make proper introductions. "Lord Kinsworth, may I present your future father-in-law, Lord Barrington."

My fiancé and father perform the English gentleman act, bowing to one another, but only as much as is socially required, exchanging forced smiles like two seasoned thespians.

"Won't you join us, Lord Barrington? I'm told the fish soup is quite flavorful today." Miss Stranje reseats herself.

My father does not sit. He broods and shifts from one leg to the other. "A young lady on Napoleon's ship—accompanied by the Prince Regent, no less. Everyone knows his abysmal reputation. It wasn't a suitable place for a delicate young lady. My wife feels this entire situation is beyond scandalous."

"Oh, yes. I'm familiar with your wife's opinions." Miss Stranje spreads mustard on her ham. "And what do you hear other people saying about your daughter?" With her pinky finger, Miss Stranje indicates the Times in Sera's hand. "What have you read?"

"They are calling her a . . ." he glances guiltily toward me. "A hero." He looks down, but when the carpet proves uninteresting, he shoots a stern glare at Miss Stranje. "But Maya is a fragile young lady."

"Fragile?" Lord Kinsworth nearly chokes. "I'll have you know, this *fragile* young lady saved my life."

"And she kept England from falling into Napoleon's hands." Georgie scoots back her chair as if she is ready to do battle for me. "Did the papers tell you that?"

Sera scans the Times on the table beside her. "They allude to it, but they aren't giving the details. The Cabinet must be keeping the accord secret."

My father stares at Sera and Georgie, then back again to Lord Kinsworth. His lips are pressed almost white with frustration until he blurts, "She never ought to have been in such a violent situation! It's . . . it's unseemly."

"*Unseemly?*" Miss Stranje sighs and clears her throat. "I believe the word you are looking for is dangerous."

"Yes! Dangerous. Precisely the point."

"I understand." She carefully sets down her silverware. "And you would very much like to protect your daughter from danger, correct?"

His shoulders wilt. My big strong father slumps. "I would." He glances at me, and I hear it again, a lute, this time plunking low notes of regret.

"So would I." Miss Stranje stands, waiting until he meets her gaze. "You were acquainted with my father, were you not? When you were a young man in India."

Papa tugs at his collar as if it is inordinately hot inside the Ship, despite the windows allowing the ocean breeze to waft through. "Yes, I knew him. An extraordinary man, your father. He was largely the reason I entrusted Maya into your care."

He knew her father. I lean in, listening closer, scarcely able to believe it. My father did not abandon me to a stranger.

Miss Stranje speaks to my father in a kindly manner, as if they are old friends. "And were you aware of the sort of business my father conducted for the Foreign Office?"

"I, uh..." He exhales loudly. "I had some notion of it."

She traces her finger on the tablecloth, marking the

facts. "You admired my father. You understood something of the life he led, and that I assisted him from time to time."

A warm shade of red creeps up my father's neck. "I did." He glances apologetically at me.

"You knew all these things, and yet you trusted me to train your only child—your fragile young daughter." Still standing, Miss Stranje plucks the top off of a strawberry and sets it on her plate. "How very puzzling."

"Because she was—" He turns to me. "Because she *is* a remarkable young woman." No regret rings from him now, only pride. "I thought if anyone could guide her, it would be you. Her stepmother . . . wasn't . . ." He looks away. Shame breaking strings, muddling his music until he shutters it away. Like always.

Except now, I know.

He sent me to Miss Stranje, not because he didn't care, but because he respected her and thought it the best place for me.

"If this is true, Lord Barrington, why you are questioning my ability to do so now? Especially when, and I do not say this lightly, your daughter has shown herself to be extremely capable. And she has done so in dozens of situations." She gazes at me with approval she rarely displays. "Miss Fitzwilliam spoke the truth. Maya kept our country from falling into Emperor Bonaparte's clutches. Most of Britain will never know it, but they owe her a debt of gratitude. Yet, here you are, wanting to remove her from my care. I am perplexed."

Lord Kinsworth reaches for my hand as if he expects my father to try and snatch me away at any moment. "She belongs here. With us. With Miss Stranje." Ben uses a deep manly tone. “And someday, when the time is right, she belongs with me—as my wife.”

That sounded awfully much like a real proposal.

“This is all highly irregular.” My father looks to me as if the decision is better left in my hands. “I worry for your safety, Maya.”

“Ooh,” Lady Jane sighs as if his sentiment is the tenderest thing she has ever heard, but then Lady Jane coos the same way when our wolf puppies yip. “My lord, we all love your daughter. Parting with her would be excruciating. She is like a sister to us. Rest assured, any of us would give our lives to protect her.”

Sera reaches for my other hand. “It’s true.”

“And she protects us.” Georgie rises and comes to stand beside me.

“So, I see.” My father’s eyes begin to mist ever so slightly. “Maya?”

My heart is singing in ways I never thought it would. How can I find the right words? I did not even realize I was humming until all of them stare at me expectantly.

There is only one thing to say.

“I love you, Papa.” I try to smile as stoically as Miss Stranje does when her heart is overflowing.

But I cannot.

My lips spread even more broadly, and instead of being brave, the smile breaks me open, and a chorus of joyous tears pour out. “I’m so happy you came, Papa. And I am pleased you brought me to Miss Stranje. Grateful. This is where I belong. Here. With them.”

I open my arms out to my friends, who wrap me in their warmth.

“I see.” My father slowly turns to Miss Stranje. “You

have done well by her. Thank you. Will you send me regular reports?"

"You may count on it. Will you join us for nuncheon?"

His marching music returns. "No, thank you, though." He puts on his hat with a brusque tap. "My lady wife awaits in the carriage."

I rush to catch him before he can leave and throw my arms around him. I do not care if he is unprepared for such an *unseemly* show of affection.

"No matter where you are," he whispers in my ear and pats my shoulder. "Keep singing, daughter, and I will hear you."

He will?

Can it be?

He leaves, and I stand in my father's wake, astonished. Those were the same words my grandmother said when I left India.

AFTER OUR NUNCHEON, Lord Kinsworth offers to take me for a stroll along the embankment. Arm in arm, we walk out one on of the small piers, and back again atop the seawall. Waves lap up on empty beaches. Bathing wagons sit unrented, tucked up against the embankment, even their purveyors are nowhere to be seen.

Kinsworth whistles softly through his teeth. "Everyone knows about the Prince, don't they?"

"So, it would seem." His cuts are healing quickly, and I cannot help but wonder how long it will be before he rushes off to join the others in fighting Napoleon. "Do you think the war will get worse?"

I glance up at him, waiting for the answer. Half angel,

half rogue, I cannot determine which he is. I only know I adore the way his blue eyes match the sky, and how the golden sun dances across his brown curls. Most of all, I relish the inviting notes of his violoncello. It plays so mellow and deep that I could fall into his arms this very minute.

"I expect it will," he says. Although, he does not sound as eager for adventure as he once did. Perhaps the reality of battle changed him a bit. He smooths his hand over mine as it rests on his arm. "I will have to serve. You know that, don't you?"

"Yes."

Of course, I knew.

He needn't have said it aloud. I wish he hadn't.

"But not today!" I say firmly, refusing to let the future darken today's happiness. "Today we have the beach all to ourselves."

I let go of his arm and scamper down the embankment steps. He follows, and we make our way toward the water, laughing as we try to keep our balance walking across piles and piles of sea-polished stones exposed by low tide. Finally, we cross over all the rocks and come to a broad stretch of sand where we can stand comfortably and stare out at the ocean lapping so tamely on the shore. Except now, I know better. The sea is not tame. She is both dangerous and amazing, a vast nursery swarming with life and an equally unfathomable crypt.

One that nearly claimed our lives.

He bumps his arm against me, rousing me from my morbid thoughts. "Shall I hire a bathing wagon for the afternoon?" He sweeps his arm out. "We have our pick today. I'm sure you agree, I need to learn how to swim more proficiently."

"Most assuredly." Hands on my hips, I struggle to maintain a stern expression. "Except the surgeon ordered you to keep the dressing dry, and Miss Stranje will lop off my head if you come back with a wet bandage. Aside from that, we ought to start back if we are to return to the inn before she does."

"Not just yet. You worry too much. They'll be shopping for hours." There is mischief brewing in his eyes and impish bassoons playing hide and seek. "We're alone, Maya. I don't hear a single soul on this entire stretch of beach. Do you?"

I fail to answer. He stands so close I can smell the sun warming his skin.

The corner of his mouth curves up waywardly, and he lowers voice till I must lean in to catch his next words. "You know what that means, don't you?"

My breath catches, and I cannot keep from smiling.

He means kissing.

Kinsworth draws back as if I have shocked him. "Why, Miss Barrington, I am surprised at you for thinking such a thing."

I did not say it aloud.

At least, I don't think I did.

I cross my arms and frown. "I was not thinking anything amiss."

"You were." He picks up a stick of driftwood. "And here I was exulting in the fact that we have the perfect opportunity to practice our sword fighting. That is the only thing I had in mind."

"It is not." I fume.

"It most certainly was. *Sword fighting*, I said to myself.

A good joust will be just the thing. Besides, you know how Miss Stranje feels about our kissing." He tosses me the smooth stick and steps back to pick up another one. A much longer one.

Ben pulls his arm out of the sling and poses in the quarte stance. "*En Garde.*"

"You are forgetting about your stitches." I sulk and tap his nonsensical sword out of the way. "Aside from that, you have the longer branch. It isn't fair."

"Fair? Why, of course, it is. I'm taller and bigger. It's only natural that I should require the larger sword."

"*Wretch.*"

"Names will get you nowhere. This is a game of skill and wits." He steps forward challenging me again.

"And, apparently, bigger swords." I strike his ridiculous piece of driftwood, and he parries. Tap, tap, we drum back and forth in a satisfying tempo. Our swordplay almost becomes a dance, until he breaks rhythm and tags my shoulder.

"Ha! Wounded you." How is it Kinsworth can seem so charming, while at the same time behaving like a remorse-less rogue?

"The long sword gives you the advantage."

But does it?

Madame Cho's training rushes back to me. How silly I'm being. She taught us how to put long swords at a disadvantage. So, I whirl toward him, too close for him to strike, and with my mythical short sword, I chop off his arm. "You just lost your arm."

"Hmph. So, I see." He pauses to scowl at his make-believe wound.

"Do you yield?"

"Never!" He rebounds in a flash, his inner music racing happily. "Don't worry. I can fight one-handed. Watch this." His eyes flash impishly, and he lunges forward with a stab that would've ended the game had I not reflexively dodged.

That lunge will leave him exposed, so I spin in close and tap his heart. "I just ran you through, my love."

Instead of pretending to be mortally wounded, he tosses his sword away, and reaches for my waist, pulling me closer. "I yield," he says huskily.

Does he mean to yield *kissing*? Because if he does not, there may be dire consequences.

"Do you?" I ask in a breathy whisper.

"Don't you know, Maya?" He laughs, and the cello inside him plays chords that ease all the sore knotted places in my soul.

The make-believe sword slips from my fingers and falls in the sand. And the nightingale wings freely. The lioness rests quietly within me, waiting until the next time she must rise and protect those she loves. The storm has gone, disappeared over the mountains. In his arms, I feel raw and warm and sheltered.

He brushes a lock of hair from my cheek and murmurs in my ear, "My heart belonged to you since the first moment I heard you sing."

He yields then, covering my lips with a symphony of kisses.

Sera will reveal her story
when the Stranje House saga
continues
in

SANCTUARY FOR SEERS

AFTERWORD

Dear Reader,

Thank you for experiencing Maya's story with me. Learning to hear the world, as Maya does, rather than perceive it primarily through sight, was illuminating. And challenging. It stretched my writing skills, and the deeper I got into her story, the more the world of sound intrigued me. That is probably why it took me so long to write it. I still feel I have not fully captured the concept of sound vibrating from our emotions.

If you have thoughts on this, I would love to hear them. My email is:

Kathleen@KathleenBaldwin.com

Readers often ask whether Maya's gift of manipulating her voice, is real.

Short answer, yes. All of my characters are amalgams (blends) of people I have known, and Maya is, too. Her gift is based on a real person. I mentioned the inception story of Maya's voice on my blog, but I will share it again here with you.

My neighbor is from India, and one day I intruded on a breakfast she was preparing for friends. With typical Indian graciousness, Rashmi invited me to join them. Every time her friend spoke, I found myself mesmerized. Her voice was enthralling, almost magical. She relaxed us as we listened, and yet all of us were riveted to her words. She conveyed emotion with a simple shift of tone and cadence, and something about the musical quality of her voice made everything she spoke about come alive. We could *see* her stories.

Since then, I have met others with this fascinating gift. A young lady at our local high school, who helps me get some of my facts right about India, assures me that her mother shares Maya's gift. Apparently, her mother can be extraordinarily persuasive.

Another question readers ask is, "Can the gift of voice be learned?"

Yes, with practice, I believe we can all learn to use our vocal cords more effectively. Speech-givers and politicians study cadence and tone, as do hypnotists. *How* something is said is as important as *what* is said. There's far more to communication than the sum of our words.

You may have heard me say, "You are changing the world around you. The decisions and choices you make today impact the people in your life tomorrow, and have a far-reaching effect." After writing Maya's story, I am convinced that how we speak, the tone we use, and the emotional force behind our words is equally important. Whether we are called upon to speak forcefully as the lioness, or to soothe as the nightingale, there is power swirling behind and in our words.

May your life be filled with love, peace, and joy!
—Kathleen Baldwin

Kathleen loves hearing from readers. Her contact info, Readers Guides, and other insights about the world of Stranje House are on her website:

KATHLEENBALDWIN.COM

Also By Kathleen Baldwin

The Stranje House Novels

A School for Unusual Girls

Exile for Dreamers

Refuge for Masterminds

My Notorious Aunt Series

Lady Fiasco

Mistaken Kiss

Cut from the Same Cloth

The Highwayman Came Waltzing

Diary of a Teenage Fairy Godmother

For Reader Guides and Story Extras, visit:
KATHLEENBALDWIN.COM

CPSIA information can be obtained
at www.ICGtesting.com
Printed in the USA
LVHW031623061119
636549LV00004B/835

9 780988 836440